"Perhaps the best of Stephen Coonts's six novels about modern warfare." —*Austin American-Statesman*

"Coonts delivers some of his best gung-ho suspense writing yet." —*Kirkus Reviews*

FORTUNES OF WAR
"*Fortunes of War* is crammed with action, suspense, and characters with more than the usual one dimension found in these books." —*USA Today*

"A stirring examination of courage, compassion, and profound nobility of military professionals under fire. Coonts's best yet." —*Kirkus Reviews* (starred review)

FLIGHT OF THE INTRUDER
"Extraordinary! Once you start reading, you won't want to stop!" —Tom Clancy

"[Coonts's] gripping, first-person narration of aerial combat is the best I've ever read. Once begun, this book cannot be laid aside." —*The Wall Street Journal*

"Kept me strapped in the cockpit of the author's imagination for a down-and-dirty novel." —*St. Louis Post-Dispatch*

SAUCER
"A comic, feel-good SF adventure . . . [delivers] optimistic messages about humanity's ability to meet future challenges." —*Kirkus Reviews*

Also in this series

Novels by STEPHEN COONTS

Nonfiction books by STEPHEN COONTS

STEPHEN COONTS'

DEEP BLACK:

Sea of Terror

Written by Stephen Coonts and William H. Keith

St. Martin's Paperbacks

This is a work of fiction. All of the characters, organizations, and events portrayed in this novel are either products of the author's imagination or are used fictitiously.

STEPHEN COONTS' DEEP BLACK: SEA OF TERROR

Copyright © 2010 by Stephen P. Coonts and Deborah B. Coonts.

All rights reserved.

For information address St. Martin's Press, 175 Fifth Avenue, New York, NY 10010.

ISBN: 978-0-312-94696-8

Printed in the United States of America

St. Martin's Paperbacks edition / February 2010

St. Martin's Paperbacks are published by St. Martin's Press, 175 Fifth Avenue, New York, NY 10010.

10 9 8 7 6 5 4 3 2 1

PROLOGUE

Pacific Sandpiper
Harbor Channel
Barrow, England
Thursday, 0745 hours GMT

SHE WAS A BLUE AND WHITE monster slipping slowly down the deep-water channel on a gray and rainy early-fall morning. To port were the sprawling facilities of the Roosecote Power Station and the neighboring Centrica Gas Terminal at Rampside. To starboard, toward the south-west, was the clawlike hook of Walney Island, the South End. North, blocked at the moment by the towering mountain of the *Pacific Sandpiper*'s superstructure, the port of Barrow-in-Furness slowly receded into the morning haze.

Through his binoculars, Jack Rawlston looked straight across the low-lying strand of Walney Island and could just make out the slender white towers of the BOW on the southwestern horizon, seven kilometers offshore. British Offshore Wind was a joint project of Centrica and a Dan-ish energy group, a wind farm consisting of thirty wind-mill turbines harvesting ninety megawatts from the winds blowing across the Irish Sea.

Energy. It was *all* about energy these days.

Rawlston stood at his assigned post on the ship's bow,

his assault rifle slung over his shoulder as he watched the Walney shoreline creep past. Seabirds wheeled and screeched against the overcast. A foghorn lowed its mournful, deep-throated tone.

And he could just make out another noise behind the normal sounds of the sea. A mile and a half ahead, hoots and honks and bellowing horns sounded in a slowly gathering maritime cacophony that made Rawlston's skin crawl.

Idiots, he thought. *As if their pathetic little demonstration could stop* us.

He turned to give the blockading line a disdainful look, and added to himself, *The bastards wouldn't dare*.

A ponderous 104 meters long, with a beam of sixteen meters and a full-load displacement of 7,725 tonnes, the *Pacific Sandpiper* was one of just three purpose-built oceangoing transports currently owned and operated by Pacific Nuclear Transport Limited, a British firm headquartered in Barrow, in the northwest of England. Her cargo, bolted to the decks in five large and independent storage holds below her long main deck, consisted this September morning of fourteen TN 28 VT transport flasks, each 6.6 meters long and 2.8 meters wide, weighing ninety-eight tonnes and each holding, stored carefully in separate containers, between 80 and 200 kilograms of mixed plutonium oxides, more colloquially known as MOX.

The fact that plutonium is, weight for weight, the single most poisonous substance known to man, and that there was enough on board the *Sandpiper* to construct perhaps sixty fair-sized nuclear weapons, did not bother Rawlston in the least. He'd served as security for other PNTL shipments and knew exactly how stringent the safeguards and precautions were. *He* was one of those safeguards, in fact.

But the demonstration now picking up at the mouth of

the channel had him uneasy. What did the fools think they were playing at, anyway?

Less than three kilometers ahead lay the exit of the Barrow Channel into the Irish Sea. From north to south, a half mile of open water separated Roa Island and the southern tip of Rampside from Piel Island in the middle of the channel, and another half mile from the southern tip of Piel to the north-curved tip of Walney. The deep-water channel ran to the right of Piel Island, an utterly flat and grassy bit of land capped by the ruins of Fouldry Castle.

That channel was narrow, only about two hundred yards wide. Spread now along that gap were dozens of small craft, pleasure boats, fishing boats, even a few yachts. They'd been gathering all morning, lining up across the channel entrance. Closer at hand, Zodiac rafts hopped and bumped ahead of churning white wakes as they moved to intercept the slow-moving mountain of the transport.

"Jesus Fucking H. Christ," Jack Rawlston said.

Folding his arms, he leaned against the portside railing forward, watching the show.

Timmy Smithers slung his "long," SAS slang for his SA80 rifle, over his shoulder and joined him from farther aft along the forecastle railing. "Quite a party, huh?"

Rawlston spat over the railing and into the sea. "Fucking idiots," he said.

"Shit, mate," Smithers replied with a grin. He was former Australian SAS, and his words oozed outback affability. "Things just wouldn't be the same if we didn't have our little embarkation party, right? Lets us know they *care.*"

Straightening, Rawlston raised his binoculars to his eyes, massive Zeiss 15×45s that snapped even the most distant of the boats into crisp, close-up detail. He'd purchased them on eBay rather than relying on his service-issue set. Several of the larger small craft out there sported banners draped festively from their sides. "STOP NUKE SHIPMENTS," a particularly garish red and green sign read above a crude drawing of a human skull. "NO MOX," read another.

"Pretty wild, ain't it, mate?" Smithers said. "Playing up to CN-bloody-N, I suppose."

"Just so they move the hell out of our way," Rawlston replied after a moment. He focused on a pair of Zodiacs that appeared to be closing with the *Sandpiper* off her bow. Each carried two men wearing wet suits, bent low to keep their craft stable as they skipped off the waves.

"Looks like they're siccing the dogs on 'em as we speak," Smithers said, pointing. To starboard, the *Sandpiper*'s escort was leaping ahead, lean and white, a shark to the *Piper*'s lumbering whale. She was the *Ishikari* of the Japanese Maritime Self-Defense Force, the numerals 226 prominent on her knife-edged prow.

"Some of them're already inside the exclusion zone," Rawlston said. "Serves 'em bloody right if the *Ishi* runs 'em down!"

"Yeah, but then if she does, you have all of those lawsuits and demonstrations and newspaper editorials," Smithers replied. "So tiresome."

Rawlston lowered the binoculars and looked at the other man. Like Rawlston, Smithers wore civilian clothing, though the tactical vest, boots, and floppy-brimmed hat were all military issue. As with Rawlston, a small radiation meter hung from his tactical vest. In fact, both men *were* civilians, but until four years ago Rawlston had been in the British SAS. Now he was a contract employee for Pacific Nuclear Transport Limited, more usually called simply PNTL. He and the twenty-nine other security personnel on board the *Sandpiper* had been referred to more than once and disparagingly as "rent-a-cops." That, he thought, might be true . . . but they were very *dangerous* rent-a-cops, the very, very best that money could buy. PNTL had a great deal riding on these radio-active cargoes, and could not afford to hire anyone who was less than the absolute best.

"There they go!" Smithers shouted, and he gave a whoop. "*Run*, you green little bastards!" The *Ishikari* was swinging to port, now, putting herself between the demonstrators and the slow-moving *Sandpiper*, using her sheer tonnage to clear a path through the line of demonstrators, scattering them. Overhead, a Royal Navy helicopter, a Sea King off the RNS *Campbeltown*, roared south with a clattering thunder of rotor noise. Under threat from sea and air, the demonstrators appeared to be losing their nerve.

"You'd think," Rawlston said with just a shadow of a smile, "that they'd be happy to see our backs! We're hauling the radioactive crap out of their backyards, after all!"

"Aw, the cobbers're more worried about saving the bloody whales, ain't that right? Don't matter if a city or two gets fried . . . but we can't hurt the *whales*!"

One of the approaching Zodiacs, Rawlston saw with approval, had been capsized by the *Ishikari*'s surging wake. Raising his binoculars again, he studied the scene with a grin as two wet-suited swimmers floundered in the chop. The occupants of the other Zodiac had been attempting to deploy a large banner reading: "GREEN-PEACE," no doubt for the benefit of news cameras ashore, but the sudden dunking of their comrades had interrupted the operation.

This sort of thing, Rawlston knew, happened around the world in dozens of other ports. Greenpeace and similar anti-nuke organizations liked to create demonstrations and photo ops any time a military nuclear vessel put to sea or, as in this case, when radioactive material was being shipped from port to port. These shipments of processed radioactive material had been carried on between Britain and France on one side and Japan on the other since 1995.

PNTL had completed almost two hundred shipments during those fourteen years, with not a single accident, not a single release of radioactivity, not a single hijacking or act of piracy, not a single problem of any type.

But Greenpeace and the others still had to put their tuppence in.

Ishikari was through the channel entrance now, and the *Pacific Sandpiper*, slowly gathering speed, followed in her wake. Rawlston watched the lines of civilian craft milling about to either side, continuing the honking and tooting of horns, the wail of sirens, the clang of bells. He could hear voices now, chanting, though the distance was too great for him to make out the words.

But the way was open as *Pacific Sandpiper* nosed through the channel entrance and into the chop of the Irish Sea. The wind was brisker here, kicking up whitecaps beneath the gray scud of the sky.

"At least," he told Smithers, "that's the *worst* part of the voyage behind us!"

★ ★ ★ ★

Some eighty yards aft of Rawlings and Smithers, the main deckhouse superstructure of the *Pacific Sandpiper* bulked huge and white above the main deck. On an open wing of the superstructure, high above the main deck, two other men leaned against the railing and watched the demonstrators falling astern.

"Jikan desu yo," one said.

"Hai!"

Both men were Japanese and, so far as anyone else on board the ship was concerned, were representatives of the Japanese utilities company that owned 25 percent of PNTL. They certainly had the requisite papers and ID, though the *real* Ichiro Wanibuchi and Kiyoshi Kitagawa were now dead, their bodies hidden in two separate Dumpsters on the outskirts of Sellafield, twenty-five miles north of Barrow.

The second man pulled an encrypted satellite phone from his windbreaker, punched a code into its keyboard, and began speaking rapidly into the mouthpiece.

1

"MY GOD, MITCHELL!" CHARLIE Dean said, shaking his head. "You have *got* to be freaking kidding!"

"You know better than that, Mr. Dean," Thomas Mitchell said. "MI5 *never* kids."

Dean was sitting with the three security people at a console at the center of a large room, hanging one floor above the security checkpoint leading from the Royal Sky cruise ship terminal out to the dock. In front of them was a giant flat-screen TV monitor, on which the black-and-white image of a naked man could be seen walking through a broad, white tunnel. To one side, a much smaller security monitor showed the same man, this time from a high angle near the ceiling and in color, wearing dark trousers, a yellow shirt, and a white nylon jacket.

"Yeah," Dean agreed cautiously. "When it comes to a sense of humor, you're worse than the FBI and CIA put together. But since when did you guys turn into porno-graphic voyeurs?"

"Believe me, Mr. Dean," the woman sitting next to him at the console said. Her name badge bore the name "Lock-wood," and she was, Dean knew, a technical specialist with X-Star Security, the company that manufactured the equipment. "There is *nothing* whatsoever pornographic about this!" She sounded prim and somewhat affronted.

"That's right," David Llewellyn added, grinning. "After the first couple of hundred naked bodies, you don't even notice!"

Thomas Mitchell was an operative with MI5, Great Britain's government bureau handling counterintelligence, counterterrorism, and internal security in general, while David Llewellyn was the head of the Security Department on board the cruise ship *Atlantis Queen*. Dean had met Mitchell in Washington a week earlier, and knew him to be a dour and somewhat unimaginative British civil servant; he'd met Llewellyn and Lockwood only that morning, when Mitchell had escorted him into the Royal Sky Line's Southampton security section.

"That hardly matters, does it?" Dean said. "It's *their* privacy at stake, not how many naked people you've seen in your career."

Interesting, Mitchell thought. Llewellyn was seeing bodies. Dean was seeing *people*.

"I needn't remind you, Mr. Dean," Mitchell said, "that conventional metal detectors simply cannot pick up plastic bottles containing explosives or petrol, hard-nylon knives, or anything else made of plastic. Richard Reid walked through metal detectors several times before he boarded Flight Sixty-three."

Richard Reid had been the infamous "shoe bomber" who'd been subdued by passengers on board an American Airlines Boeing 767 in December of 2001. He'd been trying to light a fuse in one of his shoes, which had been packed with PETN plastic explosives and a triacetone triperoxide detonator. Ever since, airline passengers in the United States had been required to remove their shoes at airport terminal security checkpoints.

Charlie Dean had considerable experience with antiterrorist security technologies of all types. A senior field officer of the U.S. National Security Agency's top-secret Desk Three, he'd circumvented quite a few of them while on covert missions overseas, and he'd gone through more than his fair share at secure installations back home. In fact, he'd read about *this* technology some years ago, though he'd never seen it in operation. It was called backscatter X-ray scanning, and it was the latest twist in high-tech security screening . . . as well as the most controversial.

"I seem to remember seeing this sort of thing in a movie, once," Dean said. "Slapstick stuff."

"*Airport*," Lockwood said, rolling her eyes. "Yes, we've been told. Numerous times."

The man on the screen was somewhat pixelated by the digital imaging process, but every detail stood out with startling clarity, from the frames of his glasses to the zipper of his open jacket—every detail except his clothing, which had been rendered invisible. His face seemed a little blank; Dean could see his eyeballs and eyelids easily enough, but the iris and pupil were almost impossible to distinguish.

But the rest! The guy was heavy, his belly bulging strangely over an invisible belt. His belt buckle appeared to ride tucked in beneath the bulge just below his navel, and he was wearing a small, bright crucifix on a chain around his neck. His pubic hair, the trail of hair up his belly to his navel, and the thicket on his chest and back all had a crisp, wiry, almost metallic look to it. Dean could just make out the zipper in the trousers at the man's crotch, and it was clear, as an older generation of men's tailors would have put it, that he "dressed to the left."

"I thought," Dean said, "that there was supposed to be a software algorithm that blurred faces and . . . other body parts."

"Oh, sure, some places still do that," Llewellyn replied. "But that rather defeats the purpose, doesn't it? People have tried smuggling guns or drugs hidden at their crotch or between their butt cheeks, where they think a pat-down wouldn't find them." He made a face. "You Americans are *so* squeamish about this sort of thing."

Lockwood typed a command into the keyboard in front of her, and on the big screen the man's computer-processed image seemed to freeze, then revolved in space for a moment, showing his body from all possible angles. At the right of the screen, a column of data appeared as it was forwarded off a security card the man was carrying—his name, passport number, cell and home phone numbers, Social Security number.

"Show us level two," Mitchell told her.

Lockwood typed in another command, triggering a small flood of data. James Gullabry, it seemed, was American, was visiting England on business, and was a sales rep for Del Rey Computers. He lived in Westchester, just outside of Boston; he had a wife, Anne, and two children . . . and was on medication for depression and for type 2 diabetes. Apparently, he was taking the long way home, by way of a Mediterranean cruise. *That*, Dean thought, was unusual.

"What . . . you don't have his credit history?"

"We can call that up for you, if you want," Mitchell said.

And Dean knew the man wasn't joking.

It's not that Americans are squeamish about nudity, Dean thought, watching the image on the screen, though that *was* of course a factor. The whole privacy issue had become a hot button on both sides of the Atlantic in the paranoid years since 9/11. MI5 itself had been called on the carpet back in 2006, he recalled, when a member of Parliament had disclosed that the security agency maintained extremely detailed and highly secret files on 272,000 British subjects—the equivalent of 1 in every 160 adults.

How far did you go to stop the threat of terrorism, and to protect your citizens?

Where did you draw the line between protecting your citizens . . . and spying on them?

The man on the screen walked off to the left. A moment later, he was replaced by an attractive young woman. She was wearing a bracelet, a watch, two rings, a single-strand necklace, and small, bright bits of jewelry in her navel and through both nipples. Quite obviously she was not carrying a gun . . . or anything else for that matter, not even a book of matches. Hurriedly Dean looked away, focusing instead on the security cam image that showed a pleasant-looking woman in her twenties, wearing a skirt and a bright green blouse and with an exuberant cascade of long blond hair hanging down past her waist.

Damn it, he *was* embarrassed.

And yet Mitchell had a point. Dean remembered a humorous but half-serious comment that had floated about in the aftermath of the 9/11 terror hijackings . . . something to the effect that the only way to ensure passenger safety on an airline flight would be to strip every passenger stark naked and handcuff them to their seats.

Technology had all but delivered the first of those two requirements.

Lockwood used her keyboard to call up the woman's information.

"O-*kay*, then, Miss Johnson," Llewellyn said, reading her name off the screen. "Here, Mr. Dean. Watch this."

He turned a dial on his console, and on the big screen the young woman's hair faded to a pale transparency, then vanished completely. A plastic hair clip continued to hang unsupported behind her now completely bald head, and Dean noticed that her tuft of pubic hair had vanished as well. Somehow, if possible, the complete lack of hair made her appear even more shockingly naked.

"We can adjust the strength of the X-ray beams," Mitchell explained. "We've had people try to hide stuff in long hair, men and women both." He glanced at Dean, and seemed to read his expression. "Look, I *know* it's intrusive . . . but most people would rather have *this* than have security guards frisk them . . . or put them through a strip search!"

"Both of which slow down the queue," Lockwood added, "and make for unfortunate delays at the security checkpoints."

"Do they have a choice?" Dean asked.

"Oh, yes," Llewellyn told him. "They can walk through the machine, or they can submit to a hand search. Of *course* they have a choice!"

Dean wondered if most people knew they even had that option. That had been a problem with trials in the United States, he remembered . . . that, and the fact that most people simply didn't know how graphically revealing this sort of device actually could be. They heard "X-ray" and immediately thought of *medical* X-rays, black-and-white transparencies showing decidedly non-erotic shadows of bone and translucent tissue.

"So how much radiation are those people getting, anyway?" Dean asked. He knew the answer but wondered what the security people would say.

"About as much radiation as you would pick up walking outdoors in full sunshine," Lockwood replied. "Not an issue."

Dean looked back at the main screen as the computer froze the shockingly bald woman's image momentarily, then rotated it in three dimensions before going back to a real-time image. Her hair, clearly not hiding anything dangerous, faded back into view, and she stepped off-screen.

"I see you leave no fig leaf unturned," Dean said. "You could make a fortune putting these up on the Internet, you know."

"The data are *immediately* discarded, Mr. Dean," Mitchell told him.

This backscatter unit, Dean noted, was an upgraded

model, much improved over the first such devices of a few years ago. The first one had gone into service back in 2007, at the Sky Harbor International Airport in Phoenix, Arizona. With that unit, airline passengers had stepped onto the painted outlines of footprints in front of a cabinet the size and shape of a refrigerator and stood there for ten seconds. Fast-improving technology had soon made this new model possible, with a computer imaging the body in real time, manipulating viewing angles, and even adjusting its sensitivity to peer down through successive layers of leather, cotton, nylon, and silk. Privacy concerns had delayed the widespread adoption of the technology; there'd been talk about having the computer blur sensitive parts of the body, or even redraw it as a kind of cartoon image that wasn't so completely graphic.

As Mitchell had pointed out, though, there were problems with that approach. New types of high-velocity explosives in a plastic container the size of a pack of cigarettes were powerful enough to kill several people, or depressurize an airliner's passenger cabin. That had been Reid's intent, obviously, with his PETN-laden shoe.

And if you *could* look at each and every passenger boarding an aircraft or, in this case, a cruise ship and be able to see with absolute clarity and perfect certainty whether or not just one person out of some hundreds or thousands was smuggling a bomb or other weapon . . . didn't simple common sense demand that security forces make use of that technology?

It is, Dean thought, *an increasingly strange and difficult world.*

"Uh-oh," Mitchell said, sitting up straighter in his swivel chair. "We've got a live one."

"Ah!" Llewellyn said. "I see it. Okay, Mr. Dean! *There* is why we don't have the machine put a blur over 'body parts,' as you put it!"

Another man had just walked into the tunnel. He was skinny, his ribs showing clearly. He was bearded and, though his facial features were somewhat vague and blank-eyed on the X-ray image, his movements appeared jerky and seemed nervous or uncertain. Hanging above his genitals were what appeared to be three semitransparent bags, each the size of a man's fist. His hips were oddly pinched by an invisible cloth belt cinched tightly against his skin. As the image rotated, two more bags came into view, one flattened over each buttock. On the security camera, the man was wearing loose-fitting trousers and a shirt with the long tail hanging down outside the pants halfway to his knees. To an unaided eye, there was no way to see the bags secreted underneath.

" 'Nayim Erbakan,' " Mitchell said, reading the data on the right as Lockwood called it up. "Turkish national, German visa."

Llewellyn reached up and touched his communicator headset. "Fred? David. Hold this one! Looks like a mule."

On-screen, the man looked up, stopped, then took a backward step, raising his hands as if to push someone away. Two security guards entered the screen, one from the left and one from the right. Closing on Erbakan, they took him by either arm—with holstered semiautomatic pistols at their hips, with extra ammo clips, plastic belt pouches, badges, ID cards, wallets, radios, handcuffs, flashlights, nightsticks, zippers, buttons, the bills and internal structure of their caps, and other paraphernalia all dangling unsupported from their otherwise nude bodies.

Dean stood and walked across to the slanted windows looking down onto the terminal concourse and security area. The two guards, fully dressed in blue and white uniforms, were escorting the man away from the white tunnel toward a door marked "Private" and "No Admittance."

The security process had been efficiently streamlined, Dean saw. A line of civilians, most of them in appropriately garish vacation clothing, stood in line waiting to go through the backscatter scanner. Each person in turn would stop beside a conveyor belt and deposit wallets, handbags, cameras, cell phones, and other devices and carry-on items into baskets for conventional X-ray scans, then walk first through an old-fashioned metal detector and then through the smoothly sculpted white tunnel of the backscatter X-ray machine. Security guards stood at strategic points to control the traffic or to administer, as with Erbakan, more detailed and personal attention. Under the guards' watchful eyes, they retrieved their personal items at the end of the conveyor, on the far side of the backscatter device. Once they were cleared through the checkpoint, they filed through glass doors leading to the dock outside and the immense white cliff of the newest addition to the Royal Sky Line's fleet of luxury cruise ships, the *Atlantis Queen*.

Another young woman, looking harried and a bit impatient, stepped out of the tunnel below Dean's window, holding an infant on one arm. She turned, and held out her free hand, fingers impatiently waggling. A moment later a dark-haired girl walked out and took her hand. The girl couldn't have been more than ten.

Disgusted, Dean turned away and watched Lockwood, Llewellyn, and Mitchell at the console but did not walk back to where he could see the screen.

"Just how long have you been using this device?" he asked. He was trying not to think about the ten-year-old . . . or about a world gone so sick and paranoid that this kind of thing was thought necessary.

"Do you mean here in England?" Mitchell asked. "Or Royal Sky Line? We've had them operating at Heathrow International for a couple of years now."

"That's where I got my training," Llewellyn told him. "We started using this unit here just yesterday. The upgrades are amazing."

"We've already screened over a thousand of the *Queen*'s passengers," Lockwood added.

"Really? How many opted for a hand frisk?"

As he spoke, his right hand peeled a three-inch strip of

black, sticky plastic from the back of his tie, the movement blocked from the others by the screen itself.

"A couple of hundred," Lockwood told him. She shrugged. "Like Tom said, most people prefer this. It's less obtrusive. Less . . . *personal*."

"So what is the CIA's interest in our little peep show?" Llewellyn wanted to know.

Dean had introduced himself that morning as a security analyst with the CIA, though he'd used his real name. The National Security Agency remained not only the largest and best-funded intelligence agency in the United States but also the most secretive. Its operatives rarely admitted who they really worked for. NSA employees jokingly referred to the acronym as "No Such Agency" or "Never Say Anything," and, even yet, few people in the general public had ever heard of the organization, or knew anything about it.

But *everyone* had heard of the CIA.

"We're interested," Dean said carefully, reciting from a memorized script, "in how new transportation security technologies might be interfaced with various international databases, passport records, and police files, so that we can track known criminals and terrorists before they can even enter the United States or Great Britain."

Unobtrusively he pressed the tape, sticky side down, against the back of the freestanding console. The tape had a meaningless ten-digit number printed on it in white letters; if a security sweep found it later, it would look like just another serial number.

"Royal Sky Line," Dean added as he finished, "is introducing some . . . novel concepts along those lines."

"Ah. You mean the passenger tracking chips," Llewellyn said, nodding.

"Among other things."

"Makes sense, actually. As you saw, Ship's Security personnel can pull everything necessary in a person's jacket into a database when they check in, or even when they first buy their ticket. When they check on board, they receive a key card with a magnetized strip and an embedded microchip. It serves as the key to their state-room, but it also holds all pertinent data about that person, *and* lets them be tracked wherever they go on board the ship. At any given moment, Ship's Security can determine the exact location of everyone aboard. If someone goes ashore at a port of call but doesn't come back aboard for some reason, Security knows about it."

"Scanners in the passageways and public areas ping the cards' strips every few seconds," Lockwood added. "A computer in Security tallies up where every card is at any given moment, and which cards are missing. Or it can isolate, identify, and pinpoint the location of any one particular card, anywhere on board."

"Very convenient," Dean said. "What if someone for-gets and leaves his card in his stateroom?"

"Then a steward very politely informs him of the fact," Llewellyn replied, "as soon as he tries to go ashore or to enter a monitored public area. If he loses his card, he is es-corted down to Security, where his identity can be veri-fied, and he is issued another card."

"And how do you safeguard the data?"

"I beg your pardon?"

Dean gestured at the back of the big screen. "You've got a lot of sensitive, personal information there. I'm not saying you, necessarily . . . but what's to stop one of your security people from misusing it?"

"I'm *sure* I don't know what you mean," Llewellyn said.

"You liked the looks of that one woman who just went through . . . what was her name? Miss Johnson? And here, right at your fingertips, you have her age, her marital status, her address, her phone number, her Social Security number, what she does for a living, where she works, health conditions. For all I know, it tells you whether she

prefers Harvey Wallbangers to scotch on the rocks! Are
you telling me you don't see how that much personal information could be misused?"

"*All* data here are destroyed, Mr. Dean," Mitchell insisted.

"No, they're not! Those X-ray images are erased—or
so you tell me—but the personal data are still there. And
why should the public accept your word that even the
naked pictures get shit-canned?"

"Mr. Dean," Lockwood said. "There are professional
and legal standards here. We are professionals, no less
than doctors or therapists! And our clients, the companies
using X-Star's equipment, I assure you are self-policing.
A scandal—"

"In other words, Mr. Dean, we're *not* going to do anything that would generate lawsuits or right-to-privacy in-
junctions," Llewellyn said, interrupting.

"Maybe not," Dean said, shrugging. "But what about
outside access? Hackers?"

Lockwood patted the keyboard in front of her. "This
network is completely isolated from the Internet. Hackers
can't get in."

"Oh? What kind of protection software do you use?"

Lockwood hesitated, and Mitchell answered, "They're
not supposed to tell you, but you've been cleared. It's a
software package called Netguardz."

"Ah, right. I've heard of it."

"Since when is the American CIA so interested in protecting the privacy of individual citizens?" Mitchell asked.

"There's a difference between what I do for a living,"
Dean replied slowly, "and what I feel and believe on a
personal level."

"Really?" Lockwood said. "Maybe you're in the wrong
line of work."

"I've often thought so."

The door to the security room opened and a young
man in the blue uniform of the Royal Sky Line walked in.

He was young, in his mid-twenties, perhaps. "Hey there," he said. "Shift change!"

"About time," Llewellyn said, standing. He turned to Lockwood. "Can I get you anything, Ellen? Tea? Coffee?"

"I'm fine, thanks," the woman said. "I'll be breaking for lunch in a little bit."

"Suit yourself. How about you gents?"

"Thanks, no."

Mitchell stood up as well. "Well . . . you wanted to see the operation here, Mr. Dean," he said. "Are we done? You got all you wanted?"

"I think so," Dean said. He nodded at Llewellyn and Lockwood. "It was nice meeting you both. Thank you for your help."

He turned for one last look down through the windows onto the concourse again. There was someone he'd been watching for. . . .

Yes! There she was. He resisted the urge to wave.

"See anyone you know?" Mitchell asked.

"Yes, actually. A . . . friend."

"More CIA?" Mitchell frowned. "Just how many of you are there here today?"

Dean grinned. "Just me. She's not Company." Which was true enough. "She's just a friend, and I happen to know she's taking your cruise to the Med and was going to check in through your queue today."

"Really?" Mitchell said, joining him at the window and looking down at the line of tourists. "Who is it?"

"*I'm* not going to tell you that!" Dean said. "You're about to strip her naked and peer up every orifice in living black and white! She can just remain anonymous, thank you very much!"

Lockwood snorted. "If his friend was CIA, you don't think he'd *tell* us so, do you?"

The young man sat down at the console in the seat Llewellyn had vacated. "What's all this? CIA? Cloak-and-dagger stuff?" The others ignored him.

Dean turned away from the window. "What's next on the tour?"

"Lunch, actually," Mitchell said, standing by the door. "After you?"

As Dean walked out, he heard the young man's voice behind him. "Coo! Now *there's* a sweet bird!"

"Jesus!" Lockwood said. *"Grow up!"*

Royal Sky Line security queue
***Atlantis Queen* passenger terminal**
Southampton, England
Thursday, 1202 hours GMT

Carolyn Howorth couldn't resist. She stepped into the yawning mouth of the white tunnel and struck a sexy pose, hips cocked sharply to one side, left hand on her hip, right arm straight overhead. "See anything you like, boys?" she asked.

Dropping her arm, she swished out of the tunnel, smiling sweetly at the cruise line security guard waiting outside.

He looked puzzled. "Did you say something, ma'am?" he asked.

"Not really," she said. "Just checking to see if these things are equipped for sound."

"No, ma'am. It just takes your picture."

"Oh, I see. Is that all?"

She glanced up over her left shoulder. She could see the line of windows up near the ceiling of the cavernous room, the office where Charlie Dean was making nice with the Royal Sky Line security people, and wondered if he'd just gotten an eyeful. She didn't see him, however, and so she walked on down the line to the end of the conveyor, claiming her handbag, her camera, and her laptop computer. She asked the guard for a hand check on her camera. He had her remove her camera from its case and looked down into the lens, but Carolyn noticed that his eyes were watching hers, checking for nervousness or other telltale clues.

"Open the computer, please, miss," the guard told her, setting the camera aside. "Thank you. Now turn it on for me."

She pressed the power switch and they waited for the machine to boot up. "Damned Vista," she told him. "It tries to boot everything at once and takes forever."

Finally, though, the screen came up. Satisfied, the guard motioned to her to close it up and put it away. "Thank you," he said, apparently satisfied. "Have a nice cruise!"

"Thank you," she told him. She was wondering if he had any idea what was possible in computer technology these days. It wouldn't be hard at all to have a working laptop exactly like this one, which booted to a full screen and yet had free space enough inside for a disassembled gun or high explosives or almost anything else she cared to smuggle onto the ship.

Presumably, they'd checked for that sort of thing when her laptop had gone through the carry-on scanner . . . but still.

In fact, her machine wasn't at all what it appeared to be, or not entirely, at least. The computer part *did* work.

Technically, Carolyn did not work for the NSA as Charlie Dean did. She was GCHQ, one of the Menwith Girls, as they were known, an employee stationed at Menwith Hill, in Yorkshire, of the highly secret British eavesdropping agency that was closely partnered with America's NSA. Carolyn had worked with Dean before, in an op targeting the Russian mafia.

Through the double glass doors and onto the dock. A gangway festooned with bunting extended up to the entry port on the *Atlantis Queen*'s port side, where a ship's officer waited for her.

He checked the electronic pad he was holding. "Good

afternoon, Ms. Carroll," he said with a pleasant smile. "May I see your ticket and your passkey, please?"

"Certainly." She fished into her handbag and produced both. For this operation, Carolyn was traveling as Judith Carroll and all of the electronic information about her in the system, save for her nationality and her gender, was completely false.

The officer swiped her card through a reader and handed it back to her. "Here you are, Ms. Carroll. We'll keep your ticket for you in the bursar's office. Your passkey serves as your ticket and your ID during your cruise. You have your ID bracelet?"

"Oh, yes. Somewhere here." Again she fumbled through her bag, producing a slender strip of white plastic with a small metal clasp.

"I don't need it, miss," he told her. "All of your information is in the ship's computer. I was just going to tell you that you should keep your passkey with you at all times during the cruise . . . but that if you want to go to the pool, the spa, the sauna, or any of the other shipboard facilities where you might not want to have to carry the key along, you can wear that bracelet instead."

"But what's it all *for*?" she asked him, giving him her best wide-eyed innocent's look.

"Security, miss. It's for your safety." He pressed several keys on his electronic pad. "Right, then! You're all checked in. Stateroom Six-oh-nine-one. That's straight ahead to the elevator, then up to Deck Six and follow the signs. Have a nice voyage!"

"Thank you . . ." She glanced at his name badge. "Mr. Norton, is it?"

"*Lieutenant* Norton, miss."

"Maybe I'll see you around the boat?"

He grinned at her. "Could be. But it's a *ship*, not a boat."

She started to reply, but he was already turning to greet the next person coming up the gangway.

Not a problem. Norton wasn't part of the security staff in any case. She needed to see if she could run into Foster, Ghailiani, or Llewellyn sometime during the course of the voyage.

In the meantime, she was going to enjoy this assignment. A four-week cruise to the eastern Mediterranean? With stops in Madeira, Greece, Turkey, and Israel? And all at the Company's expense! Now *that* was luxury!

She was looking forward to checking out her accommodations for the next glorious month.

Yeah, this was going to be *fun*!

Lower Mortimer Road
Woolston, England
Thursday, 1215 hours GMT

Mohamed Ghailiani trudged up the steps leading to his flat, one flight up from the street just across the Itchen Toll Bridge from the center of Southampton. He was tired and he was worried. He'd tried phoning home earlier that morning, but Zahra hadn't answered. With all of the craziness going on at work lately . . .

He turned his key in the lock and stepped through the front door. "Zahra?" he called.

There was no answer. Odd.

Pocketing his keys, he walked through to the living room. "Zahra? I'm home!"

Mohamed Ghailiani was Moroccan, but his family had moved to England in 1973, when he'd been five. He was a Crown subject and thought of himself as British. He was not particularly religious, though he did go to mosque most Fridays. It was a formality, something that gave him a social connection with other members of Britain's Moroccan community.

He'd worked for Royal Star Line for six years, now.

Before that, he'd worked for a computer company in London, and before that he'd been an electronics technician in the British Army. He was *good* with computers.

He supposed that that was why Khalid had approached him two days ago.

Finding no one in the living room, he continued through to the kitchen. The men were waiting for him there.

"*What are you*—," he began, but stopped when the two men pointed handguns squarely at his face.

"Shut up, you," one of the gunmen said in heavily accented English. He pointed at one of the white-painted kitchen chairs beside the table. "Sit down. Someone wants to talk to you."

Trembling, Ghailiani did as he was told.

2

"I DON'T LIKE IT," DEAN SAID.

"You're not being paid to like it," the voice of William Rubens whispered in Dean's ear. "It's necessary."

"Oh, yes. *Necessary.* And all in the sacred and most holy name of national security."

"Are you having a problem with this op, Mr. Dean?" Rubens asked. "Something *personal*?"

Rubens was the head of Desk Three, Deputy Director of the National Security Agency, and Dean's boss. A tiny microphone and bone-conducting speaker surgically implanted behind Dean's left ear picked up his own voice—which could be pitched just above a sub-vocalized murmur and still be clearly heard back at the Art Room, the black chamber beneath NSA headquarters that ran Desk Three operations—and played Rubens' replies in his head. The antenna and power supply that gave Dean a direct satellite comm link back to Fort Meade, Maryland, and the headquarters of the NSA was coiled up in his belt. His handlers in the Art Room had been able to listen in on his entire conversation with Mitchell, Llewellyn, and Lockwood.

The strip of plastic he'd left in the Security Office, however, was a bit more sophisticated.

"No, sir," Dean told Rubens. "Nothing that will affect the mission, anyway. But I *don't* like spying on an ally, and I *don't* like spying on ordinary people."

It was after lunch, now, and Dean was sitting on one of the plastic couches in the main waiting area just outside of the security checkpoint, a laptop computer open in front of him. Several hundred people, most in casual tourist dress, sat elsewhere on the concourse, gathered in small groups talking, or were lining up to go through the checkpoint. He stared at the laptop's screen, his lips moving slightly as he continued to speak with Rubens three thousand miles away.

"Okay. This should do it." Dean pressed the return key on his laptop. "Initiating. Are you getting the signal?"

"Wait a second."

There was a long pause. Transatlantic encrypted transmissions had been more and more uncertain of late. Communication satellite coverage wasn't as good these days as it had been ten years earlier, thanks to an aging infrastructure and some serious budget cuts. Even the NSA, with the largest budget of any branch of the U.S. intelligence community, had been feeling the bite lately.

"Okay," Rubens' voice said. "We've got it."

Dean was seated only a couple of hundred feet from the upstairs room housing the backscatter X-ray security system, a deliberate positioning that kept him inside the range of the sophisticated surveillance device with which he was working. Inside his laptop case was a black plastic box with two long power cords—apparently an AC adapter for the computer. Although it *could* serve as an adapter, most of the space inside the box was taken up by a unit that could transmit low-power signals to the microcircuitry embedded within the piece of tape Dean had left in the security office, initiating an information dump. The batteries were disguised as screws in the casing, while the coiled-up power cords served as an antenna. Dean's laptop, in turn, took the incoming data and boosted it along, via satellite, to Fort Meade.

The plastic strip adhering to the back of the computer console upstairs included a microphone only a little thicker than a human hair, and a simple-minded computer chip that could store a few seconds' worth of incoming sounds, then transmit them when Dean's remote unit pinged it. Power for that transmission came from the ping itself, so routine security scans of the upstairs office shouldn't pick it up, not even active scans by units designed to pick up feedback from more conventional microcircuitry.

"We're getting clear keystrokes," Rubens told him. "Don't move for a bit."

"I'm not going anywhere," Dean told him.

Upstairs, someone—either Lockwood or, God help them all, the young punk with the big mouth—was typing on the console keyboard, calling up names and other data on the passengers as they filed through. Each keystroke made a distinct sound, as individual as a fingerprint. As the strings of keystroke clacks and clatters were beamed across the Atlantic, they were processed and stored at the Tordella Supercomputer Facility on the grounds of Fort Meade.

Over the space of several hours, the NSA computers would gather more and more keyboard information. Space bars, for example, made a very different sound when struck than regular keys. So did the return key, and it was always struck at the end of a string of characters representing a command. Individual letters and numerals were slightly different from one another, and certain strokes— the numerals 1 and 2 and the letters *e* and *a*, for instance— were statistically more common than others. In the course of an afternoon, the NSA's powerful decryption algorithms could with fair to high reliability assign an ASCII code to each distinct keystroke click, producing a transcript of Lockwood's typing that would be almost as clear as it would have been if the Art Room had a camera peering over her shoulder. By tomorrow morning, the Art Room would be able to watch as she or whoever else might be on duty in the security office entered the passwords that gave them access to the entire system at the start of the workday.

And the NSA would then have that access as well.

That access wouldn't give direct access to all of the Royal Star Line's security and financial records, but it *would* give them direct access to the security software running on the company's internal network. Netguardz was one of several commercial and industrial software packages originally written by coders working for the NSA under a black project called Trojan Horse. Sold worldwide to government and business clients in over eighty countries, each program included built-in back doors allowing the NSA to bypass firewalls and security passwords as easily as if they weren't even there.

And since Royal Star Line *did* have computers that talked to the Internet for credit card transactions and taking reservations, Netguardz could use wireless technology to give the NSA direct access even to an internal system that was not hooked up to the Internet.

A tall, lanky man in a rumpled suit walked up and sat down on the plastic couch a few feet to Dean's right, unfolded a copy of the *Sun*, and began to read. Ilya Akulinin was relatively new to Desk Three. The son of naturalized Russian immigrants and a native of Brooklyn, New York, Akulinin spoke fluent Russian that had led to his running numerous ops with America's new Russian Federation allies, first as a Green Beret in the Army and now as an NSA officer working out of the agency's Deep Black ops department, and Desk Three.

"So what happened to your British nanny?" Akulinin

asked, his voice pitched low enough that only Dean—and the electronic eavesdroppers in the Art Room back at Fort Meade, of course—could hear.

"Who, Mitchell?"

"Yeah. Looks like he was sticking pretty close to you all morning."

"He took me to lunch in the employee cafeteria," Dean said. "Then he said he had work to do, we shook hands, and he left me on my own. Get the Art Room to read you the transcript, why don't you?"

"I would if you had anything interesting to say."

"See the guy at two o'clock, gray suit, leaning against the wall next to the ladies' room?"

"Yeah."

"He showed up five minutes after I sat down here. Pretending to wait for a friend in the rest room, but I think he's a tail."

"Wouldn't be surprised. He has the MI5 look."

What griped Dean was the perceived need to play these damned games. His time, he thought, could be used a hell of a lot more effectively tracking al-Qaeda operators, Russian mafia bad guys, or even putting in some time and rounds blowing holes in defenseless paper targets on the firing range back at Fort Meade. Spying on the Brits, on a *cruise ship* line, of all things, took international paranoia to a whole new low.

Ignoring Akulinin, Dean leaned in his seat and let his gaze move along the line of people checking on board the *Atlantis Queen*. Most of them, to judge by their occasionally loud but always upscale clothing, were well-to-do. Poor people did *not* book vacation cruises to the Mediterranean.

Some looked like businesspeople . . . with plenty of lawyers and doctors and a few accountants thrown into the mix. Most of the men were accompanied by wives, and a few by one or more kids as well, though, again, couples with small children didn't often take vacation cruises. The majority appeared to be older people, retirement age and above, which made sense. If you were retired, you might actually have the *time* to take a four-week cruise . . . to say nothing of the money.

There were exceptions, of course—with human beings there were *always* exceptions. A few older men were accompanied by *much* younger women who didn't look much like wives, for instance—and there were those two young men holding hands while they waited in line. There were even some more swarthy-skinned, black-haired individuals who might have been Middle Eastern, Pakistani, or Turkish, like the would-be drug smuggler he'd seen apprehended earlier.

But looking at individuals in the queue and trying to pick out the ones who might be terrorists simply didn't work. Not all terrorists looked Middle Eastern, which was why X-Star and its peep show, as Llewellyn had called it, was necessary.

And yet lots of what was going on back in the States had the smell of snooping for the taste of snooping, and there'd been concerns that the Patriot Act had been misused ever since its inception immediately after the destruction of the World Trade Center. Charlie Dean tended to believe, though, that if backscatter scanning prevented even one 9/11-style terror bombing, the invasion of privacy would be worthwhile.

He was less sanguine about the need to covertly infiltrate the commercial computer networks of the British government, or of British-based companies like Royal Sky Line. Great Britain was America's closest ally in the War on Terror and with GCHQ was an intimate partner in electronic eavesdropping and counterterror operations worldwide.

The rationale, as Dean understood it, was that the British government was coming under increasing fire for its own steady erosion of privacy rights. If the *Sun*, the *Guardian*, or another British newspaper found out that the NSA was sneaking peeks at British T and A—with London's active knowledge and participation—the firestorm of public reaction could be catastrophic. That, at least, was how the NSA's legal department saw it. By penetrating British security systems covertly, Washington gave London the absolute deniability it required.

Dean wondered if MI6—London's equivalent of the CIA—was performing similar black-bag ops in the United States.

Friends spying on friends. He was reminded of Henry L. Stimson, President Hoover's Secretary of State, who shut down the State Department's cryptoanalytic office in 1929 with the words "Gentlemen don't read each other's mail." That had certainly been a simpler and more innocent era. A more *naïve* era.

And, Dean reminded himself, even Stimson had reversed his views later.

"Okay, Charlie," another voice whispered in Dean's ear. Jeff Rockman was one of the handlers in the Art Room. "We have a solid link. Looks like the same command set over and over. You have a place to plant the unit?"

"Yes, we do," Dean replied. He began packing up to leave, slipping the laptop into its case and, as he did so, removing the AC power adapter from its Velcro-sealed side pocket and setting it on the seat beside him. "Any word on Carrousel?"

Carrousel was Carolyn Howorth's code name for the op.

"Just a ping from her laptop. She's on board and in her stateroom. Nothing else to report."

Technically, because of need-to-know restrictions, Dean wasn't even supposed to know Howorth was on the op, but he'd met her for dinner the night before and they'd compared notes. And the Art Room knew all about the rendezvous, since they'd been there electronically. Howorth, "CJ" to her friends, had been tapped for the op because she didn't have the hard-wired circuitry in her skull of her Desk Three counterparts. The embedded mike was supposed to be small enough and to use little enough metal that it wasn't supposed to trip security metal detectors, and it couldn't be seen by the X-Star scan, but Desk Three operators were not taking chances. Besides, the belt with its embedded antenna *would* be picked up by backscatter scanning, which meant Dean would have had to leave it in a suitcase and risk having the X-ray scans of his luggage tag him as an intelligence officer.

After a few more motions of getting things together, he stood up and walked off toward the terminal entrance.

★　★　★　★

Akulinin continued to pretend to read his newspaper, lingering over the page 3 girl, a half-naked young lady smiling seductively for the camera. One wag had noted that readers of the *Sun* didn't care who was leading the country, so long as the girl on page 3 had big breasts.

Dean, Akulinin noticed, had placed the AC adapter on the seat close enough to Akulinin that the tail couldn't see it. Good tradecraft. After a few moments, the gray-suited man by the ladies' restroom glanced at his watch, then followed Dean, staying well back to remain lost in the crowds.

Akulinin waited several minutes to be sure the MI5 agent was gone, then folded his paper, picked up the black box, and walked toward the security checkpoint.

"Excuse me," he said cheerfully.

A security cop eyed him with the cool, impersonal suspicion of his breed. "Yes?"

Akulinin handed him the adapter, its cables wrapped

around the black box. "I found this on the couch in the waiting area over there. You think someone lost it?"

The guard's eyes widened slightly, and he actually took a step back. "You found it? You shouldn't pick up abandoned packages, sir. . . ."

"Oh, for the love of—" Akulinin made a face. "It's not a *bomb*, for Christ's sake! Some guy working on his laptop left it there, okay? I think he just forgot and walked off without it. He'll probably be back looking for it any moment now. Is there a lost-and-found or something here?"

Gingerly the guard reached out and took the box, scowling at it as though it might bite him. "I'll have to check this out, sir."

"Sure, sure. You do that." Akulinin waited while the guard ran the box through the carry-on luggage X-ray machine, confident that the guts of the device looked like what they were supposed to be.

The woman operating the machine nodded at the first guard. He picked the box up at the other end of the conveyor. "Looks okay," he said, returning to Akulinin. "We'll lock it up in security and see if the guy comes to claim it."

Which, of course, was exactly what the Desk Three operators had expected the man would do.

"Great. You guys *are* careful, aren't you?"

"Better safe than sorry. You have a nice day, sir."

"I intend to."

From a safe vantage point, he watched as the guard took the device into a back room marked: "No Admittance," almost directly below the upper-floor security room where Dean had planted the microphone. Perfect! Better than they'd hoped. The Art Room reported that it still had a clear signal.

The best plants were those you could get your target to make for you.

Akulinin checked his watch. He would rendezvous with Dean back at the hotel. This op was going slick as grease, just the way he liked them.

There wasn't a thing now to worry about.

Lower Mortimer Road
Woolston, England
Thursday, 1315 hours GMT

The two thugs had kept Ghailiani waiting for almost an hour and a half, ignoring his increasingly frantic pleas for news of his wife. Finally, though, the front door banged open, and a third man entered, carrying a briefcase.

Ghailiani knew him. His name was Yusef Khalid and he was another employee of the Royal Star Line. He'd approached Ghailiani two days before, telling him that a number of crates would be delivered to the *Atlantis Queen* the day before she sailed and that it would be in Ghailiani's financial interest to accept those crates aboard without checking their contents.

The Moroccan had refused the offer, of course, at which point Khalid had become abusive and threatening. "You'd better change your mind, Mohamed," the man had told him. "Play it our way, and you pocket some extra money. Report this, and something *very* nasty could happen to your family. Understand me?"

It had been the threat against his family that had kept Ghailiani from reporting the incident to his bosses in the company security office. Khalid was an Arabic name. He might be Jihad.

Ghailiani desperately hoped that it was something else. Mafia business, maybe. Or the Camorra or the 'Ndrangheta. Some criminal underground group involved in smuggling something out of England to Greece or the Near East.

Please! he thought. *Not Jihad! . . .*

"What . . . what have you done with my wife?" he demanded. Zahra was always home at this time of the day. His long wait with the two gunmen had convinced him that they'd done something with her. "If you've hurt her—"

"Be quiet, Mohamed," Yusef Khalid said with a deadly, oily calm. "I am going to talk. You are going to listen. Understand?"

Ghailiani nodded, the movement a sharp jerk of his head. Terror warred with rage, but as he looked up into Khalid's hard eyes, terror began winning.

"You disappointed us the other day, Mohamed," Khalid said. "I asked you for help in the name of Allah, and you refused. I told you that you might wish to reconsider. And what did you tell me, Mohamed?"

"Th-that I would see what could be done."

"And I told you that you *would* do what we required, or your family might suffer. You remember?"

Ghailiani nodded.

"I gave you a cell-phone number to call when you were ready to cooperate."

"Please, Mr. Khalid. What you ask simply is not possible!"

"It *is* possible. All I need are the appropriate clearance codes, and an approval from the Purser's Office. You have them in your computer on the ship. I am afraid you are going to force us to use . . . stronger measures."

"Please, sir," Ghailiani said. "Please, for the merciful love of Allah!"

"The *love* of Allah has very little to do with this, Mohamed," the man said. He began opening his briefcase. "This is about jihad. It is about the martyred dead in Afghanistan and Iraq. It is about *justice*."

"Please . . . please . . . I *tried* to do what you told me, Mr. Khalid," Ghailiani said, sputtering. "I really did! But the security measures are simply too tight! I cannot—"

"Mohamed, you are the second-ranking security officer on board that ship, are you not?"

"Yes, but . . ."

"Then you will find a way to do this. If not, the consequences might well be unfortunate. For you . . . and for both of *them*."

"Wha—" Mohamed blinked, confused. "Both of . . . ?"

Fresh terror took him. He'd been so focused on Zahra, he'd forgotten about their daughter. She was supposed to be at school for several more hours, but . . .

Khalid dropped the photographs on the kitchen table in front of Ghailiani. There were three of them, horrifying and brutal, digital photos printed out in color on white stationery. Each showed a slightly different angle of two women sitting on a bed in an unfamiliar room. Both had their hands tied behind their backs, and both had strips of white cloth pulled tightly between their teeth and knotted behind their heads. Nouzha's blouse had been ripped open, exposing her bra. Zahra had what looked like a bruise on her right cheek, dark beneath the gag.

They stared up at the camera, the fear and the pleading evident in their moist eyes. To one side, a standing man was partly visible, though his head was cropped in each photo. He was holding a newspaper—the *Sun*—folded so that the date, today's date, was visible.

"Zahra and Nouzha," the man told Ghailiani. "We picked up your daughter on the street this morning, as she was walking to school." He shook his head sadly. "Education is wasted on females, you know. And it is *such* an unwholesome environment for an innocent girl." He gave a theatric sigh. "In any case, Mohamed, their lives truly are in your hands now."

For an instant, rage flared in Ghailiani, overpowering the fear, and he started to rise. "Where are they, you devil? What have you done to—"

One of Khalid's men put his hands on Ghailiani's shoulders and slammed him back down on the chair.

"They are in a safe place, and we've done nothing . . .

yet." Khalid's emphasis of the final word was chilling. "But if you do not get us the results we require, we have several interesting options."

Mohamed's momentary defiance shriveled. He knew he could not fight these men, and he knew that he would do anything, anything, to secure the release of Zahra and Nouzha. "Please . . ."

"Do we need to discuss those options? Which one of these two shall we begin to work on first, Mohamed? Your wife?" He turned one of the pictures to look at it. "She really is quite attractive. Or shall we begin with your daughter?"

"*Please*, I beg of you . . ."

"I imagine our people will want to start with your daughter. So pretty. She is what, sixteen?"

"Fifteen! She's . . . fifteen. Look, Mr. Khalid—"

"Fifteen? Such a tender age. It would be a shame to see her . . . spoiled."

"Please, no! I'll try to do what—"

"You will do more than *try*, Mohamed! You will do everything we demand of you! *Everything!* Otherwise, the next things we show you will be photographs demonstrating step-by-step *exactly* what we are doing to them . . . and perhaps one of your daughter's fingers as well! Or an ear? A nose?"

Ghailiani screamed. The man standing over him swung his arm, catching Ghailiani's face with a vicious open-handed slap. The seated man subsided into a series of deep, choking sobs.

"The first shipment will be arriving late this afternoon," the man told Ghailiani. He nodded, and one of the others scooped up the photographs and put them back in the briefcase. "If you want your wife and daughter back again, *unspoiled*, you will see to it that that shipment gets on board the ship, with no questions, no alarm. If you fail, or, most especially, if you approach the police or your employers with any of this, your wife and daughter will suffer terribly, I promise you! Do we understand one another?"

"Yes. Allah . . . yes!"

"Good."

The three visitors let themselves out Ghailiani's door. Behind them, the man continued to sob.

3

"WOW, MOMMY! THIS MUST be the biggest boat in the whole world!"

"Well, I don't know about that, sweetheart. But it *is* big, isn't it?"

"And Daddy's going to meet us here, right?"

"That's what he said, dear."

Nina McKay leaned against the railing on the main promenade, looking down at the line of passengers coming up the gangway and checking in with the ship's officer standing at the entrance. She still wasn't at all sure this cruise idea was a good one. Her mother could be . . . *commanding* at times, and often going along with her pronouncements was the simplest course of action.

"Mommy?"

"Yes, dear."

"When is Daddy going to come back and be with us?"

She sighed. "I don't know if that's going to happen, Melissa. We talked about that, remember?"

"I know, but I want him to come back home."

"I don't want to talk about that right now."

"You *never* want to talk about that."

"That's enough, Melissa. Mommy's tired!"

She looked up into the gray overcast, watching the wheel and plunge of seabirds. She *didn't* want to talk about it. Maybe it was time for that last phone call to her lawyer. It was time to end this.

"Daddy!" Melissa shrilled, standing on tiptoes and waving wildly. "I see Daddy!"

Nina looked down and saw Andrew McKay emerging from the glass doors to the cruise ship terminal and security area.

She resisted the momentary urge to wave.

It didn't look like he'd seen them up here in any case.

Andrew McKay crossed the pier toward the banner-bedecked gangway leading up to the *Atlantis Queen*'s quarterdeck, and wondered again what the hell he was doing here.

Well, of *course* he knew. Nina's mother had explained it all to him quite carefully, in words a three-year-old could understand. The woman could be incredibly force-ful when she put her mind to it—the perfect image of the rich, southern matriarch.

Nina had left him four months ago, and taken Melissa with her. Eleven years of marriage, flushed down the pipes for no rational reason that he could see at all. Nina's mother apparently thought that a little Mediterranean cruise was all that he and Nina would need to rekindle the romance and find each other again.

Fuck *that*. . . .

Seabirds darted and shrieked, drowning out all else. He stopped and looked up at the enormous ship.

According to the travel brochure, the *Atlantis Queen* was 964 feet long, 106 feet wide, and displaced some ninety thousand tons, making her the largest, as well as the newest, of the Royal Sky Line's fleet. She was a damned floating city, with a passenger complement of almost three thousand and a crew of nine hundred, with so much glitter and glitz that passengers could spend two weeks on board and never see the ocean, never even know they were at sea.

Rich people doing rich-people things. He shook his head and continued up the gangway.

At the top of the ramp, a uniformed ship's officer greeted him with a public-relations-perfect smile. "Good afternoon, Mr. McKay," he said. "May I see your ticket and your passkey, please?"

McKay handed them across, and the officer made a note on his electronic pad with a stylus. "You're in Four-one-one-four. That's fourth deck, on the port side. Your wife and daughter are in Four-one-one-six, the adjoining stateroom, as requested." If he thought the living arrangements were strange, he gave no sign of it. "They both checked in about an hour ago. Would you like for me to page them?"

"Uh . . . no. That won't be necessary."

"Very good, Mr. McKay." He began explaining the need to keep his key card on him and that he should wear the plastic bracelet if he wanted to use the pool, the spa, or some other ship's surface where he might not have a pocket handy. McKay listened to the spiel, thanked the man, and walked on past into the ship.

He wasn't sure he was ready to see Nina just yet. Perhaps a drink at one of the ship's several bars first . . .

★ ★ ★ ★

For Adrian Bollinger, this cruise represented a chance at a whole new life.

Tabitha Sandberg clung to his arm. "Oh, look at her, Adrian! Isn't she *gorgeous*?"

"She's all of that," Bollinger replied. "Not as gorgeous as *you*, of course."

"Oh, you . . ." She gave him a playful slap on the arm. "You're just saying that."

"No, Tabby. I'm not. Not now. Not ever."

They stepped through the glass doors and started across the dock toward the gangway.

A new life.

Bollinger had to admit to himself that he'd pretty much wrecked his old one. Trading shares on the floor of the New York Stock Exchange had been a lucrative life but an ungodly high-stress life as well. Too much money, not enough sense . . . He'd made mistakes. Bad ones. And he'd ended up as a guest for three years at a state correctional institution. His wife had left him; his daughter refused to talk to him. And they hadn't wanted him back at Tarleton Financial, not a guy with a prison record.

Somehow, though, *somehow* he'd managed to fight his way back. A friend with another firm, one of Bollinger's old competitors, in fact, had gotten him back on the trading floor at 11 Wall Street. He was damned good at what he did . . . and this time he was determined not to let the adrenaline or the stress get to him.

One day at a time. He'd been clean and sober for almost ten years, now.

At the bottom of the gangway, he stopped and turned Tabby to face him. "Happy us," he told her. "Not happy birthday, not merry Christmas. Happy *us*."

"You're the best there is, Adrian," she said. "Happy us!"

She sounded as though she meant it completely. Sincerity, Bollinger realized, was a damned rare commodity these days.

He'd met Tabitha at a party in New York City just a year ago, and she'd become an incredibly important part of his life . . . a constant reminder that there was more out there than Wall Street, more than stock quotes, more than *work*. She'd agreed to move in with him two weeks ago, and as a kind of celebration he'd surprised her with tickets for a flight to England followed by a cruise on board the *Atlantis Queen*. Tabby was something of an armchair historian, and a two-week cruise through the Mediterranean, stopping in at ports rich with history from Marseilles to Alexandria, was just what the stockbroker had ordered.

And why not? He could afford it. He'd gone from well-off to impoverished and fought his way back to wealthy. Money, he'd learned, definitely was *not* everything.

And now that Tabby was in his life, he could use his money to celebrate that fact.

"Good afternoon, folks," the officer at the top of the gangway said. He gave them his spiel and handed them their keys. "Stateroom Five-oh-eight-seven," he said. "That's four decks up, starboard side and aft. Enjoy your cruise!"

"Thanks," Adrian Bollinger said, grinning as he gave Tabby a squeeze. "We certainly intend to!"

Rubens' office
NSA Headquarters
Fort Meade, Maryland
Thursday, 0825 hours EDT

"*Shit*," Rubens exploded. He stared at the bright blue screen on his computer monitor for a long couple of seconds. "Not again!"

Of the sixteen agencies operating within the U.S. government, the National Security Agency arguably was the most technically advanced. From the mammoth machines of the Tordella Supercomputer Center, to the secure internal server networks within the agency itself, to the various shared networks and databases theoretically connecting all of the various government and law enforcement agencies and departments both in the United States and abroad, the NSA had long prided itself as having the very best IT systems, personnel, and equipment of them all.

So why the hell did they have to put up with these system crashes that were becoming more and more routine?

He touched an intercom button. "Pam? NCTC is offline again. Get me Lowell on the phone."

"Yes, sir."

Charles Lowell was the closest thing the National Counterterrorism Center had to an IT head; he was in charge of the complex tangle of databases, some classified, some not, that were intended as a resource to be shared among all government agencies taking part in the War on Terror.

And the project had been a nightmare from the start.

It wasn't Lowell's fault, of course. The problem was that the database project itself was simply so big, so complex, and involved so many different programmers and design tracks that it was almost impossible for any one person to see all the parts and how they had to work together at once.

The NCTC had spent half a billion dollars to upgrade the foundering system through a project called Railhead, and things rapidly had gone from bad to disastrous. At the moment, the system was nearly useless, and a lot of data collected through enormous cost and effort had gone missing.

The Counterterrorism Center had been trying to address the issues for several years, but things looked little better than they had when a Congressional oversight committee had flagged the project in 2008.

Rubens had come up to his office from the Art Room to run the name Nayim Erbakan through the sieve. It seemed strange that the man was smuggling what appeared to be a kilo or so of drugs—heroin, most likely—from England *back* to the eastern Med, and on a cruise ship no less. Maybe the guy just hoped to sell his wares to the rich tourists, but after a while intelligence officers developed a hyper-paranoid sixth sense about *anything* out of the ordinary, and Rubens was curious about this one.

But as soon as he'd tried to run the search through the TIDE database, the Center's network, one of several connecting various government agencies, had crashed.

"Mr. Lowell on the secure line, sir."

He picked up the handset. "Lowell? Rubens."

"The system's down," Lowell said. "I *know*. We're working on it."

"You've been working on it for six years. When is *it* going to work?"

"You've seen the schedule. The upgrades are supposed to be complete by 2012."

"*If* they come in on time. Can you put someone on a special search for me?"

Lowell sighed. "No promises. What is it?"

"A name. Nayim Erbakan." He spelled it out, waiting as Lowell jotted down the letters and repeated them back. At least the Turkish used the Western alphabet. One of the serious problems with the TIDE database was the problem in transliterating Arabic names. Was it "Mohammed," "Muhammad," or "Mohamed"? The answer, often, was *yes*, and cross-referencing numerous alternate spellings as well as aliases all for the same terrorist was part of the reason the database project wasn't fulfilling expectations.

"Got it," Lowell told him. "Any background?"

"He was just detained by MI5 in Southampton," Rubens told Lowell. "He was carrying five concealed plastic bags that might be drugs. I'd like to know if he's working with one of the major drug cartels over there . . . or if he has terrorist connections." Numerous terrorist operations financed their operations with drugs, especially lately, since the United States had begun aggressively freezing the bank accounts of organizations connected with al-Qaeda.

"I'll see what I can do, Rubens," Lowell replied. "But I can't keep taking my assets off important projects just to do your homework for you."

"You're there so we *can* do our homework," Rubens

growled. "And right now you're the dog that's eating it!" He hung up the phone, scowling. Usually he was more diplomatic than that, but Lowell's bureaucratic pettiness had provoked him.

Sometimes, Rubens thought, it was a toss-up as to who your worst enemies were in this game—the terrorists or the turf-guarding bureaucrats right here at home. TIDE's effectiveness depended on each of the U.S. agencies tasked with counterterrorism to feed data into the TIDE database, but those agencies shared a long history of mistrust and miserly secretiveness with regard to one another . . . and with good reason. An intelligence agency's funding depended, at least in part, on its success as perceived by Congress. If your operatives gathered a key piece of intelligence, handing it over to a competing agency might mean that they got a bigger slice of the budgetary pie, possibly at your expense.

There wasn't *supposed* to be any competition. The FBI was responsible for domestic threats, the CIA for gathering intelligence overseas, the DIA for military intelligence, the NSA for electronic eavesdropping worldwide, and so on, but with terrorists ignoring international boundaries, responsibilities inevitably overlapped.

It is, Rubens thought, *a hell of a way to run a railroad, or a war.*

Turning back to his computer monitor, he backed out of the screen showing the NCTC system's baleful error message and connected with the network serving the NSA's Deep Black program.

At any given time, Desk Three might have six or eight operations going worldwide. He tried to keep up with them all, of course, but some were decidedly low priority. They had a field team in Lebanon now, and he called up a status report. Maybe they could be diverted to Ankara for a look at Turkey's police records.

The team had been assigned to Operation Stargazer, a routine and low-risk op being conducted in conjunction with the CIA, designed to slip an electronic Trojan horse into Syrian intelligence.

Here they were. Howard Taggart and Lia DeFrancesca. Good. . . .

Security gate
***Atlantis Queen* dock**
Southampton, England
Thursday, 1412 hours GMT

"You are sure this will bypass the main gate?"

"Yes, sir. It's an access for heavy equipment, but it's rarely used." Ghailiani was sweating heavily, squeezed into the cab of the six-ton lorry between Khalid and the driver as they made the final turn off Herbert Walker Avenue and into an alley between two enormous warehouses. The terminal was a hundred meters to the left, the gate just ahead.

"Pray you are right, Mohamed."

The truck squeaked to a stop, the way ahead blocked by a padlocked chain-link gate. "I need to get out."

Khalid opened the passenger door and stepped down into the alley. Ghailiani followed. He fished inside the pocket of his slacks for the key he'd taken from the terminal security office forty minutes ago.

He'd been hoping to find the gate guarded. Security around the Royal Sky Line dock in Southampton had been tight, lately, and it was possible that an armed guard would have been posted, if only to foil would-be smugglers from reaching the dock and the *Atlantis Queen*'s hold.

But there was no one here. He unlocked the heavy padlock, pulled the chain from the fence, and swung the gate open. Khalid waved the truck through.

The truck turned left and kept going as Ghailiani closed the gate.

Ghailiani and Khalid would follow the truck on foot.

Atlantis Queen passenger terminal
Southampton, England
Thursday, 1418 hours GMT

"Everybody stay together!" Donald Myers fluttered his hands, trying to get the group's attention. "*Please* stay together! We still need to go through the security gate!"

He was, Myers thought, getting too damned old for this nonsense. A docent of the Walters Art Gallery in Baltimore, Maryland, he'd been guide and nanny for more tour groups now than he really cared to think about. Lately, it seemed, his job had been less about lecturing on eastern Mediterranean culture than it had been about herding rich little old ladies from one point to another and trying to keep them all together, a process uncannily like attempting to herd cats.

This time around, he was responsible for a group of eighteen, fourteen of them women, four of them men, and all of them over sixty. They'd signed up for the *Atlantis Queen* tour to Greece and the Near East, and he was there to give lectures on a variety of topics, from art in ancient Greece, to the Bible as history, to the writings of Homer; but sometimes he felt that he was little more than a poorly paid babysitter.

Leading the way, he stepped through the metal detector, then turned and waited for the rest. Ms. Jones and Mr. and Mrs. Galsworthy stepped through okay, but the alarm sounded as Ms. Dunne, waved through by an impatient security guard, set off the metal detector with her walker.

"Oh, dear," Ms. Dunne said, looking about. "Did I do that?"

"Over here, please, ma'am," the guard said. He began using a wand to check Ms. Dunne from head to toe, to make sure that it had been her walker that had triggered the device and not, Myers thought with wry amusement, a bomb hidden beneath her knit cardigan.

The others followed, one by one.

"Mr. Myers?" one elderly woman said after she'd stepped through.

"Yes, Ms. Caruthers?"

She pointed. "What does that sign mean?"

Just beyond the metal detector they were faced now by a somewhat ominous white tunnel and several blue-uniformed security guards. A sign on a metal pole to one side read:

PLEASE FORM SINGLE LINE FOR
X-RAY SECURITY SCREENING.
PROCEDURE IS SAFE AND UNOBTRUSIVE.
PASSENGERS MAY REQUEST HAND SEARCH
IN LIEU OF X-RAY SCAN.
THE PROCEDURE IS FOR YOUR SAFETY.
ROYAL SKY LINE REGRETS THE
INCONVENIENCE, AND HOPES YOU HAVE
A WONDERFUL CRUISE. THANK YOU.

"Just another security precaution," Myers told her. "Like it says. It's 'for your safety.' "

"X-rays can be harmful," Caruthers told him. "My doctor told me so."

"Ms. Caruthers, I'm very sure they wouldn't do it to people if there was any chance of harm."

"It's just like in that movie, Elsie," Ms. Jordan said, placing a reassuring hand on Caruthers' arm. "*The Terminator*, I think it was. The one with Arnie Schwarzenegger, before he became governor of California? The security people could see him on a big screen as a moving skeleton, remember?"

"That wasn't *Terminator*, Anne," Caruthers snapped back. "It was *Total Recall*. And that's beside the point."

"But they could see he was carrying a gun!"

"Well, I'm *not* carrying a gun," Caruthers said with a defiant upward lift of her chin. "And I'll keep my skeleton to myself, thank you!"

Myers sighed. He didn't like Ms. Caruthers, and she didn't like him. The woman had once had the effrontery to correct him in the middle of a lecture he'd been giving back at the Walters, part of a Western arts lecture series presented by the museum foundation. She'd actually interrupted to correct him on some fine point about Doric and Ionic columns in front of the rest of the class.

The fact that, when he'd looked it up, he'd found she'd been correct only made it more irritating.

"You *have* to go through, Ms. Caruthers," Myers told her. "Either that, or let the guards frisk you. It's for your *safety*."

"Young man, I don't *have* to do anything! They want to frisk me like I was some kind of criminal? I won't stand for this!"

"Well, if you wish to leave the group—," Myers began, but she cut him off.

"As tour guide you can make special arrangements," Caruthers told him. "People like us shouldn't have to go through these machines like we were riffraff! And *you* should have known that, and made those arrangements in advance!"

"What seems to be the problem here, folks?" a security guard asked, joining them. The tour group was piling up now in front of the X-ray machine as they came through the metal detector, bringing progress to a halt.

"I'm sorry, Officer," Myers told the man. "Ms. Caruthers, here, has some concerns about the safety of this X-ray scan."

"It's *perfectly* safe, ma'am," the guard said. "You'll get more X-ray radiation walking outdoors on a bright, sunny day."

"My sunblock," Caruthers told him with an acid touch to her voice, "is over there, in my carry-on luggage, which you people seem to think is hiding bombs or drugs or something!"

"Ma'am—"

"On my flight from Baltimore, they confiscated my knitting and a plastic bottle of water, and then they made me take off my *shoes* so they could see if I had explosives hidden inside them!"

"I'm sorry, ma'am, but—"

"Young man, I am sixty-nine years old and I'm not a threat to anybody! *Except,* perhaps, to certain overzealous civil servants and incompetent tour guides!"

"Please, Ms. Caruthers!" Myers said. "If you make a scene—"

"So now I'm making a scene, am I? Good! I *refuse* to be frisked like a common criminal, and I refuse to be zapped by X-rays! What are you going to do about it?"

"I'm going to ask you to step outside the line, ma'am," the guard said, "so we can allow the other passengers to continue boarding."

"What's the matter, Elsie?" Nancy Haynes asked, grinning. "Don't want your picture took?"

"I don't know about this," Mabel Polmar said, looking worried. "Elsie's right about X rays. My doctor told me when I had my hip surgery last winter that I couldn't have too many X-rays, or else I'd—"

"It's *safe*, Ms. Polmar," Myers said. He turned to the guard. "Look, is there anything else we can do?"

"Company rules, sir. *Everyone* goes through the scanner, or they allow themselves to be searched."

"I'd better discuss this with your supervisor, then."

"Very well, sir. But can we get the rest of these people moving? They're holding up the line."

"Okay. Let me go through and show them it's okay."

He walked into the white smooth-surfaced tunnel, turned, and held out his arms. "See, everyone? Nothing to it!"

One by one, the members of Myers' tour group followed him through the tunnel, some hesitantly, some with dogged determination, some fearfully, some with good-natured banter. Judy Dunne hobbled through step-by-step with her walker. Myers hoped that the security personnel were getting a good look at all of their skeletons, or whatever it was that they were looking at. A more unlikely terrorist group he couldn't imagine . . . though Ms. Caruthers did come close. She was, in his opinion and at the very least, a royal pain in the ass.

A few—Caruthers, Polmar, Jones, the Kleins, Kathy Morton—chose to follow the security guard off to the side and were engaged in a spirited discussion with him.

The Elderly Ladies' Home Terrorist and Sewing Circle, Myers thought. With a grimace, he turned and walked back to join the discussion.

This really *was* going to be his last time as a tour group guide.

Atlantis Queen pier side
Southampton, England
Thursday, 1420 hours GMT

The gray morning's overcast was breaking at last, giving way to bright sunlight. Several hundred feet aft from the *Atlantis Queen*'s boarding gangway, the garage-sized doors to her main cargo hold on A Deck had been slid open and another lorry filled with crates of provisions drove up alongside.

Chester Darrow picked up his electronic clipboard and walked down the loading ramp to meet with the driver. "Good afternoon!" he called cheerfully. "What do you have for us?"

"More food," the driver said with a disinterested shrug. "Where do you want it?"

"Let's see what it is first," Darrow said. "What's the lading number?"

A cruise ship the size of the *Atlantis Queen* had a population as large as many towns—almost three thousand in all. The amount of food and other consumables required for a two-week cruise was staggering in its amount and in its variety. So far, Darrow had checked aboard twenty-five tons of beef, five tons of lamb, five and a half tons of pork, four tons of veal, a ton of sausage, seven and a half tons of chicken, three tons of turkey, nine tons of fish, and two tons of lobster . . . and the loading was continuing as more and more shipments arrived at the pier. In two weeks, the four restaurants on board the *Queen* would run through almost twenty-five tons of fresh vegetables, four thousand liters of ice cream, four tons of rice, five tons of coffee, fifteen tons of potatoes, twenty tons of fresh fruit, five tons of sugar, and twenty thousand liters of milk. Her alcohol lockers routinely stocked over four thousand bottles of assorted wines, three hundred of champagne, four hundred of vodka, five hundred of whiskey, and a thousand of assorted liqueurs . . . not to mention some eighteen thousand cans or bottles of a bewildering selection of beers.

The *Atlantis Queen*'s guests and crew wouldn't consume all of that vast mountain of food and drink in two weeks, of course. A percentage was held against the possibility of a delay somewhere along the line and as a precaution against the unthinkable—that the ship's larders would actually run out of something toward the end of the cruise. The ship's commissary department would also have the opportunity to buy fresh provisions along the way—in Greece and Turkey, especially—if anything in the ship's computerized lists of stores appeared to be running low.

Odd, the manifest the driver handed Darrow was in a different format than the one routinely used by the Royal Sky Line. It listed the truck's contents as two tons of rice, three tons of potatoes, and one ton of sugar . . . but he'd already checked four tons of rice on board that morning and they weren't scheduled to receive any more. There'd been a screwup somewhere down the line.

"I'm sorry," Darrow said, handing the clipboard back.

"I can't take this. I'll need to check it with the commissary office."

"Is there a problem here?"

Darrow looked around and saw two of the ship's Security officers approaching along the pier from aft. He recognized one as a guy named Ghailiani. He didn't recognize the other one, though that was hardly surprising. There were nine hundred Royal Sky employees on board this ship; you couldn't possibly know them all.

"Nah, not a problem," Darrow told him. "I think this shipment is for someone else, though."

"What makes you say that?"

"It's not our inventory form, for one thing. And I can't tell if it's been screened. I don't see a customs stamp, either." All shipments of cargo and provisions were carefully checked before they were loaded aboard ship, by security personnel, by customs officers, and even by public health inspectors. Bombs, smuggled contraband, and diseases were three things that could give the company a *very* bad public image, and every step was taken to make sure that none of those got on board. "Come to think of it," he added, paging through the manifest, "I'm not sure how he even got in here."

"Let's take a look," the second security man said. "Maybe the right papers are in the back."

Darrow shrugged. "Sure."

The lorry had been backed up until it was directly alongside a huge Dumpster on the pier, and Darrow had to turn sideways to squeeze through the narrow passage. The truck's tailgate came down with a bang, and Darrow pulled himself up onto the cargo bed. It was dark inside, the space filled with a number of large crates masked in deep shadow.

"You have a torch?" he called back. "It's bloody dark in—" He caught movement out of the corner of his eye. "What the hell?"

"What's wrong?" the security officer called from outside.

"I thought I saw—"

Someone grabbed Darrow from behind, a hand clamping down over his mouth, an arm pinning his arms at his sides. A second shadow emerged from behind the crates in front of him, and he felt something hard and metallic rammed against his ribs.

He tried to scream.

Three sound-suppressed gunshots, sharp, hissing chirps, cut through the close darkness. Darrow bucked once, then sagged in the arms of the man behind him.

"Merciful Allah," Ghailiani said in the light outside the truck. "Forgive me."

4

Royal Sky Line security queue
Atlantis Queen passenger terminal
Southampton, England
Thursday, 1439 hours GMT

ARNOLD BERNSTEIN STEPPED through the metal detector, then stopped, reading the metal sign in front of the big white tunnel. "What's this?"

"X-ray scan, sir," the security guard standing next to the tunnel said. "It's completely harmless. Just step through like you did with the metal detector."

"Bernie!" Gillian Harper said, coming up behind him. "Why do they need to x-ray us?"

"They *say*," Reggie Carmichael said with a knowing leer, "that it looks right through your clothes, and lets them see you naked!"

"*Who* says?" Harper demanded. "I'm not getting naked for anybody!" They were standing in the short stretch between the metal detector and the white tunnel, confronted by a security guard and the metal sign. The rest of the Harper entourage was continuing to step through the metal detector, and the line was piling up.

"That's right, baby!" Jake Levy said. He was one of Harper's agents, and always had his eye on the bottom line. "Not unless they pay you for the peek."

"I'm sure it's nothing like *that*," Bernstein said. "See? The sign says it's not intrusive. It's just security!"

"Well, *I'm* no terrorist!" Harper said, her voice taking an unpleasant edge to it. "Bernie, you can get me in another way. I'm a *star*, for Christ's sake!"

"What seems to be the problem?" the guard asked. He looked weary, as though he'd been handling recalcitrant passengers all day.

"Do you have *any* idea who I am?" Gillian Harper demanded.

"No, ma'am, I have no idea. I'm sorry, but I have my orders. *No* exceptions."

"Gillian, I think we'd better do as the man says. You can let yourself be x-rayed, or you can let them feel you all over looking for . . . whatever it is they're looking for. Which is it going to be?"

"You can't talk to me that way, Bernie!"

God. Another temper tantrum coming on. "I'm sorry, Gillian. Rules are rules." *Even for you, you strung-out little bitch*, he thought. *No* amount of money was worth this.

Bernstein was disgusted. Gillian Harper's bad-girl image played great at the box office, but her attitude made her increasingly difficult to work with. Damn it, she was just another in a long line of high-visibility, high-maintenance models, movie stars, and MTV pop idols, no different, really, from Spears or Lohan or any of the rest. What was it about a little fame that made these people think they were immortal?

But Bernstein was her manager . . . as if anyone could *manage* the brat. Getting her to do anything that wasn't her idea first was damned near impossible. It had been her idea to do this latest gig—shoot segments for her new music video, "Livin' Large," on board a luxury cruise ship and at various landmarks in the Mediterranean: on the beach at Majorca, in front of the Parthenon, along the Turkish coast. "Livin' Large" held the promise of being a top-of-the charts blockbuster, bigger than "Material Girl," maybe . . . *if* the bitch could control her temper, stay sober, and keep her mind on the job. Her idiot boyfriend wasn't helping; Carmichael was a minor actor with delusions of grandeur, a pretty boy who'd hit it lucky in a film or two and now seemed bent on destroying himself. *And* her.

The drug use worried Bernstein.

Arnold Bernstein had already decided that he was through with this insane business. Let him get just one more big hit under his belt and he could say good-bye to Gillian Harper and all of her parasites. He had a fair amount of money tucked away. Maybe he would produce dinner theater somewhere, some place far away from the glitz and the lights and the high-living idiots.

"Gillian," he said sharply, "it's not like half the male population of this planet hasn't already seen you naked. *Get* your ass through that machine!"

He strode through without looking to see if the rest were following him.

Bridge, *Atlantis Queen*
Southampton, England
Thursday, 1444 hours GMT

"Captain?"

Captain Eric Phillips was leaning over the chart table, reviewing the latest met print-out. Several hours ago, a low-pressure cell had begun forming off the West African coast, and by the time the *Queen* reached the Strait of Gibraltar in another four days, it might make for some rough weather.

"Can it wait? I'm busy—"

"Sir, we have a problem. A *real* problem."

"Now what?" Captain Eric Phillips looked up, exasperated. Why did problems always begin multiplying exponentially the closer the ship came to debarkation?

His staff captain, Charles Vandergrift, stood a few feet away, holding the bridge phone against his ear. "It's Ghailiani, sir. Security. One of our officers has been found . . . dead." He sounded as though he couldn't quite believe the report.

That got Phillips' full attention. "Dead? My God, who? How?"

"Chester Darrow, sir. Ghailiani says he's been shot!"

"Sweet Christ Jesus! Give me that!" He took the handset from Vandergrift. "Ghailiani? This is the Captain."

"Y-yes, sir." The man's voice sounded weak over the phone, almost dull, as if he was dazed, or in shock.

"What the devil happened?"

"We're not sure, sir. Mr. Darrow was checking provisions into the aft A Deck cargo hold. I came down here to check something, and found him on the pier, dead."

"You said he's been shot?"

"Yes, sir. Several times, sir. In the chest."

This *had* to be some sort of sick joke. *Please let it be a joke!* he thought. "Ghailiani, if this is some kind of prank—"

"*No*, sir! It's *not*! Darrow's dead! There's blood everywhere—"

"Where are you?"

"On the pier. Just opposite the A Deck cargo gangway. There's a big green Dumpster there? We found him between the Dumpster and the main warehouse wall."

"Okay. Stay there. Don't let anyone touch the body. The police will be down there soon."

"Yes, sir."

Several thoughts and emotions battled one another in Phillips' mind. One of his men murdered! Who was the killer? A member of the crew? Or someone ashore? Had anyone seen what had happened?

Phillips didn't know Darrow well. The man had only joined the *Queen* a month ago. Phillips would have to check with Personnel to see if the man had any family.

He would have to write a letter, at the very least. Oh, *God.* . . .

Other, more selfishly motivated thoughts crowded in, jostling with the others. Could the incident be kept from the passengers? And, even more critically, would the murder prevent the *Atlantis Queen* from sailing on schedule?

Like a hotel, a cruise ship depended on filling available vacancies with paying customers. If the *Atlantis Queen* was kept in port by a police investigation, people would start canceling their reservations, and passengers already aboard might begin making other plans for their tightly structured vacations—and demanding refunds.

With the economy the way it was right now, a company like Royal Sky Line could go under with the failure of a single cruise—the profit margin was that slim.

A small and unworthy part of him was already wondering if the death could be covered up, at least until the ship was out of port . . . but he shoved the thought viciously aside. No, they would play this by the book.

He began punching numbers into the handset. First he would call Sir Charles Mayhew, the member of the board of directors who was Operations Director for the *Atlantis Queen* and Phillips' boss.

And then he would call the police.

Atlantis Queen **pier side**
Southampton, England
Thursday, 1446 hours GMT

Ghailiani snapped his cell phone shut. "It's . . . it's done," he managed. He felt weak, on the verge of falling over. His initial terror was being submerged in a paralyzing numbness that made it hard to think, hard to know what to think.

They were within the narrow, deep-shadowed corridor between the Dumpster and the wall of the warehouse.

Ghailiani was leaning against the wall, trying to keep from falling as his knees trembled. Yusef Khalid squatted in front of him, crouched over the body. Two of Khalid's men stood guard in the sunlight outside.

It had happened so quickly! Khalid's men had materialized out of Allah-knew-where almost at once—members of the ship's deck gang, Ghailiani thought. Dock wallopers, tough, hard-looking men who'd been helping to shift stores on board the ship. Careful to stay in the shelter offered by the back of the truck, they'd dragged poor Darrow's body out and bundled it around into the narrow alley behind the Dumpster.

He'd also seen them produce a briefcase from inside the truck's cab, which they'd tossed into the Dumpster.

None of this was making sense.

"Are they sending someone down here?" Khalid demanded. He'd removed Darrow's wallet from his hip pocket. At first, Ghailiani assumed Khalid was robbing the dead man . . . but no, apparently he was stuffing something inside.

Khalid was wearing nylon medical gloves.

"He . . . the captain just said to stay with the . . . with the body," Ghailiani managed to say. "He said the police would be here soon. Allah! The police! . . ."

"Calm yourself, Ghailiani," Khalid told him. "You are doing well."

"You didn't tell me you were going to kill him!"

"That is correct. I did not."

"You're going to take the ship." Ghailiani was on the verge of tears. He felt like he was going to be terribly sick. *"You're going to kill everyone on the ship!"*

Khalid stood suddenly, turned, and grabbed Ghailiani's collar with one blue-gloved hand. *"Listen* to me, Mohamed! You have heard of al-Qaeda, yes?"

Ghailiani managed a jerky nod.

"Yes. We are going to take that ship. By arranging for

the truck to get past security and onto the pier, you have helped us do so."

"You're going to blow up the ship—"

"No!" Khalid released him, then, shoving him back a foot. "No, we are not! I promise you, by the word of the Prophet, *no*. We intend to take that ship, yes. We will *threaten* to blow it up, yes . . . but I promise you that we will not. The people on board are innocents, women and children, and the holy Qur'an tells us not to shed innocent blood."

Ghailiani looked down at Darrow's body. Blood continued to ooze from the chest, soaking the uniform, pooling on the concrete beneath. *He'd* been an innocent. . . .

Khalid seemed to read Ghailiani's mind. "As a man, he was responsible for his actions, for ignoring the words of the Prophet. Understand? We are at war, we are engaged in holy jihad, and men will die in this war . . . but we will *not* kill the innocents on board that ship, I promise you! Do you believe me?"

"I . . . I don't know what to believe—"

"Then listen to this, and believe it, Mohamed Ghailiani. You have already helped us in this operation. You will continue to help us."

"I can't!—"

"You *will*! You can't pull back now."

"You're going to kill us all anyway!"

"I give you my word, upon the holy Qur'an and if Allah wills, that I will not. If we succeed in this, the governments of Great Britain and the United States of America will pay us one-point-five-*billion* euros. Think of that, Mohamed! Two *billion* American dollars! And we will arrange for a small percentage of that . . . say, one million euros? To be transferred to a private numbered account in your name. You will be a very wealthy man."

"I don't . . . I don't want money—"

"If we fail, you will be arrested as a co-conspirator. They will find a record of what you have done to help us . . . getting those security keys, and getting the truck past the security checkpoint."

"Please—"

"And I am certain that I don't need to remind you of your wife and daughter. If *you* fail us, I promise you that both Zahra and Nouzha will suffer terrible pain and terrible humiliation before they finally die. Their deaths will take a very long time. Your Zahra will be forced to watch *everything* we do to your daughter first. It may take a week, perhaps more. And then, when Nouzha is finally dead, we will start working on her. Do you understand me?"

For just a moment, defiance stirred within Ghailiani. "I . . . I thought you said you didn't hurt women and children!"

Khalid seemed to think about this for a moment. "This is war. Terrible things must be done in war. I am willing to die to see this thing through . . . and I *am* willing to shed the blood of innocents to accomplish this. We require your help, and this is how we have chosen to get it. But our goal, the goal of this mission, is to take from the governments of America and Great Britain the sum of two billion American dollars in order to finance our operations elsewhere. It will *not* further our goals to slaughter the people on board the ship. You must believe me on this. Help us and we accomplish our mission, you will become wealthy, and your wife and daughter will be released to you unharmed. This, God willing, I swear to you upon the word of the Prophet!

"But if we fail, or if you betray us or refuse to help us, you will die, and your wife and child will die. If it is possible, you will be there to watch both of them die first. I swear this by Allah! I swear this by Allah!" Khalid leaned forward, speaking directly into Ghailiani's face as his voice dropped to a whisper. *"I swear this by Allah!"*

Mohamed Ghailiani did consider himself to be Muslim, though he was not an observant one, and he had little interest in the fine points of the Sharia, of Islamic law.

Still, he knew that a man who swore by the name of God three times was in earnest; lesser oaths, by other things than Allah Himself, often were not considered binding, especially if the oath taker added the words "if God wills" to his promise.

He knew that Khalid would carry out his threat if Ghailiani crossed him in any way. There was no way out . . . no way out for him, no way out for Nouzha or Zahra, save to do exactly what he was told.

"I . . . yes. I understand."

"We are absolutely willing to do whatever must be done to achieve our aims. You hear what I am saying?"

Again, Ghailiani nodded. His moment of rebellion was fast fading. There was no way he could fight men like these.

"Good." Khalid turned away and walked out from behind the Dumpster. Ghailiani followed. The truck, he saw, was gone. He'd heard one of Khalid's men moving it a few moments ago, and assumed it had been driven onto the ship.

He wondered what was on the truck. Explosives, possibly. He looked back at the Dumpster. What, he wondered, had been in that briefcase?

He wouldn't ask. He *couldn't*. He wanted to know as little as possible about these terrible men, and their plans for the *Atlantis Queen*.

He would do everything they told him, praying that they would be satisfied, that they would release Zahra and Nouzha unharmed.

And then he would die, because he knew these men would never let him live even if they succeeded in their scheme. Khalid had said "if Allah wills" and sworn upon the Qur'an when he'd promised that Ghailiani would be rewarded, which meant it was not a binding oath.

Not as binding, at least, as Khalid's solemn three-times invocation of Allah, promising what would happen to Ghailiani and to his family if he failed.

Ghailiani's stomach gave a sudden, sharp twist. He turned away, doubled over, and vomited on the pier.

Atlantis Queen **passenger terminal**
Southampton, England
Thursday, 1505 hours GMT

Fred Doherty said, stepping through the glass doors onto the *Atlantis Queen* pier, "Jesus, is that a police car down there?"

"Flashing lights, anyway," Sandra Ames said, following him outside. "Let's check it out!"

"We don't have our equipment," James Petrovich said. He hefted the small video camera in its case that he'd just rescued from the conveyor belt at the security checkpoint. "Just this."

The three of them were a reporter team for Cable News Entertainment. Doherty was the field producer and director, Ames the reporter, and Petrovich the camera and sound man. From here, just outside the terminal door in front of the ship's gangway, they could see the flash of amber and red lights a hundred yards away, toward the right and near the aft end of the ship.

Technically, they were a part of Gillian Harper's entourage, though neither Harper's people nor CNE outwardly acknowledged the liaison. They'd been assigned to this cruise to shadow the rock diva; Terry Carter, Gillian's publicist, wanted the exposure, while Doherty's bosses at CNE hoped that Harper would have yet another major and public meltdown and provide even more highly profitable sound bites and video clips for their celebrity news broadcasts.

Not exactly an inspiring way to make a living, Doherty thought, but it *was* a living, and a pretty good one. The challenge, of course, was getting close enough to Harper at the right time to get the right footage. She was traveling with her entourage, of course, which included several beefy personal security guards. Despite the arrangement CNE had with Harper's support people, the bodyguards seemed to have the impression that the CNE field team were some kind of paparazzi.

Which, perhaps, they were. Doherty didn't even know if Harper herself knew the news team was dogging her. It was, he decided, all part of the game, a means of titillating CNE's viewers and making them come back for more. How close can we get this time?

Maybe by the end of the cruise they could arrange a real interview. Carter had promised something of the sort . . . or at least suggested that an in-depth interview was possible.

But no matter how that worked out, CNE's viewers expected the hot steaming inside shit on media stars great and small, and Doherty's team was there to give it to them—even if they had to follow the Harper slut around with a pooper-scooper.

She was also traveling with her latest lover, so at the very least they might manage a telephoto shot or two of the lovebirds lounging by one of the ship's pools in thongs. Show the viewers how the glitzy-rich set lived in a thirty-second segment.

And with luck the bitch might do something *interesting*. Journalism at its finest.

What a crock.

He studied the flashing lights for a moment. The three of them *were* news professionals, and they knew how to work a story. Police lights suggested that something newsworthy was happening down there—maybe someone hurt on the docks. They could chase that story even if it didn't involve Ms. Harper.

"Sounds good, Sandra," he said after a long pause. "Let's go see what's shaking."

"I'm sorry, sir," a big man in a camouflaged uniform

and a red beret said. He had an assault rifle slung from one shoulder, and he'd just stepped out from wherever he'd been lurking to block their path. "That end of the pier is closed."

"I'm a reporter," Ames said, producing her press card and flashing it at the soldier. "This is my crew. Let us through, please."

"No, ma'am," the soldier said. "I can't do that."

"Look," Doherty said, holding up his ID as well, "you don't understand. We're the news media! We have clearance, and we have a *right* to see what's going on!"

"No, sir. I can't allow you through here, sir. Orders."

"*What* orders? By whom?"

"Sir, if you will just board the ship—"

Doherty had already pulled out a notebook and a pen. "What's your name, soldier? And who do you report to?"

The soldier told him, carefully spelling out both. Neither name meant anything to Doherty, but he took them down. He would file a complaint later.

The soldier was wearing a radio on his jacket. It crackled, and Doherty heard something about an ambulance coming through. Interesting.

"Hey, Fred?" Petrovich motioned him closer. He was holding a cruise booklet open to a deck plan of the ship.

"What?" Doherty leaned over so Petrovich could whisper in his ear.

"If we go on board, it looks like we can follow the Promenade Deck aft, maybe get a good look at what's happening from the ship. Good camera angle, anyway."

Doherty considered this. Of course, Sandra wouldn't be able to interview anybody from up there, but they clearly weren't going to be able to interview anyone down here, either. The soldier seemed blissfully content to ignore their protests and keep them away from the incident for the rest of the evening. They could film from up on deck and come back ashore later and get comments from

Royal Sky personnel, the police, and maybe even this soldier. It might be worth it questioning the ship's security officer, too.

"Okay," Doherty said. "Let's go." He glanced at the soldier. "You'll hear from us again later, Sergeant," he promised.

"As you wish, sir. Security, sir. I'm sure you understand."

They jogged up the gangway, brushing past the ship's officer as he started in on his welcome-aboard spiel. Doherty hung behind to get the passkeys for all three of them, then excused himself and hurried after the others. Into the luxurious Grand Atrium and up the sweeping curve of the Atrium stairs to the Promenade Deck.

Gillian Harper could wait.

This smelled like news. *Real* news.

Infirmary, *Atlantis Queen*
Southampton, England
Thursday, 1506 hours GMT

"Hey, Doc!" Johnny Berger's voice was shrill with excitement. "You hear what happened outside?"

Dr. Heywood Barnes looked up from his paperwork. "Eh? What commotion?"

"They say Mr. Darrow got shot!"

"Good God!" Barnes rose from his desk, automatically reaching for his first-aid kit. "Where?"

"On the pier! Outside of the main A Deck hold! There's cops and an ambulance and everything!"

"I'm on my way." He followed young Berger out into the main passageway heading aft. If an ambulance was already on the scene, they wouldn't be needing his services, but he brought the first-aid kit just in case. A ship's officer shot! How the hell had that happened?

The *Atlantis Queen*'s infirmary and doctor's office was

amidships on A Deck, the first deck down from the first passenger deck and the only area below the First Deck open to passengers. A security door blocked the way aft, but Berger already had his passkey out, swiping it through the magnetic reader and pushing the heavy, watertight door open. Beyond that door, the character of the ship's décor changed radically, from soft pastels and fastidious cleanliness to institutional green paint on the bulkheads and a somewhat depressing sensation of claustrophobia.

In general, the crew and staff lived and worked on A Deck and below, while the passengers saw only the gleaming and luxurious fantasy of the upper decks, First through Eleventh. The main A Deck passageway ran past the main galley, a steaming, clattering industrial complex located immediately below the ship's Atlantia Restaurant. Beyond that was the main A Deck hold aft, a cavernous compartment known to the crew as "the Pantry," since that was where most of the dozens of tons of foodstuffs for the voyage were stored. Another passkey swipe gained entrance to the hold. Ahead and to the right, sunlight spilled in from outside in a dusty shaft, where the hold doors stood open to receive shipments of stores.

As Barnes rounded a stack of supply crates, he noticed a six-ton lorry parked inside the hold, up against the port-side bulkhead. A half-dozen workers lounged around the back of the truck, watching him jog past with dark, incurious eyes.

That was odd. Cruise ships occasionally carried vehicles on board. There were always the few rich people—celebrities and millionaires—who brought their own Porsche or Mercedes or Rolls along for joyrides at various ports of call, but those generally were carried in the A Deck *forward* hold.

In any case, this was the first time he could remember seeing a *truck* down here.

And it seemed odd that the deck personnel were here,

rather than at the cargo loading doors fifty feet away. Several other crew members were gathered there as well, staring out into the sunlight.

Barnes pushed past these last and jogged down the ramp onto the pier. Three police cars had pulled up alongside the *Queen*, and an ambulance was backed up next to a green Dumpster alongside the warehouse opposite the ship. Yellow police line tape had already been strung around the area, and nervous-looking policemen in black-and-white checkered caps and several soldiers in camouflaged uniforms and red berets were patrolling the area.

A policeman stopped Barnes as he approached the tape barrier. "Sorry, sir. You can't go through here."

"I'm the ship's doctor," Barnes said. He hefted his first-aid kit, as if it provided proof of his identity. "Has someone been hurt?"

"He won't be needing *that*," the officer told Barnes, nodding at the kit.

"Who's that, Constable?" another man asked. He was tall and lean, and unlike most of those at the site, he wore civilian clothing.

"Ship's surgeon, sir.

"I'm Dr. Barnes," he added. "Can I be of help?"

"I don't know," the civilian said. He reached inside his sports coat, pulled out an ID case, and flipped it open. "Mitchell," he said. He flipped the ID card away quickly, but not before Barnes saw that the man was MI5. "Did you know a man named . . ." He stopped and consulted a small notebook in his other hand. "Chester Darrow?"

"Darrow? Yes. He's the ship's fourth officer."

"You know him well?"

"No, can't say that I did. He only came on board . . . let's see . . . would've been maybe last month. Quiet guy. Kept to himself. Seemed to know his stuff."

"And what was his 'stuff'?" Mitchell asked.

"He supervised the hotel staff on board. Cargo and

provisions. Worked with the Security Department and the Purser's Office screening cargo. That sort of thing."

"You said you're the ship's doctor?"

"Senior doctor, yes. There are three of us, and a medical staff."

"Tell me something, Doctor. Is there a drug problem on board this ship?"

"Drugs? *No*, sir! Every person in the crew is screened regularly! It's part of the employment contract!"

"Okay. Thank you very much." Mitchell made a final entry in his notebook. "We'll get back to you if we have any more questions."

A couple of attendants brought an olive-drab body bag out from behind the Dumpster and slid it onto a gurney. From there it was a short trundle across the concrete pier to the back of the waiting ambulance.

Chester Darrow dead? And the MI5 officer's questions seemed to suggest a drug connection. That was *not* good. The Royal Sky Line board of directors was going to have a collective cow over *this* bit of news. A very *mad* cow.

Dr. Barnes wondered if they were going to cancel this cruise.

5

Cairo Street
Northern Beirut, Lebanon
Thursday, 1755 hours GMT + 2

"RIGHT," LIA DEFRANCESCA said, her eye against the eyepiece of her camera's viewfinder. "Aquarius One. I have Sagittarius in sight."

She knelt on the rooftop of a five-story office building in Beirut's Hamra District, not far from the Paradise Residence hotel, on Cairo Street. To the west, late-afternoon sunlight flashed from the azure waters of the Mediterranean. North, hundreds of pleasure craft, sailboats, and yachts bobbed and shifted in the St. George Marina. Nearby, the clatter and rattle of heavy construction continued, incessant and pounding. Beirut was busy rebuilding itself from the devastation of its civil war twenty years earlier.

"Aquarius Two," Taggart's voice sounded in her ear. "Sagittarius acquired."

Lia shifted, following the target. She appeared an unlikely field intelligence operator at the moment. She'd hiked the skirt of her conservative business suit up around her waist so she could kneel and crouch more easily behind the wall, and her fashionable heels were on the roof beside her, her feet bare. She'd gained access to this building by looking the part of a Western-dressed businesswoman.

Resting on the wall in front of her, mounted on a small tripod, was the Sony camera, equipped with a powerful telephoto lens. Though it was impossible to tell through a casual inspection, the camera had been extensively rebuilt. While it could still take digital photographs, the image on the viewfinder was simultaneously appearing on computer monitors back in the United States, both in Desk Three's Art Room beneath NSA Headquarters at Fort Meade and in the Operations Center at CIA Headquarters in Langley, Virginia.

Leaning against the concrete wall beside her was a Mark 11 Mod Spec rifle, a weapon one observer had called an M16 on steroids. The weapon had been left for her, concealed in one of the building's rooftop ventilation ducts.

Howard Taggart—Aquarius Two—was across the street on top of the new Holiday Inn, farther up the street and only three floors up. Both Lia and Taggart were linked into the field satellite communications network through their com implants.

Through the powerful lens, Lia saw Michael Haddid from above and behind as he walked along Cairo Street toward the Paradise hotel. She raised the instrument slightly, sighting ahead along Haddid's path, and saw a man with sunglasses and a heavy mustache seated at a sidewalk table in front of a café.

"Aquarius One," Lia said. "Target acquired. I have Scorpio in sight." As she watched, the man dropped some coins on the table, stood, glanced around, and then began walking toward Haddid. "Scorpio is now moving. He's approaching Sagittarius." She estimated they were a hundred feet apart, now, walking briskly toward each other through the heavy late-afternoon foot traffic on the sidewalk.

"Aquarius, Crystal Ball," Debra Collins' voice said in Lia's ear. "Any sign of the opposition's overwatch?"

"None visible," Lia replied. "But they're out there. Count on it."

Lia and Taggart had been in Lebanon for the past month, setting up this meet, which had been dubbed Operation Stargazer. Technically, this wasn't an op for Desk Three or the NSA at all. The CIA was running Stargazer; Debra Collins was the Agency's Deputy Director of Operations, and the rumor was that Stargazer was her baby. Desk Three had been brought in to the op, however, because the NSA's highly specialized technical skills had been needed, especially as they applied to electronic intelligence.

It was not a comfortable alliance. Collins felt—and perhaps with some justification, Lia admitted to herself— that the NSA's Deep Black operations department, Desk Three, should properly answer to the CIA's Directorate of Operations. There were some at Desk Three who wondered if Stargazer might not be an attempt to wrest control of Desk Three away from the National Security Agency.

"Sagittarius, Crystal Ball," Collins' voice said over the net. "Scorpio is right in front of you, another thirty feet."

"Copy that, Crystal Ball," Haddid replied. Haddid didn't have the implants of the NSA operators, but he was wired, with a radio receiver that appeared to be a tiny hearing aid.

Damn it, Lia thought. *The bitch is micromanaging. Shut up and let the man do his job.*

Haddid was a CIA officer, and cupped in his right hand as he walked along the busy Beirut sidewalk below was a 40-gigabyte thumb-drive, a device actually half the size of a man's thumb that could plug into any computer USB port.

Scorpio was the target of the operation—Colonel Assef Suleiman, a high-ranking officer of the Idarat al-Mukhabarat al-Jawiyya (IMJ), Syria's air force intelligence service.

Despite the name, the IMJ was not primarily responsible for gathering intel for the Syrian Air Force. It was, rather, the most secretive, the most efficient, and the deadliest of Syria's four intelligence services. For thirty years, until his death in 2000, Hafez al-Assad had ruled Syria, President in name, dictator in style. When he'd first taken control of the country in 1970, he'd naturally given the most sensitive departments of his intelligence service to friends and trusted cronies in Syria's air force, which he'd once commanded, and the IMJ had become his favorite spy agency. The IMJ was primarily responsible for tracking down and eliminating Islamist opposition groups within Syria, but it also played a major role in terrorist operations covertly supported by Damascus, such as the well-publicized attempted bombing of an Israeli airliner at Heathrow International in 1986.

"Sagittarius, Crystal Ball. Ten feet!"

"I see him."

After occupying Lebanon for years, Syria's military had finally been forced to leave Lebanon in 2005 after the dramatic popular uprising known as the Cedar Revolution. That didn't mean that Syria had lost interest in its diminutive neighbor, however, or that it didn't continue to maintain a watchful presence in the country. All of the Syrian intelligence agencies were still well represented in Beirut. The CIA believed that Colonel Suleiman was running all IMJ operations inside Lebanon, including one designed to suborn Hezbollah and several other independent terrorist networks in the region and bring them firmly under Syrian control.

Haddid, a twenty-eight-year-old American of Arab descent, was a relatively junior CIA officer working out of an Agency sub-station at the American Embassy in Beirut. He'd been contacted five months ago by an IMJ agent at a cocktail party, and Collins had decided to use the opportunity to pull off a Trojan horse.

At stake was nothing less than an opportunity to penetrate the IMJ.

Lia watched through the camera as Haddid and Suleiman approached each other, carefully not making eye contact . . . and then they brushed past each other, right shoulder bumping right shoulder. For just an instant, their hands touched.

The technique was called a brush pass and was a standard bit of tradecraft. As they'd bumped, apparently by accident, Haddid dropped the thumb drive into Suleiman's waiting fingers.

"Pass complete," Haddid said.

"Okay," Taggart said. "Let's see if Scorpio takes the bait."

Haddid continued walking until he reached the sidewalk café where Scorpio had been waiting. Casually Haddid sat down, back to a hedge in a position where he could watch the street.

Almost directly below Lia's position overlooking the street, Suleiman got into the front passenger seat of a red Mazda. Tilting the telephoto lens to look almost straight down, she could just make out Suleiman's shoulder and thigh through the vehicle's open window.

"What's he doing?" Collins demanded.

"Aquarius One. Hard to see from this angle."

"Aquarius Two," Taggart said. "I can see the front seat from my position. Looks like he has a laptop . . . he's plugging it into the cigarette lighter. Yeah! Now he's plugging in the thumb drive."

The Art Room and Langley would be getting a better view through Taggart's camera. Lia shifted her camera back to Haddid, who was now talking to a café waiter. Over his communicator, she heard Haddid asking for Turkish coffee in Arabic.

"Aquarius One, this is Magic Wand." The voice was Kathy Caravaggio's, and she was the Deep Black handler watching and listening from the Art Room. "Can you pull back a little on your telephoto? We'd like to see more of the background."

"Copy that." Lia pressed the rocker switch on the barrel of her camera's lens, zooming out to show more of Haddid's surroundings. She could see past the hedge now, see the crowds of people on the sidewalks on both sides of the street.

One person in particular immediately stood out. He was behind Haddid and across the street, leaning against the side of a green Volkswagen, perhaps fifty feet away, though the foreshortening created by the zoom lens made him look much closer. Despite the warmth of the day, he wore a dark overcoat; despite the late hour of the afternoon, he wore sunglasses. And his gaze, judging from the angle of his face, never left the back of Mike Haddid's head.

Her nose wrinkled. Security types. You could always spot them.

"Thanks, Lia," Caravaggio's voice said. "You see him?"

"The guy by the Volkswagen? Yeah."

"He may be the paymaster. Or the trigger. Keep him in sight. We're designating him as Echo Whiskey One."

"Copy that." Echo Whiskey—EW. Enemy Watcher.

"Bingo!" Collins said. "We're in! We're online!"

The USB thumb drive was a highly sophisticated bit of engineering from the NSA's technical support center, with an even better software package from the Agency's programming department. A tiny 40-gig external drive, it looked and acted like a 10-gig drive, with the extra memory invisible behind a virtual wall. Stored on the accessible portion of the compartmented drive was data, *lots* of data, all of it pertaining to CIA operations out of the U.S. Embassy in Beirut.

A lot of the data was even true.

The NSA and CIA technical operations departments had collaborated on that data, compiling page after page listing Agency assets in Lebanon, Israel, Turkey, and Syria, as well as giving details on a dozen different sensitive intelligence operations in the region conducted since

2001. Also included were extensive lists, reports, and, in some cases, speculations on some twenty-five Islamic terrorist and revolutionary groups, from well-known and active ones such as Hezbollah to groups that were insignificant or almost vanished, like the Japanese Red Army.

What was not immediately obvious was the fact that most of that data either was obsolete or mirrored information that the CIA knew the Syrians already possessed. Some was fabricated, to create the illusion that there was new and therefore useful information on the drive; some would confirm other, earlier fabrications, such as the existence of an Iranian mole inside the Shu'bat al-Mukhabarat al-'Askariyya, Syria's military intelligence service.

But the real purpose of Operation Stargazer was to get the thumb drive and its hidden memory hooked into the IMJ's computer network in Damascus. Once there, a carefully crafted bit of software would graft itself to the operating system running Syria's military and government computer networks, creating an invisible back door through which the CIA and NSA would have complete and untraceable access.

Back at Langley, Collins was now watching Suleiman check out the thumb drive's visible contents. He would be scrolling through menus and lists of files, perhaps sampling some to satisfy himself that the information was valid.

"Aquarius Two. Scorpio is taking out a cell phone," Taggart reported. "The laptop's still open in front of him. He's placing a call."

"Echo Whiskey One is taking a cell phone out of his coat pocket," Lia said. "Three guesses who Scorpio is calling."

"Aquarius, Magic Wand," Caravaggio said, addressing both members of the NSA overwatch team. "Recommend you go to shooter mode."

"Roger that. Camera angle okay?"

"Looks good, Lia."

Leaving the camera aimed at Haddid and his immediate surroundings for the benefit of the watchers at Langley and Fort Meade, Lia shifted a bit to the left and picked up the Mk 11, easing its slender barrel with the long, vented sound suppressor over the top of the wall.

The Mk 11 did indeed look much like a standard-issue M16, though with a longer barrel and with a telescopic sight in place of the carry handle. In fact, about 60 percent of the parts were common to both weapons. The internal workings had been extensively modified, however, to create an exceptionally accurate weapon custom-tailored to clandestine operations.

Lia dropped her right eye behind the eyepiece and re-acquired Echo Whiskey One. The man was walking across the street, now, coming directly toward Mike Haddid. She could hear Collins talking to Haddid, letting him know what was happening behind his back, but Lia wasn't listening. All of her attention was focused now on Suleiman's henchman as he approached the CIA officer in the café. She let the crosshair reticule rest on the man's chest, between throat and heart. The range was just less than two hundred yards.

This sort of thing, she thought, was more Charlie Dean's line of work. Charlie had been a sniper in the Marines and, according to his service jacket, a damned good one. But Charlie had been tapped for another mission, something in England, and Lia had already been in Turkey finishing up another mission. She had the requisite training, so when Stargazer had surfaced, she and Howard Taggart had been dispatched to Lebanon.

Normally, two people were deployed in a sniper team, a shooter and a spotter, and that had been the original plan. Debra Collins had recommended splitting Lia and Howard up, however, as two independent shooters in order to give better coverage of the street, one on each side. There hadn't been time to bring in more people.

With luck, they wouldn't need to shoot. If Suleiman

had taken the electronic bait just now, Echo Whiskey was about to deliver to Sagittarius an envelope containing a bank note for 45 million Lebanese pounds—a bit under thirty thousand U.S. dollars.

Lia did not believe in luck. If Syrian intelligence suspected something was wrong, Echo Whiskey might have just been dispatched to eliminate Sagittarius. Hell, even if Suleiman had accepted the thumb drive's contents as genuine, the man was perfectly capable of eliminating Haddid simply to wrap up some untidy loose ends. The hope, of course, was that the IMJ would choose to keep Haddid alive and available as a regular source of intelligence inside the U.S. Embassy, but according to the jacket compiled by the CIA over the years, Colonel Suleiman was a paranoid and psychopathic thug. It was anybody's guess how the next few seconds were going to play out.

Which was why Lia and Taggart were there as overwatch. If Echo Whiskey produced a weapon from inside that overcoat, he was a dead man. If he produced an envelope, he would live. As simple as that.

She watched as he stopped next to Haddid's sidewalk table, exchanging words with the CIA man. Lia could hear words in Arabic but didn't understand them. A moment later, Echo Whiskey walked around to Haddid's right and took a seat, facing the street. One hand reached inside his coat, and Lia's finger tightened ever so slightly on the trigger.

"I've got the shot," she said.

Echo Whiskey's hand emerged from the jacket, holding an envelope, which he casually placed on the table between the two men. They continued to speak for a few moments, and at one point Haddid picked up the envelope, looked inside, then slipped it inside his jacket.

"That's it," Collins said. "Payment received. The fish bit."

"Aquarius, stay on Echo Whiskey," Caravaggio warned. "It's not over yet. . . ."

But a few moments later, Echo Whiskey stood, exchanged a few more words with Haddid, then walked back up the street. Haddid visibly sagged in his seat, rubbed his jaw, then said, "Mission complete. I'm coming in."

Lia continued to cover the man, however, as he stood, paid for his drink, and left the café. Only when he was out of sight from her sniper's perch did she lean back from the wall and begin breaking her weapon down.

She worked swiftly and with no wasted motion. The Mk 11 had been designed to disassemble into a small package, and this special modification had several extra steps to make it smaller still. The barrel and sound suppressor unscrewed, then came apart into two pieces. Then the receiver assembly unsnapped from the stock, then clicked apart into two more pieces, until Lia had five parts, not counting the magazine, none more than twelve inches long. After she pulled a tightly bundled roll of cloth and a pair of sandals from her handbag, all of the parts went into the bag, which concealed them easily. Her shoes went into the bag as well, followed by the camera and tripod.

With a final look around to sanitize her rooftop observation post, she pulled on the sandals, then crossed the open roof to the small building sheltering the top of the service stairs. Once inside, with no possibility of being seen, she slung the bag over her neck by its long strap, so that it hung over her torso just below her breasts. Unrolling the dark cloth, she slipped it over her head and tugged it into place—a traditional Muslim woman's burka covering Lia from head to foot and effectively concealing the handbag.

Down the service stairs to the main level, where she stepped out into the building lobby. None of the people there—mostly men—gave her a second glance.

Lebanon was a remarkably progressive and Western nation within a sea of conservative Islam. Women could be seen on the streets in blue jeans, miniskirts, and other Western attire, and could grace the local beaches in almost nonexistent bikinis. There was even one beach a few blocks from here in downtown Beirut, restricted to women only, of course, where they could sunbathe topless.

At the same time, most Muslim women still preferred more conservative dress, and you could see a range of fashion from colorful scarves over the head to full-length burkas like the one Lia was wearing now. Within Beirut, she was now effectively invisible.

Bowed slightly under the weight of camera and rifle, she made her way toward the safe house on Verdun Street, as planned. The eerie wail of a muezzin calling out the *adhan* sounded from the loudspeaker in a spire-topped minaret nearby, calling the faithful to prayer.

"Good job, Lia," William Rubens' voice said in her ear. It startled her. She'd not realized he was in the Art Room, or that he was watching this op. At any given moment there might be as many as three separate missions being handled through the Art Room, and a Deputy Director of the NSA could not be expected to closely watch them all.

"Thank you, sir," she murmured. "It was routine and went down as planned . . . thank God." Just another day at the office.

"When you get back to the safe house," Rubens told her, "call in. I need you to check something for me."

"In Beirut?" she asked. She liked Lebanon, and had been wondering if she might be able to grab some time as a tourist while she was here.

To be sure, that sort of thing was not usually a good idea and Rubens would never have sanctioned it. Standard tradecraft required operators to be pulled out of a mission area as soon as the op was over, just in case there were unexpected repercussions. But this op had been a walk in the park with no hostile contact and no complications. There was almost zero chance that she'd been spotted, or that any of her covers had been blown. According to the op plan, she would be going home on a commercial flight sometime tomorrow. That would give her the evening free, at least. And if Rubens wanted her to stay on for a while . . .

"Negative," Rubens told her. "Ankara. There's a company jet waiting for you at Beirut International."

So much, she thought, *for a free evening in exotic Beirut.*

"On my way," she told him.

Office of Sir Charles Mayhew
Atlantis Queen **terminal complex**
Southampton, England
Thursday, 1610 hours GMT

Sir Charles Mayhew was a vice president of Royal Sky Line, Ltd., chief operations officer, and member of the corporate board of directors. He was also the company board member nearest to hand when Thomas Mitchell and MI5 needed a high-ranking corporate officer to give him some answers.

They gathered in a small meeting room adjoining Sir Charles' office, which was located on the tenth floor of the ultra-modern green glass tower adjoining the *Atlantis Queen*'s passenger terminal. The tower also housed a hotel and a ground-floor gallery of shops and travel agencies, but the penthouse had been reserved for Royal Sky bigwigs, most of whom weren't available at the moment.

Typical, Mitchell thought. But unimportant. Sir Charles would do just fine. Mayhew was an obese man, heavy-faced but with nervous, active eyes. He was scared, Mitchell thought, scared that his company was about to be dealt a financial body blow.

That fear could be useful.

Also present were the ship's captain, Phillips, his second in command, Staff Captain Vandergrift, a solicitor for Royal Sky Line named James Alcock, and David Llewellyn, the chief of security on board the *Atlantis Queen*.

"I take it," Mitchell said, placing a photograph on the table before them, "that none of you have ever seen this man before." It was a color shot of Nayim Erbakan, an eight-by-ten blow-up of the wallet-sized photo found on Chester Darrow's body.

"Sure," Llewellyn said, grinning. "A little while ago, when they arrested him. Caught him with his pants down, as it were, in the backscatter scanner."

"I know," Mitchell said dryly. "I was there, too, remember? But how about any of you? Captain?"

"Never seen him before," Captain Phillips said. "Should we have?"

"Not really . . . but you have to admit that there are some puzzling facts about this case." Mitchell glanced at his notebook. "A Turkish national, caught smuggling one half kilogram of cocaine onto a luxury cruise ship . . . bound from England to the eastern Mediterranean. That's not one of the usual smuggling routes, you know. Erbakan has a legitimate ticket for a mid-priced stateroom, booked by a travel agency in Le Havre five days ago.

"An hour or so after Erbakan is taken into custody, your fourth officer is murdered on the dock by persons unknown," Mitchell continued. "Three shots to the chest from a handgun at point-blank range. No one hears the shots, though there are plenty of dockworkers in the area, including just inside the ship's cargo hold forty or fifty feet away. That suggests Darrow was killed by a silenced weapon, a professional hit.

"On Darrow's body, we find a small version of this photo. And in the Dumpster next to the body, right on top of the garbage as though it had just been tossed in, we find a briefcase containing thirty thousand euros. Coincidentally, that is the approximate street value of one half kilogram of cocaine . . . which is also, coincidentally, the amount of cocaine Erbakan was carrying. Anyone here want to connect the dots for me?"

None of the others replied. Sir Charles shifted uncomfortably in his seat, which creaked as he moved. The solicitor, Alcock, wrote something down in a small notebook. Mitchell shrugged and continued.

"I'll tell you how *I* see it. Erbakan was a small-time operator. Neither MI5 or Interpol has much on him. He doesn't appear to have had any organized crime connections, but he does have travel visas for half a dozen European countries, including Great Britain. I think Darrow had contacted Erbakan and arranged to buy half a kilo of coke. Erbakan gets picked up at the terminal security station. Darrow doesn't know this, and meets someone else, maybe someone pretending to be Erbakan, maybe someone claiming to work for Erbakan. Darrow takes the money for the exchange and hides it in the Dumpster before the other guy shows up . . . and then the other guy shows up and puts three bullets into him."

"It sounds like you have the puzzle pretty well put together, Mr. Mitchell," Sir Charles said. He tried to sound casual, and failed. "Exactly how does this affect Royal Sky Line?"

"It all fits together very neatly," Mitchell agreed. "Maybe a trifle too neatly, one might think."

"Did Erbakan tell you anything?" Llewellyn asked.

"A little. He seems to want to cooperate, but we're not sure he's telling us everything. He claims a man named Darrow met him a week ago in Le Havre, and arranged for him to smuggle the coke on board today."

"Well, then, it all rather seems open-and-shut, doesn't it?" James Alcock said. He was a sour, precise little man who worked in Royal Sky's legal department.

"Almost," Mitchell replied. "As I said, it's neat . . . but

there are a couple of loose ends dangling, and they just
don't make sense. Why did Erbakan try to board the ship
when he could have simply met Darrow on the pier and
not risked going through the security check? If he *did* get
on board as a passenger, why not meet Darrow when the
ship was at sea?

"And, most important, who killed Darrow?"

"The Mafia, perhaps?" Vandergrift suggested. "Or one
of the other crime syndicates? They could have seen
this . . . this transaction as competition."

"Yes. That's what we thought at first," Mitchell acknowledged. "But it's not really their style, you know. A
half-kilo deal is nothing for the big guys. Chump change.
They might've demanded a percentage, or broken Darrow's kneecaps as a warning, or even killed Erbakan and
told Darrow he needed to buy from *them* in the future . . .
but they wouldn't have just killed the guy like that. *Not
unless they thought Darrow was working for someone
else.*"

"Sir!" Phillips said, angry. "Are you suggesting that
we're operating some sort of drug ring off of my ship?"

"The thought did cross our minds," Mitchell admitted.
"Especially when we looked at the records of some of
your passengers."

"What?" Sir Charles snapped, startled. "Since when
does MI5 have the right—"

"Please, Sir Charles," Mitchell said. "There's nothing
new in any of this. We have access to police records both
here and abroad, and we use them. It's our *job* . . . and if
you have an issue with that, take it up with Parliament the
next time they pass intrusive legislation. Or the Americans with their Patriot Act.

"In any case, one of the passengers on the *Atlantis
Queen* is a Ms. Gillian Harper. American. She's been in
trouble half a dozen times. Two years ago she got a suspended sentence and a rehab order when she tested positive for cocaine.

"And there's a stock trader . . . Adrian Bollinger. Another American. He did three years for possession back in the eighties. And there's—"

"Just what is the point of this inquisition?" Alcock demanded. "That some of the people on the *Queen*'s passenger list use drugs? Or have in the past?"

"Mr. Alcock—"

Captain Phillips interrupted, his anger barely contained now. "I think the latest statistics say that somewhere between one and three percent of the adult population either use or have used cocaine. Out of three thousand people on my ship, that's at least thirty! So what are you going to do . . . question every person on board? Treat them all like criminals?"

"Mr. Mitchell," Sir Charles said. His heavy face had gone florid, and he was perspiring freely. "Are you seriously considering delaying the *Queen*'s departure? Do you have any idea how much revenue is involved here?"

"No, Sir Charles. I don't."

"Hundreds of thousands of pounds! Most of the passengers on that ship are on time-sensitive schedules! If there is a serious delay in sailing, they will . . . make other arrangements. Royal Sky will have to refund a fortune in moneys already paid. It could ruin this company!"

"Don't worry, Sir Charles," Alcock said. "He won't delay the sailing."

"And why won't I do that, Mr. Alcock?" Mitchell asked.

"Because to do so legally you will need to show cause, then get an injunction from the courts. And *we* will file to block that injunction. The ship is due to sail at nine tomorrow morning. I don't believe you could get the legal mills turning in time, sir."

"In the case of a capital crime, Mr. Alcock, there are ways to expedite matters."

"And there is also the unsavory possibility of a lawsuit

against the government. And some *very* bad publicity both for MI5, and for you, personally. I assure you that if you try to harm this company, your name and the name of MI5 will be prominently displayed on page one of every newspaper in the country, from the *Telegraph*, the *Guardian*, the *Times*, all the way down to the *Sun*! After that debacle over the files your bureau holds on ordinary, law-abiding citizens . . . is that really something you wish to call down upon yourself?"

Mitchell chuckled. "I'm terrified. Fortunately, I'm not suggesting that we delay the departure."

"Then what *are* you suggesting, sir?" Captain Phillips asked icily.

"That you take on board two additional passengers, myself and one other. There's no way we could question two thousand people, and no way we could legally hold them long enough to do so. Besides, I assure you, the government has no wish to put you out of business. But if I and an assistant could circulate among the crew and passengers for the next fortnight, we could ask our questions, carry out our investigation, and the entire matter could be kept more or less quiet."

"That seems . . . most reasonable," Sir Charles said. "What do you think, Alcock?"

"I think that the government could still find itself on the receiving end of a major lawsuit if their agents spread slanderous accusations about drug use on one of our cruise ships. I promise you, Mr. Mitchell, that *any* bad publicity whatsoever concerning this line or its employees could be actionable!"

"Mr. Alcock . . . a man is *dead*." Mitchell's face was stony. "Drugs are involved. Rattle all the lawsuit threats you want at me. I promise we will be discreet, but we *will* do our job."

They argued for another ten minutes, but in the end Mitchell got exactly what he'd wanted all along.

There were people on board the *Atlantis Queen* who knew more about Darrow's murder than had emerged from the investigation so far.

And Thomas Mitchell intended to find them.

6

Bridge, *Atlantis Queen*
Southampton, England
Friday, 0849 hours GMT

"THE DECK CREW REPORTS THE gangway has been secured, Captain," Vandergrift reported.

"Very well," Phillips replied. "Single up all lines, fore
and aft, and secure the spring."

"Aye, aye, Captain."

Phillips walked to the port side of the spacious bridge,
gazing out through the sloping windows overlooking the
bow promenade and, below it and to port, the *Atlantis
Queen*'s berth alongside the Royal Sky cruise terminal.
With the gangway pulled up and stowed, there were no
longer security restrictions along the pier. People spilled
out of the terminal to form a dense crowd alongside the
ship, families, friends, and well-wishers giving her the
traditional bon voyage send-off. Passengers lined the railing of the Promenade Deck, waving back, throwing con-
fetti, and calling down inanities to the people ashore.

Tradition . . .

To starboard, the two harbor tugs *Cornwall* and *Devon-
shire* signaled their readiness to proceed with short whistle blasts. Southampton occupied the south-pointing
arrowhead of land between two rivers, the Itchen to the

east, the Test to the west. Where the rivers joined became Southampton Water, a broad, straight channel running southeast toward the coast and the Isle of Wight. The Royal Sky Line terminal was located on the Test, only a few hundred yards from the beginning of the Water. Phillips could see the numerous white triangular sails of pleasure craft beyond the Point, along with the faster-moving specks of powerboats.

Just ahead of the *Queen*, the harbor pilot boat chugged into position, ready to guide the ninety-thousand-ton behemoth down through Southampton Water, past the Isle of Wight, and out into the English Channel beyond.

The tide had turned and was now in ebb flow. The weather was sunny, with just a hint of haze against the southern horizon. Even the met reports had been more promising this morning.

Omens of a good cruise.

The captain tried not to think of the bad omens . . . of Darrow's murder, or of the presence of two MI5 people conducting a surreptitious investigation on board his ship. He was just glad things had worked out as they had. He knew how close Royal Sky Line was running financially right now. Had the cruise been canceled or badly delayed, Phillips would have been looking for a new job . . . and there just weren't that many openings for cruise ship captains right now. It would have meant going back to piloting the Channel Ferry or skippering supply boats to North Sea oil platforms.

"Engine room reports both Azipods ready and turning," Vandergrift said. "Captain, the *Queen* is ready in all respects for sea."

He could only just barely feel the hum of the *Queen*'s powerful Sulzer ZA40 diesel plant through the deck beneath his shoes as it cranked out 63.4 megawatts of power. Azipod was the brand name for the ABB Group's azimuth thruster. The *Queen* had two, electrically powered propellers mounted in pods beneath her stern capable of turning 360 degrees to face any direction. Normally turned with the propellers leading, in a tractor configuration, the Azipods provided the *Queen* with superb maneuverability.

Captain Phillips was fiercely proud of his vessel.

He glanced at the digital clock above the bridge windows. Two minutes before nine.

"Mr. Vandergrift, you may give the order to cast off fore and aft. Mr. Cardew, signal the tugs that we are ready to put to sea."

"Aye, Captain."

The last slender tethers holding the *Queen* to the shore were flipped free from their bollards and run on board. Towering above the crowded pier, the ship gave one short, mournful hoot from her whistle . . . then another . . . and finally a third long blast. The throngs both ashore and on board cheered and waved.

Urged along by her Azipod thrusters and gently nudged by her tugs, the huge ship edged farther out into open water, the gap between ship and shore steadily widening, the bow swinging out to align with the harbor pilot ahead.

And Captain Phillips breathed a heartfelt sigh of relief.

The *Atlantis Queen* was under way at last.

Fantail, *Atlantis Queen*
River Test, Southampton, England
Off the cruise ship dock
Friday, 0901 hours GMT

At the very stern of the *Atlantis Queen,* Yusef Khalid stood with another man and watched the crowded pier slowly recede across the water. "Praise be to Allah," the other man said quietly in Arabic. "He has seen fit to bless us with success!"

"Success for the first steps, at any rate," Khalid replied in English. "We have many steps to go, yet."

"Allah will provide!"

"If you say so," Khalid replied with a shrug.

Khalid had little patience with the hyper-religious pos-
turings of some of his fellow, more passionate jihadists.
Passion could be a good thing when it came to war, especially when men were asked to sacrifice their lives to
carry out a mission such as this one. And it was useful to
pretend a passion for the Divine in order to manipulate
credulous people.

But he was not in this for spiritual reasons. Quite the
opposite, in fact.

"Your problem," Rashid Abdul Aziz told him, still
speaking in Arabic, "is that you have been too long in the
World. Your faith in the Almighty and in His Prophet,
bless his name, has grown weak!"

"And *your* problem," Khalid snapped in the same language, "is that you rely too much on God! When you fail,
you claim that it must be God's will! It wasn't that you
didn't plan enough, or prepare enough, or take the proper
precautions, or even that the enemy was too strong, or too
smart. No! It must have been God's will! Don't you see
that that is the worst kind of blasphemy, that you are
blaming God for what has gone wrong?"

Stunned, Aziz shook his head. "You . . . you are
wrong, my brother. *All* things are in God's hands. Our
successes, and our failures as well."

Khalid took a moment to slow his breathing, the
pounding of his heart. His own outburst had caught him
by surprise. Where had *that* come from?

"I am . . . sorry," he told Aziz. It would serve no purpose to berate Aziz for his misplaced faith, or to engage
in useless disputation. Let the man believe what he
wanted. "I've been under a great strain lately."

And it was true. For months, now, he'd been one of the
four team leaders involved in Operation Zarqawi, and the
planning, the preparation, had been both intense and
exhausting. There'd been a very real possibility that the

police would have kept the *Atlantis Queen* from sailing. Had that happened, his half of the plan would have failed. Operation Zarqawi would have continued—indeed, it could not now possibly be stopped—but the strike against the hated West would be so much more devastating, so much more effective, if the *Atlantis Queen* could be taken and brought into the unfolding plan.

It had been a close-run thing, but the *Queen* had sailed despite the murder of the ship's officer, had sailed exactly as he had predicted she would when he'd first laid out his plan for approval in front of the guiding lights of al-Qaeda, in that mountain cavern back in Pakistan's Northwest Territories.

And perhaps Aziz was right. Allah *was* smiling upon this venture. At least, it would do no harm to allow himself to believe that, to enjoy the warmth that came with the sincere belief that God was with you.

So long as he didn't begin counting on God's blessing. What was it the Westerners said? *God helps those who help themselves.*

"What was our final count, Rashid?" he asked. "How many did we manage to get on board?"

"Thirty-one, praise Allah!"

"And supplies?"

"Three trucks, Amir." The honorific meant "Commander." "A total of twelve tons of explosives, as well as rifles, ammunition, detonators, hand grenades. And the special weapons. Everything we need!"

"It is good. Remind them to stay out of sight. This ship has security cameras everywhere. We don't want anyone to show himself and give our presence away too soon."

"It will be as you say, Amir."

"Our man in the security office should have passkeys for everyone before tomorrow." He pointed forward with a twitch of his head. "Go, now. Tell them to stay out of sight."

"Yes, Amir Yusef!"

Khalid pulled out his phone with its encrypted satellite link.

It was time to begin coordinating events with the *Pacific Sandpiper.*

Pacific Sandpiper
St. George's Channel
51° 20' N, 5° 45' W
Friday, 0920 hours GMT

West of Saint David's Head and the coast of Wales, the leviathan plowed forward into rolling seas and a stiff breeze. The blue-and-white-painted PNTL transport had a top speed of eighteen knots, but since leaving Barrow some two hundred nautical miles astern she'd been plodding along at a mere eight, a concession to safety regulations. Sea traffic was heavy within the confined waters between England and Ireland and the chances of a collision markedly higher. The *Pacific Sandpiper*'s stringent insurance contracts required that she move slowly enough within congested waters that even rowboats could avoid her, or so it seemed. She would be required to crawl during her approach to the Panama Canal, and when she entered Japanese waters as well.

High on the ship's spacious bridge, her captain, Neil Jorgenson, stood next to the helm and studied the waters ahead. Their escort, the *Ishikari*, led the way nearly half a mile off the bow, a narrow gray silhouette rolling alarmingly from side to side in the heavy swell. To starboard rode their second escort, the Royal Navy frigate *Campbeltown*. The *Campbeltown*'s Sea King helicopter was a speck in the distance to the southwest, scouting ahead for trouble.

"Looks like the Japs'll be feeding the fishes this morning, Captain," the first officer, Roger Dunsmore, said, grinning as he lowered a pair of binoculars.

Jorgenson had been a sailor for nearly all of his fifty-two years, starting out as a boy on the family fishing boat in Norway. His parents had immigrated to Great Britain in the early 1970s, and his very first adult job had been as deckhand on board a British Petroleum supply ship in the North Sea. Compared to that, a bit of roll like this was nothing.

"That's what you get when you go to sea in a cockle-shell," Jorgenson replied with a shrug. He fished inside the pocket of his jacket, extracting a battered pipe and a tobacco pouch. There were regulations against smoking on board—there were regulations for *everything* on PNTL vessels—but at sea *he* was the master. He began filling the pipe. "I imagine they envy us our rock-solid little island now!"

The *Sandpiper* was superbly stable, ignoring the swell, which broke to either side of the ship's high, rounded bow with scarcely any lift or roll at all. Even in a full gale, being on board the *Piper* was more like standing on an oil platform anchored to the bottom than being on board a ship. She was an aircraft carrier to *Ishikari*'s canoe, a most comfortable and pleasantly civilized way of going to sea.

"Speaking of Japs, sir," Dunsmore said, "have you seen ours?"

"Wanibuchi and Kitagawa? Not since we left Barrow," Jorgenson replied. "Why?"

"Not sure. They were giving me the creeps when we were taking on our cargo, always underfoot, always watching everything we do."

"It's their plutonium," Jorgenson replied mildly. "They have every right to keep a close eye on it."

"I suppose so, sir. But I swear they crawled through every cubic meter of this ship. Looking at everything. Taking notes. Checking security measures. Asking questions. Jabbering away at one another like nobody's business."

"It *is* nobody's business, Number One. They were cleared by the head office. That should be enough for us."

Dunsmore's attitude annoyed the captain. The man was a bigot. He didn't like blacks, he didn't like Asians, and he didn't like the third-world hands who made up the majority of the deck force on board working ships. As the ship's executive officer, Dunsmore was responsible for the thirty men of the *Sandpiper*'s crew—and a good three-quarters of them were Pakistani, Malay, or Filipino. Dunsmore was an elitist of the worst type, a snob and a racist who liked to boast that an ancestor of his had been in the court of the first Queen Elizabeth.

It must, Jorgenson thought wryly, *be something of a comedown for Dunsmore, having to work with the riffraff like that.*

Jorgenson didn't care what the man thought, so long as he did his job. He was a competent first officer, and that was all that mattered.

PNTL was a British company, the *Pacific Sandpiper* a British-flagged ship. Their chief client and business partner, however, was Japan. Since 1995, Japan had been shipping radioactive wastes to France and England for reprocessing. The high-level radioactive waste, or HLW, belonged to ten Japanese utility companies using nuclear plants to produce electricity. The waste was processed and vitrified at the Sellafield reactor complex in England, north of Barrow, then returned to Japan for disposal. The last shipment from France had been completed in 2007; shipments from England would be continuing through 2016.

Since 1999, a new twist had been added, when PNTL had begun transporting used fuel rods from Japanese reactors to Sellafield, where useable plutonium was extracted from the waste and mixed with depleted uranium into fresh fuel elements, called MOX. Japan had some fifty-three reactors online that could use these fuel elements, and more were being built. They were building a new processing plant at Rokkasho-mura, in northern

Honshu, but there'd been delays. Until that plant was up and running, Japan would rely on Europe for its supply of nuclear fuel.

Pacific Sandpiper and her sisters had been custom-built for transporting radioactive waste halfway around the world, and they'd been *very* well designed for that task, and that task alone. They'd been called the safest vessels on the seas, and with good reason. With double-hull construction, double collision bulkheads, and redundant power and propulsion systems, she was designed to be as close to unsinkable as a ship could be. She was safe from attack, too. Hidden away inside her superstructure were three 30mm cannons, the first time since World War II that merchant ships had actually been armed. The guns were backed by thirty ex-military British AEF police on permanent assignment to PNTL and by the *Sandpiper*'s two escorts, the *Campbeltown*, which would escort them out of European waters, and the *Ishikari*, which would accompany them all the way to Japan.

Jorgenson puffed his pipe alight, discarded the match, and raised his binoculars for a closer look at the *Ishikari* ahead, then looked to starboard and studied the *Campbeltown* for a moment. As they left the Irish Sea for the Atlantic Ocean proper, the water grew swiftly rougher, and both escorts were making rather heavy work of it.

Yes, the crews on board the *Piper*'s escorts were certainly in for a rough ride.

Pyramid Club Casino, *Atlantis Queen*
The Solent
50° 46' N, 1° 43' W
Friday, 1015 hours GMT

Jerry Esterhausen glowered at the monitor screen, where a beautiful woman's face stared back with a blank-faced lack of emotion. "You electronic *bitch*!" he said.

"You do know how to sweet-talk a girl," Sandy Markham said.

"She's determined not to be cooperative this morning," Esterhausen said. He pushed his glasses higher up at the bridge of his nose, then began typing furiously at the keyboard in front of him. "I swear sometimes she has a mind of her own."

"Danger, Will Robinson!" Markham said, putting an edge to her voice as she imitated a famous robot from American TV. "Danger! Danger!"

"Yeah, right," Esterhausen said, still typing. He'd only heard that lame old joke a few dozen times in the past year, and it was no funnier now than it had been when he'd started. "Believe me, there'll be plenty of danger for Rosie if she doesn't behave herself."

"Rosie" was the CyberAge Corporation's latest commercial product, a robot that could play blackjack and several other card games. Named for another American TV robot, Rosie looked nothing like her cartoon namesake. She was bolted to the deck, for one thing, a slender, upright pylon capped by a moveable TV monitor that displayed her face and a small video camera. She had broad shoulders supporting a pair of spidery arms ending in finely articulated mechanical hands. Those hands, sold by the Shadow Robot Company in London, possessed a touch delicate enough to handle a wineglass, pick up a feather—or deal playing cards from a deck.

At least, she could deal cards when she was properly working.

CyberAge was an American company, located in Paterson, New Jersey, and Esterhausen was one of their service representatives. Royal Sky Line had purchased one of CyberAge's half-million-dollar machines for the *Atlantis Queen*'s Poseidon Casino, a novelty item to complement the cruise ship's ultra-modern décor. It was a dream assignment, really . . . a free two-week cruise to the Eastern Mediterranean on board a luxury liner, and all he had to do was make sure Rosie was functioning properly.

Well, she *had* been working when she'd left the shop . . . and she'd been working okay after she'd been installed in the ship's casino last week. But an hour ago he'd come down to run some test programs through the infernal contraption and she'd locked up hard. Her debut was supposed to be tonight, and he'd promised Sandy Markham, the *Queen*'s Entertainment Director, that Rosie would be up and dealing by 6:00 P.M.

He hit enter, and Rosie's arms swung protectively across what would have been her breasts if she'd had them. "*Please*, sir!" she said in a sultry, come-hither voice. "You're making me blush!"

Markham burst out laughing. "Good heavens! What are you doing to her, Jerry?"

"Trying to find out why it's hanging up." He typed in another command.

"*Please*, sir! You're making me blush!"

"That," Markham said, still giggling, "is funny as hell!"

Esterhausen ignored her and kept working. His boss had promised dire consequences if Rosie screwed up, and Esterhausen was painfully aware that he and his company's card-playing robot were both on display. If Rosie didn't perform as promised—and by showtime tonight—they might both find themselves out of a job.

"*Please*, sir! You're making me blush!"

Several other ship employees had heard the exchange and were gathering around now—one of the bartenders, a couple of janitorial types sweeping the deck, and a dark, Arabic-looking man with the badge that said he was a Ship's Security officer. "Why does it keep saying that?" the security officer asked.

Esterhauser sighed. "It's designed to banter with the customers," he said. "The program's smart enough to identify if someone is male or female—it reads the tonal qualities of your voice, actually—and to respond to a few hundred different words, phrases, and movements we've programmed into its operating system. It says that in response to four or five different risqué comments it might hear, or if a man tries to touch its . . . its chest. Right at the moment, though, it's stuck in a loop, and I can't . . . Hang on. Wait just a sec. . . ."

He typed in two more lines of code and hit enter. Rosie's arms came down to the ready position, hands slightly flexed just above the tabletop before her. "Awaiting input," she said in her sexiest voice.

"I'll just bet you are, girl," Markham said, and she laughed again.

"That's obscene," the security officer said, though whether he was referring to Rosie or to Markham's bawdy comment Esterhausen couldn't tell. The man shook his head as he walked off.

Esterhausen typed in "Run Program 1" and hit enter. The hands flexed, stretched in an eerily human way, then picked up a deck of cards nearby. The hands began moving, shuffling the cards too fast for the eye to follow. "*That's* more like it," Esterhausen said.

"When your lot gets one of these to do the housework," Markham said, "give me a call, okay?"

"When one of these does the housework, Sandy, *we'll* all be obsolete!" He began packing up the keyboard and the scattered items of testing equipment on the table.

"May I give you a hand with this, then?" Markham offered.

She was holding Rosie's body, a female mannequin torso, complete with generous breasts, and draped in the top of a black ball gown that left the shoulders bare. "Sure," Esterhausen said. "It opens here . . . snaps shut like this."

The unit closed around the robot's central pylon, creating a bizarre mix of human and machine—a woman's body with mechanical arms and hands and a TV monitor for a head.

"*Please*, sir!" Rosie said as he straightened the hang of

the gown, displaying her plastic cleavage. The monitor swiveled so that the camera and the woman's face peered directly at him. "I'm *not* that kind of girl!"

"What kind of girl are you, then?" Markham asked, grinning.

"*Expensive*, ma'am," Rosie told her, rotating her monitor to face Markham with a mechanical hum and a click. "So please keep your hands to yourself!"

Esterhausen felt a wave of relief. Maybe this cruise wasn't going to be so bad after all. When Rosie worked properly, she could utterly charm her audience, holding them spellbound.

Through the broad windows of the Pyramid Casino, he saw the sun dance off the waters of the Solent, the straits tucked in between Southampton Water and the Isle of Wight. Off the aft port quarter, he noticed the towering gray cliff of a Royal Navy aircraft carrier anchored in Stokes Bay, off Gosport and Spithead.

The ship raised some unexpected memories. *Damned Navy bastards*, he thought.

Atlantean Grotto Lounge, *Atlantis Queen*
The Solent
50° 46' N, 1° 43' W
Friday, 1022 hours GMT

Carolyn Howorth sat at one of the tables in the elegant Atlantean Club, her laptop before her. The words *Charlie: So how's it feel to be a rich bitch now?* appeared on her screen.

She grinned, and typed back her response. *I could get used to this. I feel pampered. Where R you?*

Charlie: *Back in my hotel, getting ready to check out. Can't get them to let U stay a few days?*

Charlie: *It would take that long to fill out the paperwork.*

The server brought her the tea she'd ordered. "Thank you."

"You're welcome. Will there be anything else?"

"If I think of anything, I'll give a yell."

The club offered broad, high windows looking out to both port and starboard. In front of her was the coast of southern England and the city of Portsmouth. Several Navy ships were at anchor off Stokes Bay, and the Solent Express, a hovercraft ferry, made its way across the open water in a haze of spray. From here she could make out the white point of the Spinnaker, the modern-art tower rising from the Portsmouth waterfront, designed to look like a mast supporting a billowing spinnaker sail.

Carolyn snuggled back in her padded seat and wiggled her bare toes in the carpet. Yes, she could *definitely* get used to this.

The ship maintained its own Internet service, connected to the Net by satellite, allowing Carolyn to get her e-mail, exchange text messages with Charlie, and also check in with Peters at work. Vacation this might be, but it was a working vacation, and Carolyn was expected to log in each day to keep up with things. Her laptop ran its own encryption program, so she could use it as a secure link with GCHQ at Menwith Hill—not that she expected to be beaming top secret messages back and forth with the home office. Her job was strictly one of light reconnaissance, checking out the *Atlantis Queen*'s security systems and looking for ways that GCHQ or the American NSA could use them to good advantage.

So when R U leaving? she typed.

Charlie: *Flight out of Heathrow at 2115. Red-eye to BWI.*

It was an unfamiliar expression. *Red-eye?*

Charlie: *Means I'll be up all night.*

Well, make Rubens give you some time off tomorrow.

Charlie: *VERY unlikely! Got to run. You enjoy your cruise! I intend to!*

Carolyn broke the connection, checked her tea, then poured herself a cup. The lounge was almost deserted at this hour of the morning, but she was aware of the small dark plastic domes worked inconspicuously into the ceiling at various points—surveillance cameras connected with the Ship's Security Office.

That, she decided, would be her first order of business—talking with the head security officer and seeing if she could get a tour.

Carolyn Howorth began typing, opening up the ship's home page and searching the menu for ship's officers.

There he was. David Llewellyn, Director Shipboard Security. She began composing an e-mail to him.

7

Atlantis Queen
English Channel
50° 30' N, 1° 05' W
Friday, 1400 hours GMT

UNDER WAY AT LAST, SHE WAS magnificent and she was glorious. Rounding the eastern tip of the Isle of Wight, the *Atlantis Queen* steadily picked up speed as flocks of sailboats, speedboats, yachts, and other pleasure craft scattered before her. A bright, carnival atmosphere infused each deck, though most of her passengers were either still on the broad outside promenade around the Third Deck or, if they were wealthy enough to afford it, on the private balconies outside their luxurious staterooms, leaning on the railings and, if they were in a sufficiently generous mood, waving to the lesser mortals bobbing in their cockleshells and toy boats far below.

Like all cruise ships, the *Atlantis Queen* adhered to a particular theme, in this case the fabulous lost city of Atlantis. Each of the various nightclubs, theaters, restaurants, bars, and other popular gathering spots on board was named for some icon or myth connected with either Atlantis or, with an exclusively Atlantean mythology being a bit sparse, the gods and goddesses of ancient Greece, and with just a sprinkling of ancient Egypt and Meso-america thrown in as well.

The twelve passenger decks, for instance, were named for the twelve gods of Olympus, with two notable exceptions made in the name of good public relations. The First Deck, where passengers came aboard in the Grand Atrium with its myriad shops, tour offices, and computer center, was called the Neptune Deck. The ship's owners had substituted the Roman Neptune for the Greek Poseidon, fearing that the Greek version would conjure unsettling images of the doomed ship of the popular adventure movie. And there was no Ares Deck, again for obvious PR reasons, there being no need for a god of warfare, battle, and strife on a vacation cruise ship. Instead, the uppermost Twelfth Deck was called the Ouranos Deck, that predecessor of the classical deities of ancient Greece having been promoted to Olympian status because of his traditional association with astronomy and the sky. The view of the night sky from the Atlantean Grotto Terrace while the ship was at sea, far from smog and the light pollution of cities, was fantastic.

Hades wasn't included, in part because he'd not been one of the traditional Olympian twelve and, again, due to PR reasons. The Greek god of the underworld *was* remembered in the Hades Hot Spot, however, a bar and nightclub on the Aphrodite Deck featuring a DJ, loud music, and the raucously energetic Santorini Dancers, who, after ten in the evening, performed topless.

The ship was luxuriously appointed throughout—plenty of rich wood paneling, thick carpeting, and expensively modern furnishings. Many of the windows and skylights were stained glass with intricate patterns; some decks were laid out in highly polished mosaic tiles instead of carpet, with traditional marine scenes from Greek, Roman, or Cretan artistic traditions, showing octopi, dolphins, and other sea creatures. The Grand Atrium was a cavernous circular mall with huge aquaria built into the bulkheads between the shops, and deck-to-overhead tube-pillars filled with bubbling water, the whole subtly lit to create a shifting, eerie, deep-sea feel to the place. The Cayce Library was small but well appointed, with an emphasis on books about Greece, Atlantis, mythology, history, and travel books about Mediterranean countries. The Pyramid Club Casino went for the ultra-modern look—lots of chrome, lots of flashing lights, lots of electronic gambling machines, and, of course, the newly installed Blackjack Rosie, who promised to be quite a hit with the techno-geek crowd.

The *Queen* could manage a passenger complement of three thousand. With the world economy in its current shaky state, Royal Sky Line had been hard pressed to book that many guests. Even a last-minute sales blitz offering the cruise at 40 percent off the usual ticket price hadn't been as successful as the corporate office had hoped, and during the final week they'd been offering staterooms for less than half price.

As it was, there were 2,442 paying passengers on board, enough for the company to turn a profit for this cruise, but only *just*. If anything went wrong—a delay due to weather, excessive fuel consumption, mechanical difficulties, an outbreak of food poisoning, rowdy guests getting out of hand and generating lawsuits, *anything*—then the voyage could well end up showing a loss, which would reflect badly on Royal Sky Line's credit, which was already stretched beyond acceptable limits. Failure to get another loan at the end of the year might well force the company into bankruptcy.

Kleito's Temple, *Atlantis Queen*
English Channel
49° 21' N, 8° 13' W
Friday, 1905 hours GMT

Carolyn Howorth had been waiting in Kleito's Temple for less than ten minutes, and she'd been early to begin with.

Located on the Tenth Deck—the Demeter Deck—all the way forward and two levels down from the bridge, the club bar and restaurant had been lavishly decorated to resemble a Greek or, presumably, an Atlantean temple, complete with massive marble columns, marble tables and countertops, and a bigger-than-life-sized gilded statue of a gracefully nude woman. Smaller statues, all male, occupied niches in the bulkheads to either side, and an elaborate waterfall burbled and splashed happily down rugged faux rocks into a large central pool half-shrouded in vegetation.

Legend had it that the god Poseidon had taken a human woman, Kleito, as his wife and that she'd born him five sets of twins who'd become the kings of Atlantis. A temple had been erected on the spot, or so claimed the philosopher Plato in his telling of the tale, and that temple had become the exact center of the city of Atlantis.

This club, Howorth decided, was a worthy successor to the temple described by Plato. It was a bit flamboyant for her tastes, but the broad sweep of the windows across the forward wall gave an absolutely staggering, gorgeous view of the water ahead. At the moment, the *Atlantis Queen* was sailing almost exactly due west, and the sunset—a blaze of flaming oranges, reds, and coral pinks, with cooler blues, greens, and ambers—flooded the sky with colored light.

"Ms. Carroll?" a man's voice said behind her.

"I'm Judith Carroll," Carolyn Howorth said, standing and extending her hand. "You must be David."

"David Llewellyn," he said, shaking her hand. "Director of Security. Pleased to meet you, Ms. Carroll."

"Call me Judy," Howorth said. "Everyone else does."

"Judy," he said, waiting for her to sit again, then seating himself. "Charming. A gorgeous sunset."

"Absolutely spectacular," she agreed. "I'm surprised everybody on board the ship isn't crowded in here to see it."

"It *is* a bit more crowded than it usually is," Llewellyn agreed. "And a lot of people are on the decks outside."

"I don't blame them. Thank you for agreeing to see me, David."

"My pleasure. Ah . . . your e-mail said something about you being with British law enforcement?"

Carolyn pulled her wallet out of her handbag and let it fall casually open to her ID. At least, it was *one* of her IDs, one provided for her for this specific mission. "SOCA, actually," she said.

SOCA was a relatively new agency within British law enforcement. The Serious Organised Crime Agency had been created in 2006 specifically to combat drug trafficking, money laundering, people smuggling, and organized crime, a product of the Serious Organised Crime and Police Act of 2005. Some called it Britain's answer to the American FBI, though any comparison was superficial at best. If anything, SOCA was closer in the nature of its work to the U.S. Immigration and Customs Enforcement. Unlike MI5, certain designated SOCA agents had the authority to arrest suspects. Unlike MI5, SOCA had no role in either counterterrorism or national security.

So far as Howorth or her Menwith Hill colleagues could tell, it was a political figurehead agency as much as anything else, a means of *looking* as though the government was doing something about the nation's drug and crime problems, without having to actually *do* anything about them.

But most people wouldn't be aware of that particular twist in the government's knickers. It did provide a convenient cover for Howorth. Like the American NSA, GCHQ didn't care to advertise its presence. *Ever.*

"Thank you, Judy," Llewellyn said, studying the ID carefully before meeting her eyes again. "I've heard of SOCA, of course. I gather lots of you are former MI5, MI6?"

"A lot of us are," she said. It sounded like a test question, something to perhaps catch her in an inconsistency. She'd already planned to be as noncommittal—and therefore as hard to pin down—as possible.

SOCA did draw many of its members from the existing British MI5, which handled domestic security issues, and from MI6, which handled foreign security and intelligence work, like America's CIA. SOCA's current head was a former head of MI5, and there was a lot of traffic between the two.

"I was wondering if you might know a Mr. Thomas Mitchell?"

"No, can't say that I do."

"Or a Mr. Samuel Franks?"

"Nope. Should I?"

Llewellyn shrugged. "Tom Mitchell is MI5. And Mr. Franks is MI5, but currently seconded, I understand, to SOCA. I suppose I was wondering why we have so many of you people running around on board!"

Howorth kept her smile in place. "They're passengers?"

"Of a sort. Are you aware of the . . . incident on the docks yesterday afternoon?"

"No. Should I be?"

Llewellyn seemed to relax a little. "So you're *not* with Mitchell or Franks?"

"No, Mr. Llewellyn. I'm not. I know neither of the gentlemen. SOCA has about forty-two hundred employees and operates out of over forty offices scattered all over the UK. It's impossible to meet or to remember *everyone* in the firm." *Time to change the subject*, she thought. Despite what she'd just said, the last thing she wanted was a face-to-face introduction to Mitchell or Franks, *especially* Franks, who might ask her questions only a real SOCA agent could answer. "Why? What happened on the docks?"

"Nothing important," Llewellyn told her. "And if you didn't ask to see me about that, why did you ask to see me?" His smile broadened. "Not that I at all mind meeting a beautiful woman on a romantic cruise."

"Why, Mr. Llewellyn," she said. "I didn't think ship's crew was allowed to fraternize with the paying passengers!"

"Strictly speaking, no . . . though officers have a bit more leeway than the housekeeping staff, say. And it *is* after hours. I'm off-duty. May I buy you a drink?"

"That would be great. Thank you." Her glass was empty.

"What are you having?"

"Coke."

"Nothing stronger?"

"Coke is fine. My God, will you just look at that sky?" The colors, if anything, were becoming more intense. The sky appeared to be on fire. "What is it they say . . . 'red sky at night, sailor's delight'?"

"That's what they say. Never having been a sailor, I couldn't tell you." He flagged down a server, ordered two soft drinks, and turned back to face her. "Now, you were telling me what you wanted to talk to Security about?"

"Actually, David, I was hoping to get a private tour of your security facilities on the ship. See how they work, day-to-day."

"Indeed? Why?"

"Because SOCA is concerned with smuggling into the United Kingdom. Drugs. Also people."

Llewellyn's eyebrows rose. "People?"

"Twenty-first-century *slaves*, David. People who answer ads for work in the United Kingdom in countries like Indonesia, the Philippines, Malaysia, and Pakistan. They're brought in by professional smugglers—usually by the Italian Mafia or other Mediterranean organized-crime groups, though we've been seeing a bit of activity from Russia lately, as well. The Russian *mafiya*. Men are brought in and put to work in illegal sweatshops, sometimes drug factories. Same for women and children, except they're also exploited sexually, often. They end up in brothels, or working for almost nothing as housekeepers or servants for people who abuse them. They're required to pay for their passage from their wages and, of course, somehow they never manage to get enough to buy their freedom."

"And what does all this have to do with the *Atlantis Queen*?"

She shrugged. "Nothing directly. My boss wants me to have a look at the security arrangements on board your ships. How do you know you don't have a few hundred stowaways? How do you control access to sensitive areas of your ship, such as the computers? We hope to build an intelligence network that includes *all* methods of entry through our borders—airlines, the Chunnel, Channel ferries, passenger liners—to help us monitor the people who come into the UK every day."

"I . . . see. It all seems rather comprehensive."

"It's also low-key and off the record, David. I can show you a letter from my boss authorizing me to see your system. If you'd rather not go that route, I'll let him know and SOCA can make a more . . . formal request of Royal Sky's board of directors."

Howorth could almost see the wheels turning in Llewellyn's mind. If he turned down her informal request, he might soon be dealing with a formal order—and questions from his own boss as to why he'd not been more cooperative with the government.

"If I say no," Llewellyn said, "do we have to send you home?"

She grinned. "Technically," she said, "I'm on vacation. This *is* informal."

"And if I say yes . . . will you let me buy you dinner first?"

"Plying me with food? I think I could manage that."

"Then let me see what I can do," he told her.

Pyramid Club Casino, *Atlantis Queen*
English Channel
49° 21' N, 8° 13' W
Friday, 1935 hours GMT

Rosie, bless her little Intel chip of a heart, was an un-qualified success.

Jerry Esterhausen leaned against the bar, turned on his stool so he could watch the activity at the blackjack table. On the bar in front of him, his laptop was open, the screen showing the feed from Rosie's camera as she dealt out another hand.

The *Atlantis Queen*'s onboard casino was doing a fair business this evening. Men in formal black and women in colorful gowns and plunging décolletage mingled with men and women in more casual attire, feeding coins to electronic slot machines, sitting around green-felt tables studying fans of playing cards, or hanging out at the bar. By far the largest group, though, had clustered around Rosie at her station in front of the broad, glass doors leading out to the after pool deck. Only three were playing; the rest kibitzed with raucous good humor. But when one human player decided he or she had had enough and stood up, another would slip into the vacated seat.

Esterhausen was flanked at the bar by Sharon Reilly, the *Queen*'s CD, or Cruise Director, and by William Paulson, the Hotel Manager—or "hotman," in cruise ship parlance. The CD was in charge of the staff devoted to the care and entertainment of the ship's passengers—hostesses, entertainers, stage managers, fitness instructors, teen counselors, and all the rest who provided recreation for the guests. The hotman, in turn, was a ship's officer and the CD's boss, reporting directly to the staff captain, who was the ship's second in command. The hotman ran the immense floating hotel that was the *Atlantis Queen*.

"That," Paulson said, leaning over to peer at Esterhausen's screen, "is impressive."

The screen showed a Rosie's-eye view of her hands as she shuffled a deck of cards, jointed fingers coated in a thin vinyl skin that stretched and grabbed and manipulated as skillfully as the fingers of any human dealer. The earlier programming glitch appeared to have cleared up completely.

"So, can you operate the robot from your computer?" Reilly asked him.

"Sort of," Esterhausen said. "I can type in code to make changes to the programming, and I can control some of the gross motor movements with this." He tapped the tiny, rubber-capped controller in the center of his keyboard, a miniature joystick. "I can make her turn, make her move her arms, that sort of thing. But to do *that* I would have to use the t-gloves."

On the screen the cards were almost magically scooting off the deck in Rosie's hand as her thumb flicked back and forth.

"T-gloves?" Paulson asked.

"Teleoperational gloves. They look like thin rubber gloves. You put them on, plug them into a USB port, and they sense your hand positions and finger movements, transmitting them to the robot hands. That's how we trained them to do stuff like shuffle, cut, and deal in the first place. That's just for emergencies, though." He shook his head. "I can't deal as slick as Rosie's doing there. We actually had a professional gambler come into our labs to train her with the gloves. Those are *his* hand movements she's using, stored in her hard drive."

"Hey, Rosie!" a young man in the audience called out. "I think I'm in love with you!"

The robot's monitor turned to face the speaker, the female face appearing to look him up and down. "If I weren't bolted to the floor," she said in her provocatively sultry voice, "I'd take you up to your stateroom and let you prove it!"

The audience laughed, and a few clapped their hands. They seemed as entranced by Rosie's banter as by her manual dexterity.

"Fascinating," Reilly said. "But that means, if something went wrong, you could kind of take over for her? Work her like an electronic puppet?"

"Pretty much, yeah. Of course, what we'd probably have to do is hook up a black-box shuffler."

"I've seen those," Paulson said, frowning. "You put a deck in the top, it shuffles them inside and spits cards out one at a time. Not nearly as impressive as *that*."

"But we have one along as backup," Esterhausen told him. "Just in case there's a glitch."

"Hey, Rosie!" another young man called out. "Are those hooters of yours real, or is that where you keep your batteries?"

"*Please*, sir," Rosie replied. "You're making me blush!"

"Rowdy crowd tonight," Reilly said.

"I've seen worse," Paulson said, sliding off his bar stool. "Mr. Esterhausen? An impressive show. I think I can promise that Royal Sky Line will be doing more business with CyberAge in future."

"That's good to hear, sir."

Paulson walked off through the crowd.

"The house wins," Rosie announced as the blackjack hands were revealed. Rosie held a 19; one player had a 17, while the others all were over 21.

"I think I've just been screwed by a machine," one of the players said, laughing as he stood up.

Rosie held up one mechanical arm, the fingers working back and forth. "I'm sorry, sir. All I can manage tonight is a hand job."

That one brought down the house.

Ship's Security Office, *Atlantis Queen*
English Channel
49° 21' N, 8° 13' W
Friday, 2148 hours GMT

David Llewellyn led Carolyn Howorth up the steps and into a passageway on the Eleventh Deck, one level up from Kleito's Temple.

He'd fed her lobster bisque and shrimp scampi as the last of the sunset colors faded from the sky ahead, and talked about his job as head of shipboard security. After a phone call to clear things with someone—she suspected that the call was to Vandergrift, the staff captain— Llewellyn told her that he'd obtained clearance to take her to the Security Office. A handprint scanner mounted on the bulkhead next to the door admitted them. "You have these throughout the ship?" she asked.

"Only the most secure compartments," he said. "Security. The bridge. Engineering. The Purser's Office. Places like that. And only a few key personnel have handprint records on file." He pointed up at a familiar glassy black hemisphere mounted on the ceiling. "Smile," he said. "Big Brother is watching."

Inside, the Security Office consisted of a long room with security monitors lined up along one bulkhead. Four men and two women sat at the monitors, watching them as, occasionally, the view shifted to a different camera. Most of the monitors, Howorth saw, looked down onto passageways. A few showed decks outside, or places like the restaurant they'd just left. One of the men was watching an alcove beneath a ship's ladder, somewhere outside. The light was poor, but there was enough to see a man in a jacket and a woman in a blue gown in close embrace, kissing. The man's hand was roving at the base of her spine.

Llewellyn cleared his throat. "I don't think we have any terrorists there, Jenkins."

"Yes, sir!" the man said, starting. "No, sir! Sorry, sir!" He typed an entry on his keyboard, and the scene changed to the Atlantean Grotto Restaurant on the Eleventh Deck.

"The computer cycles from camera to camera every thirty seconds," Llewellyn explained. "Or the operators can deliberately override the system and look at what they want."

"Privacy issues?" Howorth asked.

"No security cams inside staterooms, crew's quarters, dressing rooms, or public toilets, of course," Llewellyn told her. "But everything else is pretty well covered twenty-four hours a day. Yes, there are privacy issues. But it's a trade-off. If we see drunks in a stateroom passageway, or some-one locked out of their room, or an ugly confrontation, we can have security people there in a minute or two."

"How many security personnel do you have?"

"Enough," he said.

"Computer network security," she said. "You use Net-guardz?"

His eyebrows rose. "Yes, we do. And how did you know that?"

"SOCA has its ways, David." She nodded toward a closed door at the end of the compartment. "What's back there?"

"Computers, and our magnetic keying machines."

"Where you create key cards for passenger's state-rooms?"

"And every other door on the ship. Just like in a hotel."

She'd seen and heard enough. "Thank you, David. This has been most enlightening."

"So what will your report say?"

"Report?"

"You didn't con me into giving you this tour just be-cause you like security cams," Llewellyn told her. "You intimated that SOCA wants to know about how we han-dle security on board."

"At some point, SOCA will want to establish a single

security computer network, something embracing MI5 and 6, Scotland Yard, and a number of other agencies. It looks as if they could add you to the network with a minimum of fuss." She saw the look on his face and smiled. "Don't worry. It won't happen for years . . . not with funding at the levels it's been lately!"

She allowed him to take her for an evening stroll on deck, carefully avoiding the spot where the two lovers were kissing.

★　★　★　★

And in the locked IT room at the back of the Ship's Security Office, Mohamed Ghailiani pulled the last of a stack of plastic key cards from the magnetic imprinting machine and then typed in a keyboard command that erased the log record of his having made these copies. He'd gotten the password for that access from a friend in IT, Danny Smith, claiming he needed an extra master key for a rendezvous in a secure area with a very special lady friend who wanted to see how the ship *really* worked. Smith had only grinned and given Ghailani his personal password; the computer tech was known to have a weak spot for willing women, too.

There would be a record of Ghailani's computer access kept in permanent storage, and he could do nothing about that, not now. When this was all over, an investigation would note that Danny Smith had printed out twenty-five unauthorized master keys and Smith would point the investigators to Ghailiani. Khalid had promised him that the hard drive could be destroyed once he and his friends took over the ship, and that would ensure Ghailiani's anonymity.

The stack contained thirty-one master keys, key cards that gained admission to every locked room, every secure area, every stateroom, on the ship. With these, Khalid and the people he'd snuck on board the ship would have access to every compartment on the *Queen*. And he'd made the operation possible for them.

Ghailiani scarcely cared anymore.

All he could think of was Zahra and Nouzha, and whether he would ever see them alive again.

8

Pacific Sandpiper
North Atlantic Ocean
49° 21' N, 8° 13' W
Saturday, 0805 hours GMT

"GOOD MORNING, EVERYONE," Captain Jorgenson said as he walked onto the bridge, pipe in his teeth, a heavy mug of strong coffee in his hand. As long as he'd lived in Great Britain, he'd never gotten the hang of their mimsy preference for *tea*. Jorgenson had been drinking coffee, good *strong* coffee, since he was twelve. "What's our status?"

"Good morning, Captain," Dunsmore replied, rising from the high captain's seat behind the helm and stepping aside. "We lost the *Campbeltown* four hours ago. It's just us and the *Is She* now."

Jorgenson quirked an eyebrow at Dunsmore's use of the *Ishikari*'s popular nickname. Most of the English speakers in the crew, Jorgenson knew, had taken to calling the Japanese vessel the *Is She* or, more formally, the *Is She? Ain't She?* It was a harmless and typical bit of merchant marine humor. Jorgenson preferred a higher standard of propriety on his bridge, however.

Perhaps Dunsmore caught a taste of Jorgenson's displeasure. Standing with his hands stiffly at his back, he cleared his throat. "Sir. The *Ishikari* is currently eight hundred yards off our starboard bow. We are on course, on time, on a heading of two-three-five degrees true, speed twelve knots. Winds are blowing a fresh breeze from the southwest at twenty knots."

"Very well, Number One." Jorgenson walked over to the radar console, where a seaman stood watch at the large, round screen. Like an air traffic control radar, it showed the targets within range each accompanied by a six-character alphanumeric code returned by transponders on board the targets. The display currently was set to show radar contacts out to a range of twenty miles. *Ishikari*, C7D34K, was the only other target.

"Let's see out to two hundred," he said.

The radar operator touched a control, and the display changed, suddenly crowded with returns representing ships, aircraft, marker buoys, and the cluttered noise of coastlines. Jorgenson recognized the Scilly Isles eighty-five miles due east and, beyond that, the tip of Cornwall, Land's End. At this point, the *Sandpiper* wasn't seeing with her own radar, which had an effective horizon of only about forty to forty-five miles. Instead, she was tapped into an international satellite navigation system, relying on radar plots relayed from NAVSTAR satellites in orbit. At this scale, the *Campbeltown*, M4F99D, was now visible, seventy miles out, and apparently heading back toward the Bristol Channel.

A second strong return was showing thirty-six nautical miles southeast of the *Sandpiper*'s position, about a third of the way from the *Piper* to the tip of Brittany. The target showed the IFF code V5K34R.

"Who's that?" Jorgenson asked, pointing.

The radar operator didn't need to check the traffic code. "RMS *Atlantis Queen*, sir. Cruise ship out of Southampton."

"Very well." His eyes shifted to another target, one showing an ID code of XXXXXX. "Who the bloody hell is that? No IFF."

The unidentified target was eighty-five miles to the southeast, at the mouth of the English Channel, roughly between Brest and Cornwall and some forty-five miles east of the *Atlantis Queen*'s position.

"No, sir. We've already queried them. They're ALAT."

"Bloody frogs," Dunsmore said with a dismissive snort. "If there's a way to screw things up, they'll find it."

ALAT was Aviation Légère de l'Armée de Terre—French Army aviation.

"Cougar, sir," the radar operator added. "They're on maneuvers."

Cougar was the name of the military version of the Eurocopter helicopter. "Did you tell them they were flying without IFF?" Jorgenson asked.

"Yes, sir. They told us to mind our own business, sir."

"Well, screw 'em, then," Jorgenson said. Straightening, he scanned the horizon ahead. Except for the *Ishikari* a half mile off, they had the ocean to themselves.

"Very well, gentlemen," he said. He paused to take another sip of steaming coffee. "Next stop, Rokkasho, Japan, by way of the Panama Canal! Let's open her up, shall we?" He looked about the bridge, at the men standing at their stations. "Ahead full, Mr. Dunsmore. And have Sparks inform the *Ishikari* we are going to eighteen knots."

And the *Pacific Sandpiper* began increasing her speed.

Munitions storage locker, *Ishikari*
49° 21' N, 8° 13' W
Saturday, 0807 hours GMT

Taii Ichiro Inui was methodical and he was well trained. A lieutenant in the Kaiso Jeitai, the Japanese Maritime Self-Defense Force, he'd worked with the American Harpoon antiship missiles for almost ten years and knew the deadly machines as well as anyone in his service. Working with the special tools quietly and with precision, he went from missile to missile where they lay strapped into their launch pods, removing the locks, pulling the yellow keys, and arming each warhead in turn.

Five done. Three to go.

Behind him, Kogyo Yano worked at the second part of the mission task, applying a fist-sized lump of C-4 explosives to four of the warheads, inserting a detonator, and attaching det cord to each, tying all of the charges together to a single battery and timer. The Harpoon anti-ship missile, with its 227-kilogram warhead, was equipped with a safe-arm fuse that prevented detonation of the warhead until after it was in flight, but Inui knew exactly how to bypass the safeties. When the C-4 charges went off, the missiles would go off in sympathetic detonation, all of them at once, over eighteen hundred kilos of high explosive in a single, spectacular blossom of flame and destruction.

A few meters away, a young seaman, Ryoichi Ikikaga, lay motionless in a growing pool of his own blood. Yano had dragged him to the spot after shooting him in the passageway outside, where he'd been standing guard. He would be missed soon. The two men would have to complete their mission within the next few minutes.

Six done.

The ship was pitching heavily in the chop, her speed increasing. Now that the small convoy was past the Cornwall Peninsula and out into the Atlantic proper, the two ships could increase speed to eighteen knots or so. It made Inui's job more difficult, but the deadly missiles were strapped to their pallets, immobile.

He hoped. An armed Harpoon breaking free of its straps and striking the deck just now would have unfortunate consequences.

Seven done. One to go.

The two men worked in silence. They'd planned this operation carefully, and there was no need for words. Last week, when the *Ishikari* had been in port at Barrow and most of her crew had been ashore, they'd even managed a walk-through, step-by-step, to check the timing.

Ichiro Inui had been an officer in the Japanese self-defense force for eight years, but his primary personal duty, his *omi*, lay elsewhere. He was *shishon no Nihon Sekigun*, a phrase translating roughly as "offspring of the Japanese Red Army."

He would observe that duty no matter what, even if it meant that he would die within the next few minutes.

Inui pulled the last key and turned to face Yano, silently holding up the bundle of yellow tags he'd removed from the warheads. Yano nodded, completed the preparation of his last charge of C-4, then said, "Isoge!"

"There is no need to hurry," Inui replied. "We walk, as we planned it."

Yano set the jury-rigged timer for 8:30, giving them ten minutes, and attached the battery. With a last look around, they locked the door behind them with the keys they'd taken from Ikikaga. Calmly they walked down the main passageway, heading forward. The munitions locker lay near the vessel's stern, directly beneath the two Harpoon missile launchers mounted on the ship's fantail. Up one ship's ladder and left, they stopped at a watertight door to pull a pair of bright orange life jackets from a rack on the bulkhead and don them, then pushed the door open, stepping into a wet and somewhat chilly, gusty breeze beneath a leaden sky.

The huge bulk of the *Pacific Sandpiper* plowed unperturbed through the rolling seas aft and to port, showing none of the roll and pitch of the smaller destroyer escort. Still at a casual walk, they made their way forward, hanging on to the safety railing with their left hands in order to maintain their footing on the pitching deck. The wind was strong enough to kick up a few whitecaps on the water, and spray came up over the ship's bow with each plunge through another swell.

The *Ishikari* was not a large vessel—twelve hundred

tonnes, with a length overall of 84.5 meters and a beam of just ten meters. It put her at the mercy of a rough sea.

"You men!" a sharp voice called. "Where are you going?"

It was Lieutenant Watanabe, the deck division leader. He'd emerged from another watertight door just behind them.

"Sir!" Inui said, coming to attention but keeping hold of the safety rail. "Commander Shimatsume told us to check on a loose vent grating at the bow!" Shimatsume was the ship's executive officer.

Watanabe considered this, then waved them on with a nod. "Carry on, then," he said. "Just be careful, and be sure to use safety lines. On a day like this, you could find yourself swimming home!"

"Yes, sir!"

Heart pounding, Inui continued making his way forward, closely followed by Yano. He forced himself not to look at his wristwatch. Either they would make it or they would not.

Either way, the *Ishikari* was doomed and their mission complete.

They trotted down a ladder to the foredeck, then walked past the forward turret with its single 76mm Oto Melara gun. At the ship's bow, they made their way to a grating over a ventilation intake duct and worked it free. Inside was a black, heavy rubber package, a rubber raft Yano had hidden here the day before. Inui looked aft and up, past the forward turret at the line of bridge windows overlooking the two men from the ship's aluminum superstructure. Inui and Yano were in full view now of the personnel on the bridge, and within moments Shimatsume or Captain Otaka would be sending someone forward to find out what they were doing here.

"You men on the forward deck!" boomed suddenly from a loudspeaker above the foredeck. "What are you doing there?"

They'd been seen. Inui raised an arm and waved. At the least, the gesture might confuse the bridge officers, might buy the two men another few seconds.

The *Ishikari*'s bow rose, then plunged, sending a blast of cold spray over the bow. Inui and Yano clung to the railing and to the packaged life raft, waiting it out. As the bow rose again, Inui finally allowed himself to look at his watch. One more minute . . .

A watertight door opening from the deckhouse beneath the bridge banged open, and two petty officers in bright orange life jackets emerged, walking toward them.

Thirty seconds . . .

Bridge, *Pacific Sandpiper*
49° 21' N, 8° 13' W
Saturday, 0829 hours GMT

Kozo Fuchida walked onto the *Sandpiper*'s bridge. He glanced at the armed security man standing by the starboard-side wing access way, half-expecting the man to challenge him, but he did not. Fuchida and Chujiro Moritomi, in their guise of Wanibuchi and Kitagawa, seemed accepted now as legitimate members of the ship's company. He saw Dunsmore give them a dark look as they came in, but the executive officer said nothing. The captain was on the bridge, in his high-backed chair with pipe and coffee, and if anyone was going to order the two of them off the bridge, it would be him.

But Jorgenson didn't seem to notice them. Both of them wore bright yellow plastic windbreakers with the PNTL logo—shipboard issue. The jackets were loose enough that when they were zipped up, the pistols tucked into the waistbands of the men's jeans were completely hidden.

Fuchida looked at his watch—synchronized earlier with Inui and Yano on the other ship. Another minute, perhaps less. He glanced out the forward bridge windows at the *Ishikari* in time to see the other vessel take a white plume of spray across the bow.

He didn't envy his KKD brothers over there.

Fuchida exchanged a glance with Moritomi, who nodded, then walked to the passageway leading aft from the bridge. The ship's radio room was located there, with one door opening onto the bridge, another onto the passageway. Moritomi took up his position outside the passageway entrance to the radio shack. A ship's officer was inside, headset in place as he monitored radio traffic over the ship's satellite and UHF links.

"Anything we can do for you gentlemen?" Jorgenson asked, swiveling his seat to face Fuchida.

"Not a thing, Captain," Fuchida replied in perfect colloquial English. He'd lived for twelve years in England and for four before that in the United States. His bachelor's in economics was from Princeton. "We were told to observe all ship operations, so . . ." He shrugged. "We're observing."

"Observe all you like," Jorgenson replied. "Just don't touch anything."

"Of course, Captain."

"Would you care for a tour?"

"If you—"

Fuchida caught the flash out of the corner of his eye and turned in time to see a black cloud shot through with flecks of orange roiling into the morning sky. Portions of the aft superstructure crumpled as though swept forward by a giant's fist as the first explosion was followed immediately by a second, a third, by several more blasts in rapid succession, each extending the billowing cloud up and out; the mast amidships with its forest of radio antennae ripped free, twisting, and slammed forward into the rear of the bridge tower. A shock wave raced out from the stricken vessel in a perfect circle, taking several seconds to cross the half mile of open water to reach the *Sandpiper*.

"*Holy Mother of God!*" Dunsmore cried suddenly, eyes widening.

As the shock wave passed, thunder boomed and the *Sandpiper* shuddered, the bridge windows rattling in their mountings. The black cloud continued to grow, engulfing most of the Japanese escort, swelling vast and horribly as the ship's fuel stores exploded as well. A volcano of orange flame boiled into the sky from the ruin of the aft deckhouse.

Splashes started rising in the water ahead. Something large and twisted hurtled out of the sky and struck the number three cargo hatch on the *Piper*'s forward deck with a thump, bounced, and toppled over the side. Other bits and pieces of debris continued to rain about the ship.

"*All back!*" Jorgenson snapped. The *Sandpiper* needed a *long* stretch of water in which to stop. They were not in danger of colliding with the other vessel, fortunately, given their relative positions, but the *Piper* would need to come to a complete stop to pick up survivors in the water, if nothing else.

"All back, aye!" the rating at the engine telegraph replied, hauling back on the levers that communicated the order to *Sandpiper*'s engine room.

"Sparks! Send an SOS! Give our position and report an explosion on board the *Ishikari*!" He hesitated. "Add that we are providing assistance."

"Sir!"

"My God!" Dunsmore said. "What happened?"

"Offhand, Number One, I'd say that ship's armament magazine just blew. Those vessels carry eight Harpoons, six 324mm ASW torpedoes, and God only knows how much ammunition for its Melara cannon."

Some of the cannon shells were cooking off, now, in the fierce blaze amidships, the sharp, flat reports banging across the water. "Sir," Dunsmore said. "Is it a good idea to get too close? . . ."

"The law of the sea, Number One." Jorgenson shook

his head. "Hell, I'm not going to *leave* those poor buggers!"

"No, sir. Of course not."

Fuchida glanced back at Moritomi, who was still standing next to the door to the radio room. They were ready to act should Jorgenson order the *Queen* to shear off, but their orders were to do nothing so long as the Britishers followed the script. The longer the Japanese could wait before showing their hand, the better.

The *Ishikari* was settling low in the water already, her stern either submerged or, as seemed more likely, completely blown away. Everything from her ruined bridge tower aft was engulfed in black smoke, which was billowing rapidly into the gray sky. A pyramid of flame continued to burn amidships; she'd had her diesel tanks topped off at Barrow for the long voyage home and she was carrying a *lot* of fuel. Some of that fuel oil was spreading across the sea's surface now alongside the sinking ship, carrying the flame with it.

He wondered if his KKD brothers on board the *Ishikari* had survived.

North Atlantic Ocean
49° 21' N, 8° 13' W
Saturday, 0831 hours GMT

Ichiro Inui literally had no memory of the explosion. One moment, he'd been standing next to Yano on the *Ishikari*'s bow, watching the seamen approach and wondering how he could delay them for another precious few seconds. The next, he was underwater, struggling to reach the shifting, silvery gleams of light rippling across the surface far, far overhead. Sound—tearing, creaking, thundering sound—surrounded him. His lungs burned, and he fought to keep the rising panic at bay. He kicked wildly, reaching for the surface.

He broke through at last, lungs bursting, and emerged into a world of booming, flame-laced nightmare. He'd hit the water fifty feet from the *Ishikari*'s bow, which loomed above him now like a great, sharp-edged gray cliff. He gasped for air and nearly strangled on the stink of hot diesel-oil fumes. Fire and black smoke erupted into the sky, and the oil-covered water close by the ship was blazing.

He saw men on the ship's deck, racing this way and that like ants on a kicked-over anthill. The heads of other men bobbed in the water closer to the ship, men struggling to get clear of the spreading fires.

A wave swept under Inui, lifting him bodily, and for a moment he had a better view of the disaster area. The oil was everywhere, the fires spreading. On *Ishikari*'s deck, a man emerged from a doorway aflame, fire clinging to his upper body as he vaulted the port side railing and plummeted into the sea like a burning meteor.

He tried to find the life raft. It had a compressed air bottle triggered by contact with seawater and should have inflated automatically when it fell into the sea, but he couldn't see it. He couldn't see Yano, either, or the men who'd been coming to get them. Then the wave passed and he slid down the back side into the trough. For a moment, he couldn't see anything but water below and flame-roiled smoke above.

By now, he knew, the *Pacific Sandpiper* ought to be on the way to pick up survivors, but she would still be half a mile away. Inui was already exhausted and half-drowned. He didn't expect to survive.

He thought of his father, and prepared for a welcome death.

Deck Twelve Terrace, *Atlantis Queen*
49° 21' N, 8° 13' W
Saturday, 0835 hours GMT

"That's damned odd," Fred Doherty said, looking aft, then up at the gray overcast.

"What is?" Petrovich asked, lowering the camera off his shoulder.

"Something's happened," Doherty said. "We're changing course. Picking up speed, too." He could feel the breeze stiffening on his face.

They were standing on the highest vantage point accessible to the *Queen*'s passengers, a stretch of open deck immediately ahead of the cruise ship's single enormous smokestack. The *Atlantis Queen*'s passenger decks were numbered from One, at the quarterdeck and Grand Lounge where they'd come aboard, up to Twelve, which consisted of this outdoor terrace overlooking the Grotto Pool. The Atlantean Grotto Lounge occupied the space immediately below, which opened onto the pool deck through large sliding glass doors.

Doherty had spoken with Bernstein, the Harper bitch's manager, last night in the ship's casino. The two men had bumped into each other while watching the incredible performance of the card-dealing robot and shared a few drinks.

Bernstein had told Doherty that Harper planned to do some sunbathing at the Forward Pool this morning but neglected to say what time. Doherty and Petrovich had decided that this might be an opportunity to get some candid footage of Harper, and if she showed up in one of her trademark almost-not-there thong bikinis, so much the better. Since they wouldn't be doing any interviewing, Sandra Ames had elected to stay in her stateroom. Doherty suspected she was feeling a bit queasy . . . a touch of mal-de-mer despite the fact that the rolling seas could scarcely be felt aboard the enormous and supremely stable cruise ship.

Unfortunately, the weather was gray and somewhat cool . . . not cold, but not exactly bikini weather, either, and Harper hadn't showed up. Doherty and Petrovich had waited there for twenty minutes and had just decided to give up and go inside.

"So?" Petrovich said. "We're changing course. Ships do that."

"No . . . I mean we're going the wrong way."

"What, are you the ship's captain?"

"No, jackass. Look."

He pointed aft, past the loom of the ship's smokestack. The *Queen*'s wake curved off toward the left.

"So?"

"Don't you get it? We're headed west, out of the English Channel. From here, we're supposed to turn *south*— that's toward the left, okay? Why are we turning right?" He frowned, concentrating. "I think we're speeding up, too. Feel the engines?"

"No."

"Then look at that spray, forward. We're hitting the waves harder, now."

"Look, I'm getting cold," Petrovich said. "Let's go in and get some coffee."

"No," Doherty said. "Stay put. I have a feeling. . . ."

"You had a feeling with the police and ambulance at the dock yesterday."

"Damn it, this is *different*." He could feel it in his bones.

Bridge, *Pacific Sandpiper*
49° 21' N, 8° 13' W
Saturday, 0837 hours GMT

The *Sandpiper* was slowing perceptibly but very gradually as her engines pounded in full reverse. Captain Jorgenson had stood up from his chair and now leaned against the bridge forward console, peering out over the scene of destruction ahead.

"Helm!" he snapped. "Come left two points."

"Come left two points, aye, aye, sir," the helmsman replied, turning the wheel.

Jorgenson kept studying the route ahead, judging wave action, wind, and the *Sandpiper*'s own staggering inertia and momentum. Maneuverable for her tonnage she might be, but the huge vessel still couldn't stop on the proverbial dime. The last thing Jorgenson could afford now was to ram the sinking warship ahead, or become entangled in the mass of floating wreckage surrounding her, or come so close aboard that further explosions or munitions detonations damaged his command. By shearing off two points, he ensured that they would keep the *Ishikari* well to starboard yet still be close enough to rescue men in the water.

"Mr. Dunsmore," he said.

"Sir!"

"Put the Cat into the water. Put three volunteers on board. Have them start getting those people out of the water."

"Yes, sir." The exec reached for a telephone handset and punched out a number. "Should we arm her?"

"The Cat" was a twenty-foot, high-speed powerboat stored in an ingenious launch tube over the *Sandpiper*'s stern. The boat could be armed with a machine gun, at need, and was intended as a small auxiliary unit in case the *Sandpiper* was attacked by pirates.

"No, Number One," Jorgenson said after a brief hesitation. Breaking out a weapon and ammunition would take precious time, time those men in the water didn't have. There could be no possible reason to arm a rescue craft.

"Captain Jorgenson!" a voice called from the radio shack.

"Yes, Sparks?"

Robert Orly, the ship's chief communications technician, leaned out of the radio room door. "Sir, we have ac-
knowledgments of our SOS. *Campbeltown* has asked if
we need SAR assistance. The *Atlantis Queen* reports that
she has changed course and is on her way to assist. ETA . . .
about one hour, forty-five minutes. We also have an ac-
knowledgment from that ALAT helicopter. They say
they're on the way as well."

"Very well." Jorgenson wondered what kind of helicopter the ALAT contact might be. It was over a hundred
miles from the *Sandpiper*'s position, and the *Sandpiper*
was a good 175 miles from Brest, the nearest fair-sized
French city. Helicopters weren't known for their long range.

Well, if necessary, the *Sandpiper* could provide plenty
of deck space forward if the French helicopter ran low on
fuel and needed to set down. And a helicopter would be
invaluable in a search for survivors.

"What's the ETA on the helicopter, Sparks?"

"Forty minutes, sir. Maybe a bit less, depending on
headwinds."

"Very well. Let them know their assistance is appreci-
ated, and that we can provide a landing platform should
they run low on fuel."

"Yes, sir. What should I tell *Campbeltown*?"

Jorgenson considered the question. The British frigate
had left the convoy four hours ago but hadn't been going
at flank. If her skipper cranked her up to top speed—
thirty knots—they'd be back here in a bit over two hours.

And the *Campbeltown* was a warship, with very little
free space on board for survivors off the *Ishikari*. The
only reason to bring her back would be if there was a
threat—a *military* threat—to the *Sandpiper*. The *Campbeltown* would be of little help in a rescue operation.

"Tell her thanks, but we have the *Atlantis Queen* on
the way." The *Queen* would have tons of space on board,
not to mention a large and modern infirmary for the injured. "Tell her we may need her as an escort later."

"Aye, aye, Captain."

"And radio Barrow and let them know what's going on."

"Right away, sir."

Jorgenson began going over everything in his mind again. Had he missed anything? Other ships and aircraft would be on the scene within a couple of hours or so. In the meantime, a French helicopter and a British cruise ship would be able to provide all of the search-and-rescue support necessary.

The sinking escort was less than four hundred yards off the port bow, now, and drawing very slowly closer.

9

North Atlantic Ocean
49° 21' N, 8° 13' W
Saturday, 0850 hours GMT

INUI WAS SWIMMING SLOWLY out from the sinking ship, going nowhere in particular except away from the flames. If he was going to die, he preferred drowning to being roasted alive in the inferno behind him.

His life jacket kept him afloat. For perhaps fifteen or twenty minutes, now, he'd been considering removing the jacket and allowing himself to sink, to accept a relatively quick and merciful death, but his orders, his *omi*, his duty to those above him, kept him moving. His orders were to allow himself to be picked up by the *Pacific Sandpiper* if possible, to join the KKD activists already on board and assist them with the hijacking.

The problem was, he couldn't see the *Sandpiper* now, even when the ocean swell carried him to the top. Smoke and flame blanketed the sky, his eyes burned with fuel oil, and all he could really see besides the smoke was water.

And then a hand grabbed the back of his life jacket. He spun, lashing out.

"*Easy*, Inuisan! It's me!" a familiar voice said in Japanese. It was Yano, and he was in the now-inflated life raft, leaning over the side to haul Inui on board.

Weakly he turned and tried to climb into the raft, a task that would have been frankly impossible without Yano's help. He landed in the bottom, panting hard. "It is . . . good to see you! You found the raft!"

"It hit the water not far from me, and opened automatically," Yano told him. "I had to shoot another man in the water who tried to climb on as well."

Inui nodded, then managed to sit up. He was only a little higher above the surface, now, but as the raft rode another passing swell he could see the *Sandpiper*, beyond the sinking *Ishikari* and partly obscured by smoke. "We'll have to paddle that way," he said, indicating a direction well away from the *Sandpiper*, "so we can stay clear of the *Ishikari*."

"Yes. And quickly. The ship is going down swiftly, and we don't want to be caught in the back-current!"

There were two folding plastic paddles stowed inside the emergency rafts. Yano had broken out one to begin his search for Inui. Inui unshipped the other and assembled it, and together the two men began paddling away from the dying ship.

Deck Twelve Terrace, *Atlantis Queen*
49° 21' N, 8° 13' W
Saturday, 0852 hours GMT

"This is nuts," James Petrovich said. He looked at his watch. "Can we go back inside yet? *Please*?"

For fifteen minutes now, or a bit more, the *Atlantis Queen* had been bounding ahead on her new course.

"What's the matter?" Fred Doherty said, grinning. "Cold?"

"As a matter of fact, yes!" Petrovich plucked at the T-shirt he was wearing. "I'm not exactly dressed for this!"

"We're going somewhere in one hell of a hurry," Doherty said. "You know, I think we should go see if Sandra's up.

Maybe we can talk to the captain, see what's going on. Maybe even set up an interview."

"*Anything*, man, if it means getting out of this wind!"

Doherty shook his head. "You kids, these days. You have it too soft."

"Okay. I . . . what the hell?"

Doherty was looking aft, past the ship's smokestack. An aircraft was approaching from astern.

"What?"

Doherty pointed. "Helicopter. What's it doing way the hell and gone out here?"

Petrovich shrugged. "C'mon! We're not exactly at the ends of the earth. We're, what? A hundred, a hundred fifty miles from shore, maybe?"

"That's a long way for most helicopters. Quick! Get a shot!"

Petrovich perched his camera on his shoulder and panned back and forth, peering at his viewfinder screen as he tried to pick up the approaching helicopter. "Got him!" The cameraman pressed the roll button and began filming.

"And there he goes!" Doherty said. "Jesus, that guy is booking!"

The helicopter passed up the starboard side of the *Atlantis Queen*, less than a hundred yards away and apparently on exactly the same heading as the cruise ship. Doherty didn't recognize the helicopter's type, but it was *big*, with a high-up engine mount and a pair of large air intakes to either side, the type of helicopter used for transporting cargo or passengers rather than a military gunship. It had French markings, but so far as he could tell it looked like a civil aircraft, rather than military.

It was close enough that he could glimpse several people on board, looking back at him through portholes in the aircraft's body.

Not military, not coast guard . . . or whatever organization served as a coast guard for France. Doherty was curious. He wondered what the range of that type of helicopter was, and what the hell it was doing this far out in the Atlantic Ocean.

As quickly as it had appeared, the aircraft roared off toward the northwestern horizon at a speed Doherty guessed was well over 150 miles an hour. Petrovich panned with its passing, staying on it as it dwindled to a speck and vanished. "Got it," he said.

"Let's find the captain . . . or a ship's officer and see what's going on."

"Another one of your hunches."

"Okay, okay, the thing at the dock yesterday didn't pan out so well. Forget that. I have a *feeling* about this one."

They hadn't been able to see much of anything from the Promenade Deck yesterday—just emergency vehicles and a lot of British cops. Yellow crime scene tape had been strung around the perimeter, and no one had been willing to talk to the news team. They'd tried several more times to invoke privilege of the press in order to reach the scene and question people, but each time polite but firm soldiers or Ship's Security officers had turned them back.

"That's what you always say. You need to stick with the program, man. Spoiled rich rock stars and actresses, that's the ticket."

A loud, two-tone chime sounded from a nearby speaker mounted above the entrance to the Atlantean Grotto. "Ladies and gentlemen, this is your Cruise Director," a woman's sultry voice announced. "May I have your attention, please?"

"Uh-oh," Doherty said. "This'll tell us something."

"Captain Phillips has asked me to tell you that the *Atlantis Queen* has changed course to give aid to a ship in distress at sea. The ship is on fire and possibly sinking about twenty-five miles ahead of us, and we should reach her within the next hour and fifteen minutes, or so, where we will render what aid we can until rescue vessels can arrive.

"The captain asks me to tell you that this rescue will not delay our voyage. We can easily make up any lost time in our passage south to Gibraltar. He does ask, however, that passengers refrain from using the Promenade—that's the outside area on the Aphrodite Deck, also known as Deck Three—until further notice. Ship's personnel may be bringing survivors on board onto the Promenade Deck, and we may also be lowering the vessel's lifeboats to help with rescue operations.

"The captain also requests that any passenger on board with medical experience—especially people with EMT or emergency room training, as well as doctors and nurses—please identify yourselves to a ship's steward or ship's officer if you wish to be of assistance. The ship's medical staff would appreciate any volunteer help available.

"We trust that this incident will not offer any inconvenience or discomfort to our passengers, but by the ancient and sacred law of the high seas, any ship at sea is required to give aid to any other ship in distress. The crew and staff of the *Atlantis Queen* wish to thank you for your patience and for your understanding. That is all."

"Wow!" Fred Doherty said. "You hear that? What'd I tell you? *What* did I tell you?"

"You smell a hot news story."

"Hot? Hell, yeah! The *Titanic*! The *Lusitania*! The *Andrea Doria*! This could be *real* big, and we're in exactly the right place to catch it all! Interviews! Hot news footage! Story at ten!" He leaned on the terrace railing, peering at the horizon in front of the ship's bridge. He wasn't sure, but he thought he could see something, a black smudge, perhaps, beneath the overcast on the horizon. Smoke from a burning ship, perhaps?

This could be his ticket to a producer's slot with one of the major network newsrooms, the break he'd been praying for ever since he'd gotten out of college and taken his first news job with that joke of a dinky little local TV station in Wisconsin.

"Let's go talk to the captain," Doherty said.

They would need press access to the Promenade Deck, and possibly the bridge and the ship's infirmary as well.

All it would take was one little disaster and his future career was assured.

North Atlantic Ocean
49° 21' N, 8° 13' W
Saturday, 0910 hours GMT

It still bothered Inui that he could remember nothing of the blast itself. The shock wave, he decided, must have stunned him, even knocked him unconscious for a moment. He expected his mind to *work*, however, and it irritated him that he seemed to have missed a rather spectacular flight from the *Ishikari*'s forward deck into the sea.

Yano said he remembered nothing either, or very little. "It was like being scooped up by a giant hand," Yano told him. "Then . . . I don't know. I was in the water, and the raft was unfolding nearby."

They'd been paddling hard for several minutes, now, getting well clear of the sinking ship. Inui was still coming to grips with the fact that he was alive. That he was seemed like nothing less than a miracle . . . and Inui did not believe in the supernatural.

He believed in himself. In his brothers. In the cause. In the organization.

Sekigun no Ko. It was what they called the KKD, a kind of inner-circle, private joke. *Child of the Red Army.* In Inui's case, it was almost literally true.

The Nihon Sekigun, the Japanese Red Army, had been born in the 1970s, a time of radical activism, of leftist revolution, of triumph after triumph over the crumbling shell of Western imperialism. In 1972, in a show of solidarity with fellow revolutionaries of the Popular Front for the Liberation of Palestine, three Sekigun members had carried out the Lod Airport Massacre in Israel, killing twenty-five and injuring seventy-one. Most of the victims had been Puerto Rican Christians on a pilgrimage to Israel.

One of those gunmen had been Tsuyoshi Okudaira, Ichiro Inui's father. Okudaira had killed himself with a hand grenade in the Lod Airport baggage claim area rather than allow himself to be captured.

Nihon Sekigun had expected that victory and others to rally the Japanese people behind them. Their goal was nothing less than the overthrow of the decadent Japanese government and the creation of world revolution.

And yet the revolution had never materialized. In fact, most of the people at home had refused even to believe that the Lod terrorists were Japanese at all, and when, finally, they'd accepted the truth, most Japanese had begun turning against any type of militant activism. By the 1980s, with popular support almost nonexistent, the JRA could no longer operate in Japan but was entirely dependent upon the PFLP for training, money, and weapons. In 2001, Fusako Shigenobu, the JRA's original founder, had announced from her prison cell that the unit had been disbanded, that the Japanese Red Army was no more.

Cowards. Cowards and traitors to the Cause. Ichiro Inui had never known his father, but Ichiro's mother had kept Tsuyoshi's memory alive. Kazuko Inui had instilled in the young Ichiro his father's fanatical devotion to world revolution and a seething hatred for the West and its soul-devouring ideologies of money, greed, and planetary rape. In 1992, at the age of twenty-four, Inui had joined the Kokusaiteki Kakumei Domei, the International Revolutionary League. Many of the KKD's members had had their start with the JRA and hoped that a new name, a new face, would gain the support of the masses. They still worked for world revolution but now emphasized the *Green* fight rather than the Red. United with Greenworld and other militant ecological movements worldwide, they sought to eliminate the import of radioactive material into Japan and end Japan's domestic atomic energy program.

In 1998, his militant beliefs and his association with the KKD carefully hidden, Inui had been commissioned as an officer in the Kaiso Jeitai. Last year, a cell of KKD officers within the Japanese Maritime Self-Defense Force had arranged for his transfer to the *Ishikari,* where he'd met Yano. For an entire year they'd waited, carrying out their mundane duties, until the KKD's leadership had issued them with their final orders.

The KKD had allied with al-Qaeda for a final, devastating strike at the hated West. The target of the operation was one of the plutonium shipments returning to Japan after reprocessing in England. And the *Ishikari*, with her two KKD sleeper agents, would be escorting the freighter home.

A hundred yards away, the *Ishikari* groaned, then shrieked, her gaping stern sliding under swiftly now, dragging down shattered deckhouse, bridge, the forward gun, and finally the bow, which sliced up out of the sea as a geyser of water and escaping air erupted aft. For a few seconds the bow hung suspended above the waves, and then, gracefully, it, too, slid down and submerged in a final, oily rush of churning water.

The *Ishikari* had been an ultra-modern design, highly automated, and with a crew of just ninety. A number of those crewmen struggled now in the water, oil-coated, exhausted, and in shock. There'd been no time to clear or lower lifeboats, though a few rafts were in evidence.

A small boat was putting out from the approaching *Pacific Sandpiper.*

Inui and Yano began waving their arms, trying to attract the boat crew's attention.

Bridge, *Pacific Sandpiper*
49° 21' N, 8° 13' W
Saturday, 0919 hours GMT

"Helicopter off the starboard quarter astern, sir," the port side bridge lookout reported. "Six hundred meters."

"Very well," Jorgenson said. "Sparks! Raise that chopper. Tell them we need help spotting survivors in the water."

The *Ishikari* had gone down in a boiling fountain of water just five minutes earlier. In seas this heavy, with the surface covered with oil and debris, it was tough to spot human heads floating among all the flotsam, and the helicopter would be invaluable in the search.

Captain Jorgenson turned back to the bridge windows, looking down onto the ship's long forward deck. Since the explosion on board the *Ishikari*, members of the ship's crew—security troops and off-duty personnel, for the most part—had gathered on the foredeck along the starboard side railing. The security people were at their assigned posts, but the others were simply playing tourist. Some of them had cameras around their necks, for God's sake.

"Mr. Dunsmore," he said sharply. "Pass the word that the decks are to be cleared *immediately*. Only security personnel or crew members actively engaged in the rescue are to be on deck!"

"Aye, aye, sir."

It was only natural, Captain Jorgenson supposed, for the crew to go out and rubberneck, but it was damned unprofessional.

"I'd like the guns opened up as well," he added.

"I already gave the order, Captain. As soon as you said we were going to close with them."

PNTL's standard rules of procedure. The *Sandpiper*'s guns weren't normally visible from the outside, but at certain times designated by the *Piper*'s operational orders, sections of the deckhouse dropped open to expose three 30mm cannons, one at each corner of the deckhouse forward, overlooking the deck, and one at the stern, above the fantail.

Jorgenson certainly wasn't expecting an attack from the *Ishikari*'s half-drowned survivors, but inflexible corporate doctrine demanded that the guns *always* be run out should the plutonium freighter approach another vessel or if she was approached by aircraft. They'd wargamed numerous piracy and terrorist scenarios at PNTL headquarters back in the nineties, looking at the possibility of pirates pretending to be in distress at sea, or a helicopter filled with heavily armed troops landing on deck.

Actually, the captain personally disagreed with the policy of arming the vessels; adding seven tons of high explosives to an already volatile mix of radioactive plutonium and thousands of gallons of fuel oil simply didn't make a lot of sense in his estimation, an accident waiting to happen. But the rules were definitely the rules, and he intended to follow them to the letter.

"There's the chopper, Captain!" the armed guard on the bridge announced. He'd moved over to the starboard wing and was leaning out of the doorway leading to the weather deck outside. "AS 332 Cougar!"

Jorgenson glanced at the aircraft, gentling in to a slow-drifting hover less than a hundred yards abeam of the bridge. He scowled. Something wasn't right. "I thought that was supposed to be an ALAT helicopter," he said.

The AS 332, originally designed and marketed by Aérospatiale, had both military and civilian versions. The silver fuselage and the large, black tail number identified this aircraft as the civil transport version.

The side doors, he saw, had been slid back. He saw a number of men crowded inside . . .

"Sound the alarm!" Jorgenson cried. *"That's not—"*

"*Tomare!*" Wanibuchi, the Japanese liaison standing close behind the bridge security guard, shouted. He reached into his bulky yellow windbreaker and pulled out an automatic pistol with a long sound suppressor screwed onto the muzzle. "*Ugoku na!*"

It happened too quickly, was too shockingly sudden, for anyone to react. As the bridge security guard reached for his weapon, Wanibuchi swung the pistol up into line with the back of the man's head and pulled the trigger. With the suppressor, the sound of the shot was a sharp, hissing chirp that knocked the guard forward through the half-open doorway. "Do not move!"

Immediately, a second shot, followed by a third, sounded from the radio shack, and Robert Orly stumbled through the door onto the bridge, the side of his head a scarlet mass. He fell forward, the cord jerking his headset from his ears as he fell full-length on the bridge deck. The second corporate liaison, Kitagawa, stepped out, his pistol held in a tight, two-handed grip. Dunsmore lunged for the alarm klaxon on the bridge console, and Wanibuchi shot him down before he'd taken two steps.

"Nobody move!" Wanibuchi shrilled, the gun in his hand swinging wildly from the crumpled Dunsmore, to Jorgenson, to Kinsley, the helmsman, to Mathers, the navigator. "All of you! Hands up!"

Feeling a deathly cold rippling up his spine, Jorgenson did as he was told. Mathers and Kinsley raised their hands as well. Dunsmore was writhing in a spreading pool of blood, arms folded across his belly. "May I help my officer?" Jorgenson asked. "He's hurt!"

"No! Get down on the floor!" Wanibuchi shouted. "*All* of you. Lay on the floor! Facedown! Spread your arms and legs wide apart! *Do it! Do it!*"

Floor, Jorgenson thought as he moved to obey, *not deck*. These people weren't seafaring men, then. Perhaps they could use that.

Wanibuchi barked something at Kitagawa in Japanese.

"Hai!" the man replied, and left the bridge, taking the central passageway aft.

"How many of you are there?" Jorgenson asked as he spread himself on the deck. "Only the two of you? You can't possibly take over this ship!"

"Be quiet, Jorgenson," Wanibuchi replied, his English perfect. "Another word and I will shoot your navigator at the base of his spine. It's an agonizing way to die."

Jorgenson heard footsteps and then a metallic clatter. Turning his head, he saw Wanibuchi picking up the SA80 assault rifle dropped by the guard. Wanibuchi saw the movement and raised the rifle. *"Turn your head! Look at the wall!"*

Again Captain Jorgenson did as he was told, and wondered how he could fight back.

Gun Compartment Two, *Pacific Sandpiper*
49° 21' N, 8° 13' W
Saturday, 0921 hours GMT

Chujiro Moritomi had to restrain himself to keep from breaking into a run. The excitement of the moment pounded in his heart and throat and head, to the point that he was having trouble breathing. He felt powerful, though, even superhuman. Some of the radio operator's blood had splashed Moritomi's jacket, but he ignored that. He had *killed* the man, had walked up behind him and fired two bullets into the side of his head and *killed* him.

They'd located the positions of the ship's guns during their first inspection of the vessel, days ago. The number two gun was on the starboard side of the deckhouse forward, three decks down from the bridge. Holding his pistol behind his back, he reached the door, turned the handle, and pulled it open.

A cool breeze slapped him in the face. The compartment's outer panels had been dropped, converting it to a kind of outdoor balcony overlooking the forward deck to the left and the wreckage-strewn ocean off the ship's starboard side straight ahead. Two of the civilian guards were inside, one leaning against a stack of ammo cases, the other in the saddle behind the 30mm chain gun.

"Well, hello," the man by the ammo cases said, looking around at Moritomi's entrance. "Whose little wog are you? . . ."

The gunner turned, startled. "Here, now! You're not allowed—"

Except for the M230 chain gun, neither man was armed. Moritomi brought his pistol around, put two shots into the gunner's head, then shifted aim and shot the loader as he lunged for the door.

Stepping through the door, Moritomi turned, pulled the door shut, then shoved the body of the gunner out of the saddle. The M230 was aimed in the general direction of the helicopter off the ship's starboard beam.

Moritomi had trained with these weapons at the camp in Syria. He checked the ammo feed, made sure the power was on, and dragged back the charging lever with a rasping *snick*. Then he swung the weapon around to the left, depressing the barrel to aim at the *Sandpiper*'s crowded forward deck, and switched off the safety.

Forward Deck, *Pacific Sandpiper*
49° 21' N, 8° 13' W
Saturday, 0923 hours GMT

Jack Rawlston turned from the ship's starboard railing and looked at the crowd in disgust. "Here, you lot!" he shouted. "Clear the deck!"

There was, inevitably, a certain amount of friction between the regular crew and the "specials," the civilian security guards provided by PNTL and the UK Atomic Energy Authority. "Up yours," an older seaman growled. "Who made *you* captain?"

"Clear the fucking deck!" Rawlston bellowed, swinging his arm. "We need some order up here!"

He was assuming they would be bringing survivors up onto the forward deck, and this crowd of rubbernecking tourists was going to be in the way. The skipper might want that helicopter to land, too, and they would need the entire length of the deck clear for that.

"You heard the man!" Timmy Smithers shouted. "You people make yourselves useful and—"

He never finished the sentence. Rawlston heard an angry high-speed rattle of automatic gunfire, and then the *Pacific Sandpiper*'s steel deck was erupting in white puffs of smoke and hurtling shards of shrapnel. Smithers was jerked to one side, his upper chest and left shoulder exploding in a pink spray. Merchant seamen began falling as explosions ripped through the crowd with murderous detonations.

It reminded him, Rawlston thought as he dived for cover behind a hold cover, of autocannon fire from a helicopter gunship, and he assumed the helicopter was firing on them. He hit the deck, pulled his SA80 off his shoulder, and came up with his weapon aimed and tracking, ready to return fire.

But the fire wasn't coming from the helicopter, not so far as he could tell. The aircraft was circling now past the starboard bow, still a hundred yards off, but he saw no weapons pods or gun mounts on the helicopter, no door gunner or clattering minigun trailing streams of spent shell casings. If it wasn't the French helicopter . . .

More high-explosive rounds slammed into the deck, tearing a safety stanchion free and cutting down three men running toward the bow, and two shells hit the lip of the cargo hold cover a foot from his face, stinging him with specks of flying metal. The way the impacts tracked up the deck, moving forward, made him look aft.

Rawlston saw the muzzle flash from the starboard-forward chain gun as it hosed down the *Piper*'s forward deck with explosive rounds.

What the bloody hell? . . .

He twisted around, leveling his rifle at the *Piper*'s superstructure. From here he couldn't see the gunner, but if he could lay down a heavy enough fire, aimed into the open gun housing, he might drive the bastard to cover.

Before Rawlston could fire, however, bullets whined and shrieked, ricocheting off the deck beside him. He turned again. That fire *was* coming from the helicopter, which had changed course suddenly and was flying straight toward the *Sandpiper*'s forward deck. Several more security guards and seamen, caught in the open in a deadly crossfire between the helicopter and the superstructure of their own ship, jerked, spun, and fell. Rawlston saw at least a dozen men sprawled in bloody heaps across the deck, maybe more . . . some of them still moving, trying to rise, trying to seek cover.

The helicopter roared low overhead, so low that Rawlston instinctively ducked as its shadow engulfed him and then swept on. Men inside the helicopter now shot at the open port side gun mount, pouring automatic rifle fire into the opening from almost point-blank range. Rawlston changed targets again, drawing a bead on the helicopter . . . and then a savage hammer blow struck him in his side, slapping him back and away from the meager shelter of the hold cover. The 30mm chain gun on the starboard side was firing now in short, precise bursts, and a piece of shrapnel blasted from the hold cover had struck him in the side, hard.

There was no pain . . . and then he drew a breath and the pain shrieked inside his brain. A broken rib at least, and maybe a punctured lung as well. He clutched his side and his hand came away wet with blood. His gun had spun away with the impact, was lying on the deck five yards away.

Rawlston started crawling toward it, staying on his belly as the chain gun continued to fire bursts, sometimes at him, sometimes at other survivors taking shelter on the blood-spattered deck.

The helicopter was hovering now, just above the center of the long forward deck between Rawlston and the ship's deckhouse. The portside gun wasn't firing at what should have been an easy target, so Rawlston had to assume that his mates on the number 1 gun were dead . . . the number 2 gun as well, come to think of it, since neither Marty nor George would have opened fire on their own people.

The helicopter slowly descended toward the deck, and men were jumping out of the open side doors even before the wheels kissed steel. *Armed* men, lots of them. Men in kaffiyehs and combat vests, men with AK-47 assault rifles and two, Rawlston saw, with longer, heavier RPGs.

They leaped onto the deck and began spreading out, bending low beneath the still-turning rotors of the helicopter. Two headed straight for him, their rifles up to their shoulders, the muzzles aimed at his head as they screamed orders at him. He couldn't hear what they were saying over the thunderous pound of the aircraft's rotors, but he rolled onto his back with his hands up beside his head.

The impossible, Rawlston realized, had just happened.

Terrorists had just seized the *Pacific Sandpiper*.

10

CAPTAIN JORGENSON TREMBLED with shock and horror as the man who called himself Wanibuchi ordered him and Kinsley, the helmsman, to their feet. Mathers, the navigator, was on his knees in the corner, hands behind his head, with Wanibuchi's pistol pressed up against the back of his neck. Dunsmore was still whimpering on the deck, badly wounded.

"You, helmsman," Wanibuchi said. "Take the wheel."

Kinsley looked at the captain for confirmation. "Go to hell, Wanibuchi, or whatever your name is," Jorgenson growled.

Wanibuchi shifted his aim from Mathers' head to Dunsmore, several feet away, and fired a single, hissing shot. Dunsmore jerked once, then lay still. The pistol whipped back to cover Mathers.

"Captain Jorgenson, we are not going to play games with you. Your helmsman *will* take the wheel and you *will* order half ahead to the engine room. If you do not, this man dies."

Mathers flinched as Wanibuchi bumped his skull with

the sound suppressor screwed to the muzzle of the pistol. "Captain, please!" Mathers screamed. "For the love of God! . . ."

The port wing door opened, and three of the terrorists off the helicopter strode in. They were armed with AK-47 assault rifles; the two with beards wore kaffiyehs, making them look like desert sheiks in olive-drab utilities. The third, with a mustache and dangerous eyes, wore a black leather beret. He said something to Wanibuchi in a language that sounded Arabic; Wanibuchi replied in the same language.

"My compatriot," Wanibuchi said, "tells me they have eighteen prisoners. You can see them out the bridge window."

Jorgenson stepped closer to the window and looked down. Along the starboard railing, between the helicopter and the deckhouse, eighteen of his men were being prodded into line, hands behind their heads, facing away from the ship and out over the water. Arab terrorists paraded back and forth, shoving and prodding men into position, shouting orders. Several of the prisoners were obviously badly hurt; their friends to either side were allowed to hold them upright.

"I am going to give you several orders, Captain," Wanibuchi said. "Each time you refuse, each time you *hesitate*, one of your men on the deck will be shot. Do you understand me?"

"I . . . I . . ." Jorgenson shook his head, stepping back from the window. "Listen, there's no way I—"

Wanibuchi snapped something, and the man in the beret stepped back onto the bridge wing and raised his right arm. Instantly there was a crack, a puff of smoke, and the *Sandpiper* crewman standing farthest in the line from the deckhouse pitched forward over the railing and into the sea.

"Do you understand me?" Wanibuchi asked again.

"I . . . understand."

"Good. We will leave this area. Order half speed ahead."

The *Pacific Sandpiper* was almost at a halt, her engines churning at full astern to stop her ponderous forward momentum. Jorgenson grasped the engine telegraph lever and moved it to half ahead. The device was electronic these days, rather than the manual lever of the older days of seafaring, but the idea was the same. They ran the engines from down in engineering.

"What about the people in the water?" Jorgenson asked.

"I'm sure this area will be filled with rescue vessels in short order," Wanibuchi said.

The other Japanese liaison, Kitagawa, entered the bridge and said something to Wanibuchi in Japanese.

"Perhaps I was too hasty," he said. "Order the engines stopped."

Jorgenson moved the lever again.

"Now order the appropriate people in your crew to bring your small boat onto your ship. I'm told some of our friends are on board."

Realization struck Jorgenson like a fist in the gut. There must have been Japanese terrorists on board the *Ishikari*, moles or plants or sleepers or whatever the appropriate spy term would be, men who'd sabotaged the vessel and blown her up.

The scope of this attack, the planning and the detail that must have gone into it, was staggering.

He reached for the telephone handset that would connect him with the shipboard boat crew aft. Wanibuchi gestured with his pistol. "While you're at it, Captain . . . after ordering the boat brought back on board, you will pass the word over the ship's intercom, telling all personnel to surrender themselves to us. We estimate that there are still ten to fifteen of your people on board, including those in the aft 30mm cannon housing, in engineering, and in the ship's crew's quarters. We know you have twenty-eight crewmen and thirty security personnel . . . a total of fifty-eight men aboard. A number of those are dead, now, and seventeen are still lined up at the railing outside. We will be checking to make certain that *everyone* is accounted for. Do you understand me?"

"Yes."

"Very good. Cooperate with us, and no more of your men will die."

"Aren't you going to kill us all anyway?"

Wanibuchi looked surprised. "Of *course* not, Captain! We intend to make a certain strong demonstration that will result in an end to the use of nuclear power in Japan, and an end to these plutonium shipments. When our demands are met, you and this ship will be released. You have my word on that."

Jorgenson said nothing, but his dark eyebrows rose high on his forehead at that. This man had just ruthlessly killed a large number of his own crewmen, and the people working with him had killed many more on the *Ishikari* and were leaving the survivors to their own devices in the open ocean.

Wanibuchi's *word*, Jorgenson knew, was worth nothing but more blood.

Atlas Pool, *Atlantis Queen*
49° 21' N, 8° 13' W
Saturday, 0950 hours GMT

David Llewellyn stepped onto the Atlas Pool deck, located at the extreme aft end of Deck Nine, and looked around. He'd gotten the day off by logging in on-duty the night before, though as head of security he had a lot of leeway in the hours he actually spent in uniform. Technically, he was *always* on-duty. His passkey was in the mesh-net inside pocket of his swim trunks; they could find him if they needed him.

At the moment, though, things were quiet, the passengers settling into the routine of their first day at sea. The south coast of England was a gray-green smear low on the northern horizon. And according to his check of ID chips, the delicious Miss Johnson had come up to the Atlas Pool a few moments before.

David Llewellyn was on the prowl. His hopes for the evening before with that sweet young SOCA bird hadn't panned out the way he'd hoped, but he still had the files on Miss Tricia Johnson. He'd had her spotted ever since he'd seen her walk through the X-Star scanner at Southampton . . . and that prig of an MI5 bastard be damned.

He looked up. The morning was overcast, with only a few scattered patches of blue showing through, and the breeze was quite cool. Not exactly sunbathing weather, but . . .

There she was. Lounging on a deck chair in a disappointingly one-piece bathing suit, that long blond hair wrapped up in a bun behind her head. He walked toward her, pretended he was going to step past between her chair and the pool, then stopped and did a dramatic double take. "Tricia?"

She opened her eyes and looked up at him, frowning as she tried to place his face.

"Tricia Johnson!" he exclaimed. "Gosh, it's been . . . what? Five years?"

"I'm sorry," she said. "Do I know you?"

"David Llewellyn!" he told her. "Penn State University? Pennsylvania? Way up there in the mountains? My *God*, it's good to see you!"

Tentatively she shook his offered hand. She still looked puzzled, trying frantically to remember his face or his name, but she was smiling. People, Llewellyn knew, and women especially, didn't want to appear to be rude and so tended to assume they'd simply forgotten if a stranger claimed to know them. And they tended to be friendly and go along with the flow of conversation while they tried to figure it out.

"I'm so sorry," she said. "I knew a lot of people at Penn State, but . . ."

I'll just bet you did, Llewellyn thought. *A gorgeous girl like you would have been Miss Popularity.* He laughed. "You don't remember me, do you?"

Her nose wrinkled charmingly as she tried to think. "I think . . . maybe . . ."

"We had an economics class together. Professor Marston, remember?"

"Yeah! Yeah, I think I remember you now!"

Llewellyn had been a psych major during his college days—though he'd never been within three thousand miles of Penn State. It actually didn't take much to plant false memories that were as real as the real thing. All you needed was an initial hook and a confident tone of voice.

"Mind if I join you?" He gestured toward the deck chair next to hers. "If I'm bothering you, I'll just—"

"Oh, no! No! Sit down, please!"

"I was kind of a wallflower back then," he told her with a self-deprecating shrug. "I don't blame you if you don't remember. I *did* have a major crush on you, though. You have no idea how much I wanted to ask you out, but I could never get up the nerve. Anyway, you had a boyfriend . . . Tom? Ted?"

"George, actually."

Llewellyn snapped his fingers. "*George!* That was it! How *is* George? Is he with you now?"

"He dumped me for an art major. Ancient history. What about you . . . David, you said? What are *you* doing these days?"

"Ah, the heady world of international finance," he said with an airy wave of his hand. "Moved to England to take a job with a British banking firm, and it's been up, up, and away ever since!"

"Oh, really?"

"Well, I couldn't manage a cruise like this flipping burgers, right?"

It truly *was* amazing how much information could be gleaned from various sources, once you had a person's Social Security number or, in Great Britain, their National Insurance number. With Tricia Johnson's credit history, in particular the information on her student loan, he'd been able to get a transcript of her four years at Pennsylvania State University and dug up the names of several of her professors.

He knew her address—in upstate New York—and he knew she'd been working as a waitress and as an exotic dancer since college, never quite able to pull her life together. He knew she'd been briefly married, that she was now single, and that she was deep in debt. He'd also learned she had grandparents living in England—Suffolk—and that they were quite well-off, well-off enough to purchase this cruise package for her. His guess was that she'd visited them for the summer after an unhappy divorce and that they'd given her the cruise as an opportunity to "find herself," or some such.

It was a good thing he'd found her first.

He looked at the bar overlooking the pool. "May I buy you a drink?"

Bridge, *Atlantis Queen*
49° 21' N, 8° 13' W
Saturday, 1010 hours GMT

"That looks like the plutonium ship there," Vandergrift said, lowering his binoculars. "I see smoke, but I can't see the *Ishikari.*"

Captain Eric Phillips continued watching through his own binoculars. The *Atlantis Queen* was approaching from the southeast, slowing now until she was barely making headway. It was possible that the *Ishikari* was hidden behind the bulk of the freighter, but Phillips feared the Japanese escort ship had already sunk. A pillar of oily black smoke was still boiling off the sea, but as far as he could tell at this distance, still almost half a mile, the smoke was coming off of burning oil on the surface of the ocean itself.

As soon as the SOS had come in, the *Queen*'s radio room had been in touch both with the other ship, the *Pacific Sandpiper*, and with her own head office back in Southampton. Phillips had been told that the *Sandpiper* was carrying "classified cargo" and that approach to the huge vessel normally was restricted . . . but that the *Queen* was authorized now to approach and render all possible aid. The *Sandpiper*'s escort, Southampton informed him, was a Japanese destroyer escort of twelve hundred tons, the *Ishikari*, with a crew of ninety. There'd been an explosion on board the escort—no details beyond that—but the ship was believed to be in danger of sinking. Other ships and aircraft were en route, including military vessels to take over escort duty on the *Sandpiper*, but in the meantime the *Queen* was to assist with rescuing survivors and providing emergency medical treatment.

"Classified cargo" might be any of a number of things, but Phillips knew that the *Pacific Sandpiper* and her sister vessels—*Pacific Teal* and *Pacific Pintail*—were purpose-built ships for carrying radioactive materials in heavy, sealed canisters. Information on the vessels was available on the Internet, and various antinuclear protest groups routinely picketed both the ships' home port at Barrow and their destination at Rokkasho, Honshu, usually with a fair amount of press coverage. That classified cargo would be several tons of processed and highly radioactive plutonium, enough, he'd read in an article about the ships, to construct sixty nuclear weapons.

The same article had stressed how safe the shipments were—how well shielded the containers were, how comprehensive the safety features of the transports were.

"What's that on her forward deck?" Vandergrift asked.

"Helicopter," Phillips replied. "Looks like the one that passed us a while ago. Must be helping with SAR efforts."

"Doesn't look like they're doing much search and rescue now. Think they've already finished?"

"I don't know. Please pass the word to Dr. Barnes. I expect we'll have mass casualties coming on board as soon as we reach that other ship."

"Yes, sir. How are we going to take them aboard?"

It was an interesting problem in marine logistics. The *Atlantis Queen* was 964 feet long. The *Pacific Sandpiper*, if he remembered the article right, was a third of that, about 325 feet long, and her main deck would be about thirty feet above her waterline. The simplest means of getting injured men from the *Sandpiper*'s deck onto the *Queen* would be to bring the two ships close alongside, securing them together with lines and rigging a gangway across from the *Sandpiper*'s deck into either one of the A Deck cargo doors or, possibly, directly into the quarterdeck access on the First Deck. One of the cargo deck entryways would be best, Phillips decided. The ship's infirmary was on A Deck to begin with, and there'd be no need to haul injured crewmen down one of the ship's ladders.

The touchy part would be doing all of this at sea. They would put out fenders, of course, to keep the hulls of the two vessels from grinding together . . . but the seas were rough enough and high enough that there would be a certain amount of danger involved. Not enough to hole one of the ships, certainly, unless someone did something incredibly stupid, but there would be a considerable risk of injury, or of someone falling over the side.

He picked up an intercom handset. "Sparks!" he called.

"Yes, Captain?" The *Queen*'s chief radio officer was Peter Jablonsky, the radio shack just aft of the bridge.

"Raise the *Pacific Sandpiper*, please. Tell them I intend to come alongside their starboard side. Ask them if they have injured on board . . . and ask them if we should lower boats to help look for survivors."

"Very well, Captain."

"To answer your question, Number One," Phillips continued, "I'm not sure. I think the best thing to do would be to rig a gangway from their forward deck up to our port side A Deck cargo access and bring people on board that way."

"Seas are kind of high for that, Captain."

"But not *that* high. Not if we're both bow-on into the sea. And it'll save time over trying to rig a boatswain's chair, or lower people down one at a time from the helicopter."

"Yes, sir."

Cruise ships like the *Atlantis Queen* numbered their passenger decks First, Second, Third, and so on, going from bottom to top, with the First Deck generally being the level at which passengers entered from the dock. The crew decks, however, were given alphabetical identifiers, starting immediately under the First Deck with A Deck and going down to B, C, and D Decks below. On the *Queen*, A Deck was the lowest deck with portholes— though these were permanently closed—and the level for the cargo hold entry doors, while B Deck was just above the waterline. That meant that the *Pacific Sandpiper*'s forward deck would be at roughly the same level, the same distance above the water, as the *Queen*'s A Deck.

"Captain?" Jablonsky called. "They say to come on in, port to starboard."

"Let's do it," Phillips said. "Helm, bring us two points to starboard."

And the *Atlantic Queen* began closing with the smaller freighter.

Radio Room, *Pacific Sandpiper*
49° 21' N, 8° 13' W
Saturday, 1012 hours GMT

Fuchida leaned back from the console, removing the headset. Abdel Ramid was standing behind him. "What did they say?" he asked in Arabic.

"They will come alongside," Fuchida replied in the same language, "their left side to our right. They will rig a kind of bridge to cross from our deck to their cargo hold."

Ramid grinned. "They're making it easy for us."

"It's happening as we planned it," Fuchida said, shrugging. "They *have* to respond to an emergency at sea, and they have much better emergency medical services on board . . . to take care of all of those rich, pampered tourists. Do you have everyone, all of the prisoners, off the deck and out of sight?"

Ramid nodded. "The prisoners from outside all have been moved to the crew's recreation area, their hands and feet have been tied, and they are under heavy guard. The ship's crew has also retrieved the small boat, with two more of your people on board."

"Inui and Yano," Fuchida said. "Are they okay?"

"Half-drowned and suffering from immersion in cold water, but they seem to be recovering," Ramid said. "They were well enough to hold the two crewmen in the boat at gunpoint until we could bring them aboard."

Fuchida could only imagine the thoughts of the *Ishikari* crewmen still out there in the water, clinging to rafts and wreckage as they watched the *Sandpiper* take her small boat back on board and begin to move off toward the horizon. The ship was almost a mile, now, from where the *Ishikari* had gone down.

"And the crewmen on board this ship?" Fuchida asked.

Ramid jerked his head, indicating the bridge behind him. "The bridge personnel are cooperating. They don't like it—I think the captain is trying to kill us with the evil eye—but they are cooperating."

"He can glare all he wants. So long as he does what we tell him."

"We have men now in the engineering section, watching the crew there, holding them at gunpoint. And after the captain made his announcement over the intercom, several more crewmen have come out of hiding . . . including the security people in the aft gun position."

"Excellent."

They'd had to ignore the aft gun, number 3, in the initial attack. Moritomi had taken out number 2, and the men on board the helicopter had killed the gunners at number 1 from the air. *That* had been a close thing; any one of the rapid-fire cannons mounted on the *Sandpiper* could have swatted the helicopter from the sky as easily as a mosquito. The assault force had been gambling on the fact that the civilian crew of the plutonium ship would be confused, that even the former military men within the onboard security force would have been unsure of what was happening and hold their fire for that reason. Their delay had made it possible for Ramid's helicopter to get close to the number 1 gun before the ship's defenders had fully realized that the ship was under attack and kill them from the air with machine-gun fire.

"Perform a careful check," Fuchida went on. "There were a total of thirty security guards. We want to be especially certain that they are all accounted for."

"You do not need to tell me my business, Fuchida," Ramid said, his voice crisp. "You are not in command here."

Fuchida started to reply, then thought better of it, turning away. "As you say."

Technically, Ramid *was* in command of the *Pacific Sandpiper* assault group. Lines of command had been only lightly and informally sketched in, however, as the operation planning had come together. The Islamist Jihad

International—an operational arm of al-Qaeda—and the Kokusaiteki Kakumei Domei had been forced to work together, but despite the pretensions of international revolution, neither organization was fully comfortable with the other. The KKD had needed al-Qaeda for the resources to hit a target as large and as formidable as the *Pacific Sandpiper*; the Islamists had needed the KKD in order to infiltrate the crew of the *Ishikari*, destroy the military escort, and create the diversion necessary for the taking of the plutonium ship.

The goals of the two groups, however, remained quite different from each other, and neither fully trusted the other, even yet.

"Then I respectfully suggest, *sir*," Fuchida said, his voice biting as he replaced the headset over his ears, "that you put the helicopter back in the air. Our next target will be alongside within a few minutes."

Ramid said nothing, but he turned away to comply.

With the Arab's sour attitude, however, Fuchida knew there would be trouble.

Bridge, *Atlantis Queen*
North Atlantic Ocean
49° 21' N, 8° 13' W
Saturday, 1016 hours GMT

"The helicopter's taking off," Vandergrift noted. "Why are they so far from the fire, though?"

"Probably don't want to risk the ship," Captain Phillips said. He gave a grim chuckle. "With their cargo, I can't say I blame them!"

"Yeah. I'm still not sure it's a good idea going close aboard, sir."

"Your reservations are noted, Number One. Give me an alternative and I'll consider it."

"We hold back, lower boats to assist with the rescue

operations, and wait for the *Campbeltown*, the *Ark Royal*, or *La Motte-Picquet* to arrive."

The *Campbeltown*, the frigate that had escorted the *Pacific Sandpiper* clear of British waters the day before, was reportedly now on her way here from the vicinity of the Cornish coast. The *Ark Royal* was one of Britain's aircraft carriers, with a Sea Harrier squadron embarked on board, an escort of several smaller warships, and a shipboard medical facility as good as or better than the *Queen*'s. She was coming out of the Channel from Portsmouth. And *La Motte-Picquet* was a French guided missile destroyer out of Brest. All three vessels were on their way at flank, but none would be on the scene in less than an hour and a half to two hours.

"Ninety minutes before any of them arrive," Phillips said. "The sooner we get the injured to medical care, the better their chances. Especially burn victims."

"I know, sir."

"And I know what you're feeling. But it's safe enough. The radioactive material is stored inside special ninety-eight-ton flasks. Each flask has shock absorbers, massively thick walls, and it has built-in neutron shielding, gamma shielding, and heat conductors to keep the contents cool. One flask holds up to twenty-eight separate containers of plutonium, but the total in one flask is only about two hundred kilos. It's stored in separate packages, though, to prevent the possibility of the whole thing going to critical mass and exploding."

"How reassuring."

There was a sharply sarcastic edge to Vandergrift's voice, but Phillips ignored it. "They do extensive radiation monitoring on those ships," he continued. "The actual radiation exposure for the crew . . . I forget the specifics, but it's less than ordinary people onshore get just from background radiation."

"Less than you get ashore? What does *that* mean?"

"Ordinary rock has uranium in it. It gives off background

radiation, just a tiny, tiny bit. We don't even have that when we're at sea." He waved his arm, taking in the blue-gray ocean. "No rocks. And what we'll get from those flasks on board the *Sandpiper* is less than what we get when we're ashore. So don't worry about it. We're not about to start glowing if we come alongside that vessel!"

"I was just concerned about our passengers and crew, sir."

"Of course you were, Number One." Eric Phillips was watching the ship ahead as he spoke. The *Sandpiper* was off the *Atlantis Queen*'s port bow, now, and about three hundred yards ahead. The cruise ship was so much larger than the freighter that, from the bridge, Phillips could actually look *down* on the other vessel, and he was puzzled by a couple of inconsistencies.

For one thing, he'd been expecting to see a lot of injured crewmen off the *Ishikari* on the forward deck. As the silver-painted helicopter lifted off the *Sandpiper*'s forward deck, he could see that the deck was empty. For another, there appeared to be some damage forward. It was tough to tell from this distance even through binoculars, but there was something not quite right forward. It looked as though several of the stanchions holding the deck safety railing had been snapped off. He could see one dangling from a length of cable over the side of the ship, up toward the ship's raised forecastle. And there was some scarring or minor damage to the deck up there, too.

He lowered his binoculars, thoughtful. Possibly they'd ripped up the stanchions and railing in order to facilitate bringing injured people on board. Or maybe that helicopter had caused the damage. Landing a helicopter on a ship at sea was tricky business at best. That helicopter was a civilian aircraft—he could tell that from the markings— and the pilot might simply not have the experience necessary to touch down on a moving deck without clipping a railing with his landing gear, say.

There were other questions, too. The plutonium ship's

gun ports had been opened; he could see two of the guns exposed, one over the fantail, the other at the starboard-forward corner of the bridge house. Was that standard procedure for armed PNTL ships during rescue efforts? Phillips didn't know.

And why were they steadily cruising away from the disaster area? Were they that certain they'd rescued everybody in the water? Phillips knew from experience just how big the ocean actually was, when there were men in the water after the sinking of a ship. Typically, SAR efforts continued for hours, even days, after a ship went down, until the rescuers were absolutely certain that *every* survivor had been recovered.

As Phillips watched, however, and as the *Queen* drew closer, he could see a number of crewmen on the *Sandpiper*'s decks. Several of them were waving as they waited to take lines aboard from the *Queen*.

"Pass the word for line-handling parties to stand by, port side," he said.

"Aye, aye, sir." Vandergrift began speaking into a handset.

"Sparks! Tell the *Sandpiper* to come to a full stop. This is going to be tough enough without them charging across the ocean at five knots."

Phillips turned from the forward windows and walked to the starboard wing, using the binoculars to look at the smoke plume still rising from the sea. The fire appeared to be dying out, though thick smoke continued feeding the black, roiling column ascending into the sky. At this distance, it was impossible to see if there were any people still in the water, but he could make out a lot of debris on the surface.

Damn it, there could easily be survivors there still, clinging to wreckage or buoyed on life jackets. He intended to have a long talk with the *Sandpiper*'s skipper in a few moments. There was no reason for the transport ship to leave the scene and every reason for her to stay.

"Captain?" the radio operator called. "Got something funny here."

He walked away from the bridge wing to the radio shack door. Inside, three operators sat at a bank of consoles. "What do you have?"

"We have a frequency scanner going, to keep track of local traffic, right? It just jumped to a military frequency. I think it's a military radio."

"What did they say?"

"I don't know, sir. It wasn't in English."

"French?"

"No, sir. This was . . . not sure. Kind of guttural? Sounded like 'hellick.' "

" 'Hellick'? Just that?"

"Yes, sir. Repeated three times, 'hellick, hellick, hellick,' like that . . . and then there was a pause, maybe a few seconds, and it repeated three more times."

"Maybe the Germans have a ship in the area."

"Maybe, sir." The radio operator didn't sound convinced.

" 'Hallig' is the name of a German island in the North Sea," one of the other operators suggested.

"You speak German?"

"Yes, sir."

"Keep listening, then." But the North Sea was a long way from here. It didn't make sense. Perhaps *Hallig* was the name of a German ship?

"Captain!" came over the bridge intercom system.

Phillips picked up the intercom handset. "This is the captain."

"Sir! This is Carter, Security Department. We may have a situation, here."

"What kind of a situation?"

"We're picking up crewmen on our security cams. They're moving—"

"Damn it, Carter, of course they're moving! I just gave orders to stand by to pass lines to that other ship!"

"No, sir! Not that! We have . . . looks like eight or ten men coming up the passageway toward Security. They . . . my God!"

"What? What is it?"

"Captain! They're *armed*! Automatic rifles! Eight of them outside Security! Eight more on their way to the bridge! I don't know how they got past the secure doors, but—"

Carter's voice cut off, and Phillips heard a loud, hammering sound, followed a moment later by the unmistakable flat and chattering crack of automatic fire.

"Seal all security doors!" Phillips snapped, and Kelly, the security man assigned to the bridge, moved to comply.

And then the aft door to the bridge banged open, and men were storming in, some with semiautomatic handguns, some with assault rifles. "Get away from the console!" one of the intruders barked.

Kelly continued to type on a console keyboard, entering his password, and the leader of the attackers raised his pistol with a long sound suppressor screwed onto the muzzle and fired once . . . a sharp, hissing exclamation. Kelly jerked, back arching away from the shots, then collapsed on the deck, leaving a smear of blood on the console.

The leader of the attackers wore the dark blue uniform and badge of the *Atlantis Queen*'s Security Department. Turning, he leveled the pistol at Phillips' head.

"Captain," the man said calmly, "I am Yusef Khalid of the Islamic Jihad International Brigade of al-Qaeda. Your ship now belongs to us! *All* of you, down on the deck! I will shoot anyone who disobeys, or who doesn't carry out my orders instantly!"

Automatic gunfire barked from the radio room, and Phillips heard a man scream.

11

Lost Continent Restaurant, *Atlantis Queen*
North Atlantic Ocean
49° 21' N, 8° 13' W
Saturday, 1018 hours GMT

DONALD MYERS LOOKED UP from the menu as Ms. Caruthers and Ms. Jordan hurried up to join them. Myers and the rest of the tour group were already seated at the large table along the port side windows, looking down on the merchant vessel close alongside.

The Lost Continent Restaurant was the second-largest dining area on the *Atlantis Queen*, luxuriously furnished and appointed, with large windows, crystal chandeliers, imitation Mayan walls and columns, and a small rain forest's worth of potted trees and vines giving the place the romantic atmosphere of a fantasy-adventure novel. It was located on the Tenth Deck, aft, overlooking the Atlas Pool on the Deck Nine fantail and, at the moment, offering an unparalleled view of the *Queen*'s docking with the other ship.

The group had decided to come here when the announcement had sounded over the PA system perhaps forty-five minutes ago, planning on having some breakfast while watching the drama unfold outside. *A good way to keep the women out of the way of the rescue*, Myers thought. Lots of other passengers evidently had thought the same, that it would let them watch without getting stepped on. The Lost Continent was crowded with people. They'd been lucky to get here early enough to beat the rush and get seats.

"Oh, good," Ms. Jones said. "Elsie! Anne! You're just in time! They're starting to toss ropes across to the other ship!"

"It's all so perfectly *exciting*!" Ms. Dunne added.

"Never mind that," Ms. Caruthers said. "Donald! There's something wrong aboard this ship!"

Myers sighed, looking up. Both of the women appeared slightly flushed, perhaps a bit out of breath. "Such as what, Ms. Caruthers?" he asked.

"Elsie and I were just coming out of our cabin, up on the Hera Deck," Ms. Jordan said. "We were in a hurry because we wanted to come down and join you all for breakfast and—"

"I believe there are terrorists on board, Mr. Myers," Caruthers interrupted.

"Terrorists?" Myers said. He managed not to laugh out loud. Since they'd come aboard Thursday, he'd been playing with the thought he'd had about the women's terrorist and sewing circle and wishing he could share it with someone. Caruthers' blunt statement brought the humorous image back to mind.

"Terrorists," Caruthers said firmly as the two women sat down at the places left for them. "Men with guns!"

"Slow down, Elsie," Roger Galsworthy said. "What men with what guns?"

"There were three of them," Jordan said, "and they were coming down the hallway as we were leaving our stateroom, bold as you please, and one of them bumped against me and almost—"

"They were wearing ship's crew uniforms," Caruthers said, interrupting again. "And they were carrying machine guns!"

"Machine guns?" Abe Klein said, chuckling. "Seems a little unlikely."

"They were those Russian guns, like in that movie *Russian Dawn* back in the eighties," Ms. Jordan said. "Where a bunch of high school kids fight a Russian invasion of the U.S.?"

"I think you mean *Red Dawn*, Anne," Caruthers said.

"*Red Dawn*, that's right. The rifles were this long," Jordan continued, holding her hands apart, "and black, except for orange wood underneath the barrel, and back on the stock. And the . . . the thing where they keep the bullets? It was *this* long and curved. And one of the men said something to the others when the one bumped into me, and another looked like he was going to *hit* me, but another one snapped at him and they just kept on going."

"What did they say?" Myers asked.

"I don't know," Caruthers said. "It wasn't English or French."

"It sounded *foreign*," Jordan added.

Myers frowned. "Foreign languages often do."

"One of them," Jordan continued, "the one who'd snapped at the other one, just kind of looked at us and said, 'Ship's Security, go back to your stateroom.' And they kept on going down the hall. Running, almost."

"So what did you do?" Ms. Dunne asked.

"Came right down here to find you, of course," Caruthers said. Her mouth was set in a hard-lined expression of disapproval.

"Look . . . you said they were wearing crew uniforms?" Myers asked.

"That's right," Caruthers said. "White slacks, dark blue shirts, ship's logo on the left chest, where a shirt pocket would be if it had one. But they had dark skin. Not like coloreds, but dark, Mediterranean-looking. And they all had beards. Have you seen anyone in the *Atlantis Queen*'s crew with beards?"

"Yes, actually," Myers said, trying to ignore the unpleasantly racist comment. Caruthers was old and had grown up in the South of the 1940s. "Some of the line handlers when we left the dock yesterday had beards."

"I am *not* crazy, young man," Caruthers told him. "I know what we saw!"

"I'm sure you do." Myers was continually bemused by Anne Jordan's taste in movies. Schwarznegger action films . . . and now *Red Dawn*. Her description of the rifle, though, sounded very much like an AK-47, or something just like it—an AKM, perhaps. Orange stock and fore-grip, banana clip magazine . . . not a machine gun, but an assault rifle, certainly.

"We need to tell the captain!" Caruthers said.

"Ms. Caruthers, I'm sure you saw what you say you did. But I feel very sure that there's a logical explanation."

"Such as?" Caruthers said, staring him in the eye and lifting her chin. "In *my* world people don't run around with guns, bumping into decent people and talking in foreign languages!"

"These people," Myers said carefully, "take security *very* seriously on this ship. You all saw that at the security checkpoint the other day, right?"

"Up to a point," Caruthers said. She almost smiled at the memory.

Myers was still embarrassed about that scene. In the end, the security guards had settled for using a handheld metal detector to check Caruthers and the others who'd refused to submit to the X-ray scan head to toe, then waved them on through. Caruthers clearly considered that to have been a victory for moral and upstanding people everywhere.

Myers pointed out the window. "We're coming along-side another ship. I would be willing to bet any money you like that if this ship has to get close to another ship, the rules say that armed security guards take up stations where they can keep an eye on things."

"Makes sense," Abe Klein said, nodding.

"Of *course* it does," Galsworthy added. "Us former-military types have seen this sort of thing before, right, Donald?"

"Uh, right. Yeah." Galsworthy, he remembered, was ex–Air Force from the Vietnam era, and made a lot of the fact when given half a chance.

The conversation wandered on, moving on to the fine points of twentieth-century piracy and the security systems in place on board the *Atlantis Queen*—key cards to keep unauthorized personnel out of secure areas, for instance, and scanners to make sure people weren't wandering off where they shouldn't. Bored, Myers turned away and watched the docking taking place outside. Crewmen—and many of them *were* bearded, he noted—had tossed massive hawsers out and down to the far smaller ship alongside. Crewmen on the other ship had made the hawsers fast to cleats in the deck.

He could see the name of the other ship across her transom—*Pacific Sandpiper*. She looked like an oil tanker, with her superstructure all the way aft behind a long, long forward deck, but she was a lot smaller than he would have expected for a tanker. He'd seen photos of ships like this one designed for carrying grain on the Great Lakes. Maybe that's what she was . . . a grain ship.

A helicopter was circling both ships in the distance—part of the rescue operation, no doubt.

Terrorists. He shook his head and, again, suppressed a laugh. The only terrorists on board were at this table.

Turkish Interpol National Central Bureau
Ataturk Bulvari
Ankara, Turkey
Saturday, 1235 hours GMT + 2

"*Lutfin, Komutanim!*" Lia DeFrancesca said. "*Please*, sir! We really need your help on this!"

Colonel Tarhan looked up at Lia from behind his desk and rubbed at his luxuriant mustache with a nicotine-stained finger. "Well . . ."

"Everywhere I go," she told him, "the bureaucracy stands in the way. And we *must* have this information before the British have to release the suspect."

"Yes, I can certainly understand that," Tarhan replied. He picked up the wire photo of Nayim Erbakan and studied it again. He glanced up at Lia. "You say you're with Interpol?"

"*Euro*pol, *Komutanim*," she replied. The Turkish honorific was reserved for a military superior officer, rather than a civilian. It emphasized, Lia hoped, the essential fraternity of military personnel, their bond of brotherhood, whatever their country of origin. "If I were Interpol," she added, "I wouldn't need to be here, jumping through the bureaucratic hoops, *non*?"

They were speaking English, but Lia's legend called for a French accent and she knew a few words in Turkish.

"It is irregular," Tarhan said at last, "but let me see what I can do for such a *beautiful* woman."

Interpol, the International Criminal Police Organization, maintained NCBs—National Central Bureaus—or sub-bureaus in 187 member countries and had one of the largest and most comprehensive computer databases on international criminal activity in the world.

The NSA, quite naturally, had penetrated that database long ago, but its very size and complexity meant that any covert search of Interpol's records required time—days, sometimes even weeks. Things had gotten even worse since the NCTC had begun trying to do Interpol one better with its Terrorist Identities Datamart Environment. Interpol tended to be jealous of its database and didn't make it easy for other agencies to gain access; a formal request for information could take weeks, even assuming it hit the right desk and reached the right person.

Taggart had tried first earlier that morning, showing

his NSA identification and making a formal request downstairs at the National Central Bureau for Turkey, and as
they'd expected, he'd been told that his request would be
processed . . . a polite way of saying that approval *might*
be forthcoming in a week or two.

And so Lia had decided to try it *her* way. Among her
fictitious IDs was one for Captain Danielle Fouchet, former French gendarme and current agent for Europol.

Europol was not Interpol but a relatively new organization first established in the early 1990s by the Treaty of
Maastricht and the creation of the European Union. Without full executive powers, it so far was limited to the role
of support to the law enforcement agencies of the twenty-
seven member nations of the EU. As the new kid on the
European law enforcement block, it still faced considerable difficulties in finding channels with which to work
with established agencies and databases—including those
of Interpol.

Europol, she knew, struggled with many of the same
challenges as the NSA or NCTC, but assuming this role
gave her a significant advantage. As a European, she
wasn't *American*. Too many foreign police services, re-
acting to the stereotypical image of the ugly American,
the at times heavy-handed approach of the CIA and other
U.S. agencies, and the perceived arrogance of U.S. foreign
policy over the past decade, simply refused to work
smoothly with any American intelligence unit. They dragged
their feet, invoked special privilege, and threw up bureaucratic barriers, stonewalling attempts to get them to share
needed intelligence.

That attitude was the NSA's primary motivation in in-
filtrating the intelligence data networks of other nations,
even those of close allies; Lia didn't like the need for spying on allies, but that was the harsh truth of the current
geopolitcal landscape.

And so Lia was posing as a French Europol agent and

she'd chosen Colonel Tarhan of Turkey's Interpol bureau as her target.

She watched Tarhan typing away at his keyboard and smiled. Her ploy appeared to be working.

Working with the Turkish authorities could be challenging, especially if you were a woman. Though Turkey's government was defiantly secular, most Turks were Muslim and tended to be conservative to one degree or another when it came to dealing with women. An attractive woman on her own in the streets of Ankara could be subject to catcalls and harassment, even to physical assault; at the same time, many Turkish men, especially the older ones, could be almost charmingly and touchingly gallant when it came to responding to a woman's request, *especially* if she threw in just a touch of feminine helplessness.

Lia was also using Tarhan's military background to her advantage. The military dominated all aspects of Turkish society and government, doubling as the nation's police force. Individual Interpol NCBs were staffed by the national police of member nations, and so the Ankara bureau was run by Turkish military officers. By showing her credentials as a French Army officer serving with Europol, she could call Tarhan *Komutanim* instead of the civilian *Bayim* and relate to him as a superior officer.

All Turkish males were required to serve in the Army; women were not; she could tell that Tarhan was bemused by the idea of a woman Army captain and Europol agent . . . but she was counting on what would have been called machismo in a Latino country, his conservative and patriarchal gallantry toward women.

The technique required delicacy and care; it could easily backfire, especially if the target happened to be strongly Muslim or from a hyper-traditional culture like Saudi Arabia that seriously marginalized women to second-class citizenry. But the Art Room had transmitted the records of several of the officers at the Ankara Interpol bureau to her that morning, and she'd picked Tarhan as one who might be willing to bend the rules to help a woman in distress.

Especially a beautiful woman. Tarhan seemed quite taken with her, to the point that she was already wondering if she would have to fend off his advances later.

"Ah!" Tarhan said suddenly, leaning back in his seat. "Success!"

"What did you find?"

"I'm printing off the dossier." He waved a hand at the printer on the far side of his office, which had begun to buzz and whine. "It's odd, though. You say this Erbakan was picked up trying to smuggle drugs himself?"

"Yes. In Southampton, Thursday morning."

"It's not his usual modus operandi. Generally, he acts as the point man, setting up a meet and agreeing on a price. He's also never been involved with such a large amount. He really is a minor player."

"We thought so, too. That's why we're looking for any connections you might have in your records . . . Erbakan's connections with organized crime, with known terrorists, that sort of thing."

"Terrorists? Why would a drug runner be connected with terrorists?"

She shrugged. "Many terror networks finance their activities with drugs."

"In South America, perhaps. Or Southeast Asia. Not *here*."

Dream on, Colonel, she thought, but she kept the words to herself. Though the Russians had been more and more in the picture lately, Turkey remained a primary route for narcotics—especially heroin—coming from Asia to Europe, and several local terror groups used the drug pipelines to their financial advantage . . . especially the PKK, the Kurdistan Workers' Party seeking independence for Turkish Kurds. Evidently, Tarhan didn't care to air that particular bit of dirty Turkish laundry with a foreigner.

He turned back to his computer screen for a moment. "This Erbakan appears to have been involved in small sales of drugs—heroin and opium, mostly—in Germany. Cocaine is a departure for him. So is trying to carry half a kilo of it onto a cruise ship in England. But we do have this." He got up and walked around from behind his desk, went to the printer, and picked up a stack of printed sheets. On top was a color image, which he handed to Lia.

The photo was grainy, evidently taken through a tele-photo lens, but it showed two men standing outside what appeared to be a warehouse on a city street. Both men were bearded, one in a red shirt, the other in a light blue jacket.

"The man in the red shirt is Erbakan," he told her. "The other is a man named Yusef Khalid. He may be AQ."

"Al-Qaeda?"

Tarhan nodded. "This is a surveillance photo taken by German Interpol three weeks ago in Bonn. They'd been tracking Khalid, building a file, and happened to catch him at a meeting with Erbakan."

"So what do you have on Khalid?"

"Not a lot. I'm printing out his dossier for you as well. He seems to be associated with something called the Is-lamist Jihad International, or IJI. They're new; we don't have a lot on them. But the money trail appears to be through the Bank of Saud, and may connect them with al-Qaeda." As the printer finished running them off, he handed a second sheaf of papers to her. Several, she saw, showed color images of Yusef Khalid.

"You have been *so* helpful," she said. "Thank you."

"How would you like to show your appreciation? Have dinner with me tonight?"

"Oh, Colonel! I'd love to. But I can't."

"Tomorrow night, then? The kebab at the Washington Restaurant is . . . how do you French say it? *C'est fantas-tique!*"

"Ooh . . . *mon Colonel*! Here." She pulled a card out of her handbag and handed it to him. "I'm here, at the Dedeman *oteli*. Call me, okay?"

His grin came close to being a leer. "Absolutely! Tomorrow then!"

As she walked out of Tarhan's office, the dossiers in hand, Jeff Rockman's voice whispered in her ear. He'd been monitoring the entire conversation from his console back at the Art Room under NSA headquarters. "Lia, you are absolutely shameless! You have a flight out of there tonight!"

"Oh, I don't know," she murmured as the door closed behind her and she walked through the outer lobby toward the front entrance. "He's a charmer. I might be convinced to stay on an extra day."

"Not this time, Lia," Rockman said. "The boss wants you in Southampton."

"Southampton?" she asked, puzzled. "England? I'm not coming back to Fort Meade?"

"Something's breaking in the North Atlantic," Rockman told her. "No details yet, but it's tied to your friend Erbakan, and we're putting a team together. You'll be meeting with Charlie in Southampton."

That would be Charlie Dean, and her heart quickened just a bit. "And Taggart?"

"He'll be getting orders from our friends at the Company. I think he's going to be on his way to Paris."

"Okay. When's my flight?"

"We have you booked on a British Air flight out of Ankara at seven-ten tonight, your time. And Mr. Rubens wants you to scan those dossiers you just got out of lover boy and transmit them back here stat."

"As soon as I get to my hotel," Lia told him.

Damn! The round of jet-hopping was starting to catch up with her—Baltimore, to Lebanon, to Turkey, and now up to England.

But at least she would be seeing Charlie Dean.

Bridge, *Atlantis Queen*
49° 21' N, 8° 13' W
Saturday, 1040 hours GMT

Yusef Khalid stepped onto the port bridge wing of the *Atlantis Queen* and looked down at the *Pacific Sandpiper*. The smaller ship was tucked in close alongside the *Queen*, now, and fenders had been lowered over the sides of both ships to keep their hulls from smashing into each other in rough seas. Massive cables crisscrossed the space between the vessels, giving the *Sandpiper* the look of a tugboat nuzzling her far larger consort.

From his vantage point on the wing, Khalid could look down on and into the *Sandpiper*'s bridge, which only came up to about the Fifth or Sixth Deck on the *Queen*. He could make out figures inside, though without detail enough to tell who was who.

There could be no doubt, however, that the IJI was in full control there, as well as on board the *Queen*. Armed men stood on both of the *Sandpiper*'s bridge wings and on the forward deck, supervising the crewmen who'd just completed the binding of the two ships. They wore the uniforms of the *Sandpiper*'s security force now, the so-called Atomic Police, to allay the suspicions of the curious, but Khalid knew they were his.

The helicopter had been circling in the near distance, but Mohamed Darif had already sent the radio call to bring them back on board the *Sandpiper*. Had there been a problem in taking the *Queen*, the men on the helicopter would have taken out the ship's bridge and any other pockets of resistance they could see on the deck or in spaces like the casino with large windows with automatic weapons fire. Fortunately, that hadn't been necessary; the plan called for a *quiet* takeover of the *Atlantis Queen*. With over two thousand passengers on board, plus nine hundred crew, the IJI strike force had to proceed carefully. The longer the passengers and the majority of the crew could be kept in the dark as to what was happening, the better. Khalid had only twenty-four men at his command with which to control over three thousand.

Even cattle could be dangerous if they broke into a stampede.

Glancing up, he saw that the weather appeared to be breaking, with large patches of blue sky beginning to break the overcast to the west and south. The seas were gentler, too. A mixed blessing, that. Calmer seas meant fewer problems towing the *Pacific Sandpiper.* Clear skies meant they would be exposed to the snooping lenses of Western spy satellites. As with the passengers on board the cruise ship, it was important to keep the Americans and the British in the dark as to what was happening for as long as possible. The *Atlantis Queen* and the *Pacific Sandpiper* still had a long and risky voyage in front of them.

He watched as the helicopter moved in close for a landing, drifting in across the *Sandpiper*'s port side, touching down gently well over on the port side of the deck in order to keep its rotors clear of the towering cliff side of the *Atlantis Queen.*

Looking aft along the *Queen*'s superstructure, Khalid saw people, hundreds of people, watching the show. Many of the fancier staterooms on the *Queen* had exterior balconies walled off from their neighbors but providing an outside space for sun worshipping, a romantic outside cabin-service dinner for two, or simply watching the ocean and taking in the sea air. At the moment, those balconies also provided excellent seats overlooking the *Sandpiper*'s deck, and the passengers in those staterooms were taking advantage of the fact.

Let them watch. As long as there was no panic.

Yet . . .

Turning, Khalid walked back off the weather platform and into the bridge. Three of his men stood guard over Phillips and a helmsman, both of whom stood by the ship's wheel. Vandergrift and the others had been herded aft to join other prisoners in the officer's wardroom, and the security guard's body had been carried away and the blood mopped up. It was important to maintain appearances, at least for a time.

"Tell me something, Captain," Khalid said.

Phillips looked at Khalid but said nothing. Khalid saw the anger in the man's eyes, but he also saw the fear. It would be important to keep Phillips afraid until he was no longer needed.

"Our calculations were necessarily rushed," Khalid told the *Queen*'s captain, "and not many of us have much experience with the sea. I want you to come over here and tell me if you feel the two ships have been tied together securely enough to make this voyage."

Reluctantly Phillips left his station behind the helmsman and joined Khalid. Khalid let him step past him and onto the port bridge wing, pressing the suppressor of his pistol up into Phillips' side.

"I don't know what you're trying to accomplish with this insanity," Phillips growled.

"At the moment, all I want to know is the seaman's take on those ropes."

"Lines," Phillips said. He sounded tired. "They're called lines."

"Lines, then. If the seas get rough, will they hold?"

"It depends on how rough it gets. If a gale starts blowing, or a storm hits, no. *Nothing* would keep us tied together." He hesitated. "You have no idea how powerful the sea can be."

"But will it hold for now? In these seas?"

Again Phillips paused, frowning. "Yes."

"How fast are we moving right now?"

"About four knots. Enough to maintain headway."

"Will those lines hold if we increase speed to, say, ten knots?"

Phillips looked hard at Khalid, startled. "What, towing that ship like this?"

"Exactly."

"Probably. If it doesn't get rougher than this."

"How about fifteen knots, Captain?"

He shook his head. "I don't know if we can manage fifteen knots dragging the other ship."

"What if the other ship was running at fifteen knots as well?"

"Listen, mister. This ship isn't designed for that sort of thing. I don't know if we can do that or not."

"Best guess, Captain."

"I don't know!"

Khalid shrugged, then grasped Phillips' arm and guided him back inside. "Let me explain. You are going to give the order to your engineering room to make revolutions for ten knots. My men are going to watch those ropes . . . those lines, I should say. If they start to break, my men are going to go down and bring every passenger on B Deck forward to the Neptune Theater. That would be . . . how many people, do you think?"

"I'm . . . I'm not sure. Two or three hundred, perhaps."

"That's what I thought. Men, women, and children, locked inside. They will be our hostages for your good judgment."

"Damn you, man, what are you going to do?"

"If the two ships break apart, I will order my men to begin shooting the hostages. *All* of them."

"Then the lines aren't going to hold!" Phillips said quickly, his eyes wide. "The ships will break apart if you try to do more than five knots!"

"Ah," Khalid said. "I see. In that case, Captain, I want you to pass the appropriate orders to tie the ships together in such a way that they will *not* break apart, at ten knots, even at fifteen. When you have completed that, we will bring the passengers from B Deck up to the theater and lock them in. They will wait inside while we test your seamanship. If the lines hold, we will permit them to return to their staterooms."

Phillips sagged, like a puppet with its strings cut. "The lines will hold," he said.

"What was that?"

"I said the lines will hold, damn you. As they are. I told you they wouldn't so I wouldn't risk those passengers' lives."

Khalid smiled. "I thought as much. So . . . you would bet your life on the lines holding as they are?"

"Yes."

"You would bet the lives of two hundred of your passengers that they will hold? At ten knots?"

"*Yes*, damn you!"

"That is what I wanted to hear. Captain, you may give the order to increase speed—*slowly*—to ten knots. Helmsman . . . you will put us onto a course of two-zero-zero degrees."

The helmsman cast a scared look at Phillips, who nodded at him. "Yes . . . sir."

"Rashid?"

"Yes, sir!"

"Radio our people on the *Sandpiper*. Tell them what we are doing. Have them match our speed."

"Yes, sir!"

"Don't worry, Captain," Khalid added. "If you do what we say, you and every one of your passengers and crew will come out of this safely. We are making a . . . political statement. We have no wish to harm anyone. But we *are* going to make our message heard!"

"What message is that? Maybe . . ."

"Yes?"

"Maybe I can help."

"You *are* helping, Captain. Just continue following my orders and everything will be fine."

"But what is this message? What does this, this hijacking accomplish for you?"

"All in good time, Captain Phillips. All in good time. For the moment, all you need to know is that the safety of your passengers and crew rests *entirely* in your hands."

And slowly, the *Atlantis Queen* began gathering speed, her smaller consort tied close alongside.

12

IT HADN'T BEEN AT ALL DIFFICULT to talk Tricia Johnson into bed. Twenty minutes' casual small talk by the Atlas Pool had convinced her that they'd known each another for years. She even "remembered" having some drinks and a burger with him and some other friends at the Rathskeller one evening. Tricia, Llewellyn suspected, was achingly lonely after her bad marriage and on the lookout for someone new.

Llewellyn had pulled this scam several times before on the last ship he was on, but never with such spectacular success. The two of them now were stretched out in her bed after several exhausting hours of lovemaking, the sheets and blankets in a tangle beneath them, their swimsuits discarded on the carpet. Her wealthy grandparents had done well by her; 6029 was one of the mid-to-upper-priced staterooms on Deck Six, with a large ocean-view window and a sliding door leading out to a private balcony on the starboard side.

As he'd expected, she looked a *lot* better in the flesh, as it were, than she had in the black-and-white fuzziness of the X-Star scan. He held her close, stroking her, whispering in her ear how glad he was to have found her and what a remarkable coincidence it had been to meet here, three thousand miles from home . . .

His only problem through the rest of the cruise would be to stay clear of her when he was on-duty and in uniform. That wouldn't be too hard to arrange, since he could track her identity chip anywhere on the ship and always know exactly where she was.

The stateroom door swung open and two men in security uniforms walked in.

"*What the hell*?" Llewellyn shouted. He blinked. He didn't know either of these guys, though they were wearing blue and white security uniforms, and one was holding the security key that had given them access to the stateroom.

They also both held automatic pistols with suppressors screwed to the muzzles.

"Sorry to interrupt you two," one of them said with a nasty leer, gesturing with the pistol. "Get up! Hands behind your heads!"

Johnson tried to cover herself with the sheet, but one of the intruders yanked it away. "On your feet, whore!"

"You're David Llewellyn?" the other said. "Head of Ship's Security?"

The pistol was inches from his nose. "Uh . . . yeah. I'm Llewellyn."

"Ship's Security?" Johnson said, looking at him. "David? What is all this?"

"If this is a robbery," Llewellyn told the gunmen, "my wallet is back in my quarters."

"Get dressed."

"I don't know," the leering intruder said. "I think we should take them like that."

"Majnun!" the other man said. He added in English, to Llewellyn, "Make yourselves decent. You will both come with us."

National Security Council
White House basement
Washington, D.C.
Saturday, 0945 hours EST

"We believe," William Rubens said, "that we have a situation developing in the North Atlantic."

He was standing at the podium at the front of one of the sub-basement briefing rooms deep beneath the foundations of the White House. On the projection screen behind him was a satellite photograph, somewhat grainy and low resolution but with a sharp, metallic glint to both them and the surface of the water, of two ships side-by-side, one much smaller than the other.

The audience listened impassively in the twilight of the room. Major General Barton and Admiral Prendergast of the Joint Chiefs both were there, together with several uniformed aides. Debra Collins, Deputy Director of Operations for the CIA, was there as well, along with Thompson of the DIA, Carter from NCTC, Radebaugh from Homeland Security, and Dominic, the NSC's liaison with the FBI.

At the head of the table, at the far end from Rubens, was George Francis Wehrum, senior aide to the current Chairperson of the National Security Council, Dr. Donna Bing.

Rubens had crossed swords with both Wehrum and his boss more than once.

The National Security Council, or NSC, consisted of about one hundred staffers working within the labyrinthine recesses of the White House basement. Under the direction of ANSA, the assistant to the president for National Security Affairs—currently an unpleasant woman named Dr. Donna Bing—the NSC briefed the President on all potential international crises. The Joint Chiefs of Staff kept the President up-to-date on all military developments worldwide; the NSC kept him informed on unfolding diplomatic, economic, and intelligence problems and, when necessary, ran the President's White House Situation Room.

Rubens had called Donna Bing's office two hours earlier, requesting a special briefing session this morning. His audience now included Wehrum and several other NSC staffers, as well as liaisons from the Joint Chiefs, the CIA, and NCTC.

"At approximately oh-eight-thirty hours GMT," Rubens told them, "or about six and a half hours ago, now, a Japanese warship escorting the latest plutonium transport vessel from England to Japan exploded and sank in the North Atlantic, about a hundred miles off the tip of Cornwall. Initial reports were that the explosion was an accident, possibly the simultaneous detonation of her Harpoon warheads. Signals intercepts from GCHQ in northern England picked up radio traffic in the area indicating that the plutonium ship, the *Pacific Sandpiper*, was picking up survivors, that a civilian cruise ship that happened to be in the area was moving to assist, and that a French military helicopter was also moving in to look for survivors. Other ships and aircraft are also deploying to the area."

Turning, Rubens aimed the bright red dot of a laser pointer at the screen, indicating the smaller of the two ships. "This vessel is the *Pacific Sandpiper*. Three hundred twenty-five feet long, seven thousand, seven hundred twenty-five tons' displacement, with a crew of twenty-eight, plus thirty security personnel on board. British flagged, owned and operated by PNTL, out of Barrow, England. On board are fourteen TN 28 VT transport flasks, each weighing ninety-eight tonnes, containing a total of twenty-five hundred kilograms of plutonium. That's two and a half *tonnes* of highly radioactive material."

His audience shifted uncomfortably in their seats. The plutonium shipments to Japan had long given the NSC cause for concern. Some of the Council's deliberations had helped shape the regulations surrounding those shipments—such as the arming of a civilian vessel and the embarkation of large numbers of armed security personnel.

Rubens shifted the laser dot to the larger vessel, riding close against the plutonium ship's right side. "This is the civilian cruise ship that was rendering assistance," he said. "Royal Sky Line's *Atlantis Queen*. Nine hundred sixty-four feet long, displacing ninety thousand tons. A crew of nine hundred, with about twenty-four hundred passengers. British flagged, out of Southampton." He turned back to face the audience. "The escort was the *Ishikari*, with a crew of ninety."

"A terrible tragedy, I'm sure," Wehrum said from the far side of the table. "How, exactly, does this involve the NSC?"

"According to Royal Sky's records," Rubens said, "over twelve hundred of the passengers on board the *Atlantis Queen* are American citizens. Further, the United States is signatory to the international agreements surrounding the plutonium shipments, and by treaty shares the responsibility for safeguarding those shipments. And, more to the point, we now believe there is a possibility that the *Pacific Sandpiper* has been seized by forces hostile to the United States."

"If you mean terrorists," General Barton snapped, "say so."

"We don't know who is involved as yet," Rubens said. "As yet, we've been unable to make contact with either ship. But there is that possibility, yes."

"What's that on the plutonium ship's forward deck?" Prendergast wanted to know. "I can't quite make it out."

"That," Rubens said, "is part of the problem. It's a helicopter out of Brest, France. Signals intercepts identified it as French military. The French deny that it's ALAT—French Army—and ATC records identify only a single *civilian* helicopter operating out of Brest this morning. We're still checking into that."

Rubens indicated the photograph on the screen behind him, pointing to the blocks of text at the lower right, including the date and time stamps. "This photo was taken by one of our Argus satellites at ten-forty-eight hours GMT . . . that's just less than five hours ago. The image was taken by narrow-aperture radar from an altitude of one hundred twenty-nine miles. Radar has a much longer wavelength than visible light, so detail resolution is necessarily lower than what we can manage with optical sensors. The target, however, was under largely overcast skies at the time, and this is the best we could do.

"As you can see, the cruise ship appears to be secured to the freighter. At first we thought that they were taking injured aboard from the *Sandpiper*—the *Atlantis Queen* has a large and well-stocked shipboard hospital—but you'll notice here . . ." His laser pointer flicked along the metallic glitter of the V-shaped wakes frozen astern of the two ships. "Our analysts tell me that wakes of that size would be generated by ships of this size moving at a speed of between four and six knots."

Rubens flicked off the pointer. "There is something extremely *wrong* about this. Both the *Queen* and the *Sandpiper* should have remained in the vicinity of the disaster, assisting with rescue efforts. At the time this photograph was taken, they'd actually moved to a point some three miles southwest of the disaster. In the hours since, they have traveled an additional fifty miles, indicating an average speed of eight to ten knots.

"From the photograph, it appears that the *Queen* has taken the *Sandpiper* under tow. We have received no distress call from either ship . . . save for the original traffic about the *Ishikari* blowing up. Under normal circumstances, other ships are not permitted to come within a mile of the *Sandpiper*. Admittedly, the *Queen* might have come alongside to transfer injured personnel, but we don't understand why the two should be moving together now, at a fairly high rate of speed.

"And finally, there's this."

Rubens reached into his jacket pocket and produced a flat silver MP3 player. "GCHQ picked this up as a signals intercept at ten-eighteen hours GMT. It's impossible to determine the precise origin of the signal without triangulation, but we know it was from the general vicinity of these ships shortly after the sinking of the *Ishikari*." Holding the player high so everyone at the table could hear, he pressed the play button.

A burst of static sounded, followed by a harsh voice saying, "*Hallak . . . hallak . . . hallak*." There was a pause filled by the hiss of static, and then the words repeated. "*Hallak . . . hallak . . . hallak*."

"*Hallak*, ladies and gentlemen," Rubens said, "is the Arabic word for *now!*"

That caused a stir in the audience. "A signal of some sort," Debra Collins said. "*After* the sinking of the escort."

"It's difficult to see what else it might have been," Rubens replied. "It's possible that the destruction of the *Ishikari* was deliberate sabotage, designed both to take the *Sandpiper*'s military escort out of the picture and to draw the cruise ship in close to assist with SAR efforts. The helicopter was over the Channel at the time, and immediately radioed Brest that it was proceeding to the disaster site to assist . . . despite the fact that its fuel would have been critically low if it had flown to the *Ishikari* and then back to Brest, even without spending any time at the scene of the disaster."

"Obviously," Wehrum pointed out, "they were able to land on the *Sandpiper*'s deck."

"Indeed," Rubens replied. "But how would a civilian helicopter have known that a ship of the *Sandpiper*'s design was going to be available for a landing at sea? We picked up nothing on radio frequencies between ship and aircraft, other than the fact that the aircraft was on its way. And the fact that that helicopter was masquerading as a military aircraft is . . . disturbing. It suggests that after the *Ishikari* explosion, which quite possibly was intended as a diversion, people on board either the *Sandpiper* or the *Queen* carried out a hijacking, probably in concert with armed attackers off that helicopter. If so, then unknown hostile forces are now in control of both vessels, and taking them to an unknown destination."

"And just who is the enemy?" Admiral Prendergast asked. "Al-Qaeda?"

"We don't know, sir. Not yet. However, this operation has the flash and high profile we've come to associate with them."

"Al-Qaeda is a spent force, Mr. Rubens," General Barton pointed out. "Broken. They haven't been able to mount a single effective operation since nine-eleven."

"Not for lack of trying, sir," Rubens replied. "And perhaps they're not as broken as we've come to believe. Or this may be a new group with a similar signature. There's no way to tell. Yet."

"We can assume al-Qaeda until we learn differently," Collins pointed out. "Do you have any intelligence leads, Mr. Rubens?"

"A few. We're working them."

"So where are those ships headed now?"

"At last report, they were on a heading of two-four-zero. That's roughly the correct course for the *Sandpiper*—toward the Caribbean and the Panama Canal. At this point, the *Atlantis Queen* is considerably off-course. She's supposed to be headed due south, toward Gibraltar and the Mediterranean."

"I assume attempts have been made to contact both vessels," Barton said.

"Of course, sir. There's been no response so far."

"Then we need to intercept those ships at sea," Collins said.

Rubens nodded. Collins was not his favorite person. They'd actually once been lovers, a bit of ancient history on which he did his best not to dwell. As Deputy Director of Operations for the CIA, Collins had often targeted the NSA's Desk Three as an asset that properly should have fallen under her jurisdiction. So far, Rubens had managed to fend off her ambitious attempts to gain control of his department, but he remained cautious in his dealings with her.

At the moment, though, she seemed to be siding with him, making him wonder what she was up to. He was glad to have her support, though.

"One of the vessels that responded to the *Ishikari* SOS," Rubens continued, "is the *Ark Royal*, a Royal Navy aircraft carrier. She's still about eighty miles from the sinking, but her skipper has agreed to deploy a couple of Harriers to check on the *Sandpiper*. They may at least establish visual contact, even if the ships' radios are out." He checked his watch. "They should be over the *Sandpiper* and the *Atlantis Queen* within the next hour.

"It also seems we have a possible agent in place on board the *Queen*. Quite serendipitous, actually. We're making attempts now to get in electronic contact with her."

"An agent?" Collins asked. "One of yours?"

"Indirectly. She's GCHQ, which means—"

"Which means she works for one of the NSA's subsidiaries," Collins said with a throaty chuckle. "Yes, we know."

Not quite true, Rubens thought, but close enough to the truth that he let the barb pass. "She happens to be aboard the cruise ship as part of another operation," Rubens continued. "If we can make contact with her, we may be able to get some direct intelligence on what's happening on those ships.

"If the *Atlantis Queen* or the *Sandpiper* or, as seems probable at this juncture, *both* ships have been hijacked," Rubens continued, "her intelligence may be invaluable. We do need to begin making contingency plans."

"Meaning a military response?" Wehrum asked. "Both

of these ships are British. It seems to me the responsibility for any type of response should lie with them."

"Maybe so," Rubens said. "The NSA gathers intelligence. It does not set foreign policy, nor does it carry it out. *However*," he added forcefully as Wehrum began to reply, "half of the passengers on board the *Atlantis Queen* are American citizens, and it is our responsibility to protect them from hostile forces no matter where they are. We also have a treaty obligation to do whatever is necessary to safeguard the cargoes of those plutonium transport ships. At the very least, we're going to need to work closely with the British government on this one, making our military response assets available."

"If we're the ones to go in," Prendergast said, "it means the SEALs."

"Either the SEALs," Rubens said, "or Black Cat."

"Black Cat?" Prendergast said, white eyebrows arching. "What's that?"

"Combat Assault Team—'CAT.' A counterterrorist unit operating out of Desk Three and the NSA," Rubens said. "It's new."

Very new. More than once in the past couple of years, U.S. Navy SEAL units had assisted NSA operators in covert military missions in remote areas, including a recent one on the Arctic ice cap. The SEALs were unparalleled at getting into hard-to-reach places without being seen, carrying out their mission, and extracting again, often before the enemy knew they'd even been there. Not long after the op against the Russians in the far Arctic, Rubens had pushed through a Deep Black program called Black Cat—the "Cat" portion of the name suggested by the counterterrorism, or "CT," nature of their mission as well as by the term "combat assault team." A highly classified number of active-duty SEALs and Army Delta operators had been seconded to the NSA, still drawing military pay but serving with and under Agency personnel. For the past six months they'd been training with combat-experienced

NSA operators, including Charlie Dean and Lia DeFrancesca. Black Cat Bravo was based at Pawtuxet River, Virginia, and was under the command of Lieutenant Richard Taylor, the SEAL officer with whom Dean had deployed in the Arctic. Black Cat Alpha was based at the 'phib base in San Diego.

While the budgetary battles over Black Cat continued both within the Pentagon and at NCTC headquarters in northern Virginia—critics of the program insisted it wastefully duplicated already existent combat units such as the SEAL teams themselves—the unit promised to provide Desk Three with a tremendously valuable and powerful tool. *The NSA gathers intelligence*, he'd told them. *It does not set foreign policy, nor does it carry it out*. Right. . . .

Sometimes, though, to carry out its more dangerous or complex missions the NSA needed something a bit more specialized and a bit more hard-hitting than a com-wired agent with a handgun. The important point was that with its own paramilitary force on tap, there would be fewer problems getting a clean interface between Desk Three and the pointy end of the stick. Clear communications were vital in any covert operation, and more than one major op—Eagle Claw, the failed mission to rescue American hostages in Iran in 1980, was a rather obvious example—had ended in disaster in part when communications broke down between rival services.

Rubens completed his presentation and took a few more questions from the group, ending the briefing with the suggestion that Desk Three begin exploring plans for inserting a covert team onto both the *Pacific Sandpiper* and the *Atlantis Queen*. Two Black Cat teams of about six men each might be able to gather intelligence about what was actually happening on those vessels and, if the decision was made to take them down, would already be in place.

"Your suggestion is noted, Mr. Rubens," Wehrum said,

leaning back in his leather chair. "Thank you for the presentation."

And Rubens was dismissed.

He was gathering up his notes and replacing them in his briefcase when he sensed movement beside him. "Oh, hello, Debra," he said as Collins drew near.

"Bill."

"So . . . why were you being nice to me this morning?"

"What do you mean?"

"You were actually supporting me there on a couple of points."

She made a face. "Despite what you seem to believe, Bill, we *are* on the same side."

"Sometimes it's a bit hard to keep that in mind," he replied. He was surprised at the strength, even now, of his anger at this woman. It had been years, but once she'd betrayed their relationship, their *friendship*, to advance her own agenda . . .

The memory still burned.

It was necessary to keep up the façade, at least, of professionalism. But he would also keep watching his back.

"I just thought you should know, Bill," she told him, "that there will be no Black Cat op on this one."

"Indeed? So the Agency is employing psychics now, to read the future?"

"No, but I can read the weather vane. The *Sandpiper* situation was included in this morning's pickle. The President is inclined to allow the Brits to handle this one."

The "pickle" was the old name for the President's Intelligence Check List, or PICL, a ten-page newsletter prepared by the CIA each night listing the top five or six intelligence developments of interest to the President and a few other high-level personnel, including DIRNSA, Rubens' boss. The system had changed over the years and was now an internal Web page supposedly routed through the NCTC, but insiders still referred to the Agency's intelligence briefs as "pickles" and to the CIA itself as "the pickle factory."

"The British?" Rubens said. "Why?"

"They're closer, for one thing. They have an aircraft carrier less than a hundred miles from those ships. Our closest carrier battle groups are in Norfolk and in the Med, four days away, at best. The ships are both British-flagged. And, frankly, if those ships *have* been hijacked, the President would rather someone else fell on his face right now."

"I see."

"A word to the wise, Bill. Don't make waves."

Rubens considered this as he checked out past the various security checkpoints on his way to the underground White House garage. The current administration was coming under a lot of fire in the news media, lately. The energy crisis, the banking and global monetary crises, the unbearably slow ongoing extraction from Iraq and Afghanistan all had carried over from the last administration into this one, leaving scars and, worse, a bureaucratic tendency at every level of government not to do *anything* that might be construed as yet another failure in either foreign or domestic policy.

A hostage rescue was always a high-risk proposition, with a terrible possibility of innocents being killed, if not by their terrorist captors, then by so-called friendly fire as the hostage rescue team stormed in. The more hostages there were, the likelier it was that casualty figures would be unacceptably high. Even a *successful* rescue might expect a 5 percent casualty rate among the hostages. With something like 3,400 civilians at risk, 5 percent was 170 people dead and wounded.

And if the rescue turned into a clusterfuck like Eagle Claw . . .

Yeah. No wonder the President wanted someone else on point this time.

But Desk Three, Rubens decided, would begin preparing

for a hostage rescue anyway. The one thing they could *not* afford now was to be caught unprepared.

**Deck Twelve Terrace, *Atlantis Queen*
48° 25' N, 9° 28' W
Saturday, 1528 hours GMT**

"Yeah, now *this* is more like it!" James Petrovich said, his eye pressed up close to the LED screen of his camera. "I think I love my job."

"Feeling warmer, yet?" Fred Doherty asked with a sour smile.

"Oh, yeah! Big-time."

"Unfortunately, we won't be able to use the footage. *Damn* her!"

The two of them were again on the Deck Twelve Terrace overlooking the Atlantean Grotto Pool area. An hour earlier, Terry Carter had text-messaged Doherty on his cell phone—the *Queen* had her own cell network on board, since they were well out of range of shore-based systems when they were at sea—with the news that Gillian Harper would be sunbathing at the pool.

Once again, Doherty and Petrovich had trekked up to the terrace area overlooking the Grotto Pool. The sun was shining now, though there were still banks of clouds visible to the south, and the air was considerably warmer now. Gillian Harper had arrived right on cue, wearing an almost nonexistent bikini . . . then promptly removed the top and stretched out on her back on a deck chair, fully and magnificently displayed for the camera looking down on her from above as she began rubbing herself down with suntan lotion.

"Quit bitching, boss," Petrovich said. "Carter said he wanted her to get more exposure!"

"Yeah, but I think he meant something we could air on TV."

"Not a problem. It'll be late-night airtime. We'll just drop some pixilation over her titties. Blur 'em right out."

There were a handful of other sunbathers, and two or three other women had gone topless as well. It was not unusual, Doherty knew, for cruise ships to designate one of their pools—usually on an upper deck where they were not in full view of staterooms or public areas where there might be children present—as a topless area, or even as clothing optional, at least during certain hours. European cruise lines, especially, were far more relaxed about such things than American lines. There would be Ship's Security present in the Atlantean Grotto lounge, he knew, tactfully steering families with children or fully dressed male sightseers elsewhere.

Personally, Doherty didn't care if Harper ran around the ship stark naked. She *did* have a reputation to uphold in that department, after all. But right now he wanted useable footage for CNE, and the self-centered little exhibitionist just wasn't cooperating.

He'd need to text Carter back about this one.

Odd. A couple of people—they looked like teenaged boys, eighteen or nineteen, perhaps, though they could have been a couple of years older—had just emerged from the Grotto Restaurant almost directly beneath Doherty's camera position. They wore shorts, T-shirts, and sandals . . . not exactly out of place at the poolside but not exactly *in* place, either.

"Where the hell is Security?" he asked aloud. The two kids had wandered over to the starboard rail and were leaning against it, but they weren't watching the ocean. Instead, they'd turned and were watching Harper, grinning and making suggestive motions with their hands. After a few moments, one of them pulled a cell phone from his pocket, punched in a number, and started talking into it.

"Security's probably watching the show on their TV monitors," Petrovich said.

"No," Doherty said. "They should have someone

present to make sure female sunbathers don't get gawked at. Something's not right."

"Ah, they're probably just keeping a low profile. You worry too much, boss."

"Worrying is my job."

Two more teenaged boys emerged from the restaurant beneath the terrace and, a moment later, three more came out onto the terrace from the steps aft. They were laughing and joking with one another until they saw the camera crew. "Hey, man!" one said with a distinctly Midwest American accent as he leaned against the terrace rail. "You guys sure got yourselves good seats!"

"How'd you guys get past the guards?" Doherty asked.

"Guards?" the kid said, genuinely puzzled. "What guards?"

A hell of a way to run a cruise ship, Doherty thought. This was the sort of thing that could end in lawsuits— privacy violations, indecent exposure, and even corruption of minors charges.

Or were the Europeans *really* that free and easy about casual social nudity?

"Wrap it up, Pet," he said. "We've got all we can use, here."

Doherty was curious. He wanted to find someone in Security and ask what the hell was going on.

He heard thunder in the distance and turned. Off to the northeast, a pair of tiny black specks winged in low above the water.

13

**Flight Harrier Alpha
North Atlantic Ocean
48° 25' N, 9° 28' W
Saturday, 1535 hours GMT**

COMMANDER CHRISTOPHER Pryor sat in the cockpit of his
Sea Harrier FRS.2, watching the screen of his radar as
the flight vectored toward the target as the ocean's surface blurred beneath the belly of his aircraft, less than a
hundred feet below. His wingman, Commander Vincent
Spick, was parked off his right wing and slightly behind,
in the four o'clock position. The Rolls-Royce Pegasus engine at his back thundered raw power as the two Harriers
hurtled southwest at over six hundred knots.

"Alpha One, this is Alpha Two," Spick's voice called
over his helmet headset. "I have visual on the target."

Pryor glanced up. Sure enough, there it was—a cruise
ship gleaming a dazzling white in the afternoon sun, still
a good twenty miles off. "Copy that, Two," he replied. "I
see him. Throttle back to three hundred."

"One, Two. Roger three hundred."

The two Harriers slowed rapidly. In the dense, wet air
this close to the deck, moisture streamed from the upper
curves of their wings like thick fog.

"King's Palace, this is Alpha One," he called. "Visual

on target. We are on intercept approach." He flipped a switch on his console. "Cameras are rolling."

"Copy that, Alpha One," replied the voice of Flight Control back aboard the *Ark Royal*. "Get us some good pictures."

Except for a pair of 30mm Aden Mk 4 gun pods apiece, the Harriers were unarmed. Both, however, had been fitted with reconnaissance pods, streamlined cylinders slung like bombs from their bellies containing high-speed cameras at both optical and infrared wavelengths as well as forward-looking and side-scan radar. The Sea Harrier had been designed with both fighter and reconnaissance roles in mind, and it performed both well.

Pryor brought the nose a bit higher and began angling the main engine thrust down until his Harrier seemed to be floating in mid-air, drifting forward just a bit faster than the ship was moving. He peered out the side of his canopy, studying the ship.

She was huge, a third again longer than the *Ark Royal*, and riding considerably higher above the water. Her sides looked like cliffs closely pocked by balconies on the mid-decks, by portholes in long lines both higher up along the superstructure and closer to the water, and by broad expanses of glass at places like the bridge and wrapped around the aft portion of the superstructure. A large swimming pool formed a broad, rectangular patch of azure blue on her fantail; another, smaller pool was on the very top of the superstructure, between the rise of the bridge forward and the aft deckhouse and smokestack. As the Harriers slowly moved up the ship's starboard side, he could see people. Hundreds of them, appearing on the superstructure balconies, along the Promenade Deck encircling the deckhouse, and on the sundecks amidships and aft.

"King's Palace, Alpha One," he said. "I can see a lot of passengers. Some are waving. Everything looks normal."

"Copy One."

"I'm attempting to raise them now."

"Roger that. We are monitoring civilian channels."

Shifting to the radio frequency he'd been given during pre-flight on the *Ark*, Pryor began transmitting. "*Atlantis Queen, Atlantis Queen*, this is Royal Navy Harrier Flight Alpha. Do you copy, over?"

There was no reply.

"*Atlantis Queen, Atlantis Queen*, this is Royal Navy Harrier Flight Alpha. Do you copy, over?"

As he spoke, he eased the Harrier around past the *Atlantis Queen*'s bow, barely a hundred yards in front of her. As he did so, the bow, followed by the long forward deck and the high, blocky deckhouse of the second ship, edged into view. The *Pacific Sandpiper* was securely lashed to the *Queen*'s port side. Pryor could see the hawsers connecting the vessels clearly, along with what looked like a gangway with safety rails going from the *Sandpiper*'s deck into an open hatch in the *Atlantis Queen*'s side.

"*Atlantis Queen, Atlantis Queen*, this is Royal Navy Harrier Flight Alpha. Do you copy, over?" He listened. "*Pacific Sandpiper, Pacific Sandpiper*, this is Royal Navy Harrier Flight Alpha. Do *you* copy, over?"

Damn it, why don't they respond?

Kleito's Temple, *Atlantis Queen*
48° 25' N, 9° 28' W
Saturday, 1538 hours GMT

Dr. Stephen Penrose looked up in irritation as thunder rumbled outside. His audience, he saw, was paying more attention to the view out the large forward windows of Kleito's Temple than they were to his presentation.

"The tradition of Lyonesse as we now know it," he was saying, "goes back at least to the tenth or eleventh century, when it was supposed to have sunk beneath the waves of the English Channel. Only one man—one Trevellyn—was supposed to have escaped. Riding the fastest horse of the islands, he made it to Cornwall just ahead of the oncoming flood. . . ."

Several of the people in his class were standing now, and a few had actually left their seats and were walking past him to the front windows.

"As, ah, as I was saying," he continued, "the tradition goes back to the Middle Ages, but there are hints of Lyonesse at much earlier times. The ancient Bretons, for instance, tell of the fable of Ker-Ys, the fabulous city of Ys, sunken somewhere between Cornwall and Brittany in Celtic times. . . ."

More people hurried forward, speaking excitedly to one another. Penrose put down his notes and scowled at them. It was bad enough that those security people had come to him just an hour before his lecture was due to begin, telling him that the Neptune Theater was closed and that he would have to give his presentation in this gaudily decorated restaurant. Now his audience was more interested in whatever was going on outside than they were in his talk.

"I *beg* your pardon," he said as a young couple walked past his lectern toward the front of the room. "If you don't mind, I'm trying to give a talk, here!"

He'd been flattered when the Cruise Director had approached him a month before. Penrose taught European history at London College . . . but he was also known as something of an authority on Atlantis and on other traditions associated with lost or sunken continents. Sharon Reilly had proposed that he give a whole series of lectures throughout the length of the two-week cruise, with each talk timed to be given when the *Atlantis Queen* passed close to that particular site. They were paying him only a nominal fee, but a free booking on a Mediterranean cruise had simply been too good to pass up. He'd arranged for a grad student to take over his classes and taken a short leave of absence from the college.

This morning, as the *Queen* cruised out of the English Channel with Cornwall and the Scilly Isles to the north and the Breton Peninsula to the south, he was talking about Lyonesse, a mythical island that had little connection with Atlantis save for its ultimate watery fate. *He* found the subject fascinating, especially with its rich mythic connections with the Arthurian legends. He expected others to find it interesting as well . . . or at least to show some respect for those who wanted to hear.

Turning sharply, he opened his mouth to order the small crowd forward to return to their seats and stopped, eyes wide, jaw hanging. Ahead of the ship, two gray jet aircraft appeared to be hovering in mid-air in a very un-airplanelike way. They were facing the ships, the air beneath their bellies blurred with the heat of their jet exhausts, seeming to drift backward to keep them just ahead of the *Atlantis Queen.*

"Good heavens," he said. "What do *they* want?"

His lecture forgotten, Penrose joined the other passengers at the forward windows.

Deck Twelve Terrace, *Atlantis Queen*
48° 25' N, 9° 28' W
Saturday, 1538 hours GMT

"What a shot!" Fred Doherty exclaimed.

From the terrace high above the decks of the two ships he and Petrovich had an unparalleled view of the aircraft as they slowly passed up the *Atlantis Queen*'s starboard side, then hovered for a time directly ahead, drifting backward to maintain their relative positions with the ships.

On the Grotto Pool deck below, Harper's exposure had been forgotten as both sunbathers and gawkers ran to the port side railings to watch the show. The two teenagers on the terrace leaned on the railing, pointing, jostling, yelling at each other above the howl of the two jets, and

Petrovich had to move back and lean over the railing to get a good angle past them.

What the hell is going on? Doherty thought. Those jets were British, Royal Navy, he was pretty sure. He could see the blue and red roundels just behind their enormous air intakes on the sides, the red, white, and blue roundels on the wings. He'd seen Harrier jump jets before—at an air show demonstration back in the States. The Marine Corps used those aircraft, he remembered; their ability to hover like that had always amazed him.

They were hovering now thirty or forty feet above the water, their vectored jet blasts raising clouds of swirling spray from flat-blasted patches on the sea below them.

Harrier jump jets.

What the fucking hell is going on?

Flight Harrier Alpha
48° 25' N, 9° 28' W
Saturday, 1538 hours GMT

Commander Pryor tried a few more times, then gave up. "King's Palace, Alpha One," he called. "I'm getting no response from either ship."

"Copy that, Alpha One. How about the forward deck of the freighter? Could you effect a landing there?"

He'd already been wondering about that possibility. It seemed impossible that *all* radios on *both* ships should be down, and he'd begun entertaining the notion of landing his Harrier, climbing out, walking up to the *Sandpiper*'s bridge, and demanding to know what the bloody hell was going on.

But something was nagging at him. This was more than mechanical failure, and the possibilities were making the hairs at the back of his neck stand on end. Besides, that damned helicopter was in the way.

"Ah, negative, King's Palace," he said. "There's a large helicopter parked on the forward deck, off-center toward the port side. Rotor diameter appears to be about fifty feet. The forward deck is about two hundred feet long, but he's taking his chunk out of the middle. There's also a bridge crane across the deck forward. The LZ is too tight."

The Sea Harrier jump jet was a bit under forty-eight feet long, with a wingspan of just over twenty-five feet. With its superb VTOL capabilities, he could have touched down on that deck if the ship had been stationary, but the slight pitch and roll of the vessel coupled with its forward movement through the water made the risk far greater than Pryor was willing to accept. There was also the very real danger of the Harrier's exhaust overturning the helicopter if it caught the other aircraft wrong and possibly starting a fire.

"Very well, Alpha One," the voice of the flight controller said. "RTB."

Return to base. "Roger that, King's Palace. Alpha Flight, RTB. I'll see if I can get a closer look-see on my way out."

He gentled the throttle forward, letting the Sea Harrier drift ahead. His intent was to essentially hover just off the *Sandpiper*'s port side and let the ship pass him only a few yards away. That would give him, and the electronics packed into his reconnaissance pod, an excellent close-up look at the plutonium ship and a chance to see if anything seemed wrong or out of place on board. Spick followed, keeping his aircraft farther out to give Pryor elbow room for the close-in maneuver.

As the ship passed in front of him, Pryor could see people on the bridge, shadowy figures watching him, though he could make out no details. That meant the ship was manned, however; he'd begun wondering if everyone had packed up and moved on board the *Atlantis Queen* next door. He could also see a large number of the *Queen*'s passengers watching the show from their seaside balconies and open deck spaces above the *Sandpiper*. It was eerie having all of those people watch him—just like at an air show—but with no radio contact at all.

His attention, however, was suddenly drawn to some damaged areas on the *Sandpiper*'s forward deck, between the helicopter and the crane—stanchions torn up or knocked over along the starboard side and fist-sized dents and rips in the steel deck.

Gun Mount One, *Pacific Sandpiper*
48° 25' N, 9° 28' W
Saturday, 1538 hours GMT

Abdullah Wahidi was shaking, sweat soaking his face beneath his kaffiyeh. The British warplane was less than a hundred feet away, now, and slowly drifting closer. The second aircraft was farther off, too far to see details, but the *near* one . . .

He could see the pilot's head, encased in an oxygen mask, helmet, and dark goggles, behind the clear canopy. He had the unnerving feeling that the pilot was staring directly at him.

Abdullah Wahidi had been born in the teeming camps of the Gaza, raised from infancy with an implacable hatred of the Zionists, the Jews, and taught from childhood that it was his sacred duty to die a martyr's death for Allah, the Almighty. For a time, Wahidi had rallied to the Taliban's call, fighting with the international jihadists against the Americans in Afghanistan. He'd trained at a camp in the mountains of northwestern Pakistan, where he'd learned how to operate antiaircraft weapons such as the Russian ZSU-23 and the American shoulder-fired Stinger missile.

He'd never fired anything like *this*, however, and he grasped the handle gingerly, as though he feared it would bite him. He wanted to run. . . .

The raw emotion, the terror, shamed him. He'd volunteered for this operation, knowing beyond the shadow of any doubt that he would die. He *wanted* to die. Had he not been given this opportunity to serve Allah, the mighty, the magnificent, he would have died behind the wheel of a truck laden with explosives, detonating the cargo at some embassy, military checkpoint, or other target in Afghanistan, Iraq, or Israel. Death, a glorious death that meant Paradise for him and money for his family, was what he sought more than anything else in this world.

Why, then, was he so anxious to flee?

The enemy aircraft was drifting closer. It wasn't natural for something that looked like a jet to float like a helicopter, but that was exactly what the machine was doing. His grip tightened slightly, and he moved the barrel of the 30mm cannon, tracking the target.

"Abdullah! Abdullah!" his loader cried. "He's coming closer! *He sees us!*"

"We are to hold our fire!"

The enemy aircraft began pivoting slowly, until its nose pointed directly at the gun mount, at the same time beginning to rise as the whine from its engine increased to a shrill blast of noise.

"But he *sees* us! He's going to shoot! In Allah's name, *fire! Fire!*"

Flight Harrier Alpha
48° 25' N, 9° 28' W
Saturday, 1538 hours GMT

With a dawning sense of horror, Pryor realized what it was that he was seeing. His head snapped around as he looked at the *Sandpiper*'s superstructure. A panel was hanging open just beneath the bridge level, exposing one of the ship's 30mm gun mounts at the corner of the deckhouse. The gun, sixty feet away, now, was aimed directly at him.

He knew from his preflight briefing that the *Pacific Sandpiper* was armed, but the information was strictly of academic interest, since he and Spick weren't expecting to engage the ship in combat. As Pryor stared into the black cavern of the compartment housing the cannon, however, he began to make out shapes half-masked by the shadows—two men behind the gun, looking back at him with wide and terrified eyes.

"*Tango, tango, tango!*" he shouted over the open radio channel. At the same time, he applied full right rudder and full vectored thrust, pivoting the Sea Harrier to the right and lifting it straight up. He needed to get clear of the ship before shifting to forward flight. He could feel the aircraft shuddering violently, and the view forward through his canopy was obscured by blossoming puffs of gray smoke.

The shudders grew worse, and he heard the shrill clang of metal on metal, heard the port side compressor fan shredding in a storm of metallic shards.

"Mayday! Mayday!" he called, frantically battling with the controls as his aircraft began rolling to the right and out of control. "Alpha Flight is under fire! Repeat, we are—"

And his canopy exploded in his face as the Sea Harrier began disintegrating.

Deck Twelve Terrace, *Atlantis Queen*
48° 25' N, 9° 28' W
Saturday, 1539 hours GMT

Fred Doherty heard the clatter of a heavy automatic weapon firing before he saw what was happening, and his first thought was that the two ships were grinding together, that hull metal was tearing, and he reflexively grasped the terrace's safety rail. From high up on the *Queen*'s Deck Twelve Terrace, though, he and Petrovich had an excellent view out over the *Sandpiper*'s bridge house, and they could see both Harriers hovering above the water off the smaller vessel's port side immediately beyond the freighter's bridge. The rattling thump continued as the front half of the nearer aircraft appeared to disintegrate as if in a hurricane blast; bits of metal were peeling up and off and flying away behind as the nose was engulfed in a staccato burst of small explosions.

"Tell me you're getting this, Pet!" Doherty said softly. Petrovich had been filming the approach of the two Royal Navy aircraft; his camera was locked onto the Sea Harrier as it yawed sharply right and then vanished behind the *Sandpiper*'s bridge. "*Tell me you got that!*"

Aviation fuel exploded, the fireball boiling up from behind the *Sandpiper*'s superstructure. The second Sea Harrier, farther away than the first, dropped its right wing and began accelerating rapidly, its engines howling as it streaked past the *Sandpiper* scant yards above the water. The *thud-thud-thud* of autocannon fire continued to hammer from the freighter's guns. As the Harrier hurtled toward the east, its slipstream raising a rooster tail of spray from the surface, green tracer rounds flicked toward it, throwing up gouts of spray. Petrovich had panned his camera from the fireball left past the *Sandpiper*'s superstructure, following the fleeing aircraft as it vanished toward the horizon.

Silently Doherty put one hand on Petrovich's shoulder and pointed. As the *Queen* and the *Sandpiper* continued plowing forward, the wreckage of the downed aircraft slid into view astern of the freighter, its tail sticking up out of the water at a sharp angle, aviation gasoline spreading around it and burning furiously. Petrovich kept filming as Doherty scanned the water, looking for some sign, *any* sign, that the pilot had ejected or managed to get clear. He wondered if he should throw a life ring . . . or get help . . .

Then he began to realize through the mind-clouding shock that the *Sandpiper* had *attacked* those aircraft, had deliberately opened fire on them and shot one of them down.

"My God!" was all he was able to say, his voice tightening as he choked out the words.

"We'll . . . we'll need to get this out right away by satellite," Petrovich said.

"I don't think so," Doherty managed to reply. His thoughts were racing furiously. Ever since the rendezvous with the *Pacific Sandpiper*, things had been *wrong*. The two ships lashed together and heading southwest, without explanation from captain or crew; the fact that they'd left the area where the other ship had sunk so quickly; the odd lack of security on the sundeck just now; and now *this*. "Jim, I think we've been hijacked!"

"You're shitting me!"

"Damn it, that other ship shot that plane down!"

He could see the realization working its way through the cameraman's thoughts. "Holy Christ!"

The film crew had an arrangement with Royal Sky Line to transmit footage and interviews back to CNE using the *Queen*'s onboard satellite communications system and didn't have a satellite transmitter of their own.

"Look," he said. "If we *have* been hijacked, they'll be in control of the radio room. And they might not like it that we got those pictures. We need to hide the tape."

"Yeah. Yeah. Hide the tape. . . ."

Something was happening on the Grotto Pool deck. Two men wearing blue and white security uniforms had just burst out of the Grotto Restaurant. They were carrying AK-47 assault rifles, and they were shouting at the passengers gathered at the railing, "You! You! *All* of you! Move back! *Move back!*"

The passengers were screaming. "Jesus!" Fred Doherty said. It was a hijacking, a hijacking in progress. *"Get that!"*

Doherty pointed the camera again as the gunmen herded the screaming crowd back from the railing and past the pool. At least four of the women, including Harper, were still topless, were trying to cover themselves with their arms. One of the gunmen picked up a bright red beach towel from one of the chairs and flung it at one of them. "Filthy Western sluts!" Doherty heard him scream. "Cover yourselves decently!" As the women snatched up towels or bikini tops, the gunmen waited, then started herding all of the passengers toward the restaurant.

One gunman glanced up and saw Doherty, the two teenagers, and Petrovich with his camera on the terrace above. The gunman aimed his rifle. "You, up there! Do not move!"

Doherty slowly raised his hands and took a step back from the railing. "I think we'd better do what he says."

A moment later, he heard the sound of running footsteps at his back.

Promenade Deck, *Atlantis Queen*
48° 25' N, 9° 28' W
Saturday, 1539 hours GMT

Carolyn Howorth was on the Promenade Deck, on the port side forward, just in front of the *Queen*'s towering white superstructure. She'd come out here for a better look as soon as she'd heard the thunder of the two approaching jets and seen them move past her stateroom porthole on the starboard side. She'd jogged down three decks, cut across the atrium and the onboard shopping mall, and emerged on the Promenade just as the two Sea Harriers began drifting past on the far side of the *Pacific Sandpiper.*

Hundreds of other passengers were already on the Promenade, and she had to shoulder forward a bit to get a good view. Deck Three, the Promenade Deck, was above the Sandpiper's deck alongside, but about at the same level as the freighter's bridge. She reached the railing just as one of the Harriers came apart in a hail of 30mm cannon fire.

Passengers around her began screaming, some streaming back for the imagined shelter of the *Queen*'s interior, others just pushing away from the port side railing, as if they were afraid the *Sandpiper* was about to turn those unexpected guns on them next. Turning, she looked up at the *Queen*'s bridge high overhead, but she was too close to see in through those high, slanted windows.

She wasn't certain what was happening, but she knew she had to get back to her stateroom. She needed to use her laptop to get in touch with either GCHQ or their American cousins, the NSA, and she needed to do it *now*.

Once back inside the *Queen*'s superstructure, however, Howorth found the passageways too jammed with humanity for her to make any progress. By the time she reached the Atrium and the Grand Staircase, she wasn't able to move at all. Instead, she ducked back into the ship's Starbucks and began considering her options.

Her laptop was in her stateroom, on Deck six, three levels up. There was a service stairway behind her, she remembered, that would take her up to six and, better still, on to Deck eleven, and Security. If it was less packed than the Grand Staircase in the Atrium, maybe she could find David Llewellyn.

That staircase would also take her down two decks, to the First Deck, where, she remembered, a computer center offered Internet access to passengers.

Two decks down was better than either three or eight decks up.

Emerging once more into the current of panicked passengers, she headed for the computer center.

14

Deck One, *Atlantis Queen*
North Atlantic Ocean
48° 25' N, 9° 28' W
Saturday, 1539 hours GMT

THOMAS MITCHELL AND SAMUEL Franks were in the ship's computer center when Mitchell heard the far-off drumroll of thunder. On this sunny Saturday afternoon, the two of them were the only people in the computer center.

The center, located off the large, broad atrium on the First Deck through which they'd first entered the ship, provided shipboard passengers with a large number of computers and access, by way of the *Queen's* own server system, to a satellite link and the Internet.

Franks was using that access now to check SOCA, Interpol, and Europol databases for names he'd gotten from the Purser's Office that morning, a list of the roughly nine hundred crew and staff people who worked on board this floating hotel. Mitchell was using another computer to complete and transmit a report for MI5 on what the two agents had accomplished so far on this cruise, which was, essentially, nothing. When he was done with that chore, he planned to help Franks divvy up the names and start searching, looking for anyone with previous convictions for selling drugs, smuggling, association with criminal elements, hell, for failure to use the zebra crossing zones at Piccadilly Circus if he had to. There had to be *something*.

Mitchell dismissed the sound at first as thunder, but after a few moments he realized that he could still hear it. "Hey, Franks? You hear that?"

"Huh? Whadjasay?"

"That rumble. You hear it?"

"Sounds like a jet."

"Yeah. Out here? I'm going up on deck and have a look."

"Suit yourself," Franks said, submerging again into his monitor display.

Mitchell emerged from the computer center and into chaos. The broad, sweeping curves of the Grand Staircase to his left was packed with people, some going up, some going down, all looking panicky. The Atrium itself was a mob scene. He estimated that there were two or three hundred people packed into that space, all of them going *somewhere*, but looking as though they had no idea as to where.

He looked around for a security uniform. Whatever had just happened, shipboard security was going to need some backup. He doubted that they had the training or the experience to deal with a full-fledged riot, and this crowd had the look of a riot in the making.

God, what had happened? Was the ship sinking? Unlikely in clear weather, and there would have been an announcement over the PA system if there was a problem.

Reaching out, he grabbed the arm of an older man in a bright-colored T-shirt and white slacks; a much younger woman beside him was clinging to his other arm, her face streaked with tears. "Hey!" Mitchell shouted, trying to make himself heard above the noise of the crowd. "What's going on?"

"They shot down that plane!" the woman shrieked. *"They shot down that plane!"*

The man shook his head, his eyes distant, as if he was in shock. "God!" he said. "Oh, God!" The two pulled away from Mitchell and kept pushing ahead through the mob.

He thought he saw the blue and white uniform of a shipboard security man going up the Grand Staircase. Plunging ahead, Mitchell elbowed through the crowd, making his way after the man. Around him, people shouted and screamed, and he caught occasional fragments in the racket: "Those were *guns*! Big *machine* guns!" "Why would they shoot down Royal Navy jets?" *"They shot down those planes!"*

The guns, Mitchell decided, must be the 30mm cannons carried by the *Pacific Sandpiper*. The *Queen*, he knew, was unarmed. But Royal Navy aircraft?

Halfway up the staircase, a voice boomed from the PA system, "Attention! Attention, please! May I have your attention, please?"

The surging, jostling crowd slowly came to a stop, voices falling silent, faces turned toward the ceiling as though they were searching for the source of that voice.

"May I have your attention, please?" the voice continued, sounding louder now as the crowd noise dwindled. "Everything is under control. There is no need for panic. Repeat . . . there is no need for panic!"

The crowd had stopped moving, now, but the rumble of voices was beginning to rise once more. People were murmuring to one another, still uncertain, still frightened. A few continued to push ahead through the stalled mass of humanity.

"The freighter *Pacific Sandpiper* possesses an automated antiaircraft weapon system," the voice said in measured, reassuring tones. "It's a kind of robot that automatically tracks aircraft with radar and, when the safety is off, it automatically shoots the aircraft down.

There has been some kind of *terrible* accident, which many of you witnessed just now. One of the British jets came too close to the *Pacific Sandpiper* and one of those automatic weapons locked on and shot it down.

"There is absolutely no cause for alarm. Everything is under control, and the malfunctioning weapon has been locked down. Our ship's officers are assisting in investigating what went wrong.

"The best thing all of you can do is return to your staterooms immediately and stay there. We will keep you updated on developments as they occur. Due to the serious nature of this emergency, however, Ship's Security personnel have special police powers. Please cooperate fully with anyone wearing a blue and white security uniform, or the uniform of a ship's officer.

"Return to your staterooms immediately, please."

Mitchell felt rather than heard something like a collective sigh arising from the hundreds of people around him and crowding the Atrium just below. The crowd collectively seemed to sag, like puppets relaxing against slackened strings.

"Special police powers?" Special police cock was more like it. There was something decidedly not right about that announcement.

From the sound of things, a Royal Navy aircraft had just been downed outside, but blaming it on an accidental firing of a robot antiaircraft system was also cock.

There was, Mitchell knew, an automated weapons system like the one described just now. It was called CIWS, for close-in weapon system, and was pronounced "sea-whiz" in military-speak. It consisted of a multiple-barreled Gatling gun mounted inside an upright cylinder with an astonishing rate of fire—as high as fifty rounds per second. It was used as a missile defense system, particularly on aircraft carriers. It was *never* installed on a civilian vessel.

He decided to make his way up to Security and see if he could find David Llewellyn.

Security Office, *Atlantis Queen*
48° 25' N, 9° 28' W
Saturday, 1558 hours GMT

Yusef Khalid leaned over the shoulder of one of his men, studying the TV monitor on the console before him. At the moment, the camera was looking down onto the Atrium on Deck Two, as the crowds slowly thinned. Nearby, another monitor showed the length of a long passageway on Deck Seven, where people were unlocking their stateroom doors and stepping inside. The fantail was clear now, as was the Atlantean Grotto high atop the ship's superstructure. "Security guards" had also been sent out onto the Promenade Deck to herd the sightseers inside.

Six of Khalid's men were sitting at the line of monitors along the console, using security cameras mounted throughout the ship to watch as the crowds dispersed. It was bad, *very* bad, that some idiot on the *Pacific Sandpiper* had lost his nerve and shot down that Harrier, and Khalid had already sent word to Abdel Ramid to have the responsible person sent to the *Atlantis Queen*'s bridge to see him. He hadn't decided yet what punishment to mete out for that extraordinary lapse of judgment. . . .

The operational plan was divided into five distinct phases. Phase one had been the actual infiltration of both the *Atlantis Queen* and the *Pacific Sandpiper*, with IJI members disguised as security personnel or deckhands and staying very much out of sight. Phase two had commenced with the destruction of the *Ishikari* and the takeover of the bridge, security, and engineering sections of both target ships.

Phase three had involved tying the two ships together

and proceeding southwest as quickly as possible, and was actually rather open-ended in terms of the operational time line. Khalid was all too aware that the operation could easily fail at this point for the simple reason that it would be all but impossible for twenty-four armed terrorists to control the nearly three thousand crewmen and passengers on board the *Atlantis Queen* if they panicked or if they got wind of what was happening too early.

The longer the passengers on the cruise ship could be kept ignorant of what was going on, the better; Khalid was determined not to have a repeat, on a far larger scale, of the debacle of Flight 93.

If that Palestinian idiot on the *Pacific Sandpiper* had not lost his nerve and opened fire, those Royal Navy fighters would have snooped around for a bit, helpless to do anything but look, then returned to England, where the information gleaned by their reconnaissance pods could be analyzed. Khalid fully expected the two hijacked ships to be intercepted by naval warships, but with luck that wouldn't have happened before mid-day tomorrow.

The hijackers had maintained radio silence, knowing that there might be key phrases or code words that would reassure the ships' owners in England that all was well; Ghailiani had told Khalid that there were such codes, but that only the ship's captain and senior security people knew them. Rather than risk having those people give him the wrong codes under interrogation—there would be no way to check what they told him even if they were tortured—he'd ordered radio silence. The enemy might suspect something was wrong, but they wouldn't know.

And the longer Khalid could maintain that balance of uncertainty, the better for the operation.

Khalid straightened up, then walked down the line of terminals, looking at each glowing screen.

"Wait a moment," Khalid said, pointing at one monitor. "Who is that? What is he doing?"

The screen showed a single man in a rumpled suit

coat, sitting alone in a room filled with computer screens and keyboards. He appeared to be alone at the only live monitor.

"Computer center, sir," Inan Al-Shafi replied. "Deck One. He's been in there all morning. There was someone else with him a little while ago."

"Can you zoom in on the screen?"

"Maybe," the man said. He typed a command into his keyboard, then held his mouse, turning the wheel with his forefinger. The camera view began closing in, peering over the passenger's shoulder. The monitor flickered with a bright, fluorescent glare. Khalid felt he could almost see what was on it—it looked like a list, in neat blocks of text, each with a small graphic or photograph. But the resolution was too poor to make out what it was.

"I have a list of people who've checked into the computer center this morning," Hamud Haqqani, at the next workstation over, announced. "There were only two. Samuel Franks . . . SOCA. And Thomas Mitchell, MI5."

"Well, well," Khalid said. "SOCA and MI5? What are *they* doing aboard?"

"There is a note attached to their passenger records, sir," Haqqani said. "They were given passage two days ago so that they could investigate the murder of a ship's officer on the Southampton docks without delaying the departure." His hands began clattering over his keyboard. "I should be able to call up what he's looking at."

"Do it."

Hamud Haqqani was an IJI Brigade member recruited from Islamabad, Pakistan, where he'd worked for a major international banking concern as an IT specialist. Khalid had several computer experts on his team—six of them were sitting here in this room—but Haqqani was undoubtedly the most brilliant, and the most skillful.

He typed in a final line of code, and his monitor flashed over to a ship's personnel record. Each member of the ship's crew had an entry, complete with security clearances, a bio that included their employment history, drug-testing records, police, health, and pay records, and a small black-and-white photograph. The image on the screen scrolled up suddenly, without input from Haqqani. The passenger—Mitchell or Franks—appeared to be going through the entire list of nine hundred personnel.

"What is he looking for?" Khalid wondered.

"If he's on board investigating the death of that officer," Haqqani said, "he may be looking for police or arrest records. They probably suspect someone in the crew of being involved in drug smuggling."

For Khalid, that incident on the docks two days ago had been the weakest point of the operational plan. Involving the police and even SOCA in an investigation of the drugs and money found on the pier might well have delayed the *Atlantis Queen*'s departure, which would have complicated her role in the operation with the *Pacific Sandpiper* and possibly eliminated her from the plan entirely. By employing that Turkish smuggler Khalid had hoped to throw the British authorities off the track, convince them that the case had been solved, or at least was on its way to a solution, with the Turk's arrest.

And there'd simply been no other way to sneak several tons of high explosive on board the *Atlantis Queen*.

"Keep an eye on him, and on what he's reading," Khalid said. He turned and left the Security Center, making his way up a level to the bridge. Tatari, Musa, and Nejmuddin were among the men there, standing to one side, wearing shipboard security uniforms, including gun belts. "You three," Khalid said to them. "Go down to Deck One, the computer center. There is at least one man there, possibly two. They may be armed, so be careful. Bring them to me here."

"Sir!" the three Brigade soldiers snapped in near unison, and then they hurried off the bridge.

Ever since the assault group had taken over the bridge, they'd been finding the *Atlantis Queen*'s security personnel, the *real* ones, and taking them, one by one, to the Neptune Theater, where they were being kept under close guard. The ship's officers were being held in one of the ship's two conference centers on Deck One, as were those few crew members who'd realized something was wrong and come to the bridge or to Security to report it. At this point, the *Atlantis Queen* was completely under the hijackers' control. Only the passengers, the hotel staff, and a few dozen crew personnel on the engineering levels and in the service sections remained free, and with a little luck they could be kept ignorant for a few precious hours more.

And after that, it wouldn't matter *what* they knew.

That would be the beginning of phase four.

**Bridge, *Atlantis Queen*
48° 25' N, 9° 28' W
Saturday, 1614 hours GMT**

They led Fred Doherty and James Petrovich forward to the bridge, passing through two separate checkpoints where one of the men had to slide a card through a reader. He wondered how they'd managed to get those security IDs. At the final checkpoint, the gunman who appeared to be in charge slid his card through a scanner *and* pressed his thumb against a print reader; somehow, these people had gained high-level security access throughout the ship.

They *had* to be terrorists. Nothing else made sense—men with assault rifles herding passengers around like cattle, the shoot-down of that Harrier. And his assumption was validated the moment he stepped onto the bridge.

Doherty and Petrovich stepped into a small whirlwind of drama. A bearded man in a blue and white security uniform was screaming into the face of a man in what looked like combat fatigues and with a red-and-white-checked Arab-style kaffiyeh over his head.

"Majnun! Mahbul!" the security guard screamed. He glanced around as Doherty walked in, opened his mouth, then seemed to reconsider. "Idiot!" he said in English, his voice lowered. "Because of you the entire operation has been jeopardized! I think, for you . . . the special technical unit."

The color appeared to drain from the other man's swarthy face, and his eyes grew large. "Ia!" he screamed. He then dropped to his knees and loosed a babbling torrent of a foreign language far too swift for Doherty to catch more than isolated syllables. The security guard looked at one of the other uniformed men and jerked his head. Two security men came forward, grabbed the kneeling man, and hoisted him to his feet. Doherty and Petrovich stepped aside as the security men marched the blubbering man off the bridge.

The leader of the group nailed Doherty with a glare. "And you are . . . who?"

"Fred Doherty. CNE. This is my cameraman, James Petrovich."

"CN . . . CNN?"

"Not quite. CNE. Cable Network Entertainment."

"My men thought you might be television reporters. They saw your camera."

"Yeah, and I'll ask you to tell them to be careful of it," Petrovich said. "That thing cost eighty grand and I'd rather it not come out of my paycheck!"

"At the moment," the leader said slowly, "you two have more important things to be concerned about than paychecks."

"You're terrorists," Doherty said with what he hoped was an emotionless, matter-of-fact delivery. "You've hijacked these ships."

"You're very perceptive, Mr. Doherty."

Doherty's mind was racing frantically. "And you *need* us!"

"Oh? And what makes you think that?"

"Easy. Your men spotted the camera, and promptly hauled us up here to see you. I figure you're going to want to transmit some sort of ransom demand to the world, right? We can help you with that!"

"Actually, we brought our own cameras along, and we have the transmission facilities of this ship. Had we known *you* were going to be on this voyage, perhaps we would have planned otherwise. This . . . CNE. What is it?"

"It's like CNN. Main offices in Hollywood, not Atlanta. Not as big as CNN, of course. Not as well known. But we have connections! And a news studio. We could set you up with a live feed, interview you, let you put your demands to the right people, the whole schmeer! Like I say, you *do* need us."

The leader took three swift steps forward, and suddenly his face was inches from Doherty's, the man's eyes glaring into his with a dark heat, the voice low and dangerous. "Do *not* presume to tell me what I need, Mr. Doherty. This operation has been planned for years, with attention to every detail. You and your tall friend here are two passengers among two thousand. Two *hostages* among two thousand, I should say. And if you get in my way or simply make me angry, I will have you executed instantly. A number of people have been killed already to carry out this plan. Two more are *nothing*! Do we understand one another?"

"Y-yes."

"Good. Because, as it happens, we may take you up on your kind offer of help." He nodded at one of the guards. "Room ten-oh-two. Watch them."

And they were taken off the bridge and into the passageway leading aft.

Deck One, *Atlantis Queen*
48° 25' N, 9° 28' W
Saturday, 1617 hours GMT

The crowds in the ship's public areas were dispersing by
the time Carolyn Howorth reached the First Deck and
walked aft toward the computer room. She'd paused in
the stairwell to listen to the PA announcement, then continued on her way down. That bit about "special police
powers" didn't sound right, nor did she believe that what
had happened to that Harrier outside was an accident.

She was walking past the *Atlantis Queen*'s Sea God-
dess Hair and Beauty Salon, the Interconnexions computer center just ahead.

Something was wrong. Three men in khaki uniforms
and black berets were ahead of her, opening the center's
door. Two, she saw, had AK-47 assault rifles slung over
their shoulders, a most un-British weapon to bring aboard a
British cruise ship. The third held a drawn automatic pistol.

Fading back a few steps, she moved into the entrance
of the hair salon, watching as one of the armed men stood
guard and the other two pushed the door open and vanished inside. Several tense moments passed, and then the
two reappeared, with a civilian between them. The man
was short and had the look of an accountant, with glasses,
sports coat, and a balding scalp, but as he struggled in
their grip, his coat fell open and she noticed that he had a
shoulder holster rig on underneath . . . and that the holster
was empty.

Not an accountant, then, but police . . . possibly a de-
tective investigating the Darrow murder. Then she remembered her conversation with David Llewellyn the
previous night and him talking about two MI5 men on
board, one of them seconded to SOCA.

They'd used a plastic zip strip to tie the civilian's wrists
behind his back.

Quickly she reached into her hip pocket and pulled out

her mobile—her cell phone as her American colleagues would have called it. Pretending to look up a number, she snapped several photos with the camera function before putting the phone to her ear and pretending to talk to someone.

Someone back at GCHQ or Fort Meade might be able to get an ID on one or more of those thugs. They *weren't* security; of that much she was certain.

The fact that they'd grabbed that man in the computer room led her to suspect that it wouldn't be safe using the ship's Internet center to call home; the ship's Security Department likely was able to monitor computer use, and that might have been what brought those three down here. She continued pretending to talk on her phone as the three armed men marched their prisoner off, passing her just a few feet away.

She waited until they were gone, then found a stairway and started climbing back to Deck Six and her stateroom.

Back in her stateroom, minutes later, she opened up her laptop, which was slightly more than it seemed. The battery pack was actually a powerful satellite uplink unit that would allow her to communicate directly with both Menwith Hill or with Fort Meade. A slender cable unreeled from a spool inside; laid out across the desk, it served as the satlink antenna.

Strange soldiers on board the ship, rounding up select people, binding their hands, and leading them off. PA announcements invoking special police powers.

The ship had been hijacked. Of that Howorth was certain. And it was up to her to get the word out.

All regular communications to and from the ship, she knew, went through the radio room adjacent to the bridge, which was why she couldn't simply use her mobile to call Menwith Hill. The TV sets in the staterooms were not working—she'd already checked—probably because the people on the bridge now didn't want the passengers seeing news broadcasts from ashore right now.

Typing swiftly, Carolyn Howorth entered her code designation, routing code, and an urgent flag. She attached the photos she'd taken with her phone, then began writing her report.

Terrorists have taken control of the cruise ship Atlantis Queen *and the freighter* Pacific Sandpiper she wrote. *The terrorists are well armed and the operation appears to be well planned. . . .*

Security Office, *Atlantis Queen*
48° 06′ N, 9° 37′ W
Saturday, 1619 hours GMT

Thomas Mitchell emerged from a stairwell on the Eleventh Deck forward, just down the passageway from Ship's Security. A dozen feet down the corridor was a locked steel door with security check hardware beside it—an ID card reader and a thumbprint scanner.

There was also a push-to-talk intercom that would let him request to see someone from Security, but he hadn't yet decided whether he should take that option. He was moving cautiously and once, on the way up the stairs, he'd stopped when he'd heard a door bang open far above him and waited until the sound of footsteps receded again.

Something was very, *very* wrong on board this ship. The more he thought about it, the more suspicious he was of that PA announcement a few moments before. He was determined to track down David Llewellyn and find out what was happening.

But he also wasn't convinced that it was a good idea to call attention to himself just now.

He heard something rustle behind him, and he turned sharply. Someone was coming around the corner of an intersection down the passageway aft, and an instant before they came into view, he ducked back into the stairwell.

There was a small, square window in the door. Mitchell

pressed himself up against the door and edged his head just enough to one side to glimpse movement in the passageway outside. Two figures strode past, their shadows cast by overhead fluorescents momentarily sweeping across the glass. Stepping to the other side of the window, he pushed his face up against the glass in time to see the backs of two men walking toward the security checkpoint.

Both men were wearing khaki uniforms. Both had AK-47 assault rifles slung over their shoulders and had small, military-type radios clipped to their belts. One wore a black beret, the other a white and gray head cloth, an Arab kaffiyeh, held in place by the braided cord called an *iqal*.

The one with the beret pulled an ID card out of a breast pocket and slid it through the reader. He then pressed his thumb against the scanner, and Mitchell heard the metallic click as the steel door popped open.

Terrorists, with ID cards and thumbprints on file giving them access to Ship's Security. Mitchell reached inside his jacket and pulled out his pistol, a service-issue SIG P226, and quietly pulled the slide back, chambering a round.

Think! Think! . . .

If terrorists were in control of Ship's Security, they were already in control of the bridge, and probably engineering as well. The freighter tied up alongside must belong to them now as well; probably terrorists had come aboard the *Queen* from the *Sandpiper*. This operation clearly had been carefully planned and orchestrated, and must involve a large number of well-armed men.

Think it through! Think!

The Ship's Security personnel must all be dead or have been captured, if the terrorists were this much in evidence. Mitchell realized at that moment that he might well be the only free man on board the *Atlantis Queen* who was armed and alert to the terrorist threat. He couldn't take on the entire terrorist group . . . but perhaps he could get intelligence on the hijackers that would help a CT team. If he could get in contact with MI5 or military intelligence, he might be able to pass them critical information about the takeover, including the very fact that the *Atlantis Queen* and the *Pacific Sandpiper* had been hijacked at sea.

First he needed to find Sam Franks and bring him into this.

Carefully he began tiptoeing back down the stairs.

15

Satellite Imaging Center
National Reconnaissance Office
Chantilly, Virginia
Saturday, 1248 hours EST

"WE'RE ABOUT ONE MINUTE out, Mr. Rubens."

William Rubens nodded, looking up at the large flat-panel screen dominating one wall of the Imaging Center. The room, with its high-tech collection of SPARC work-stations and large-screen monitors, was located in the ultra-secure underground levels of the NRO's new head-quarters in Chantilly, Virginia, one of the most highly secret offices in an entire sprawling complex of top-secret installations. It was here that real-time imagery from space was processed and displayed.

"This is from Argus Twelve?" Rubens asked.

"Yes, sir." Chris Atwilder was an assistant director of the NRO, in charge of digital imaging. "We put it onto a new orbit fifty-five minutes ago. We should have a good look at the site in . . . thirty seconds."

Argus 12 was part of a constellation of seventeen highly classified surveillance satellites, each orbiting the Earth once each ninety minutes at an altitude of between 120 and 160 miles. Although both the NSA and the National Reconnaissance Office continued to vigorously deny it, Argus—named for the hundred-eyed guardian of Greek myth—could give better than one-centimeter resolution in real time, day or night. Using synthetic aperture radar, Argus could image a basketball through any weather, making it an invaluable eye-in-the-sky shared by the NSA, the CIA, the DIA, and several other U.S. spy and law enforcement agencies.

At the moment, the screen showed a wide-angle view of the ocean, as if seen from a considerable height. The weather in the target area was clear at the moment, though the software could blend incoming data in several radar, infrared, and ultraviolet as well as optical wavelengths in order to build up a composite image of what was on the ground, peering down through clouds, fog, and all but the heaviest rain.

Though there were special secure channels by which Rubens could have watched processed feeds from the NRO back in his own office or on the Art Room main screens, he'd driven out to Chantilly after his briefing session at the White House that morning specifically to see the raw feeds as they came down from the satellite. General Ronald McLean, DIRNSA, the Director of the NSA, had personally phoned Rubens before he'd left for the White House that morning. If there was a problem with that British plutonium transport, McLean wanted to know about it yesterday. Plutonium ships made the trip from Britain or France to Japan about once a year, and the National Security Agency made each voyage a high priority. With plutonium enough on that one ship to manufacture sixty fair-sized nuclear weapons, every intelligence organization on the planet was likely keeping close tabs on it.

"We have the target on radar," a technician reported from a nearby console. "Cameras are slaved and locked."

"High-speed recorders are running," another technician reported.

And there it was, drifting across the screen from top to bottom, with blocks of technical data winking on in columns at the upper left, giving time and date, range, coordinates, and camera resolution data. The resolution was crystal-sharp, the image computer enhanced to show every detail.

"That's the *Pacific Sandpiper*," Atwilder said. "What's that bigger ship tied up alongside?"

"The *Atlantis Queen*," Rubens replied. "Cruise ship. She was last reported on her way to assist in SAR at sea."

"They're lashed together. Look . . . you can see the hawsers."

"And that helicopter still on the *Sandpiper*'s forward deck," Rubens added. "That *is* odd."

"Crewmen on the decks of both ships," Atwilder said. "Can we zoom in close on them for a closer look?"

"We could . . . but let's wait. We have only a few seconds on this pass. Once we have the whole pass recorded, we can process the imagery and give you a zoom look at anything you want, for as long as you want."

"Understood."

The first Argus shot of the two ships, the photo Rubens had used in his briefing at the White House, had been a single shot, one of a series designed to keep loose tabs on the *Pacific Sandpiper*. There'd been enough anomalies in that image—the helicopter, the two ships lashed together—that McClean had ordered a detailed run with the next available Argus satellite, gleaning mountains of data at the highest resolution possible.

Still, there didn't seem to be anything overtly wrong or out of place, nothing except that civilian helicopter where it didn't belong and the fact that those two ships were lashed together and steaming southwest at ten to fifteen knots, if that double wake was any indication. The *Sandpiper* was on course; the *Atlantis Queen* decidedly was not. Maybe they'd been tied together during the SAR operation a few hours ago—it would make sense if injured people had to be transferred from one ship to the other—but there was no reason the two should have kept racing for the horizon together. There was every reason not to do so, in fact; the last report from GCHQ indicated that a dozen or so ships had reached the spot where the *Ishikari* had blown up and sank hours before, and they were still finding survivors, miraculously, clinging to bits of flotsam in the water.

No, as he'd told the NSC people, there was something *very* wrong here. He'd already given orders to put Black Cat Bravo on full alert. If he had to, he'd put a team on board covertly and have them check things out.

With two and a half tons of plutonium at stake, it was best to be certain.

The two ships slid off the bottom of the screen, and the eye-in-the-sky was again staring down at blue water. "Thanks, Chris," he said. "Route that through to Desk Three as soon as it's processed, will you?"

"Will do, Mr. Rubens. The Company's on my back for a copy, too. So's the NCTC."

"Of course they are."

Rubens checked out through several levels of security and walked back to his car in the NRO's north parking lot. As he walked, he pulled out his cell phone and saw that there was an urgent message waiting for him. Cell phones had to be switched off *and* surrendered to security inside the NRO's precincts; someone had been trying to reach him while he was inside.

That someone was Jeff Rockman, back in the Art Room.

"Rubens," he said after calling back and getting Rockman on the line. "What do you have?"

"We have all hell breaking out in the Atlantic, sir," Rockman replied. "The *Pacific Sandpiper* just shot down a Royal Navy aircraft that was checking them out. A second aircraft made it back to its carrier with some rather interesting film footage. The working assumption is that terrorists have hijacked both of those ships."

"And NCTC has just put us all on a Broken Arrow alert."

Broken Arrow. That was a holdover from the Cold War era, but still in force today. "Broken Arrow" was the code for any unexpected event involving nuclear weapons or radiological nuclear weapon components, including, among other things, the theft, seizure, loss, or destruction of significant quantities of weapons-grade plutonium.

"I'm on my way," Rubens told him. He did a fast calculation; he was in plenty of time to beat the Washington Beltway rush as he made the trek from northern Virginia to Fort Meade. "I'll be there in forty minutes."

PNTL Headquarters
Risley, Cheshire, England
Saturday, 1725 hours GMT

"Lia!" Charlie Dean exclaimed, faking surprise. "What's a gorgeous woman like you doing in a place like this?"

"Same as you, probably, Charlie," she said with an impish smile. "The voices in my head told me to come here."

Dean grinned back at her. Like him, Lia had a communications implant in the bone behind her ear that linked her to Desk Three's Art Room back at Fort Meade. Rubens himself had called both of them earlier, directing them to the small town of Risley, just south of the M62 in Cheshire, England, and the gleaming offices of Pacific Nuclear Transport Limited. After they had been checked through the security booth upstairs, an armed guard had escorted them down several levels to a second checkpoint, then through to this large and expensively furnished waiting room. Large photographs of the PNTL fleet adorned two of the oak panel walls, while a third featured a Mercator projection of the world showing PNTL's global shipping routes.

Only moments after Charlie and Lia arrived, a male secretary appeared to usher them through into the offices of Sir Vincent Wallace, the vice president in charge of PNTL security. With him was another peer, Sir Charles Mayhew, vice president and Chief Operations Officer of Royal Sky Line, and a military officer, General Alexander R. Saunders, representing the UKSF, the British Directorate of Special Forces.

"Mr. Dean, Ms. DeFrancesca," Wallace said cordially, "welcome to England."

"Thank you, Sir Vincent," Dean replied. "Good to be here. I'm sorry it couldn't have been under more pleasant circumstances."

"I confess, Sir Vincent," General Saunders said, "that I'm somewhat at a loss as to just *why* these people are here. No offense to you two, but we are quite capable of handling our own piracy problems."

"Of course you are, General," Dean replied. He'd already been briefed by the Art Room on Saunders and his refusal of a formal offer of help from the American President. "But perhaps the U.S. intelligence community can offer you a bit of technical assistance along the way."

According to Rubens, the British Prime Minister had agreed to Desk Three's participation in what was now being called Operation Harrow Storm earlier that afternoon, and Saunders had already effectively been overruled. It would still be necessary to handle the man carefully; he had the reputation for being something of a prima donna and a fierce defender of his own bureaucratic turf.

"What technical assistance?" Saunders demanded. "We have your NRO satellite data, and we know where the two target ships are. All that remains is to put together an assault team to go in and secure those vessels."

"What we have in mind," Lia said, "is actually getting a small reconnaissance team on board the cruise ship. That team will then be in a position to inform and coordinate the main assault."

"Wouldn't . . . wouldn't you be risking everything that way?" Charles Mayhew asked. He was perspiring heavily, his face florid. "I mean, if the terrorists get wind of what's happening . . ."

"Having decent intelligence going in increases the chances of success with the primary assault by at least threefold," Dean said. "We also have a unique opportunity here. There are enough civilians on board the *Atlantis Queen* that our recon team might be able to slip in among them unnoticed."

"Wait, wait," Wallace said, interrupting. "You're saying that your team could be on board that ship and the terrorists wouldn't even know it?"

"And just how would you manage that, may I ask?" Saunders said.

"These people aren't cleared for Black Cat," the voice of Jeff Rockman whispered in Dean's ear.

I know what the hell I'm doing, Dean thought, but he couldn't make an audible reply. It was tough, sometimes, trying to hold a conversation with invisible people looking over your shoulder, second-guessing you every step of the way.

"We've had combat teams looking at the problem already," Dean told the others. "We essentially have three options for I&I."

" 'I and I'?" Mayhew asked. "What's that?"

"Insertion and infiltration," Wallace told him.

"Although some military types will tell you it stands for 'intoxication and intercourse,' " Dean put in. *Wallace must have military experience,* he thought. That made sense if he was the VP of security for a company that processed nuclear fuel. "Our choices are to board the *Atlantis Queen* up the side from an ASDS, to approach from astern in a silenced helicopter, or to drop onto an open part of her deck by parachute."

"Aren't you forgetting something?" Saunders said. He sounded irritatingly smug. "Your target is moving at fifteen knots."

"He didn't say it would be *easy*," Lia said.

"What is an . . . what you said," Mayhew asked. "A-D something?"

"ASDS," Lia told him. "Advanced SEAL Delivery System. It's a small, dry-deck submarine that can carry sixteen Navy SEALs and their equipment."

"A larger submarine," Dean said, "one of our *Ohio*-class special warfare subs, would carry the ASDS close to the *Atlantis Queen*. We'd probably have to disable the target vessel, at least temporarily, possibly by fouling her screws." He glanced at Mayhew. "Unfortunately, the *Atlantis Queen* is driven by two azimuth thrusters—Azipods—rather than conventional screws. They're shrouded in such a way that it will be *very* difficult to foul them with a net or length of line, and we would have to damage or destroy both at the same time. That makes that approach very difficult, and extremely high risk."

"Even if you took out the *Queen*'s Azipods, the *Pacific Sandpiper*'s screws would be intact," Wallace pointed out. "The speed of the two ships together would be greatly reduced. I'm not sure how well the *Sandpiper* would manage pushing both the *Queen* and itself—that's almost one hundred thousand tonnes—but they would still be making way."

"Exactly," Dean said. "Which is why our ops planning team has suggested going in by parachute.

"The team would use a HAHO drop from several miles off and several miles up.

"HAHO is 'High Altitude, High Opening,'" he added for Mayhew's benefit. "They would use ram-air steerable chutes that would let them fly in to the target."

"But . . . but the ship is *moving*," Saunders insisted.

"It also has extremely good security systems," Mayhew added. "Cameras overlooking all of the public areas, the Promenade Deck, the swimming pool decks. How could you land your team without being seen?"

"The ship's movement is not a major problem," Dean said. He held up his hand, palm down, demonstrating an approach to the tabletop. "Ram-air chutes let you come in at a very flat angle, like this, and you can adjust your forward speed easily enough on the approach. Have you ever seen the Leap Frogs?"

"Leap Frogs? What are those?" Wallace asked.

"The exhibition parachuting team of the U.S. Navy SEALs, Sir Vincent," Lia said. "They put on exhibitions at air shows, sometimes. They'll jump out of a plane two miles up, fly circles around and over the air show crowd, and walk in for a landing directly on top of a one-meter bull's-eye staked out on the ground."

"An experienced team can pretty much step down out of the sky onto any exposed, flat piece of the deck they choose," Dean said. "They'd be wearing night-vision devices, so they'll see exactly what they're doing, and their approach would be completely silent. The tangos would never know they were there. The biggest *technical* problem in that approach would be the ship's slipstream, the disturbance its superstructure makes in the air behind it as it moves forward. Our team will have to fly up that slipstream to touch down on the fantail deck. That could be dicey . . . but we have people experimenting with the problem now off the coast of Virginia.

"We're also looking at the possibility of inserting a force by helicopter onto the ship's stern. We know it's possible to approach by helicopter—especially a covert ops aircraft with near-silent rotors—and not be noticed from the bridge. Unfortunately, we have two ships to worry about here, and the likelihood of the *Queen*'s fantail being guarded by sentries and monitored by cameras. A helo op appears too risky.

"Sir Charles, your point about the security systems on board the *Queen* is our primary concern right now. We have two things going for us there, though. First off, the *Queen*'s security people—or, rather, the terrorists, assuming they've taken over the Security Office—can't possibly be watching everywhere all the time. There are hundreds of security cams on that ship, and only so many monitors."

"If I were a terrorist who'd hijacked a ship," General Saunders said, "I would expect the opposition to try to put an assault team onto the ship. I wouldn't worry about using the security cameras to watch places like the ship's hold, or the galley, or the shopping mall. I'd probably herd all of the hostages into one place, where I could keep an eye on them with just a few men. And I'd set the cameras to watch the Promenade Deck and the fantail."

"We agree, General," Dean told him. "And that's where our second ace comes into play. We have at least one and possibly three people on board the *Atlantis Queen* who may be in a position to help us. One of them is a young Englishwoman who works for GCHQ. The other two are SOCA and MI5."

Mayhew nodded. "Agents Mitchell and Franks," he said. "They're on board investigating the Darrow murder. Who's the woman?"

"One of the Menwith Girls. She happened to be on board checking out aspects of the Ship's Security systems. She has a laptop computer with a direct satellite link, so she's not dependent on the ship's communications systems. I'm told she got in touch with GCHQ about an hour ago."

"Why the hell weren't we told this?" General Saunders demanded.

"I'm sorry, General," Charlie Dean said, looking him in the eye, "but this whole things has been unfolding *very* quickly. We're having trouble getting around the compartments."

Compartmentalization was both the strength and the bane of modern intelligence organizations worldwide. The idea was simple enough. If a department, unit, or person didn't *need* to know something, they weren't cleared to know it. Sensitive information could be easily controlled, kept in its own separate box, and any leaks in that box could be identified and stopped before too much damage was done.

But that also meant that it was tough to disseminate important information to the people who needed it. It took time to get special security clearances, or to be sure that the routes for transmitting that information—phone lines, computer networks, distribution lists—were secure, and that unauthorized personnel didn't have access to them.

"Compartments my arse," Saunders growled. "What is a British subject doing working for American intelligence?"

"General," Wallace said carefully, "we all know that GCHQ has a, um, special relationship with the American NSA. I, for one, don't care where the information is coming from, so long as we have it. What does the young woman have to say, Mr. Dean? What's going on aboard those ships?"

"She confirms that armed men, probably Middle Eastern, are in control of the *Atlantis Queen*. The same group is also likely in charge of the *Pacific Sandpiper*. She watched the *Sandpiper* shoot down that Royal Navy Sea Harrier earlier today. She also believes that one of the British intelligence agents on board has been captured. She saw armed men enter the ship's computer center and take him into custody."

"Is she sure he was one of ours?"

Dean shrugged. "She saw an empty shoulder holster. Unless he was plainclothes security of some sort . . ."

"If he was, he wouldn't have been armed," Mayhew said. "This is terrible . . . *terrible* . . ."

"What is it the hijackers want?" Wallace asked. "This seems to be a lot bigger than the usual antinuke protest, people chanting slogans and waving signs from Zodiacs."

"That is our feeling as well," Lia said. "This operation doesn't have the flavor of Greenpeace or any other environmentalist group we know. Different M.O. It's big and it's flashy, which suggests al-Qaeda. The agent on the *Atlantis Queen* saw AK-47s and Middle Eastern dress, which supports that idea. The operation is large, well planned, and well funded."

"They don't appear to have made any demands as yet," Wallace said.

"They will," Dean told him. "Count on it. Right now, they'll be consolidating themselves, making certain that they're in control. Their biggest problem at the moment is having . . . what, Sir Charles? Three thousand hostages?"

"Twenty-four hundred passengers," Mayhew said. "And nine hundred crew and hotelier staff."

"Thirty-three hundred, then. There can't be more than a few dozen terrorists on board. They'll be limited to however many they were able to infiltrate at the Southampton docks and at Barrow, plus maybe seventeen or eighteen more squeezed onto that Eurocopter."

"We know they had two people in the *Sandpiper*'s crew," Wallace said. He looked grim.

"How do you know that?" Saunders asked.

"There were two men on board who were representing the Japanese utilities company that owned that plutonium shipment," Wallace said. "Kiyoshi Kitagawa and Ichiro Wanibuchi. Their bodies were discovered early this morning on the outskirts of Barrow. Both were killed execution-style—a 9mm bullet behind the ear. The bodies were deposited in two different Dumpsters near the waterfront. We're assuming that terrorist agents took their place."

"Wait a minute," Saunders said. "You're talking about *Japanese* terrorists?"

"I imagine the *Sandpiper*'s crew would have noticed something wrong if Wanibuchi and Kitagawa had been replaced by Englishmen," Wallace said dryly. "They hadn't met them yet, but they knew their names and had their security clearances from the home office. We're now assuming that there was at least one terrorist agent among the Japanese escort vessel's crew as well."

"Why would Japanese terrorists be helping Middle Eastern terrorists?" Saunders said, shaking his head. "That just doesn't make sense."

"Of course it does, General," Lia told him. "We've seen this before. Remember the JRA?"

"The Japanese Red Army was declared disbanded in 2000," Saunders said.

"By one of the founding members, who was in jail at the time," Lia said. "We know. But the Japanese Red Army never had serious support at home, and ended up financed and equipped by the PFLP, in Lebanon and Syria. We're operating under the assumption that some JRA members may have hooked up with another dissident group, or reorganized themselves into something new. And we assume they still have solid contacts with the PFLP, and maybe Hamas, al-Qaeda, and other Mideast terror groups as well."

"Yes, but to what end? Why would a Japanese terrorist group want to help Muslim extremists?"

"We'll have to ask them," Dean said. "Just as soon as we get them off those ships."

"I think you people are making too many unwarranted assumptions," Saunders told them. "We don't even know for sure that the ships have been hijacked . . . just a wild story from one woman. We need confirmation."

"Which is precisely what we intend to get by inserting a team on board the *Atlantis Queen*," Dean told him. "We will have a covert ops unit deployed and ready to go in within forty-eight hours . . . possibly twenty-four. Once on board, they can blend in with the passengers, report to us the actual situation, and be in place to support the actual takedown."

"What if the passengers are being held sequestered someplace on board?" Wallace asked. "Under guard."

"According to our informant," Dean said, "that hasn't happened yet."

"Hostages who don't know they're hostages?" Wallace asked.

"Essentially. At least for now." Dean glanced at Saunders, who was scowling. "While it's possible that eventually they'll do what General Saunders suggested—herd everyone into one place and keep them under guard—they haven't yet taken that step. If we *are* dealing with just a few terrorists, they're going to try to keep their hostages in the dark for as long as possible. They can't afford the manpower to watch over three thousand prisoners—not if that means feeding them, giving them water, getting them to the restroom a couple of times a day . . . at least until they show their hand."

"Or they may hold a few prisoners as assurance for the good behavior of the rest," Lia said. "But at the moment, the passengers are just being told to stay in their staterooms. If that doesn't change, we have the opportunity to slip a team inside."

"And what if it changes?" Saunders demanded. "What if they *do* round everybody up and hold them at gunpoint?"

"Then we'll still have a team on board," Dean told him, "that can adapt to the situation as it changes. The *Atlantis Queen* is a big ship. Lots of places to hide."

"I don't think you can do it," Saunders told him. "Parachute a recon team onto a ship held by armed and fully alert terrorists? It's unprecedented."

"It's *not* unprecedented," Dean told him. "There's the *Achille Lauro* in 1985. Terrorists on board an Italian cruise ship hijacked the ship and threatened to kill everyone on board."

"But there was no CT assault on the *Achille Lauro*," Saunders said. "The terrorists negotiated with the Egyptian government by radio, took the ship into Port Said, and went ashore peacefully."

Dean's mouth worked in what was almost a smile. "There's considerably more to the story than that, sir. First off, there *was* a U.S. Navy SEAL team at sea, just a few hours away from boarding that ship."

"I know. Those were the SEALs who tried to capture the terrorists after they flew to Sicily."

Dean nodded. The *Achille Lauro* hijackers had boarded a 737 bound for Tunis after coming ashore at Port Said. U.S. Navy Tomcats had forced the plane to land at the NATO naval air station at Sigonella, in Sicily, where the SEALs surrounded it—and had very nearly gotten into a firefight with Italian carabinieri who'd demanded jurisdiction. Ultimately, the two leaders of the hijackers, Muhammad Abu Abbas and Ozzudin Badrack Kan, had walked away free, released by Italian authorities.

"Second," Dean continued, "it's not common knowledge, and it can't ever be confirmed, but the unofficial word in the intelligence community is that the Israelis already had *two* CT-recon teams in place on board the *Achille Lauro*, and that they were just waiting for the go order. It's possible that the hijackers knew this—or suspected it—and that that's why they suddenly decided to turn around and go to Port Said after only three days."

"This recon force of yours," Saunders said. "I assume it's one of your SEAL teams?"

"I can neither confirm nor deny that, General," Dean told him. "But they *are* good. *Very* good."

"The SAS is good as well," Saunders said. "I cannot countenance this plan."

"What is it you propose instead, General?" Wallace asked.

"We've already deployed Royal Navy vessels to shadow the *Sandpiper* and the *Atlantis Queen*. We send in a couple of our destroyers or frigates to block the target vessels, force them to stop. While we're negotiating with them over the bow, a couple of helos off the *Ark Royal* come in from astern, and we put a platoon of SAS commandos down on the stern of both ships. Another helicopter drops a stick of commandos abseiling down onto the *Queen*'s bridge. Sweet, neat, and simple."

"You may be forgetting something, sir," Dean said. "The 30mm cannons on the *Sandpiper*? They've already shot down one Royal Navy aircraft. Those helicopters would be sitting ducks."

"So we send in a flight of helicopter gunships just ahead of the transports," Saunders replied with a shrug. "That's just a minor operational detail. We hit those gun positions with rockets or chain guns before the terrorists even know we're there."

"I must admit to some . . . concern about firing live weapons at the *Sandpiper*, General," Wallace said. "Her cargo is highly radioactive."

"It's also well shielded and well protected, if your corporate propaganda is to be believed," Saunders told him. "Besides, those gun positions are nowhere near the ship's cargo hold."

"But accidents do happen," Wallace said, "*especially* in combat. The Home Office has already insisted that no action be taken that would jeopardize the passengers on the *Atlantis Queen* . . . or risk the release of radiation from the *Pacific Sandpiper*."

"The recon teams," Dean suggested, "would be in a position to take those guns out ahead of time. They could coordinate their strikes to take out the bridges of both ships and all three guns, then send a signal to bring in the helicopters."

"I still must protest," Saunders said. "Remember . . . *those ships both technically are British soil.* It should be British troops who carry out the rescue."

"General Saunders," Dean said, "forgive me for saying so, but this is not the time for fucking politics!"

"*Mister* Dean, I would remind you there's a lady present!"

"That's okay, General," Lia said. "Charlie is fucking right! You want to beat your manly chest and play your testosterone-sodden games, go ahead, but if you do, you're an idiot, putting at risk three thousand civilians *and* a very great deal of dangerously radioactive material to salve your wounded national pride."

"Charlie! Lia!" Rockman's voice whispered in Dean's ear. "Pull in the horns. We have to stay on this guy's good side!"

"The SAS can have the publicity, General," Dean added, standing up suddenly. "No one will ever hear about our people being there . . . or if they do, they'll assume they belonged to you. But we're ready to go and can get a team on board those ships with a minimum of delay. I suggest you consult with your superiors and then get back to us." He turned and walked away from the table. Lia stood as well and followed.

"*Charlie, you're screwing this deal up!*" Rockman called.

Dean did not reply as he strode out the door.

16

DAVID LLEWELLYN SAT IN one of the plush theater seats, his wrists tightly strapped together at the small of his back, another zip strip binding his ankles, a strip of cloth tightly cinched between his teeth and tied at the back of his head. An entire afternoon of cautious struggle had done nothing but chafe the skin of his wrists raw.

He glanced to his right, where Tricia Johnson was slumped in the theater seat next to his. At least the bastards had let them get dressed before hauling them down here; she was wearing shorts and a T-shirt. Llewellyn, though, was distinctly chilly. All he'd had available to put on in Tricia's stateroom was his swim trunks.

She met his gaze, and he saw her eyes darken with anger before she sharply turned her head away. They hadn't been able to talk much since the intruders had broken into her stateroom and hauled them out of bed. Clearly, though, she knew he was Ship's Security and not a rich passenger who'd known her at Penn State. Presumably she was also angry that he'd not done anything to stop this . . . this invasion.

He looked around the theater, an enormous bowl-shaped auditorium located at the extreme forward part of the ship's superstructure, occupying Decks One, Two, and Three. With two levels of balcony above the main floor, the theater was large enough to hold a thousand people or more. At the moment, however, it held perhaps a hundred or so—a few passengers but mostly men and women wearing Royal Sky uniforms. Perhaps twenty or thirty wore security uniforms; clearly, the hijackers had spent the afternoon rounding up shipboard security personnel and anyone else who might pose a problem. All of them, like him and Tricia, were bound hand and foot, and gagged, and all were clustered in the front-center few rows of seats, just below the stage. There were four men in khaki uniforms and carrying AK-47 assault rifles stationed in the balconies, giving them a perfect view of their prisoners.

Llewellyn was trying to think the situation through. This was a hijacking, obviously enough. Their captors looked Middle Eastern, and the Russian-made weapons suggested they were from one or several of the old Soviet Union's Arab clientele. Al-Qaeda, perhaps? Or Hamas? There was no way to tell. Whoever they were, they continued to bring people into the theater, singly or in small groups.

He heard a door bang far up the aisle behind him and turned in his seat, trying to see. A soldier was walking down the aisle, guiding a woman with a grip on her upper arm. Llewellyn's eyes widened slightly when he recognized her as Sharon Reilly, the ship's Cruise Director, her normally perfectly coiffed blond hair in disarray, her expression one of sheer fury. She struggled against the man's grip, her hands bound behind her back, but the guard forced her along quickly, bringing her down the aisle to the row where Llewellyn was sitting. "Let *go* of me, you bastard!" Reilly said, her voice piercing in the otherwise silent theater.

Roughly the soldier shoved her into the seat next to

Llewellyn's, and she landed heavily against his shoulder. Twisting, she tried to kick the soldier, but he laughed and grabbed her ankles, pinned them with one hand, and fished inside a combat-vest pouch for another zip strip.

"No . . . *no*! . . ."

With a slick, practiced motion, the soldier tied her ankles together, dropped her feet, and then pulled a strip of cloth out of another pouch. "Quiet, whore," he told her, reaching to tie the gag around her head.

With a sick shock of recognition, Llewellyn recognized the soldier as the leering one of the two men who'd broken in on him and Tricia. The soldier finished knotting the cloth behind Reilly's head, then grabbed her jaw and turned her face toward his, just inches away. "You just wait, whore," he told her, his accent thick. Releasing her chin, he dropped his hand to her thigh, nakedly exposed as her short skirt rode up on her hips. "Wait, and maybe we have much fun in later." His eyes shifted to meet Llewellyn's. "So now you getting two girlfriends, eh?" Reaching across in front of Llewellyn, he grabbed Tricia's left breast and squeezed, eliciting a muffled yelp through her gag. "Enjoy yourselves good!" Chuckling, he turned and strode back up the theater aisle. Reilly struggled for a moment, then slumped in resignation.

"May I have your attention, please?" a voice called from the PA system overhead. Llewellyn straightened in his seat, looking up and around, though he knew the speaker wasn't here. Likely, it was someone either on the bridge or in the Security Office.

The voice carried a trace of an accent and sounded cultured, well educated.

"Again," the voice continued, "we regret any inconvenience you might have suffered. The ship tied up alongside us, the *Pacific Sandpiper*, is carrying a very important and very secret cargo. The soldiers you may have seen on board the *Atlantis Queen* are a part of the *Pacific Sandpiper*'s security force.

"Because of certain problems incurred by the *Pacific Sandpiper* when her escort ship exploded this morning, Royal Star Line has volunteered to render all possible assistance. The soldiers are on board the *Atlantis Queen* while we take on board some of their cargo.

"There is no emergency, and no reason for alarm. We urge the passengers of the *Atlantis Queen* to remain calm and, if possible, to remain in their staterooms. The dining rooms are open, however, for those of you who wish to eat.

"We do not expect the problem to last more than a very few days, and we do not expect that it will interfere with your cruise. The officers and crew of the *Atlantis Queen* thank you for your understanding and for your cooperation."

Llewellyn wondered if anyone in the theater was going to get to eat . . . or be allowed to go to the restroom. He and Tricia had been brought here hours ago, and there was no indication that their guards were going to let them take care of any bodily needs.

The hijackers apparently were determined to keep as many people among the passengers and crew in the dark as they could, for as long as they could.

He wondered how much longer they could maintain the charade, until *all* of the passengers were tied up down here with him.

Forward Hold, *Pacific Sandpiper*
47° 14' N, 10° 40' W
Saturday, 2025 hours GMT

Abdullah Wahidi stood before the gleaming titanic cylinder and tried to get his breathing under control. The sight of the thing, looming, massive, aglow with reflections of the fluorescent light tubes overhead, filled him both with awe and with terror.

"Let's get on with it," Chujiro Moritomi said in thickly accented Arabic. He pointed. "Cut there . . . there . . . and there."

Wahidi exchanged a long, nervous glance with the other Arab member of the team—a kid from the Damascus slums named Musab Bekkali—and then dropped the welder's helmet down over his face and slowly raised the cutting torch.

Allah will protect me, he thought. The thought became a mantra, repeated over and over and over again. *Allah protect me! Allah protect me! Allah protect me! . . .*

He struck the spark, and the torch flared to life. A scaffold had been erected for the men in front of the face of the cylinder so that they could reach the locking bars located at three points around the cylinder's cap, inside the seal. He lowered the sharp-pointed blue-white flame to touch the metal, and white light exploded, dazzling even through the heavy visor of his mask.

He didn't want to die.

Then what are you doing on this ship? The thought was defiant, even angry. *You volunteered for this. You wanted to be a martyr . . . and one of Allah's blessed chosen!*

Silver metal began running down the line of the seal, dripping on the deck beneath.

The reality, of course, was more complex than a hunger for the blessings of Paradise. His mother, his brother, and his sister back in Gaza would receive the equivalent of nearly ten thousand American dollars after his death— more money at one time than they could otherwise expect to see in their entire lives.

The first locking bar was cut through. Kneeling, he began cutting the second.

But he'd been expecting his martyr's death to be instant and painless—a single, sharp shock, a bright light . . . and Paradise would be opened to him. His understanding of radiation, however, was somewhat limited. He thought of it as a kind of poison that would seep from the container and slowly burn him, as if by a slow, roasting fire. Mustafa Abu Sayiq, who'd first recruited him in Gaza months before, had assured him that his death would be clean and mercifully swift. At the time, that has hardly seemed important; he would be providing for his family and striking a heroic blow against the hated West in the name of Allah, the merciful, the powerful.

The second locking bar was cut and Wahidi moved to the third. Cables dangling from the ceiling had been attached to massive eye hooks on the cylinder's end, to pull the heavy lid free when the locks were cut. The ship's traveling crane had been moved and the hatch cover on the forward deck opened, so that the container could be unloaded.

These casks, Wahidi had been told, were strongly built affairs, manufactured to standards set by the International Atomic Energy Agency. Each weighed nearly one hundred tons and was firmly bolted to the deck of the transport ship's hold to keep it from shifting during transit. Each, after its manufacture, was tested by being dropped nine meters onto an unyielding surface, immersed in fifteen meters of water for at least eight hours, and engulfed in flame at eight hundred degrees Celsius for thirty minutes. It was said that these casks could survive even the extreme pressures of the ocean's depths.

Inside those massive containers, the nuclear material was safe from just about anything Wahidi or the others could do to it. If they piled up all of the explosives they'd brought on board the *Atlantis Queen* and set them off at once, they might fling the cylinder into the air but still fail to breach it.

And so the contents of at least two of these forged steel canisters had to be removed from the layers of protective shielding and transported to the *Atlantis Queen*. Several forklifts waited on the *Sandpiper*'s deck now to effect the transfer.

The final locking bar was cut through. Wahidi switched off the torch, and he and Bekkali grabbed hold of the handles on the cylinder's end and pulled. With a slow sucking sound, the seal was breached and the metal disk came away.

Wahidi had been expecting fire or lightning bolts or *something* as evidence of the radiation spilling from the breached container, but he felt . . . nothing. Nothing at all. He looked at Bekkali again, and the other man shrugged and shook his head. He and Moritomi stood ready with a cargo sling, getting set to begin hauling the cylinders out and up to the ship's forward deck.

The interior of the large canister was dark. Wahidi had also been expecting some sort of magical blue glow.

There was nothing. No light. No fire . . . no death.

Grinning now with relief, Wahidi began to slide the first of the internal canisters out of the larger container.

Bridge, *Pacific Sandpiper*
47° 20' N, 10° 28' W
Saturday, 2025 hours GMT

Alarms shrilled suddenly on the *Sandpiper*'s bridge. Jamal Hasan, at the ship's wheel, and Abdel Ramid, beside him, both jumped at the sound, but Kozo Fuchida merely smiled.

"Radiation alarm," he said, reaching past Ramid to flick a switch. The shrill ringing stopped. "They have the first cylinder open."

"I didn't realize it would reach us *here*!" Ramid said. He sounded scared.

"It won't," Fuchida told him. "Or very little will, at any rate. The alarm is connected to sensors inside the ship's hold, to detect radiation leaks there. There actually will be little leakage when they transport the inner canisters across to the cruise ship."

"How much is 'very little'?" the shaken Ramid asked.

"Not enough to harm you. The inner containers are also well shielded against neutron radiation."

"Oh. That is good."

Another alarm shrilled, and Ramid switched it off, the motion almost casual.

Fuchida didn't bother telling Ramid that, in fact, the three of them on the bridge were now receiving a fairly sizeable dose of hard radiation. It wasn't enough to make them sick, not yet. That would come with accumulated exposure over a period of time . . . in this case, a period of several days or even as much as a week.

And a week from now they would be at their final destination, and nothing would matter to any of them anymore.

Of course the men in the special technical unit— Chujiro Moritomi and the volunteers from among Khalid's Muslims—were already dying.

Stateroom 4116, *Atlantis Queen*
47° 08' N, 10° 36' W
Saturday, 2120 hours GMT

Nina McKay leaned against the railing of her private balcony, looking down into the night. An overcast sky and night-shrouded ocean surrounded her, but bright work lights on the deck of the smaller freighter immediately below her stateroom cast dazzling pools of light over the other ship's deck and illuminated several men working beside the open maw of one of the large deck cargo hatches.

She had a deeply uneasy feeling about all of this. Those men—many in military uniforms and carrying weapons openly—and the presence of that other ship still tied to the *Atlantis Queen*'s side, plus the sudden, terrifying drama of that jet plane shot down earlier in the day, all of it added up to one thing: something was terribly *wrong*.

Nina hadn't seen the downing of the aircraft; she, Andrew, and Melissa had been in the mall on the first deck, where the only windows were huge stained-glass panels high up in the gallery's overarching walls. But she'd heard about it from other frightened passengers and from the announcement over the ship's PA. She was still shaken by that nightmare crush, by the pounding fear that Melissa might be trampled in the crowd.

Turning, Nina looked back into the stateroom, lit now by a single night-light. Melissa was asleep on the huge bed with her favorite stuffed animal, a war-weary, much-patched, much-loved gray tiger kitten, cuddled tight against her cheek. When the panic had begun, Andrew had scooped Melissa off the deck with one arm, grabbed Nina's hand with the other, and plowed his way through the press of bodies by sheer brute strength.

Andrew could be . . . *dominating* sometimes. He had what she'd laughingly called a white-knight complex, a need to gallop in full tilt, take charge, and *fix* things whenever there was a problem. It had driven her nuts throughout the eleven years of their marriage and was a large part of why she'd left him, that and his need to always know everything and always be *right*. She didn't like other people taking charge of her life and telling her what to do, what she needed to do to straighten out her life. It was so much . . . so much like her *mother*. . . .

Right now, though, Nina thought she would appreciate some macho counsel, or a bit of well-meaning knight-errantry. Protecting her daughter, keeping her safe, was Nina's single driving need right now, and she had no idea how to do it. She knew something was wrong, but she didn't know what, and with all that black and empty ocean out there, she had no place safe to run.

The men on the deck of the small ship alongside were hoisting something out of the hold—a bundle of cylinders each perhaps six feet long, dull-gleaming under the work lights like lead.

Pirates, looting the ship's cargo? It was all she could imagine, and the guns those men had slung over their shoulders made the thought credible.

Leaving the balcony, she quietly slipped across the stateroom, first checking on Melissa's quiet breathing, then moving to the door that connected them with the stateroom next door.

Very, very softly she rapped on the door. "Andrew? Andrew, we need to talk."

The door swung open a moment later.

Pyramid Club Casino, *Atlantis Queen*
46° 59' N, 11° 08' W
Saturday, 2212 hours GMT

As Jerry Esterhausen sat at the Pyramid Bar in his tweed jacket and blue jeans, watching the crowd in the casino, he was becoming more and more worried. There was something *wrong*.

Rosie was functioning brilliantly, dealing out the cards at the blackjack table with slick, sure precision, bantering with the customers as she did so, but the problem was that there weren't that many players. Most of the people in the casino that evening were gathered in small groups, clustered around dining tables or at the bar or within the faux jungle at the front of the room. Not even the patter of a stand-up comedian on the stage an hour earlier had lightened the atmosphere, which felt oppressive and claustrophobic.

People were scared.

At first, Esterhausen had been primarily worried that Rosie wasn't drawing in the players as CyberAge's marketing department had promised. A failure at the tables on this cruise, a lack of rich suckers willing to put their money on the table and bet they could come closer to 21 than a vivacious machine, might translate as a lack of orders for CyberAge's products, and even a cancellation of the contract with Royal Sky Line.

Sitting at the bar watching the customers, though, had convinced Esterhausen that the problem wasn't Rosie. Snatches of overheard conversation whispered about the crash of that Royal Navy jet, the mysterious activity on board the freighter tied up alongside, and the appearance of ominously garbed and armed security guards. Esterhausen turned his head to look aft through the huge glass doors and windows there, out onto the *Queen*'s Deck Nine fantail. The ship's Atlas swimming pool was located out there, along with two hot tubs. Normally, both pool and spas would have full complements of swimmers and soakers taking advantage of the night air. There were no passengers out there at all, however, not now.

But there *were* two of the bearded, khaki-clad guards standing near the glass, with their black berets and black and orange assault rifles very much in evidence. They lent a sinister presence that overshadowed the crowd in the casino. Esterhausen saw how people at the tables nearby kept glancing outside, and how worried they seemed when each glance confirmed that the guards were still there.

Security guards off the *Pacific Sandpiper*, the announcement earlier that evening had claimed. But the *Sandpiper* was British-flagged, and these guys didn't look British. They weren't American or Israeli, either. Esterhausen would have guessed they were Egyptian, Jordanian, or from some other Middle Eastern nation.

He caught movement out of the corner of his eye and turned in his bar seat as Sandy Markham sat down next to him. She looked scared, and her eyes were red, as if she'd been crying.

"What's wrong, Sandy?"

"Hi, Jerry," she said. "I . . . I'm not sure. Things are kind of crazy."

He nodded toward the glass doors. "You mean with those armed thugs on board?"

"Among other things."

"Something's happened," he told her, sensing that she was holding something back. "What?"

She glanced around the room. "I think—" She stopped. "You can't tell the other passengers, Jerry. I don't want to start a panic. Or a massacre. . . ."

"A *massacre*! . . ."

She laid a hand on his arm. "Shh! Jerry! Please!"

"Sorry. But what the hell are—"

"About four hours ago, some of us were getting worried, you know? Calls to the bridge weren't being answered. And we couldn't find some of the crew. David Llewellyn, the head of Ship's Security? We can't find him anywhere!"

Esterhausen frowned. "Don't you guys have some sort of super high-tech ID locator on this ship? A way to tell where everyone is at any time?"

"Yes. That's why we were looking for David! The Security Office wasn't answering calls! And the passageways up on Deck Eleven, leading to Security, have all been closed off. There are armed guards up there!"

"Shit."

"So the CD, Sharon Reilly? She said she was going up to the bridge and talk to Captain Phillips. That was four hours ago, and she hasn't come back! We've tried calling her, and she's not answering her phone. Jerry, I don't know what to do!"

Esterhausen was watching the guards outside. He nodded slowly. "Well, the first thing, Sandy, is not to panic."

"But what's happening? What does that ship tied up alongside have to do with us? Are they pirates? Terrorists?"

"I think," he said slowly, "that we've been hijacked, and the bad guys just haven't bothered to tell us yet."

"Hijacked!"

It was Esterhausen's turn to lay a cautioning hand on Markham's arm. "Like I said. Don't panic. There are a couple of thousand of us, and only a few of them. We can *do* something about this."

"Jerry, they have *machine guns!*"

"Yeah. But there still can't be more than a few dozen of them. They can't possibly control all of us. And if we know what's happening, maybe we can . . . I don't know. Hide someplace. This is a big ship, lots of hiding spaces. We can figure out how to strike back."

"You're forgetting something."

"What?"

"If they're in control of security, they know where all of us are. They'd know immediately if some of us tried to hide."

"Then we'll have to figure something out. Flight Ninety-three."

"Flight Ninety-three? What's that?"

"Nine-eleven?"

"The World Trade Center bombing?"

"You remember the airliner that crashed in Pennsylvania?"

"I'm English, Jerry. And I was a teenaged girl in Woking then."

"Oh. Right. The terrorists hijacked four planes that morning. Two crashed into the World Trade Center. A third hit the Pentagon, in Washington. The fourth was Flight Ninety-three. It was hijacked over Ohio someplace. They turned it around and were flying toward Washington, D.C. We're not sure, but the terrorists were planning on crashing into either the White House or the Capitol Building.

"Anyway, the passengers knew something was wrong, and they used their cell phones to talk to friends and family on the ground. They learned about the WTC and Pentagon attacks, and figured out that their airliner was a part of it.

"So they stormed the cockpit. One of the passengers was heard to say, 'Let's roll.' It became a kind of a battle cry for the whole nation."

"What happened?"

He shrugged. "We'll never know. They broke into the cockpit. There was a struggle. And the plane crashed in a field in western Pennsylvania. Everyone on board was killed."

"God. . . ."

"The point is . . . the passengers of that airliner refused to just roll over and be victims. They *did* something. And we can, too."

He continued to watch the guards outside, his mind turning furiously.

Bridge, *Atlantis Queen*
46° 59' N, 11° 08' W
Saturday, 2212 hours GMT

Khalid stood behind Captain Phillips, who was leaning over the large electronic chart table at the back of the bridge. At the moment, the table's display showed in glowing blues and yellows a stretch of ocean 600 miles across. The tip of the Brittany coast of France lay 250 miles to the east, while the Scilly Islands and Cornwall were slowly receding astern, 270 miles distant.

"This is our position," Phillips told him, pointing to the end of a yellow line stretching southwest into the North Atlantic. "About forty-seven degrees north, about eleven degrees west."

"I see. And how far are we from New York?"

Phillips looked startled. "New York? New York City?"

"Yes."

The ship's captain appeared to wrestle with this information for a moment, then used a stylus to touch the ship's current position and dragged it across the plastic surface of the map. The software automatically zoomed out until the curvature of the Earth came into view on the screen, showing the coastlines of Europe as far as Greece and Scandanavia, much of northwestern Africa, and, to the west, half of Canada and the United States, as well as much of the Caribbean.

As Phillips dragged the stylus, a yellow line extended with it, connecting the *Queen*'s current position with Manhattan. The line bowed slightly, following the Great Circle, passing just to the south of Newfoundland and Nova Scotia, then down past Cape Cod and Long Island.

"How far?" Khalid asked as Phillips straightened up.

Phillips tapped a menu box, and the answer appeared on the navigation screen. "About twenty-seven hundred nautical miles," he said.

"And how long will that take?"

"At fifteen knots?" He tapped out the calculation on the display and read the result. "One hundred eighty hours," he said. "That's about seven and a half days."

"A week. And how much faster could we get there if we increased our speed?"

"Increased it by how much?"

"The *Pacific Sandpiper* seems to be riding alongside quite well," Khalid said. "I propose we increase speed to, say, twenty knots."

"I don't know if we can manage that."

"I understand. But if we could?"

Phillips tapped out another calculation. "Five-point-six days. Say . . . five days, fifteen hours."

Khalid's mouth worked silently for a moment. "So, at twenty knots, we could reach New York by next Friday, sometime in the afternoon?"

"Yes. But I can't recommend that."

"Why not?"

"I can't predict the stress on this vessel caused by dragging that freighter. And it will take a lot more fuel to move that much weight, at that much higher a speed."

"Would you have enough fuel to make it?"

Again Phillips worked out the calculation. "Yes." He said the word reluctantly. "Barely, but yes."

"Then that is what we will do," Khalid told him. "Give the order, please, to come to this new course."

"Helm," Phillips said, his sense of dread growing swiftly deeper. "Come to new heading . . . two-six-zero, please."

"Coming to new heading two-six-zero, Captain. Aye, aye."

The helmsman put the wheel over, and the liner slowly began to edge onto her new course.

After several moments, the helmsman announced, "We're on new course two-six-zero, sir."

"Increase speed . . . *slowly* . . . to two-zero knots."

"Coming to two-zero knots, slowly, Captain. Aye, aye."

God, what did this man want with them, steering a course for New York City?

The *Pacific Sandpiper* was carrying radioactive nuclear material. The men who'd captured both vessels were obviously Islamic fanatics.

The only conclusion Phillips could imagine was that these men intended an attack against New York City, a *nuclear* attack, an attack that would make the horror of 9/11 pale by comparison.

And Captain Phillips realized now that he might well have to choose between trying to save his crew and passengers . . . and saving New York City.

17

KOZO FUCHIDA SAT NEXT TO Moritomi's bunk. "There are doctors on the other ship," he said earnestly. "They might be able to help."

"There is a doctor on *this* ship," Moritomi replied. "Believe me, my friend. There is nothing any of them can do."

Chujiro Moritomi had begun showing signs of radiation poisoning only hours after the radioactive canisters had been transferred to the passenger ship. His face was flushed; the skin of his hands and arms was red and shiny, as though he'd received a bad sunburn.

During the night he'd started vomiting.

Fuchida didn't understand the science of it. That had been Moritomi's area of expertise, since he'd worked for several years at the Rokkasho nuclear plant. "I thought you had to breathe the powder to be hurt by it," Fuchida said.

The principal danger inherent in those metal tubes of plutonium oxides, Fuchida had been told, came with breathing the stuff, which had been described as *the* most toxic material known to man. Conventional high explosives would throw a cloud of dust into the air above Manhattan, and prevailing winds would carry the stuff in a deadly footprint up the New England coast.

But apparently those cylinders were leaking fairly high levels of gamma radiation as well, radiation enough to cook any unprotected individual who handled them.

"We weren't told . . . everything," Moritomi said. "The Arabs were terrified. They thought the radiation would kill them right away." He started coughing, and a smear of blood appeared at the corner of his mouth. "They're going to wish it *had* been right away."

"Khalid lied to us?"

"He may simply not have known what to expect. Or perhaps some of those cylinders hold something more concentrated, more deadly, than simple MOX powder, and our intelligence wasn't good enough." He shrugged. "None of it matters now, of course."

Fuchida's gaze slipped to the small table beside Moritomi's bunk, which was empty except for the compact deadliness of a Walther P5 pistol. "Of course."

"Our *omi*," the sick man said, "remains."

Fuchida nodded. He touched Moritomi's shoulder. "I'll be back to check on you after a while."

Moritomi didn't answer, and Fuchida wondered if he'd fallen asleep. Fuchida let himself out of the cabin, one of the single berthing compartments for the ship's officers, quietly.

But as he was walking away down the passageway, he heard a single loud, sharp shot from the room.

Bridge, *Atlantis Queen*
North Atlantic
47° 11' N, 14° 57' W
Sunday, 0940 hours GMT

Captain Phillips and helmsman Jason Miller walked back onto the bridge, escorted by the terrorist Khalid had called Aziz. Phillips felt dirty and tired; he'd gotten little sleep the night before.

Since the takeover of his bridge almost twenty-four hours earlier, Miller, Phillips, and four others of his regular bridge crew personnel had been kept imprisoned in the officer's wardroom aft of the bridge. An adjoining bunkroom used by duty officers served for sleeping and hygienic considerations, and members of the ship's catering staff brought meals—under guard—up from the forward galley.

Staff Captain Vandergrift, four more bridge officers, eight security and ship's computer personnel, and two surviving radio operators had all . . . vanished. Khalid had ordered them taken away at gunpoint, and, so far, Phillips had been unable to learn what had become of them.

As the hours passed, their safety weighed more and more heavily in his thoughts.

Apparently, the hijackers were determined to keep the bulk of the ship's passengers and crew in the dark concerning what had happened. The armed guards wore military-style uniforms, and a few were wearing shipboard security uniforms. Khalid or one of his men made occasional intercom announcements from the bridge or radio room, announcements crafted to convince the floating city of the *Queen* that all was well, that the *Atlantis Queen* was rendering assistance to a vessel in distress, that the ship soon would be back on her regular course.

"Good morning, Captain," Khalid said as Phillips was led onto the bridge. He was standing next to the electronic chart table. "And it *is* a good morning, I assure you."

Miller replaced Fisher, another regular bridge crewman, at the helm. Aziz led Fisher back toward the wardroom.

"Where are my people?" Phillips asked, blunt. "The rest of my bridge crew?" His questions yesterday had been ignored, but he was determined to push the issue as far as he could.

"They are safe, Captain," Khalid told him. "Safe and being well looked after. We no longer need them on the bridge, and they would just be in the way."

"And there are some other of my people I haven't seen. David Llewellyn, my chief security officer. Where is he?"

"Safe, Captain."

"Their safety is my principal responsibility," Phillips said. "I want to *see* that they're all right."

"In time, Captain. In time. For now, your principal responsibility is the safe navigation of this ship. And to obey my orders."

"What is it you want of me?"

Khalid gave a negligent wave. "Run the ship. Continue as if nothing was happening out of the ordinary."

"And my crew?"

"Later, Captain Phillips. After I know whether or not you can be trusted."

Phillips sagged a bit inside. He could push the issue no further.

Khalid, he saw, still wore the blue and white shipboard security uniform he'd been wearing when he took over the bridge, as did several of his men.

This hijacking, Phillips had decided, had been an enormous undertaking. It had taken a lot of money—that French helicopter demonstrated that—as well as a lot of planning, preparation, and advance work. Poor Darrow's murder, he now realized, must have been planned to help the hijackers get on board, and the terrorists had shown an astonishing knowledge not only of the Ship's Security systems but of shipboard routine as well.

His face darkened with a scowl. One of the regular security officers, Mohamed Ghailiani, evidently had been a mole, the means by which these armed thugs had gotten on board in the first place and penetrated Ship's Security.

So far as Phillips was concerned, the blood of two men, now—Security Specialist Kelly and Radio Operator Farnham—was on Ghailiani's hands.

And Phillips was determined that there *would* be a reckoning.

The question was how best to fight back. Khalid seemed utterly confident of his control of the ship. He held the bridge, obviously, as well as the radio room, Security, the IT department—the entire suite of departments and rooms on Deck Twelve, and in the forward portion of Deck Eleven, just below. From comments Phillips had heard, they had at least one man watching over the engineering crew on D Deck, and someone watching the catering staff in the forward galley.

That left a very great deal of ship and about three thousand passengers and crew unaccounted for, and from the sound of it most of them weren't even aware yet that the ship had been hijacked.

If those three thousand could be warned somehow . . . a handful of terrorists might kill some of them, but not all. Maybe he could arrange some sort of uprising . . . a mutiny, of sorts.

Except hundreds might be killed in such an attempt.

And if he did nothing, how many would die in New York City? Phillips was convinced, now, beyond any shred of doubt, that Khalid planned more than a simple shakedown of the American and British governments with these ships as hostage. The presence of the *Sandpiper* alongside suggested a scenario so dark that Phillips could scarcely bring himself to think about it.

His passengers and crew, or the life of a major city.

Whatever he did would have to be more subtle than an uprising among the prisoners. And there just might be a way. . . .

Casually he walked over to the chart table and checked the ship's course . . . still on a bearing of two-six-zero, still at twenty knots. Turning, he walked over to the ship's compass binnacle, checked the heading, then began punching some numbers into the keyboard mounted on the binnacle's face.

Khalid might be in control, but he was *not* a sailor. Phillips remembered their conversation on the bridge yesterday, where Khalid had committed the landlubberly mistake of calling the lines securing the *Sandpiper* alongside *ropes*. On board ship, the only rope was *wire* rope, the steel cable used for specific tasks such as lifting heavy cargo from a hold—or to secure the two ships together as they now were. But the lines first passed between the two ships had been "lines," and a sailor, someone with naval or merchant marine training, would have known that.

Phillips thought he saw a way to use that.

"What are you doing?" Khalid asked.

"Checking the compass," he replied. He kept his voice even, though his heart was pounding in his chest. "Recalibrating it. The navigator usually performs the task, but he seems to have disappeared."

Khalid walked closer and looked at the compass heading. It read 250.

"According to this," the man said slowly, "we are off-course."

"By ten degrees, yes. The navigation officer checks the compass with our GPS twice daily, to make certain this sort of thing doesn't happen. We've been having some trouble with it."

"What kind of trouble?"

Phillips shrugged. "Nothing serious. We just need to recalibrate for the currents, the tides, the wind, for the changing angle on magnetic north. That's what I just did."

"But this means we're headed too far south, yes?"

"Then I would suggest that you bring the ship ten degrees north."

"Order it."

"Helm!" Phillips said. "Come right ten degrees."

"Come right ten degrees," Miller replied. Phillips saw the sweat on the young man's face. "Aye, aye."

Gently the *Atlantis Queen* edged onto her new, more northerly course. As minute followed agonizing minute,

Khalid said nothing more, content with staring out the bridge windows forward at the bright blue sky above the endless violet-gray blue of the horizon.

They might just be able to get away with this. . . .

Neptune Theater, *Atlantis Queen*
North Atlantic
47° 12' N, 14° 58' W
Sunday, 1020 hours GMT

David Llewellyn paced up the aisle of the theater, deliberately testing the bounds set on the prisoners. Halfway up the aisle, a bearded man in khaki had stepped out of the shadows, pointing an AK at Llewellyn, barking something in Arabic. He raised his hands and took a step back. "Easy, man, easy!"

The guard barked again, and a second armed man appeared. "You need piss?" the man demanded.

"Uh, yeah," Llewellyn said.

"Come."

The man led Llewellyn through the double doors at the top of the aisle and down a short passageway toward the mall. Several men's and ladies' rooms were located here. The guard led Llewellyn inside but let him use one of the stalls in privacy.

At least, he thought, their captors had seen fit to come in last night and cut those damned plastic strips off their wrists and ankles. As each man or woman was cut loose and their gag removed, they'd been led away, and at first Llewellyn had thought they were being taken away to be killed. Some of the captives had thought the same and began screaming and struggling. When that happened, they would be released, and the guards would choose another to release. And those who were led away were brought back safely after a few minutes.

As each prisoner was returned, as they rejoined the

others and began talking in hushed, urgent whispers, Llewellyn had realized that they were being taken, one by one, to one of the restrooms just outside the theater. The process had taken a long time; there were almost a hundred people being held in the theater, now, and only a handful of guards.

Eventually, it had been his turn. He'd scarcely been able to walk after hours of being tied, and he'd been afraid that they would be tied once more afterward, but when the guard had brought him back from the head, he'd been released. Later, a couple of catering staff people had brought box dinners in—sandwiches, fruit cups, and small cartons of juice—not quite the usual sumptuous fare on board the *Queen*, but at least the hijackers didn't intend to starve them all.

He finished up, flushed, and washed his hands at one of the sinks as the guard watched impassively. "So, what's your name?" Llewellyn asked brightly.

"No talk."

"Not very friendly, are you?"

"No talk!"

The guard had led Llewellyn back to the theater, then, and he took the opportunity to look around. There didn't appear to be anyone in the bit of the ship's mall area visible down the passageway. Two men in Ship's Security uniforms stood to either side of the doors into the theater.

Inside, he took a moment to study the situation from the top of the aisle. Only the overhead lights illuminating the stage were on, and the prisoners were huddled together there, lying or sitting on mattresses.

At around ten the night before, a dozen crew members had been led away at gunpoint. Again the prisoners left behind had begun talking among themselves, wondering what was happening. The chosen prisoners had returned twenty minutes later dragging mattresses from the ship's housekeeping stores. Llewellyn and a number of other men had volunteered to help, then, and they'd spent the next hour and a half making trips down to B Deck Forward, dragging out blankets and more mattresses and hauling them up in the main forward service lift. The mattresses were laid out side by side across the theater's stage, with more on the deck between the front-row seats and the stage, and others in the side aisles.

At the time, Staff Captain Vandergrift had first suggested that the men and women take opposite sides of the theater for sleeping. Llewellyn had looked at Tricia and Sharon Reilly, who were huddled together now side by side in the front-row seats, and shaken his head. "I think a better idea, sir," he'd said, "would be to put the women in the middle, the men around the outside."

Several of their captors—the ugly, leering one especially—seemed to be eagerly anticipating a chance to rape some of the women.

Vandergrift had thought about it and agreed. The prisoners had passed an uncomfortable night on the mattresses, many of them clinging together for warmth and for at least an illusion of security. Their guards had watched impassively from the balconies, their shifts changing once in the twelve hours that had passed since.

There were, as near as Llewellyn could tell, four guards in the balconies—one on the left above the stage, one on the right, and two in the rear balconies above the door—as well as the two at the top of the aisle. One of those, his escort to the restroom, now nudged Llewellyn with the muzzle of his rifle. "You go!"

"Okay, sunshine," Llewellyn said. "Don't get your camel in a twist."

He walked back down to the mattresses. Vandergrift sat on the stage, his legs dangling over the edge as he ate a banana. More food had been brought in that morning, and prisoners who needed to use the restroom facilities could do so by asking one of the guards to walk them out and back. Llewellyn joined him.

"Guards outside?" Vandergrift asked, his voice low.

"Two that I could see just outside the doors," Llewellyn told him. "Not good."

"No. . . ."

Arnold Bernstein picked his way over the mattresses on the deck and joined them. He was an older man—in his early sixties, Llewellyn guessed—and was the manager of a minor celebrity among the passengers. "You fellows still talking about how to break out of here?" he asked.

"Maybe," Vandergrift said. "You have any ideas?"

"I have an idea," Bernstein replied, "that these people are going to kill us if we don't do *something*."

"We're open to suggestions, Mr. Bernstein," Llewellyn said. "But right now I don't think there's much we can do."

During the long night, Llewellyn, Vandergrift, and a few other men had discussed the possibility of trying to overpower the guards and break free. The numbers, certainly, were in the prisoners' favor—a hundred of them against six guards inside the theater.

But even if the prisoners could find a way to take out all six simultaneously, there would be noise, there would be gunfire, and the two outside would alert the bridge.

"We outnumber them," Vandergrift said, "but eight automatic weapons against a hundred unarmed men and women are no odds at all. The way I see it, we might, *might*, be able to take out two of the guards, maybe three, and turn their weapons against the others, but the end result is sure to be a bloodbath. The rest of the hijackers will fire into the crowd before we can get close to them."

"There's also the possibility that the terrorists have rigged explosives around the theater," Bernstein added.

"Have you seen any sign of that?" Llewellyn asked.

"No. But that's what they did at Entebbe."

Llewellyn nodded. Entebbe was the Ugandan airport where 250 crew and passengers off of Air France Flight 139 had been imprisoned by terrorists and Ugandan soldiers after their plane had been hijacked in 1976. The prisoners had been locked up in an old airport terminal, given mattresses, and held under guard . . . just as was being done here. Explosives had been prominently placed around the terminal as an added threat.

As he looked at Bernstein, Llewellyn was forcibly reminded of another aspect of the Entebbe hijacking. At one point, the terrorists had gone through the prisoners' passports and separated out the ones with Jewish-sounding names. Those had been led to another room in a selection process eerily and nightmarishly reminiscent of the selection lines at Nazi death camps.

And there'd been the Jewish passenger on board another hijacked cruise ship, the *Achille Lauro*, an elderly man in a wheelchair shot by the hijackers and tossed overboard.

Llewellyn wondered if Bernstein was thinking about those incidents now.

"There's been no sign that they're wiring us with explosives," Vandergrift said. "The way I see it, they figure they can keep us under control just with the threat of those rifles."

"Unfortunately, they're right," Llewellyn said. The doors leading to the balcony stairways from inside the theater had been locked. Llewellyn could see no way to get at the men in the balconies other than swarming up the outside, using curtain ropes or the Baroque decorations covering the walls as climbing aids. "If we rush them, it'll be a slaughter. We can't risk it."

"If we take down the two up there by the doors," Bernstein pointed out, "we'll have their guns. We could shoot the ones in the balconies, then."

Vandergrift shook his head. "We wouldn't make it halfway up the aisles before the people in the balconies started shooting into the crowd. Damn it, we can't risk it!"

"The passengers on Flight Ninety-three risked it!" Bernstein said, angry, his voice rising.

"*Please!*" Vandergrift said, putting a cautioning hand on the man's shoulder. "Keep your voice down!"

"Flight Ninety-three," Bernstein said, more quietly. "Nine-eleven? Does that ring any bells? I say we should *roll*!"

"The hijackers on Flight Ninety-three were armed with box cutters and knives," Llewellyn pointed out, "not AK-47 assault rifles. They were also in close quarters, with the terrorists locked inside the cockpit." He shook his head. "We try that kind of hero stunt and we'll be cut to bits!"

"Bernie!" A piercing female voice echoed through the theater. Llewellyn turned and saw a tall, slender, big-breasted woman in a bare excuse for a bikini standing on the other side of the theater seats, hands on her hips. "Bernie! Where are you!"

Bernstein sighed. "The mistress calls," he said. "Look, if you guys decide to actually *do* something other than waiting to get shot or beheaded or whatever these clowns decide to do to us, count me in! And I suggest you hurry!" Turning, he tiptoed across mattresses and over passengers to rejoin the woman.

"Who is that?" Vandergrift asked.

"Some rock star or singer or something," Llewellyn said. He tried to remember the passenger records he'd seen. He recalled that several staff people had been complaining about the woman, her complaints about her suite, her meals, and the service on board. "Hopper? No, Harper. Gillian Harper. High maintenance. Thinks the world revolves around her."

"I gather she's learning otherwise."

She appeared to be telling Bernstein off. "Maybe."

"So what do you think, David?" Vandergrift asked. "Should we . . . 'roll'?"

He shook his head. "Whatever these people are planning on doing, they're ready for the long haul."

"What makes you say that?"

Llewellyn raised his hands, exposing his wrists. "They untied us. They let us use the loo . . . and gave us mattresses to sleep on. Not the *Queen*'s usual luxurious accommodations, certainly, but it shows they're going to keep us for a while."

"How long, I wonder?"

"Depends on where we're headed, I guess. America? The Med? Maybe back to England?"

"We were on a westerly heading," Vandergrift said. "I got a glimpse of the sun when they brought me down here. America."

"So that's five days to a week, depending on our speed."

"You think they're going to hold us down here that long?"

"I think they're prepared to. I think we're here to guarantee the good behavior of the skipper and maybe the rest of the passengers."

"Which suggests we need to make a break somehow. . . ."

"Not if it gets us all killed, Charles," Llewellyn said, shaking his head. "Anyway, before too long, somebody's going to notice that we're not on-course for the Med anymore. They may stage a rescue mission."

"You think so?"

"I *hope* so. I think this is one we need to leave to the professionals."

Vandergrift looked again at the guards watching from the balconies. They seemed to be interested in an argument developing between Bernstein and the Harper woman.

"That could still get bloody," Vandergrift said. "Commandos storming in here? The terrorists might open fire on the crowd."

"We'll need to think about ways we can minimize casualties," Llewellyn said, thoughtful. "Maybe try to disperse everyone in small groups, as much as they'll let us. Warn them not to jump up in the line of fire if shooting starts."

"We could do that, yeah," Vandergrift said. "Make a list of things to do and not do. Pass the word on a few people at a time."

"And we can think about grabbing weapons when the time comes," Llewellyn added. "It's all a question of being ready when things go down."

"I agree."

Llewellyn found himself looking across the theater, halfway up the ranks of seats. Tricia was up there, sitting in an aisle seat, and one of the terrorists was talking with her. The man said something . . . and Tricia *smiled*, the expression startling Llewellyn. *What the hell?* . . .

The terrorist, he saw now, was not one of the two who'd broken in on the two of them in her stateroom yesterday. This one was young, with little more than fuzz on his cheeks instead of the beards or heavy mustaches sported by most of the others.

It was tough to see their captors as individuals. The guns, the attitudes, the broken English all combined to turn them into faceless, threatening shadows.

But there were differences. That one, for instance, was almost painfully young, and he seemed to be treating Tricia with a measure of deference. The two who'd captured them—especially the leering one—had been quite different. There was an interesting difference. The leering terrorist had been all but drooling over the attractive women; that kid looked like he was almost afraid of them. From what Llewellyn knew of Arab cultures, there was a tendency to treat women as second-class citizens . . . but the teachings of their Qur'an, he'd heard, tended to stress women's equality. Most of the Muslim men he'd known in England seemed to think of women as *almost* their equals; he suspected that the real difference lay not in the religion but in the myriad native cultures beneath the Islamic overlay, in peoples as mutually alien as Moroccans, Egyptians, Syrians, and Afghans.

This lot seemed pretty diverse. Ghailiani was Moroccan. He thought Khalid might be Egyptian . . . or possibly Saudi. Was there a way to use that, to drive wedges between their individual captors?

Was that what Tricia was doing?

She glanced his way and caught his gaze. He saw again the anger flash in her eyes.

Maybe, he thought, *they should be thinking about the wedges driven in between the individual captives instead.* He didn't like to think it, but it might be necessary to be careful when it came time to sharing escape plans with the others.

The guard said something and Tricia laughed. . . .

**Bridge, *Atlantis Queen*
North Atlantic
47° 59' N, 18° 14' W
Sunday, 1730 hours GMT**

Khalid leaned over the electronic chart table and drew the line again, just to be certain. He nodded, satisfied, then looked up at Aziz. "Is everything ready?"

"Yes, Amir." He nodded toward the bridge window. On the *Atlantis Queen*'s forward deck, two lonely figures stood next to the starboard side railing. "As you ordered."

"Bring him here, then."

Aziz left the bridge and returned a few moments later, leading Phillips at gunpoint. He watched the captain's eyes as the man saw him standing next to the chart, saw those eyes widen ever so slightly. *He's afraid. Good. . . .*

"Perhaps, Captain, you would be so good as to explain something to me."

"Perhaps you would tell me what you are doing with my people! Your thugs just came up and dragged Jason out of the wardroom."

"*First*, Captain," Khalid snapped, "you will tell me why you tampered with the compass this morning!"

"I . . . I told you. It needed to be calibrated."

Khalid sighed. "Captain Phillips . . . do I *look* stupid? Or do you simply assume Arabs don't understand technology?" He touched a control on the chart table, and a yellow line drew itself across the curve of the Earth's globe, sliding just south of Newfoundland, Nova Scotia, and the hook of Cape Cod, before coming to a halt a few miles south of Long Island and the entrance to New York Harbor. "This is the course I ordered you to set."

He touched the control again and drew a second line, one that diverged slightly from the first, to the north, a line that diverged farther and farther as the miles slipped past until it came to a halt smack against the coastline of Newfoundland, well to the north of Cape Race.

"And this is the course you recalibrated for us this morning. Do you notice a difference in our destination?"

Phillips said nothing, his jaw tightening.

"Did you think I would fail to notice, Captain? Your change would have put us over a hundred miles too far north. Were you planning some sort of distraction, to keep us from realizing you were attempting to run these ships aground?"

"Please, Amir Khalid," Phillips said. His voice quavered just a bit. "Please. I'm afraid that . . . that you intend to use these ships as a weapon, somehow. An attack on New York City. If that's true, my passengers and crew are dead no matter what."

Khalid seemed to consider this. "Come here," he said after a moment. "Look out the window. What do you see?"

Phillips looked out over the forward deck. Hijazi had the prisoner on his knees, facing away from him, his hands zip-stripped behind his back. "Who . . . who is that?"

"That is one of your helmsmen, Captain. Jason Miller. He was at the wheel, I believe, when you changed the compass."

Khalid pulled a handheld radio from a belt holster, pressed the send key, and said something in Arabic.

"Wait!" Phillips said. "Please—"

A sharp crack sounded from outside, the shot slightly muffled by distance and the glass. Jason Miller flopped forward, striking the ship's railing, then slumped back in an untidy huddle at his executioner's feet. The gunman slung his AK, then proceeded to lift Miller's body up, press it against the railing, and topple it over and into the sea far below.

"You murderer!" Phillips snarled, turning suddenly from the bloody scene. Several of Khalid's men on the bridge stepped forward, weapons coming up.

"Do you wish to die as well, Captain?"

Phillips stopped in mid-stride, his fists clenched, breathing hard.

"If you wish, I will kill you as well, and bring your second in command up here in your place." His head cocked to one side. "Or . . . it may even be that I don't need you any longer. The ship continues to run smoothly and well. It will be simple enough to get it back on its proper course." He paused, as though thinking about it. "I choose to let you live for the moment, Captain," he said at last. "I may have need of you when we reach New York."

Reaching for a small device in a second holster on his belt, he extracted a handheld GPS receiver. "I have my own means of determining our position, Captain. And I can easily compare this with the numbers on your various instruments here. I can read a map, and some of my people are quite good with computers.

"In short, Captain Phillips, this operation has been most carefully planned and orchestrated. We know what we are doing. Do not attempt to trick me again! Do you understand?"

Phillips said nothing.

"I said, do you understand? Or shall I bring another member of your crew onto the forward deck? How many must I shoot before you obey me?"

"All right! All right! I understand!"

"Good." He looked at Aziz and jerked his head. "Take him back to his room," he said in Arabic.

When Phillips was gone, Khalid stood for a moment

looking out over the ocean. Five more days and then it would be over. It was going to be hard keeping the majority of the crew and passengers ignorant of what was happening . . . and sooner or later they would find out or figure it out, and then it would be a matter of keeping them all cowed.

Just five more days . . .

And then none of it would matter anymore.

18

National Security Council
White House basement
Washington, D.C.
Monday, 1030 hours EST

"THE PRESIDENT," DR. BING said, "was most emphatic. Both ships belong to Great Britain. The problem is theirs as well."

Rubens' jaw tightened, and he made an effort to keep his voice calm. "Madam Chairperson," he said, "I cannot stress this enough. That decision is shortsighted and it is wrong. If I could just have ten minutes with the President—"

"That is not going to happen, Mr. Rubens," Bing told him, and the tone of her voice had the finality of a slamming door. "He was very clear on the matter."

"London has indicated that they are ready to go in with an SAS assault sometime tonight," George Wehrum added. "We will support their operation by sharing intelligence, by providing logistical support, and by making available ships and helicopters to evacuate crew members and passengers from those vessels and to provide medical support when and if that becomes necessary."

"How are you going to evacuate over three thousand people in the middle of the North Atlantic?" Rubens asked. He looked around the room, trying to gauge the mood of the rest of the people at the conference table. It was crowded here, more crowded than it had been on Saturday morning.

"By aircraft carrier, of course," Wehrum said. "The *Ark Royal* is in pursuit of the target vessels now. And the USS *Eisenhower*—she was en route from Norfolk to the Med—she's been redirected and should rendezvous with the British squadron within twenty-four hours."

"What, are you planning on building a tent city on the *Ike*'s flight deck?" Admiral Prendergast asked, his tone sarcastic and possibly angry as well. Rubens wondered if the order to the *Eisenhower* had bypassed Prendergast on the way down.

"If necessary," Bing told him. "However, it almost certainly will not be necessary. The SAS is very, very good at what they do."

Rubens could only shake his head. While an aircraft carrier was big enough to carry several thousand people— the *Eisenhower* had a complement of over fifty-six hundred—it would be an absolute nightmare trying to house, feed, and care for the needs of thousands of civilians as well. And that didn't even begin to address his original question, which was how the Navy would get those civilians off of the *Atlantis Queen* and onto the *Eisenhower* in the first place. They would not be able to transfer directly, not without risking a lot of damage to both ships. Personnel could be transferred by helicopter, but there would be only a few of those available, and each could carry only a handful of people—perhaps twelve to fifteen—at a time.

There was also a serious logistical question. If the *Eisenhower*'s flight deck was covered with refugees, there wouldn't be room to handle flight operations—and there would be no place for the necessary small fleet of helicopters to land. No wonder Prendergast was pissed.

Of course, Bing was right in one respect. It probably *wouldn't* be necessary to evacuate the *Atlantis Queen*.

Either the SAS assault would be successful and the cruise ship secured . . . or the terrorists on board would push a button and blow her up.

There was also the question of the *Pacific Sandpiper* and her deadly cargo. The terrorists must be planning on using the plutonium somehow, if only as a bargaining chip.

"What about the *Pacific Sandpiper*?" General Barton said, as if he'd just read Rubens' mind. "Suppose the terrorists are using the nuclear material on board to make a bomb?"

"I believe Dr. Cavenaugh has a report on that issue," Bing said. "Doctor?"

Dr. Bruce Cavenaugh was a member of the Atomic Energy Commission and served as an advisor on nuclear threats both to the NCTC and to Homeland Security. A rumpled man in a tweed jacket, the very image of an elderly professor, Cavenaugh stood to address the group, moving around to the lectern at the front of the room with a double handful of notes and folders before him.

"We've been reviewing the possibilities," he told the group, "given PNTL's cargo manifest for the *Pacific Sandpiper*. While it's been widely reported that the ship carries enough plutonium to manufacture as many as fifty or sixty nuclear weapons, there is almost no chance at all that terrorists on board those two ships could create such a weapon themselves. For a nuclear explosion to be generated, two sub-critical masses of plutonium must be brought together *very* suddenly and *very* precisely. This requires precision tooling, and a means of reshaping the plutonium elements to achieve maximum effect. Usually, this means two hemispheres—imagine a ball cut in half—positioned so that conventional explosives slam the two halves together." He brought his hands together in a sharp clap, and several people at the table jumped slightly. "They achieve critical mass, and a nuclear explosion is the result. A second method is to machine a sphere of plutonium with a precisely drilled hole into which a plutonium cylinder is fired. A third would be to have one sphere of plutonium positioned inside a larger, hollow sphere, with conventional explosives around the outside to create a powerful implosion.

"But the plutonium on board the *Pacific Sandpiper* is carefully packaged in one-hundred-ton canisters bolted to the cargo hold deck, in such a way that the plutonium always remains sub-critical. It might be possible to use cutting torches to remove the storage containers inside each canister, true, but the plutonium is stored as plutonium oxide, an extremely fine powder. The terrorists simply don't have the facilities to transform that powder into pure, solid plutonium. If they slapped a critical mass of plutonium oxide together, the worst that would happen would be the release of a tremendous amount of heat . . . enough heat to melt through the bottom of the ship and sink her . . . what became known as the 'China syndrome' back in the 1980s. There would be extensive contamination of the sea in the ship's immediate vicinity, of course, but no explosion."

Rubens could feel the others at the table relaxing. Since the beginning of his crisis, the major concern had been that terrorists were attempting to seize the *Sandpiper* in order to either gain access to enough plutonium to make atomic bombs or threaten the United States with the possibility of a nuclear explosion.

"Dr. Cavenaugh," he said. "What about the possibility of a dirty bomb?"

"Ah! Yes. That is one possibility we've been looking at that *does* appear to pose a very real threat in this situation. The plutonium oxide is already in a fine powder form, as I said. If it were to be removed from its protective containers, a sufficiently powerful *conventional* explosion—an explosion big enough to destroy the ship, say—might hurl most of that powder into the atmosphere, where prevailing winds would carry it out over a large footprint. Any ships downwind of the explosion would be contaminated."

"Then we will recommend that our British friends stay well upwind during their assault," Bing said.

"How big of a footprint, Doctor?" Debra Collins wanted to know.

"That depends on wind speed, humidity, and several other factors," Cavenaugh replied. "But potentially five or six hundred miles long, perhaps fifty to one hundred miles wide."

"Enough," Rubens said, looking squarely at Bing, "to blanket all of Manhattan and Long Island with radioactive dust, if they blow that ship up inside New York Harbor. *That* is what I want to be certain the President understands. Those ships changed course thirty-six hours ago, and are on a heading that appears to be aimed straight at Boston or at New York City, or, if they come further down the coast, Philadelphia or Washington, D.C. Our crisis assessment team at the NSA believes the enemy's target to be either Boston—it's the closest major city on the new course—or New York City.

"Right now, the *Sandpiper* and her cargo are nineteen hundred nautical miles from New York. That's *four days* at the speed they've been traveling since Saturday night. That makes it *our* problem as well as the Brits'."

Bing shifted uncomfortably in her chair but said, "The President has already been *fully* informed, and it is his decision that this situation be resolved by the British."

"We have a special operations unit ready to go in," Rubens said, "on twenty minutes' notice, but they will need approximately twelve hours to redeploy to the *Eisenhower*. Once there, however, they would be available to provide special combat intelligence to the SAS commander on-site."

Bing appeared to consider this, then shook her head. "The President has decided that this situation will be resolved by the British."

Rubens heard the warning in Bing's voice and in the way she kept repeating her words: do *not* push. The harder he fought to have the NSA's combat action team included in the assault, the more deeply entrenched and stubborn Bing and her cronies would become.

He wondered, though, if the President really was dead set against U.S. forces participating in the op . . . or if this was Bing's way of defending her turf. Whichever it was, Bing had just slammed the door shut on Rubens, or she thought she had.

He was not willing to concede the victory to Bing and Wehrum, however, not yet. Rubens had tremendous respect for the British SAS. They were well trained and battle-tested. Some claimed they were the equals in most respects of the U.S. Delta Force.

But Rubens knew too well that no combat op ever goes down exactly the way it was planned, and if the hijacking of those two ships *was* the prelude to a terrorist nuclear attack against the U.S. East Coast, he wanted to have all of Desk Three's available combat assets on the scene and ready to go.

Just in case.

Deck Eleven, *Atlantis Queen*
48° 32' N, 27° 19' W
Monday, 1640 hours, GMT

Carolyn Howorth carefully stepped up to the door, pressing her face against the tiny window in order to see as much of the passageway beyond as she possibly could. For two days, now, yesterday and today, she'd been "skulking," as she'd described it in her reports back to GCHQ, slipping through the huge cruise ship passageways and access corridors in an attempt to garner every scrap of information she could on the paramilitary force that appeared now to be in total control of the *Atlantis Queen*.

In some thirty-six hours of skulking, she'd learned quite a bit. The hijackers appeared to be Arabic speakers, though she'd heard some speak English—including a few with no trace of an accent. She'd actually seen at least twelve different men but suspected there were others she'd not seen—up on the bridge, in the Security Office one deck down, and in places like engineering and the ship's holds, all of which were barred to anyone without a properly programmed key card.

Two guards stood outside the doors leading to the ship's Neptune Theater at all times, and she'd watched other guards escort bound crew personnel and passengers through those doors and emerge again without them. The theater, then, was a secure holding area for people the terrorists needed to take out of circulation, quite possibly because they'd seen or guessed something they shouldn't have. She hadn't been able to find a way in, yet, to see how many people had been taken there, but the traffic suggested that the number was fairly high. There were probably several terrorists inside the theater as well, keeping an eye on the prisoners.

She'd come up the forward stairwell hoping to see if there was a way to get to the Ship's Security Office. The place was sure to be guarded, she thought, but if she *could* get inside, she might be able to learn a bit more about the size and disposition of the hijackers' force.

It was the Ship's Security systems that worried her most. The *Atlantis Queen* was enormous, with mile upon mile of corridors, maintenance tunnels, and compartments that guaranteed that she could move around the ship unseen, if the hijackers weren't watching the Ship's Security cam screens, and if they didn't know how to use the onboard tracking system. According to Llewellyn's description of the system Friday night, passengers carrying key cards or the small tags with their embedded computer chips could be tracked by sensors inside the bulkheads. Worse, passengers without cards or tags could still be sensed—and a warning flashed to the Security Office that someone was wandering where she shouldn't without her ID.

She'd elected to carry her ID tag with her, on the assumption that with it, she was just one of some three thousand colored blips on the security monitor screens, and so might be overlooked even if she was now on the Eleventh Deck where she had no right to be, officially. If the sensors picked up a warm body moving in a restricted area with no ID, an alarm would sound, and that would bring the bad guys down on her like an avalanche.

The terrorists, clearly, had circumvented the security system somehow and were traveling everywhere through the ship with impunity. The question was—were they using the ship's sophisticated security systems to monitor and control their hostages?

Through the tiny door window, Howorth could just see the security checkpoint in the passageway beyond and to her right, a sealed massive steel door with a card reader and a thumbprint scanner set in the bulkhead to one side. There were no guards as there were one deck up, in front of the security door leading to the bridge and radio room. She put her hand on the door handle to open it, then ducked back when she heard the boom of another door closing somewhere down the passageway to her left. A shadow passed the window, and when she edged closer to look, she caught a glimpse of a uniformed man pressing his thumb to the scanner plate, then opening the door to the Security Department.

If she could find a way through those doors, she might be able to get to the computer room behind the Ship's Security Office. But . . . what then? It would be more effective, actually, if she could somehow get the passwords that would let her break into the ship's computer network. Or possibly the Netguardz trapdoor might give her access.

David Llewellyn, she thought, *would have those codes, or be able to get them*. But she'd not seen him since Friday.

She'd been wondering if the ship's senior security officer had fallen afoul of the terrorists and been killed or marched off like the SOCA agent she'd seen outside of Connexions.

With chilling suddenness, a man's hand slipped around the right side of her head, clamping down tightly over her nose and mouth, drawing her backward as a second hand and arm grabbed her from the left, pinning her arms to her sides. Howorth struggled wildly, trying to break free, trying to kick back against the kneecaps of her captor, but her foot struck empty air as the man squeezed more tightly. She tried to scream, but the smothering hand blocked all sound, threatening to drag her into unconsciousness.

Security Office, *Atlantis Queen*
48° 32' N, 27° 17' W
Monday, 1641 hours GMT

"There it is again, sir," Hamud Haqqani said, pointing at the display. Khalid leaned over the man's shoulder for a closer look.

The display screen was long and narrow, running left to right, and was touch sensitive. At the moment, it was showing Deck Eleven as yellow lines on a black background, the various compartments and passageways marked with coded alphanumerics translated by an inset table. Deck Eleven was divided into two sections—the aft sundeck around the ship's smokestack aft, and the superstructure forward housing security, the computer center, and, on Deck Twelve, the bridge.

Khalid touched the screen next to the forward superstructure, and the schematic expanded. Six red dots were clustered inside the Security Office—marking Khalid himself, Haqqani, and the other four with them. Just outside of the Security Office area, however, lay a passageway and, off to one side, the service access stairwell connecting several of the upper decks forward, including the bridge and Deck Eleven. A red dot hovered inside that stairwell and, when Khalid touched the screen again, expanding the schematic further, the single dot became two pressed closely together. He touched one of the dots, and a name and ID number appeared: Judith Carroll. One of the passengers. He tapped the other dot, and his eyes opened wider when he saw the ID.

Khalid looked up. Ghailiani and another member of the security team, Mahmoud Amin Rawasdeh, were seated at the security console near the door. "You two," Khalid snapped. "We have inquisitive intruders in the stairwell next to the passageway outside. Two of them. Bring them in!"

Rawasdeh picked up his AK-47, leaning against one bulkhead, and snapped back the charging lever with a harsh *snick-snack*. "Alive?" he asked.

"Any way you can get them," Khalid replied.

Rawasdeh nodded, and he and Mohamed Ghailiani hurried from the Ship's Security Office.

Deck Eleven, *Atlantis Queen*
48° 32' N, 27° 17' W
Monday, 1641 hours GMT

"Do not scream," the man's voice whispered in Howorth's ear as he clamped a hand down over her mouth. "I'm a friend! Okay?"

She nodded, and the hands released her. Turning, furious, she looked into the creased face of a rough-looking man in a dark suit jacket and tan slacks—probably in his forties, stocky, and with thinning hair. He didn't look much like an Arab terrorist.

"What are you doing up here?" he asked. "Who are you?"

"I might ask you the same thing."

"Mitchell," he said. "MI5." He quirked an eyebrow. "You?"

Before she could decide whether to answer or not, the door to the stairwell banged open and two men walked in on them.

The one in the lead wore a Royal Sky Line security uniform and appeared to be unarmed. The second man, with a bushy mustache and pocked skin, wore a khaki uniform with an Arabic kaffiyeh over his head, and was holding an AK-47 assault rifle in both hands.

Mitchell reacted immediately and decisively, stepping past Howorth, snapping his right arm out, hand open flat, to catch the first man beneath his jaw with the heel of his palm and slam him backward into the gunman. As the two collided, Mitchell reached inside his jacket and dragged out his handgun.

The gunman, though, was fast and strong. He knocked the unarmed man aside with a sweep of his rifle butt, smashing the muzzle down across Mitchell's right wrist with a sharp crack and sending the pistol clattering and skittering across the deck. Mitchell stepped inside the reach of the weapon, pushing the muzzle aside as he swung a vicious uppercut with his left, uninjured hand, then grabbed the gun's muzzle and yanked forward, hard, tugging the gunman off-balance.

Howorth, standing to one side, thought first about grabbing Mitchell's pistol, but it had skittered to the other side of the stairwell and was balanced precariously on the top step, with Mitchell and the gunman between her and the weapon. The unarmed man was on his hands and knees; Howorth leaped at the gunman's back, grabbing his kaffiyeh and the *iqal* cord that held it in place from behind with both hands and dragging them down over his eyes.

The gunman spun, teetering at the edge of the steps,

holding the AK with his right hand as he fumbled with his left to pull the checkered cloth off his face. Howorth raised her right leg, planted her deck shoe on the man's chest, and kicked, hard, sending the gunman, arms flailing, backward and off the top step.

He screamed going down, the cry echoing down the stairwell as he slammed into the steps halfway down and completed an awkward backward roll to the first landing below. Mitchell flew after him, vaulting into space and landing on the gunman's chest five feet below with a sickening thud. Reaching down, Mitchell pulled the AK from unresisting fingers with his injured hand while drawing his other fist back to deliver a final blow—

"Stop!"

Howorth turned at the voice. The unarmed man, ignored for the opening seconds of the fight, had scooped up Mitchell's P226 and now held it aimed straight at Howorth.

"Don't move or I'll shoot!" the man shouted, his voice cracking on the last word. He held the pistol with a manic intensity, both hands on the grip, arms stiff, the gun's muzzle wobbling in his unsteady grasp. Howorth raised her hands as Mitchell dropped the AK, dangling uselessly backward in one hand.

"Don't shoot!" Howorth said. She was close to the now-armed man, close enough to see the beads of sweat rolling down his cheek. If she could get a *little* closer . . . "Please, don't shoot!"

"Shit!" the man said. "Shit! Shit! *Shit!* . . ."

Howorth was startled to realize that it wasn't sweat she was seeing on the man's face but *tears*. He was crying. The pistol's muzzle wavered, then dropped to point at the deck as the man sagged, his shoulders heaving with his sobs.

Swiftly Howorth stepped forward and snatched the pistol from the man's hands. Mitchell retrieved the AK, then stooped to check the terrorist sprawled at the bottom of the steps. He looked up to meet Howorth's eyes. *Dead*, he mouthed. The tumble had broken the man's neck.

Their prisoner continued to cry.

Atlantean Grotto Lounge, *Atlantis Queen*
48° 31' N, 27° 31' W
Monday, 1702 hours GMT

Dr. Heywood Barnes stepped into the lush tropical ambiance of the Grotto Lounge and walked forward, toward the big sliding glass doors opening onto the Deck Eleven pool area. The restaurant, curiously, was deserted. Normally, it was one of the busiest social areas on the ship. A "Closed" sign had been hanging at the front entrance, but he'd ignored it and come inside anyway. The lounge was supposed to be open all hours.

Barnes rarely got up here. His quarters, along with those of the other medical personnel on board, were on A Deck, just forward of the infirmary, and while there were no rules against his coming up into the passenger areas, fraternization was discouraged, save for very specific instances—when ship's officers dined in the formal Atlantia Restaurant on Deck One, for instance, or up on Deck Nine, in the Lost Continent.

Generally, Barnes was a solitary soul who disliked crowds and social mingling, preferences that years ago had led to his taking the position of ship's doctor when he could easily have had a thriving practice ashore.

For the past several days, however, the infirmary had been anything but quiet. Members of the ship's crew and staff kept gathering there, hanging out in the waiting area or in the staff lounge, drinking tea and coffee, and discussing *them*.

"Them," of course, were the foreign soldiers, presumably Arabs, who were now everywhere on board the

Queen and who appeared to be in control of the ship. Two of them were in the main galley now at all times, flanking the big double doors leading to the aft A Deck hold. Galley personnel who had to go into the hold for supplies were escorted in and out and kept away from the area near the loading bay and external doors. But Johnny Berger and several other members of both staff and crew had been back there and seen a number of trucks parked near the doors and a large number of armed and uniformed men.

PA announcements and a memo from the bridge had spoken of helping the *Pacific Sandpiper* and of security personnel from the other ship protecting a top-secret military cargo . . . but no one really believed any of it. Phone calls to the bridge had gone unanswered. Personnel who'd physically gone to the bridge or to the Security Office to talk to someone in charge had never returned. The mess stewards, though, had been ordered to take boxes of food—cold cuts and sandwiches, mostly, and hundreds of bottles of water—up to the doors leading to the Neptune Theater, where gruff and uncommunicative uniformed guards had taken them inside. Rumor had it that the missing crew members were being held prisoner inside the theater.

Earlier that afternoon, Barnes had made his way up to Deck One and found an out-of-the-way alcove in a deserted Starbucks on the mall. From there, he could see down a passageway leading forward to the theater, where he could just make out one of the guards at the entrance without being seen himself. After an hour of waiting, another guard had led a woman out of the theater and steered her to the left, toward the restrooms. After perhaps ten minutes, the two had reappeared, vanishing once more into the theater.

So . . . there *were* prisoners being held in the theater. They were being fed and being taken to the nearest restrooms, but they were under heavy guard. Barnes had considered going up to Security but decided against it. The terrorists, if that's what they were, must be in control of the Security Department and the bridge, and if he called attention to himself, he would end up with that woman and God knew how many others tied up and under guard inside the theater.

And so, using back service access ways and emergency stairs, Barnes had ascended all the way up to Deck Eleven and the Grotto Lounge. Partly, he wanted a look at the *Pacific Sandpiper*, which some of the staff said was still tied up alongside as the *Queen* clipped ahead through the ocean at a good twenty knots—an insane pace if they were, indeed, towing another vessel. Barnes' cabin was on the starboard side of the ship, and he couldn't see anything from there. From the Deck Twelve Terrace, though, he would be able to see clearly in all directions, and be able to look down onto the *Sandpiper*.

He also wanted to check for himself the ship's course. Rumor had it that the ship had changed direction two days ago, late Saturday, and was now heading due west, instead of south toward the Strait of Gibraltar.

He heard a clatter of noise from just ahead and froze, then stepped back into the shelter of a spray of palm fronds. The restaurant's tropical jungle décor had always seemed rather silly to him, but he was glad to have the cover now. Several men were talking to one another just ahead. There was a long string of almost guttural words, followed by a loud thump. "Iyak!" one voice cried, the voice sharp, even threatening.

Barnes had spent a year in Kuwait, during his stint as a medical officer with the British Army, right out of medical school. He didn't speak the language, but he knew Arabic when he heard it. Easing forward, he tried to get a better view.

Four uniformed men were at the glass sliding doors leading out to the pool area, and they were manhandling a large flatbed handcart piled high with wooden crates under an olive-drab tarp. The cart had just become entangled with a table as they'd tried to position it in front of the door, and the men were trying to pull the cart free. "Yallah!" the one in charge cried. "Yallah!" Two more armed men, Barnes saw, were standing outside by the pool, apparently guarding a stack of identical tarp-covered crates.

Abruptly the cart bounced free of the obstruction and three of the men wheeled the cart out onto the deck while the fourth, the leader, stood to one side, gesturing to the others. In that moment, Barnes noticed two critical things.

First of all, the afternoon sun was streaming through the broad glass windows of the Atlantean Grotto Lounge. Those windows faced forward, and if the sun was coming in that way, it meant the ship was sailing west, into the late-afternoon sun.

And as the soldiers bullied the cart out the door, the tarp had been tugged aside just enough for Barnes to see letters stenciled in black on the side of one of the cases.

"FIM-92 STIN" was all he could read, the letters centered above a portion of a serial number.

But that glimpse was enough to chill Barnes' soul.

My God! he thought. *I've got to tell someone!*

But who? And how?

And was it already too late?

19

"IT'S *OKAY*," HOWORTH TOLD their prisoner. "It's okay! We're not going to hurt you!"

But the man continued to sob. *"Zahra!"* he finally managed to say. *"Zahra! Nouzha!"*

"What language is that?" Mitchell asked. "Arabic?"

"Maybe," Howorth said. She frowned. "Actually, I think they're names."

They'd brought their prisoner down to Deck Eight, the highest deck on the liner with staterooms, and used a security passkey they'd found in the man's shirt pocket to open the door to an empty cabin. The other terrorist, the one who'd broken his neck on the stairs, had been dragged to a janitorial closet on Deck Nine and stuffed inside. They had his passcard now, too, as well as his AK-47.

Now they had the prisoner between them on the bed as they tried to get some kind of sense out of him. His emotional breakdown had been startlingly swift and complete; Howorth doubted that he was one of the terrorists. He'd not been armed, and he was wearing a Royal Sky uniform. Possibly he was as much a hostage as the rest of the *Queen*'s passengers and crew.

"My . . . wife . . . ," the man finally managed to say, shoulders heaving. "My wife, Zahra. And . . . my daughter. . . ."

"What about them?" Mitchell asked. Standing suddenly, reaching down, he grabbed the front of the prisoner's blue security force uniform and bunched up his other fist. "You'd best start talking, raghead, or—"

"*Stop* it!" Howorth said, pushing the fist aside. "Damn it, Mitchell, this isn't an interrogation!"

"Like hell it isn't!" But he relaxed slightly, backing off.

"Tell us about Zahra," Howorth asked the prisoner.

"My . . . wife. They have her. And my daughter . . ."

"Who? Who has her?"

"Yusef Khalid. The leader of Islamist Jihad International. The men who . . . who have taken over this ship."

"Are you a part of this group, then?" Mitchell demanded.

The prisoner shook his head. "No. Or . . . I wasn't. Not at first. They made me help them. They *made* me. They have Zahra and Nouzha. *I had to help them!* . . ."

Slowly, they managed to drag the whole story from their prisoner. He was Mohamed Ghailiani, and he was a Moroccan emigrant, now a British subject and an employee of Royal Sky Line, living in Woolston, just across the river from Southampton. Khalid's people had abducted Ghailiani's wife and daughter, were holding them to ensure Ghailiani's cooperation.

"Do you know where they're keeping them?" Howorth asked.

Ghailiani shook his head. "No. But they've been e-mailing me . . . pictures. To show me they're still alive. And to . . . to remind me." He closed his eyes, his face screwing tight with rising panic. "Oh, God! I'll never see them again!"

"You *will*, Mohamed," Howorth told him. "We can help you! But you'll have to help us."

"When they know I've helped you," he said, pain etching his voice raw, "when they know I've *talked* to you, they'll—" He broke off, sobbing again.

"This is useless," Mitchell said.

"No," Howorth told him. "This may be the one big break we need. You *know* they're going to be putting together some kind of rescue op. Mohamed, here, will be able to give us all the intel we need. We just have to show him we can help his family."

"They . . . they're going to kill them," Ghailiani said, miserable. "They're going to kill them. . . ."

"Not if we have anything to say about it," Howorth told him. "We need to get to my stateroom and get my computer. And we'll need your e-mail account information, Mohamed. Address and password. Can you do that for us?"

Slowly, Ghailiani nodded.

"I think we'd better get out of here anyway," Mitchell said. "They'll be tracking this guy and his buddy. And *us*."

"Too right." Together, they helped Ghailiani stand and move toward the door.

**Infirmary, *Atlantis Queen*
48° 31' N, 27° 44' W
Monday, 1720 hours GMT**

Dr. Barnes sat down at the console in the back of the infirmary and switched on the power. Slipping the headphones on over his ears, he dialed up the volume slightly, listening to the hiss and crackle of ionospheric static.

The shortwave radio had been installed in the cruise ship's infirmary as a lifesaving measure, a means for the medical personnel to communicate directly with a hospital ashore in medical emergencies without having to run all the way up to Deck Twelve and the radio shack aft of the bridge.

He'd first tried using his cell phone, of course. The *Atlantis Queen*'s onboard cell network connected via satellite to shore networks, enabling passengers to make calls and connect with the Internet. However, when he tried to make a connection, all he got was a recorded voice telling him the system was temporarily unavailable. That, he reasoned, would have been one of the first things hijackers would do—shut down the phone network so that the hostages on the ship couldn't call out.

But, just possibly, the hijackers didn't know about the infirmary shortwave.

"This is Delta Charlie Sierra One-one-three Echo," he said. "To any station hearing this call. Mayday, mayday, mayday . . ."

The danger, of course, was that they might monitor the call from the radio shack. But it would take them time to get down here, or to disable the antenna on the radio mast.

"To any station hearing this call, mayday, mayday, mayday . . ."

Security Office, *Atlantis Queen*
48° 31' N, 27° 44' W
Monday, 1722 hours GMT

"Where are they going?" Khalid demanded.

"It's hard to tell," Haqqani replied, studying the liner's deck schematic. "They were on Deck Eight, but they're going down, now." He pointed. "This stairwell."

"Who do we have near there?"

"No one, sir. It's . . . it's a big ship."

Khalid scowled. That had been the problem from the beginning. With only thirty-one men on the *Atlantis Queen*, plus the fifteen or so he might be able to borrow from the *Pacific Sandpiper* at any given time, his personnel assets were sharply limited. There were so many places on board where he *had* to have people at all times—the bridge, engineering, watching the prisoners in the theater, the aft hold on A Deck, the fantail, the Deck Eleven Terrace. Most of the men had been awake for thirty hours straight at this point, and he needed to let them start rotating shifts to get some sleep.

But the two he'd sent aft to deal with the intruders on Deck Eleven had run into trouble. They should have returned almost immediately with two prisoners or word that the intruders had been dealt with . . . but according to the monitor, they were moving down and aft through the ship. Deck Six, apparently.

"Call up the records on the Carroll woman," he said.

Haqqani did so.

"Her stateroom is Six-oh-nine-one," Khalid said, reading the entry. His eyes narrowed. "Another SOCA agent, no less. Show me Mitchell's records." He scanned through those as well. "He's on Deck Four—Four-oh-seven-two. Obviously they're working together, however."

"We have six men on the Deck Twelve Terrace, sir," Haqqani pointed out. "We could send some of them down to deal with these two."

"No. I need them where they are." He was not going to allow these . . . these rats in the walls to sidetrack the plan or divert his people from their mission.

"Amir Khalid!" a voice called from the Security Office intercom speaker. "Sir, are you there?"

"I am here, Fakhet," Khalid replied. "What is it?"

"Sir, someone is transmitting from inside the ship!"

"How? The satellite phone network has been disabled!"

"This is shortwave radio," Abdul Agami Fakhet replied from the radio room, one deck above. "It's coming over the scanner."

"Let me hear."

Khalid heard a rustle, and a burst of static as Fakhet

turned up the gain on the radio scanner. "To any station hearing this *call*," a voice said, crisp and close. "Mayday, mayday, mayday . . ."

"Can you tell where the call is coming from?"

"No, sir. Somewhere on board."

Khalid thought it through. Passengers wouldn't have shortwave radios. It had to be a crew member somewhere, perhaps down in engineering. A Deck or below, certainly.

In fact, it scarcely mattered. He'd hoped that the implementation of the next phase of Operation Zarqawi might be put off a little longer, but everyone in the IJI command group had acknowledged that the assault team would have to come out into the open sooner rather than later . . . perhaps as early as today, certainly by tomorrow.

But *another* rat in the walls. With so few men to call upon, Khalid felt as though he were engaged in a colossal juggling act, trying to keep a dozen balls in the air at once.

And the first of those balls were starting to fall.

"Fakhet!" he said. "You were a radio operator in Afghanistan." He and two others had been picked for this operation because of their technical experience, so that they could man the ship's radio room.

"Yes, Amir."

"You know what shortwave sets look like. What the antennae look like."

"Yes, Amir!"

"Take Obeidat up to the ship's mast. Use the ladder and deck hatch behind the radio shack. See if you can find the shortwave antenna and cut it or pull it down."

"It will be done, Amir!"

This particular rat wouldn't be able to reveal too much to the world outside that hadn't already been guessed, but it was time to move to the next phase. In any combat, a critical aspect of battle management was the pacing, the ability to keep moving and to always stay one step ahead of one's opponent.

Khalid returned his attention to the ship's schematic. According to the data carried by the small moving red dots, both Ghailiani and Rawasdeh were traveling with Mitchell and Carroll. The four of them emerged from the stairwell onto Deck Six, now.

The most likely reason for this was that Ghailiani and Rawasdeh were dead, and the two SOCA agents had taken their ID cards with them. Like Khalid himself, Rawasdeh was a veteran of both Afghanistan and Tanzim Qaidat al-Jihad fi Bilad al-Rafidayn, the branch of al-Qaeda fighting in Iraq. He would never surrender, never betray the Cause.

Ghailiani, however, was an unknown quantity. The Ship's Security officer had been kept in line so far by threatening his wife and child—the operatives holding them e-mailed a new photograph to his account each day, proving his wife and daughter were still alive but still very much at their captors' mercy. But it was possible that Ghailiani had broken completely; for several days, now, the Moroccan had been showing the enormous stress he'd been working under, the staggering load of fear. Had he been pushed too hard? Had he elected to help the two British agents?

If the SOCA agents had managed to kill Rawasdeh and Ghailiani, they had Rawasdeh's assault rifle, and they probably had handguns of their own.

"How many men do we have guarding prisoners in the theater?" Khalid asked.

"Six, Amir Yusef," Haqqani replied. "Four inside, two at the doors outside."

"Alert the two at the doors. Send them up to Deck Six to kill those two."

"Yes, Amir."

"They are to use caution. The targets are armed. They are *not* to attempt to capture them. Just kill them as quickly and as efficiently as possible. I don't want to lose any more men."

"It will be done, Amir!"
"It had better be!"

Stateroom 6091, *Atlantis Queen*
48° 31' N, 27° 49' W
Monday, 1728 hours GMT

"Nice place you got here," Mitchell said as they stepped inside Howorth's stateroom. "I didn't get an ocean view."

"Maybe you don't know the right people," Howorth replied.

"Maybe. Who *are* your people, anyway?"

"Let's go into that later," she told him. She tossed her ID card and Ghailiani's onto the bedside table. "Watch the door, will you? If they're tracking us by these ID cards, they may be on their way here already." All business, Howorth walked to the desk set into one corner of the compartment, next to the sliding glass doors opening onto an enclosed balcony.

"Yeah. And they know our staterooms, too. Why the hell do we need to come here? We need to find a place to lay low."

She was already booting up her laptop. "Because my computer is here," she told him. "And it has its own satellite link, so we don't need to go through the ship's communications suite."

"And that right there rules out MI5 or SOCA," Mitchell said. "So . . . MI6? CIA?"

"Something like that." She glanced at Ghailiani, who was sitting on the bed now with a dazed and vacant look on his face. "Let's leave it there, shall we?"

Mitchell read her glance and nodded. It wouldn't do to discuss things like that in front of someone who was still, technically, a terrorist, or one of the terrorists' accomplices. He looked over the AK-47, then leaned against the door. Howorth typed in the first of her passwords . . . and then the second. After a moment, the front page for GCHQ's secure Internet connection came up. She typed in the final password and her user name, then began typing rapidly.

"Maybe we should pack that up and take it somewhere else," Mitchell suggested. "Damn it, they're going to be here any minute!"

"Not much longer," Howorth told him. "Just let me—"

There was a thump at the door, and Mitchell turned, startled as it opened slightly, hitting his shoulder. *"Shit!"*

Howorth glanced over her shoulder and saw him throw himself against the door, banging it shut. She kept typing. . . .

Automatic gunfire thundered in the passageway outside. Bullet holes appeared in the door, sending splinters whirling into the stateroom as Mitchell's body was smashed back a step in a spray of blood. The thunder continued, more and more holes appearing now on the inside of the door as Mitchell collapsed on the deck. Bullets slashing through the stateroom hit the balcony windows, smashing them in shattering glass. Ghailiani was hit as well, knocked back onto the bed as a booted foot smashed the wreckage of the door open.

Howorth had an instant to react. Mitchell's AK was too far, the P226 clumsily inaccessible tucked into the waistband of her jeans. Snatching up the computer, she leaped from the chair and whirled around toward the sliding door.

"Wakkif!" one of the gunmen yelled as he barged into the room, the stock of an AK-47 up against his shoulder. But Howorth was through the shattered glass door and onto the narrow balcony. The man behind her opened fire, and bullets smashed more glass and screamed off the balcony railing.

She hit the railing and hurled the computer out into the emptiness beyond. While it was unlikely that the terrorists would be able to break her laptop's security, there was no sense in handing them the computer's hard drive and the data stored there as a present. Grabbing the railing with both hands, she vaulted over, twisting to face the ship's hull as she slammed against it.

For a dizzying instant Howorth dangled a hundred feet above the ocean and the surging white wake of the ship below. The *Atlantis Queen*'s white superstructure had a slight tumblehome, and her feet and ankles, she could feel, were hanging over empty space—the opening of the next ocean-view balcony below hers. She let go.

Sliding down the tumblehome, she fell into the opening of that next balcony down, snatching at the next railing, nearly losing her grip as the shock wracked her body with pain and concussion. Somehow, though, she managed to hang on, scrambling against the railing, throwing her upper body and then her leg over the rail and onto the balcony. As she rolled up against the glass doorway, she heard voices just overhead, as the attackers came out onto her balcony.

She froze. Maybe they would think she'd fallen into the sea.

They would certainly want to check to make sure. They wouldn't follow her down the outside of the ship's hull, but they would come down to Deck Five and look, just to make sure.

At her back, the glass door suddenly slid aside. She looked up at the surprised face of a man looking down at her, and held her finger to her lips.

Art Room, NSA Headquarters
Fort Meade, Maryland
Monday, 1350 hours EST

Rubens looked up at the main display screen dominating one wall of the Art Room. At the moment it showed a shocking digital photograph blown up with punch-in-the-gut clarity—two women, one in her thirties, the other obviously much younger, lying side by side on a rumpled bed, tied, gagged, and partly undressed. A newspaper lay on their bare stomachs, folded to show the masthead logo, *The Sun*, and today's date.

"Do we have a positive ID on them?" he asked.

"Yes, sir." The reply came through an overhead speaker. Charles Gaither was an NSA analyst working at GCHQ in England and was speaking over one of the NSA's secure satellite links with Menwith Hill. He had the same image on his own monitor, thirty-four hundred miles away. "The one on the left is Zahra Ghailiani. Age thirty-four. Housewife. The other is Nouzha Ghaliani, daughter, age fifteen. Zahra's husband is Mohamed Ghailiani. Their address is a flat on Lower Mortimer Road, in Woolston. British citizens. Mohamed Ghailiani is a security officer on board the *Atlantis Queen.*"

"So the IJI is holding these two hostage to guarantee Ghailiani's compliance."

"Yes, sir. According to our informant on the *Queen,* they forced him to make security cards for them that gave them access to all parts of the ship, then forced him to help them get three trucks on board while the *Queen* was still at the dock. According to him, they've e-mailed him several photos like this since the ship left port. He's terrified for their lives."

Rubens studied the photo a moment, looking for clues in the background. The wall was dirty plaster; a piece at the extreme right edge of the photo had cracked and broken off, exposing the lath beneath.

"You'll have been analyzing this," Rubens said. "Do you have anything yet?"

"Not much. See the hole in the wall at the right? Lath and plaster construction. That means they're being held someplace pretty old, built before drywall came into general use. Almost certainly not a motel or a hotel. The bed frame is an old style, too, probably at least thirty years old."

"It doesn't look much like an upscale part of town."

"Exactly. We also know they had photos of the two women to show Ghailiani the same morning they went missing. We're operating on the assumption that they're being held pretty close to Woolston, probably in the same neighborhood, within a fifteen- or twenty-minute drive. That narrows the field for the search quite a bit. MI5 has units out now going door to door, asking people if anyone saw anything suspicious last Thursday."

"People *always* see suspicious stuff," Rubens said. "That could take a long time."

"We have one thing more to go on, Mr. Rubens. Take a look at this."

The two kidnapped women vanished from the big screen, replaced by a grainy and slightly fuzzy photo in gray-green tones. It showed a suburban street scene—rows of trees and neat, brick houses—and with a dark-colored sedan parked to the right. A man leaned on the car, smoking a cigarette and looking away up the sidewalk.

"We have a tap into the British security street-camera system," Gaither explained. "Cameras mounted on lamp-posts take shots every few seconds and forward them to the local police. Nouzha Ghailiani goes to school in the Woolston district, and we knew what bus stop she used. We dialed into several cameras in the area and came up with this."

"What about it?"

"I don't know about America," Gaither said, "but over here the police are *extremely* interested in older guys who hang around school bus stops. Nouzha's stop is just out of frame to the left. This photo was taken about fifteen minutes before her bus was due to arrive last Thursday morning."

"I see."

A white rectangle drew itself around the man's head, and the scene expanded until only the head was visible, vast and disturbing, filling the screen.

"We can't tell a lot from this shot," Gaither went on, "but the subject's mustache and skin tone are at least consistent with Middle Eastern profiling data."

" 'Profiling' is a bad word over here," Rubens said dryly, "but your point is taken."

"We got a total of thirty-two photographs of this subject," Gaither went on. "Unfortunately, the camera didn't happen to catch Nouzha."

The face vanished, the image shifting back to the street scene. The image changed, tree branches and cars in the background jumping back and forth like a choppy movie viewed frame by frame. The last three frames showed the man throw his cigarette down, grind it underfoot, and begin to walk out of frame to the right. The final image showed the car pulling out away from the curb.

"And one thing more. . . ."

The image cut back to one showing the car parked by the curb. Again a white square drew itself around the license plate mounted on the car's front bumper. The plate was partially obscured by the trunk of a small tree growing out of a planter area in the sidewalk, but as the scene zoomed in close, "E83K," the last four figures in a longer registration number, became visible.

"We have a partial plate number," Gaither continued, "and a make and model on the vehicle. MI5 is running the data through their databases now."

"Good work," Rubens said. "They may not be holding the Ghailiani family at the same address where the car is registered."

"No, but it will give us a start. We're putting together a team now to liaise with the HRT in Southampton."

"Who's running the team?"

"Edward Cartwright. Colonel, SAS."

"Okay. I'm going to send two of my agents to work with him," Rubens said. "We need to stay on top of this. I don't want to lose even thirty seconds because the lines of communication get scrambled or some idiot bureaucrat decides we can't have access."

"Right, Mr. Rubens."

"Let me know the minute you turn up anything else. Rubens out." He cut the connection.

Rubens walked over to Jeff Rockman's workstation. "Patch me through to Charlie Dean and Lia DeFrancesca," he said. "Where are they?"

"Holiday Inn, Southampton, England," Rockman told him.

A moment later, Dean's voice sounded over the speaker. "Dean. I copy."

"And DeFrancesca. What's up?"

"New assignments," Rubens told them. "Lia, you're going to the MI5 branch office in Southampton tonight, and putting yourself at their disposal. Talk with Colonel Edward Cartwright. He knows you're coming. You'll be our liaison with the SAS hostage rescue team they're assembling for an important op. Code name Imperial. Ilya Akulinin will be flying back out to join you tomorrow. He'll be your backup."

"Yes, sir. What's this all about?"

Briefly Rubens filled them in on Ghailiani and the need to find and free his family. "There's just one hitch," Rubens added. "Ghailiani may be dead or captured. We . . . lost contact with our operator on board the *Atlantis Queen* in mid-transmission."

"Who was that?" Dean demanded. "Carrousel?"

Rubens hesitated, then said, "Yes. She began transmitting over her secure link with Menwith Hill a little over an hour ago. She told us she'd hooked up with a British MI5 agent, gave us a fair rundown on the terrorists, and said they'd captured Ghailiani, one of the Ship's Security men, who's being forced to help the terrorists. But halfway through the transmission, she was cut off, mid-word. We have to assume that she and the MI5 man are dead.

Ghailiani may be dead as well." Rubens paused, then added, "I'm sorry, Charlie. I know you've worked with Carrousel before."

"So Lia's helping MI5." Dean's voice sounded hard, a bit cold. "Where do you want me?"

"You're on your way to Spithead tonight. A COD is being readied to deliver you to the USS *Eisenhower.* You'll draw CQB gear and weapons on the ship and take charge of Black Cat Bravo when it comes aboard tomorrow morning."

"Are we going to mount an assault, then?" Lia asked.

"Yeah," Dean added. "Did Saunders and the DSF come around?"

"Not yet," Rubens told them. "We're working on that."

"Meaning, Charlie," Lia said, "that they're still trying to pick up the pieces after we walked out on a British general."

"We didn't have a lot of choice," Dean said. He sounded angry. "Damn it, we were told that Saunders had been bypassed, that the Brits were going to accept American help. We go into that meeting, and there's Saunders telling us to keep our collective noses out of the UK's business. He wasn't going to play nice. So we left."

"You did the right thing, Charlie," Rubens told him. "I would have done exactly the same if I'd been there."

"What's Saunders' problem, anyway?"

"It's not him as much as us," Rubens said. "The *real* problem is that both we and London are getting mixed signals from our own people. The Pentagon wants us to go in whether the British want our help or not. A Broken Arrow alert requires a military response, and the Joint Chiefs informed London that we were prepared to handle the takedown and to safeguard the security of the *Pacific Sandpiper*'s cargo. But the President and the State Department both want to leave this to the British."

"Why?" Lia asked. "The Brits are good, yeah, but shouldn't they be looking for all the help they can get right now?"

"More to the point, shouldn't we be offering it?" Dean added.

"Of course. But the President promised to disengage from Iraq and avoid foreign military interventions. And if someone's going to try to go in shooting and fails . . . well, both the President and State would rather someone else take the fall. Right now, things in Washington are more than normally surreal."

"Hell, *that's* saying something," Dean observed.

"So what's the story?" Lia asked. "Are we going in or not?"

"This is classified, of course . . . but an SAS assault is going down tomorrow night."

"Tomorrow! They're going with Saunders' plan?" Dean asked. "A helo-borne assault?"

"We don't have the details yet," Rubens said, "but I would guess so. With luck, the commandos will get on board, take down the bad guys, and secure both ships.

"But if they don't, and assuming the terrorists don't push a button and blow both ships to bits, I want our people ready to launch a follow-up. Code name Operation Neptune. We need to find Ghailiani's family, the sooner the better, and we need to have a Black Cat team ready to insert off the *Eisenhower* if the HRT doesn't go down as planned. Understand?"

"Yes, sir," Dean said.

"Absolutely," Lia added.

"Good. Questions?"

There were none, and Rubens broke the connection.

20

Bridge, *Atlantis Queen*
North Atlantic Ocean
48° 29' N, 37° 46' W
Tuesday, 1303 hours GMT

"IS THE CAMERA ON?"

Doherty glanced at Petrovich, who had his camera riding on his shoulder, the small red light on. "We're rolling," he said. "You're on the air."

The terrorist leader actually looked a bit nervous. He pulled himself up straighter and held the microphone a bit closer to his mouth.

"I address the governments of the United States, of Great Britain, and of the world!" he said. "I am Commander Yusef Khalid of the Islamic Jihad International. As our enemies will have guessed by now, Jihad forces have boarded and captured two vessels at sea, the cruise ship *Atlantis Queen*, of Royal Sky Line, and the plutonium transport ship *Pacific Sandpiper*, belonging to PNTL. We now hold some three thousand people hostage. As you see here, we are in control of the cruise ship bridge, and we have dozens of fighters dedicated to the cause of martyrdom, positioned at key points throughout the ship." He gestured, leading Petrovich over to the starboard wing of the bridge, pointing down and aft. "You see there," Khalid continued, "the PNTL ship, tied to the side of the *Atlantis Queen*. We could blow it up, and sink the *Atlantis Queen* with all of her passengers trapped and helpless on board.

"During the past several days, we have transported a part of the radioactive cargo from the *Pacific Sandpiper* across to the *Atlantis Queen*, in effect turning that ship into a gigantic floating nuclear bomb. Any attempt to attack either ship will result in the immediate destruction of both vessels, and the deaths of everyone on board." He pulled Petrovich's arm, guiding the cameraman back into the main part of the bridge.

With the camera again on him, Khalid continued. "The United States of America has committed itself to the path of destruction, with its invasions of Afghanistan and Iraq, its tortures and barbarities at Guantánamo and the ADX, the so-called 'Supermax' prison, in Colorado.

"In exchange for the release of our hostages, we demand the immediate release of *all* Islamic prisoners currently held in the West as a result of the illegal military invasions of Islamic countries by the United States and the so-called coalition forces. In particular, we demand the immediate release of the inmates of 'H-Unit,' including Ramzi Yousef, Zacarias Moussaoui, Richard Reid, Wadih El Hage, and the other Islamic fighters held at the ADX facility in Colorado.

"In addition, we demand the payment, within four days, of one billion American dollars to agents we shall designate in Beirut, Lebanon. Upon confirmation that these prisoners have been released and that this sum has been paid, we shall release the *Atlantis Queen* and all hostages aboard it.

"We shall, however, retain control of the *Pacific Sandpiper*, and of its crew. We shall relinquish control of that vessel, its crew, and its cargo upon the confirmation of the receipt of a *second* payment of one billion dollars by our agent in Beirut.

"We are monitoring the standard marine radio channels, and are awaiting your answer. Remember! The lives of over three thousand civilians are in your hands! Any attempt at military intervention will result in their immediate execution! Any attempt to damage this vessel's propellers or otherwise cripple the ship, and everybody dies!"

Khalid made a slashing motion across his throat, ending the speech, and Petrovich lowered the camera. One of Khalid's men took it from him.

"That was . . . dramatic," Sandra Ames said, accepting the microphone from Khalid, then handing it to another of the uniformed terrorists standing on the bridge. "Would you like an interview as well?"

"Why?" Khalid said.

"I don't know. To get your message out. To win . . . understanding. I could ask you questions on the air, about you, about your cause, and you could—"

"I do not want *understanding*, woman," Khalid told her. "I want only fear." He gestured at the three CNE people. "Take them back to their stateroom. Put their equipment back in the radio room."

"Two billion dollars?" Doherty asked him. "Do you really think they'll pay you that?"

"Actually," Khalid said with a cold voice, "I don't really care."

And they led the news team back to their stateroom.

Flight Deck, HMS *Ark Royal*
48° 03' N, 35° 18' W
Tuesday, 1330 hours GMT

General Saunders was stepping onto the port flight deck elevator when his chief aide, Colonel Mabry, hurried up. "Sir! Dispatch from HQ!"

God, Saunders thought, accepting the message flimsy. *Now what?*

The elevator gave a lurch and began to rise with a shrill whine. Saunders stood between the safety railing overlooking the ocean and the bulk of an AgustaWestland AW101 Merlin helicopter transport riding the elevator up to the flight deck. The wind had freshened in the past several hours, raising the seas in swells and chop.

He read the dispatch as the elevator ground its way up, leaving the cavernous embrace of the hangar deck below. As Mabry watched, he shook his head, then read it a second time. "Bollocks," he said at last, then crumpled the message into a ball and flicked it over the railing and into the sea. "This is a hell of a time to bring this up," he said.

"Sir," Mabry said. "Is there a reply?"

"Negative," Saunders replied. "We're operating under radio silence, remember?"

"Sir!"

"This is just a delaying tactic, Mabry. They still want to bring the damned Americans into this."

"Yes, sir. But . . . if the report is accurate, sir . . ."

"It is not!" Saunders snapped. "It was demonstrated most convincingly years ago that the batteries on those weapons systems degraded without proper maintenance and storage. By now they are *quite* useless!"

"Yes, sir."

"Besides, man, consider the source! A shortwave broadcast from the hijacked ship? *Shortwave*? When they have cell phones and computers with satellite uplinks to the Internet? This . . . this message GCHQ claims to have intercepted was clearly enemy disinformation, an attempt to thwart any attempt to get close to those vessels with helicopters. And certain elements within the government are using it as an excuse to delay our op."

The elevator ground to a halt and locked with a shudder felt through the deck. The inboard safety rail dropped, and Saunders strode onto the *Ark Royal*'s flight deck. Behind him, deck personnel swarmed around the Merlin, removing chocks and attaching cables so that a tractor could tow it into position. Four other helicopters, the smaller, sleeker Super Lynx gunships, were already parked on the deck.

The *Ark Royal* was small as aircraft carriers went—nothing at all like the ponderous, angled-flight-deck nuclear monsters so beloved by the American Navy. In fact, when the *Ark Royal* had first been launched back in 1981, she and her sister ships had been designated as cruisers for political reasons.

There could be no mistaking the old girl's true design and purpose today, though. Her 183-meter flight deck with its characteristic ski-jump bow ramp for Harrier takeoffs was crowded with the readied gunships and a number of Sea Harriers; deck personnel swarmed everywhere in their color-coded jerseys, readying aircraft for Harrow Storm.

Saunders felt a surge of pride. *Damn* the politicians! He and his men were about to make bloody history!

And those damned terrorists were never going to know what hit them.

Bridge, *Atlantis Queen*
48° 03' N, 38° 15' W
Tuesday, 1405 hours, GMT

"Attention, passengers and crew of the *Atlantis Queen*," Khalid said, speaking into the PA system handset. "The governments of the United States and of Great Britain have continued to trample the rights of the Muslim peoples of the world, to wage war against us in unending crusade, to insult our holy faith, to silence our voice, and to rape our sovereign nations of our natural resources. We are fighting back. It is time now to inform you all that the *Atlantis Queen* has been commandeered by fighters in the service of Allah and of world jihad. I am Amir Yusef Khalid of the Islamic Jihad International, and all of you are my hostages until the governments of Great Britain and the United States of America surrender to our demands."

Khalid sat in the captain's chair, delivering his speech. It was amazing, he thought, that he'd been able to go this long without making this announcement, his men hiding in plain sight, as it were, as they seized the ship right under the noses of most of the civilians on board. Westerners, it was quite true, were sheep, easily misdirected, easily herded, easily managed.

Even so, it wouldn't do to underestimate them. Now that he'd transmitted his demands to the Western media, now that news of the double hijacking was appearing on every TV screen in the West, it would only be a matter of time before friends and family of the hostages ashore would begin trying to reach them. Haqqani had disabled the electronics that relayed cell-phone calls and Internet connections to and from the passengers—only on the bridge could they still get CNN—but he could do nothing about direct satellite links, rented satellite phones, and the like.

They'd discussed that possibility in their final planning session, in that dark and filthy cave in Pakistan months ago when Operation Zarqawi had first been conceived. During the al-Qaeda attack on New York and Washington, passengers on board the hijacked aircraft had learned what was happening from people on the ground. In particular, the passengers on Flight 93 had learned of the World Trade Center attacks long before the hijackers could reach Washington, D.C., and the passengers' interference had forced the airliner to crash far short of its goal.

That would *not* happen this time.

"If all of you remain calm and do what you are told," he continued, "no harm will come to you. When Great Britain and America accede to our demands, as they must, we shall depart this ship and all of you will be free to go home.

"However, to guarantee your good behavior and to keep you out of our way, some one hundred passengers and crew members have been taken to a separate part of the ship and are being held there under guard. They are unharmed, and are being well cared for. I've given orders that they be untied and given mattresses, that they be taken to the toilet facilities in small groups, that they be given food from the galley. If at any time, however, any one of you decides to 'play the hero,' as the Americans like to say, if any of you attempts to interfere with our operation in any way, we shall begin shooting them one at a time in a public place to enforce compliance.

"The rest of you may move around as you wish. I recommend that you stay in your staterooms most of the time, but you may go to the restaurants and other public areas on board as you usually do. Exceptions are the mall area on the First Deck, the theater on the First and Second Decks forward, the Promenade Deck outside, and the outside pool areas on the Ninth and Tenth Decks. Anyone who enters those areas will be shot.

"Crew members will continue to carry out their normal duties. You may go anywhere you need to go in the performance of those duties. Exceptions are the bridge, radio room, and security areas on Decks Ten, Eleven, and Twelve, the ship's holds, the theater, and the Promenade and pool deck areas outside. Any crew member who needs to go into any of those areas in pursuance of his duties must approach one of our fighters and ask permission first. Any crew member who enters any forbidden area without permission and an escort will be shot.

"*Any* attempt to harm or disarm one of our fighters or to communicate with the outside world will result in the deaths of the hostages we have sequestered for safekeeping. So stay out of our way, do not attempt to interfere, and all of you will get out of this alive." He paused, looking across the bridge at the electronic chart table. Over the past hours, enemy ships and aircraft had steadily been drawing their noose tighter.

"One thing more. At some point within the next day or

two, we expect the military forces of Great Britain and the United States to make some sort of demonstration, a hostage rescue attempt. Such an attempt would be quite foolish and doomed to fail, but your governments will feel the need to flex their muscles and try to prove to us how powerful they are.

"We are ready for them. If such an attempt is made, I strongly advise all of you to remain in your staterooms and out of danger. We cannot be held responsible if any of you are caught in the lines of fire between our fighters and hostile forces attempting to board this ship. Any attempt to interfere with our defense of these vessels, or to help an enemy boarding party in any way, or to communicate with them will result in your death and in the death of all of the hostages.

"We shall continue to address you with updates on the situation as necessary. In the meantime, stay out of our way!"

And now, Khalid thought, *for the next inevitable step . . .*

Rubens' office
NSA Headquarters
Fort Meade, Maryland
Tuesday, 0915 hours EST

"Yes, Dr. Bing," Rubens said into the telephone receiver. "We've seen it."

A wooden panel on his office wall had been opened, revealing a line of six TV monitors. All were on, now, showing the ongoing news from two CNN feeds, plus FOX, CNBC, and the major networks. One monitor now was showing a replay of the shaky footage from the *Atlantis Queen,* broadcast at just past eight that morning, Eastern Time. The others all showed talking heads.

"It's been playing on every news channel since the

transmission came through this morning," Bing said at the other end of the line. "God. CNBC already has a fancy computer-graphic logo for their special news bulletin up and running."

" 'Terror at Sea,' " Rubens said. "Yes. A bit on the tacky side."

"The terrorists are demanding two billion dollars plus the release of several hundred prisoners. The President has announced that we will not negotiate."

"I saw his press conference a few minutes ago," Rubens told her.

"He wants to know if your Black Cat team is still ready to go."

"It is." Rubens did not add that most of Black Cat Bravo was already on board the carrier *Eisenhower*, now steaming less than two hundred miles to the south of the hijacked ships. Charlie Dean was en route on board a COD C-2A—the acronym stood for Carrier On-board Delivery—flying from England to a rendezvous with the carrier in another few hours. In addition, the USS *Ohio*, a special forces–capable submarine transport, was on her way from Norfolk with Navy SEALs on board and an ASDS strapped to her afterdeck.

"The President still insists that the British go in first," Bing told him. "We still fully expect the SAS to be able to capture both ships. However, should they run into trouble, the President is authorizing a limited military response."

"A limited response? What the hell does *that* mean?"

"That we be prepared to assist British forces, but that they handle the brunt of the operation."

"Fair enough."

"The President is adamant, however, that we not risk a public relations debacle. With over three thousand hostages on board those ships, collateral damage is inevitable. We can't afford to be . . . to be associated with that."

Rubens managed to bite back an acid reply. It wouldn't do to antagonize ANSA, who, together with the Director of National Intelligence, was one of the NSA's two conduits to the Oval Office.

But the chronic Washingtonian ass-covering infuriated Rubens. Bing was right, of course. With a military assault on those hijacked ships, there *would* be "collateral damage," as she so delicately put it, almost certainly. Counterterrorist scenarios typically assumed a minimum of 10 percent casualties among any hostages present, and for the *Atlantis Queen*, that meant an appalling figure of over three hundred civilians killed or wounded in the assault, many of them, probably, victims of friendly fire. If the attack stalled on the way in, leaving terrorists guarding the hostages time to begin killing their prisoners, the figure would be much, *much* higher.

But the alternative was either paying the ransom or watching *all* of the hostages die if the terrorists had explosives on board those ships—and that was a near certainty. Carrousel's interrupted report had mentioned trucks in the cargo hold. That might mean as much as several tons of high explosives on board the *Atlantis Queen*, enough to easily sink the ship.

Enough to easily create a titanic dirty bomb with the radioactive material from the *Pacific Sandpiper*.

Paying the ransom, Rubens knew, would not be an option. Some of those talking heads on the TV monitors had been urging just that: give them what they want; too many lives are at stake to play macho games.

But the lesson learned from the turbulent seventies and eighties, when international terrorism had first exploded across the national consciousness, had been that giving in to terrorist demands guaranteed *more* terrorist demands, more hostages taken, more lives lost. If al-Qaeda thought they could bully America into paying money and freeing prisoners, they would continue to bully America in a never-ending vicious circle.

Besides, no one in either Whitehall or Washington was going to let Khalid and his people blissfully sail off with a cargo of two and a half tons of plutonium. Rogue states such as Iran and North Korea had the industrial capability to turn MOX into weapons-grade plutonium; no one wanted to see them or al-Qaeda acquire sixty atomic bombs or use the stuff with conventional explosives to spread radioactive dust clouds over Western cities. There would be a military reckoning. There was no other viable choice.

"You can tell the President that we will be most discreet," Rubens said at last, barely disguising the sarcasm. "This isn't about who gets the credit, you know. Or about who gets the blame."

"Sometimes, Bill," Bing told him, "I don't think you grasp the realities of modern global politics."

"Sometimes I'm delighted that that's the case. I would be risking my sanity otherwise."

She ignored the riposte. "Tell me about this message your people picked up yesterday."

"Your office has a copy. As does NCTC and CIA."

"Yes, but what do you make of it?"

"Our listening station at Menwith Hill picked it up about sixteen hours ago. Shortwave broadcast. It purported to be from one of the *Atlantis Queen*'s doctors. It pretty much verifies what we already know of the situation . . . but adds that he saw a number of crates on an upper deck with 'FIM-92' stenciled on them. He thought it important enough to make a special note of it. As with Carrousel, the transmission was cut off in mid-broadcast. We haven't heard from him since."

"I was told you informed General Saunders directly."

Her voice was cold, colder than usual. *God*, he thought. *She's going to make it into a turf war.* Within the intelligence community, information was power. ANSA would see his decision to bypass the NSC, the NCTC, and the President himself as undercutting her authority.

"Actually, Dr. Bing, I told Menwith Hill to pass the

information on to Saunders. It is military intelligence critical to his operation, first, and second, I thought it would help mend fences if I made sure he heard it from a *British* intelligence source, rather than from us. I gather Saunders is sensitive about the . . . relationship we have with GCHQ."

He didn't add that he doubted that Saunders would have accepted any information from an American source in the first place, or that Rubens had also transmitted the information to Lia and Akulinin in Southampton, just to be certain.

He could almost hear the wheels turning in Bing's head on the other end of the line. "That was good thinking, Bill," she said at last. "And appropriate. Just remember that the President is *very* concerned about the diplomatic angles of this situation. You'd be best advised to keep the NSC in the loop with all of your decisions to disseminate information. We have protocols for controlling that sort of thing."

"Of course, Dr. Bing."

"We'll talk again after Harrow Storm."

She hung up, and Rubens turned again to watch the talking heads on his wall. On NBC, a noted psychologist was discussing the sense of helpless anger within the Palestinian community that led to their feeling of betrayal and abandonment by the West.

On Rubens' computer screen, a map showed the North Atlantic, with several points marked by red and blue dots, and by thread-thin lines showing the courses of a dozen ships over the course of the past several days. The red symbol pinpointing the *Atlantis Queen* and the *Pacific Sandpiper* had been maintaining a steady heading of almost due west, toward America's eastern seaboard. They were now less than eighteen hundred nautical miles from New York City.

Blue symbols were closing in on the red from three

directions—the *Ark Royal* and her consorts from the east, the *Eisenhower* battle group from the south, the *Ohio* from the west. Aircraft were shown as well, forming a ring around the hijacked vessels a hundred miles out. Two British frigates, the *Campbeltown* and the *Sheffield*, had closed to within about fifty miles of the two hijacked vessels. The rest were farther out, strung out from one hundred to two hundred miles away.

"So what's your *real* mission, Khalid?" Rubens asked aloud. "You have to know we're not going to let you get anywhere near the U.S. coast with that plutonium, hostages or no hostages."

If it was straight extortion—money for ships and hostages—they could have managed it with the *Atlantis Queen* alone and a few trucks full of high explosives. Why the added risk and complication of hijacking the *Pacific Sandpiper* as well?

Nor was it about hijacking the plutonium alone. The NSA had known almost immediately three days ago, on Saturday evening, when Khalid's people had begun transferring several hundred pounds of MOX from the *Sandpiper* to the *Queen*. Each large storage flask had a GPS tracking unit mounted on its casing, and each internal container had one as well; they could be tracked by satellite with superb accuracy, to within half a meter. If they tried to load even a single one of those containers onto another boat, the Agency would know and be able to track it anywhere in the world.

So this wasn't about trying to acquire plutonium for some rogue state's nuclear weapons program, either.

The *Queen* had radar. Khalid must know those ships and aircraft were out there.

What are you up to?

The records people at Langley had already pulled a fat dossier on Yusef Khalid, or, rather, on Rahid Sayed as-Saadi, which appeared to be his real name. As Yusef Khalid, he'd been hired by Royal Sky Line three months earlier. He'd claimed to be Egyptian, born and raised in Alexandria, and had come with sterling references, of course, including a letter from the Egyptian Ministry of Culture. His excellent English—he also spoke fair German and Turkish besides both the Egyptian and Syrian dialects of Arabic—had recommended him to the cruise ship company first as a translator. His training and his first shipboard assignment, however, had been with ship's security. *That* was an odd anomaly that would need to be investigated.

So much for the man's legend—the intelligence community's word for his fictitious background and identity. Royal Sky Line and MI5, it seemed, simply hadn't dug deep enough.

The man whose bearded face had appeared on all of the news channels this morning had been positively matched by the CIA's Office of Image Analysis with another identity entirely—Rahid Sayed as-Saadi. Like Osama bin Laden, he was Saudi, a native of Riyadh. He might have known bin Laden at the King Abdulaziz University. He'd fought with bin Laden and other mujahideen against the Soviets in Afghanistan and probably been in on the formation of al-Qaeda in the early 1990s. He was still wanted for questioning in regards to the *first* World Trade Center bombing back in 1993; he'd been photographed by the FBI in several meetings with Ramzi Yousef, who'd masterminded that attack. After 9/11, Rahid had gone first to Afghanistan, where he'd been captured by American forces at Tora Bora and questioned by the CIA . . . before being mysteriously released by Afghan Northern Alliance troops.

After that, he'd gone to Iraq, where he'd helped Abu Musab al-Zarqawi create the Tanzim Qaidat al-Jihad fi Bilad al-Rafidayn, better known as AQI—al-Qaeda in Iraq.

He'd been with al-Qaeda from the beginning, a member of bin Laden's inner circle. The CIA's best guess was that this Islamic Jihad International was a new operations arm for al-Qaeda.

If Rahid Sayed as-Saadi was running this show, it was very big, and very deadly.

What are you really *up to, you bastard?* Rubens asked again.

Kleito's Temple, *Atlantis Queen*
48° 01' N, 39° 09' W
Tuesday, 1550 hours GMT

"So we're agreed?" Andrew McKay said.

The others sitting around the table with him nodded. Most of them looked scared. Some looked defiant. A few— like the Hollywood agent Jake Levy—looked numb.

"Not all of us," Dr. Barnes replied.

"I knew we'd been hijacked as soon as those men came to our stateroom yesterday," Adrian Bollinger said, grim. Tabitha Sandberg, sitting next to him and holding his hand, nodded. "They were looking for that woman who came in over our balcony, and they meant business. They hit me in the face with a rifle butt when I told them to get the hell out of my cabin, and they threatened to rape Tabby. If there's any way off of this hell-ship . . ."

"Yeah, well, we all heard the PA announcement from the bridge yesterday," Reggie Carmichael said. "We all know the score, right? We know we're all gonna die if we don't *do* something!"

"They have Gillian," Levy said, "*and* they have Bernie. . . ."

"Gillian and Bernie? Who are they?" Donald Myers wanted to know.

"Arnold Bernstein and Gillian Harper," Carmichael said. "Bernie is her manager." When Myers looked blank and gave a slight negative shake to his head, Carmichael added, "Gillian Harper? The hottest MTV star ever?

'Livin' Large'? Platinum labels and music video hits out the ass?"

"Sorry," Myers said. "Never heard of her."

"Jesus! Where've you been, man? Kansas?"

"Baltimore."

"*Enough!*" McKay said. "Keep it down, all of you!" He glanced around the room, trying to peer past the clumps of tropical vegetation and faux Mayan ruins. There didn't appear to be any of *them* in the Deck Eleven lounge, but he didn't want to take the chance of being overheard, or of attracting attention. Too much was at stake.

Barnes, the ship's doctor, took a sip of his drink. "The ship has been taken by terrorists," he said. "They are well armed, and preparing to fight off any attempt by the military to retake the ship. But it still might be that our best bet is to hunker down and wait this out."

"I am getting my wife and child off of this ship, Doctor," McKay said. "The sooner the better!"

He'd left Nina with Melissa back in the stateroom. He looked at the others around the table, trying to assess their spirit.

"How about a show of hands?" Stephen Penrose asked. "Everyone who thinks we should steal a lifeboat and get the hell off this ship, raise your hand!"

Of the fourteen people around the large table, eleven voted yes.

"We can't decide something like this democratically," Barnes said. He'd not raised his hand. "My duty is *here*, looking after the passengers and crew. But I'll help you if I can."

"I can't go," Levy said. "They have Gillian!"

"Yeah, Jake? And maybe you want to join the bitch, wherever she is," Carmichael said.

"Listen," Donald Myers said. He'd not voted, either, but he seemed unsure. "I've got a whole bunch of people in my tour group. Can we bring them?"

"How many?" McKay asked.

"Nineteen total," Myers replied. "Fourteen women, four men . . . and myself."

"That's the Baltimore tour group?" Barnes asked him. "Yes."

Barnes shook his head. "Most of them are elderly," he said. "One's using a walker, isn't she? I think their chances are better here, not bobbing around in a rough ocean for God knows how long before a ship picks you up."

"I don't think that's a good idea," McKay said. "The fewer people in our party, the better, y'know? And we don't want to be held back by walkers and arthritis."

Myers nodded. "I understand."

"You're welcome to come."

He shook his head. "No. I need to stay with my people."

"It'll just be the eleven of us, then," McKay said. "That's a good number. Johnny, here, can use his key to lower one of the lifeboats. We pile in, lower away, and let the ship sail over the horizon. Then we use the emergency transmitter on board to call for help. You *know* the military's going to be listening to every frequency."

"It'll be rough," Berger warned. He was a ship's steward whom McKay had met and talked with several days ago. Berger had been instrumental in helping get this group of men and women together, passing messages and cell-phone numbers and getting them into the Kleito Lounge for this meeting. "Lifeboats aren't supposed to be dropped into the water when we're moving."

"How fast *are* we moving?" Penrose asked.

"I'm not sure," Berger said. "Eighteen, maybe twenty knots. Our top speed is closer to twenty-five, but we're dragging the *Sandpiper* alongside, so we haven't been going at our absolute max."

"We'll have to chance it," Bollinger said.

"If we release the davits just before we hit the water," Berger added, "it'll be a jolt, but it shouldn't be any rougher than an amusement park water ride, right?"

"We'll do what we have to do," McKay said. "This is about survival."

"How long will we have to wait before someone picks us up?" Sandberg asked.

"Probably not too long," Barnes told her. "My guess is that the military will be putting together a takedown as we speak. You'll be spotted pretty quick."

"If they get us soon enough, we can tell them what we know about the terrorists," Carmichael suggested. "They'll have us *all* on TV!"

"First things first," McKay said. "First we get off the ship. We worry about press conferences later."

And in hushed voices, they began to discuss the details of their escape.

Bridge, *Atlantis Queen*
47° 56' N, 40° 38' W
Tuesday, 1810 hours GMT

"Amir!" Jamel Hijazi shouted from the radar display. "They're coming!"

Khalid walked over to the display, which was set now to show everything around the *Atlantis Queen* and the *Pacific Sandpiper* out to a radius of 120 nautical miles. The display used computers to integrate the data from several radars mounted on the mast above and behind the bridge in order to show both surface and air targets. Two surface targets had been dogging their wake for two days, now, very slowly closing to a range of less than fifty miles. Their IFF codes had been changed so that the *Queen*'s computers couldn't identify them, but Khalid suspected they were a pair of British destroyers or frigates. Military aircraft were circling a hundred miles out.

But something new had appeared on the display . . . a tiny double chevron of bright green dots, four in front, four close behind, coming straight toward the *Queen* and the *Sandpiper* at 150 knots.

Helicopters.

"Tell Ibrahim to stand ready," Khalid said, "and to wait for my signal."

As Hijazi picked up the intercom handset and began speaking rapidly into it, Khalid watched the approaching targets, nodding. *It begins. . . .*

21

Helicopter Talisman One
North Atlantic Ocean
47° 48' N, 40° 46' W
Tuesday, 1843 hours GMT

"FIVE MORE MINUTES, GENERAL! Amethyst is peeling off now!" The helicopter pilot had to use his radio headset to call the information back and be heard above the roar of the rotors. The AW101 Merlin, its cargo deck crowded with battle-ready SAS troopers, screamed along less than a hundred feet above the water, and the thunder filled General Saunders' claustrophobic world.

"Right!" Saunders called back. He looked at the men with him, black-clad, faces masked by balaclavas and gas masks, torsos swaddled in Kevlar and combat vests and equipment. It gave them an otherworldly look, alien invaders bent on destruction.

It was an image deliberately fostered by the Special Air Service, an appearance not only practical in combat but also designed to terrorize hostage takers for the mind-numbing instant of confrontation, an instant these men were trained to utilize with deadly speed and precision.

His critics, Saunders knew, would attack him for his presence here, but Alexander Saunders was not the sort of man who would send his boys in while he remained behind, safe and secure in the rear. He'd been a colonel in the SAS before his promotion to brigadier and, later, his appointment to the DSF. It was important that he be here, to make a statement, to prove that Britain still had the resolve to go toe-to-toe with evil and to *win*.

Saunders let his mind move through the ops plan once more, looking for anything that might have been missed, any preparations or final orders that needed to be made. There was nothing. They were ready. They were *go*, as their American cousins might have said.

The assault code-named Harrow Storm was deploying as two waves. Amethyst was first, four HMA.8 Super Lynx attack helicopters on loan from the Three Commando Brigade Air Squadron at Yeovilton. They'd been outfitted as gunships, each mounting two 20mm cannons and eight TOW antitank missiles. Coming up on the *Pacific Sandpiper* and the *Atlantis Queen* from astern, they were swinging off to the north now to begin their attack.

One, Amethyst Three, would go straight in, firing a wire-guided missile at the chain gun mount on the *Sandpiper*'s stern. The other three would swing around past the *Queen*'s starboard side, using the cruise ship as a shield in order to loop past the vessels' bows and come down on the *Sandpiper*'s bridge house from forward. Amethyst One and Two would take out the *Queen*'s forward starboard and port chain gun mounts respectively, while Amethyst Four provided cover and backup, using its cannons to disable the terrorists' helicopter and to clear the freighter's deck and superstructure. With the chain guns out of commission, the attack helicopters would then circle both ships, using their cannons against targets of opportunity, and in particular firing into the bridge windows in order to kill the terrorist leaders. Another prime target was the A Deck cargo hold doors, which satellite surveillance imagery showed to be open at the moment, with a gangway connecting them with the *Sandpiper*'s deck. If those doors were closed, Amethyst Four would open them with a wire-guided missile.

Sixty seconds precisely after the coordinated attack began, Talisman Flight would reach the combat area, each carrying twenty battle-tested SAS commandos. Talisman Two's stick would fast-rope onto the *Sandpiper*'s superstructure above the bridge, then move to secure the bridge and communications center. Talisman Three would do the same with the *Queen*'s bridge, while Talisman Four lowered its stick onto the *Sandpiper*'s deck immediately adjacent to the gangway leading to the cruise ship's hold. Their responsibility would be to get onto the cruise ship and disable any explosives that might have been rigged around the transferred radioactive canisters.

Talisman One would be in reserve, sending its commandos wherever they were needed, but with special attention paid to the *Sandpiper*'s cargo holds forward. The op planners had felt that it was unlikely that the terrorists had planted explosives around the large one-hundred-ton canisters on the *Sandpiper*, because even an explosion large enough to blast the ship to bits would be unlikely to breach them. Intel from the NSA operator on board the cruise ship suggested that any explosives were there, in the *Queen*'s aft hold.

The plan, code-named Harrow Storm, depended on speed, surprise, and overwhelming firepower for success. If anyone on either ship had a button ready to push to detonate those explosives, it would be in the hands of Khalid himself, rather than risking premature martyrdom with a poorly trained AQ soldier. And the psych wonks had done a thorough workup on the man calling himself Yusef Khalid. He was into a power trip, they said, and would not surrender the responsibility for blowing up those ships to an underling.

He would also, they insisted, hesitate before committing suicide and ending the mission. With the ships, the hostages, and two and a half tons of plutonium, he held what he believed to be the winning hand . . . which, oddly enough, meant he would wait before playing it. The man, according to all intelligence reports on him, wasn't religious; he would want more than martyrdom at sea. If the psych profiles were accurate, he wanted to sail those two hijacked ships into New York Harbor or Boston Harbor and hold them for ransom.

So the op planners estimated that there was only a 20 percent chance that Khalid would push the button before the SAS could kill him and secure the explosives.

An 80 percent chance of success was pretty good in Saunders' estimation, better than you usually got in this business.

Less certain was the fate of the hostages on board. Some were bound to be hit when those wire-guided missiles started detonating, especially on the *Sandpiper*. Captains and senior officers might well still be on the bridges of the two vessels, and they would almost certainly be killed if they were. And the SAS assault teams would be first moving to secure the radioactive canisters and any explosives planted around them and worry about hostage rescue later. A lot of civilians might die. Any crew members still in the engineering sections deep in the bowels of both ships might be killed as well.

But what was certain was that *all* of them would die if Khalid blew up the ships and blanketed the area with a cloud of radioactive fallout, especially if his ultimate goal was to set off his bombs in Boston or New York City. The SAS troopers would save as many of the civilians as they could, but their first responsibility, spelled out most carefully in their orders, was dealing with the terrorist bomb threat, followed closely by ensuring the safety of the MOX canisters on both ships.

"Amethyst is beginning the attack run!" the helicopter pilot called to him.

"Right." He made a fist of his gloved hand and punched the air. "Showtime, people! Let's kill some tangos!"

The troops cheered as the Merlin transport accelerated, engines howling.

Security Office, *Atlantis Queen*
47° 48' N, 40° 46' W
Tuesday, 1846 hours GMT

"Amir!" Ahmad Khaled Barakat's voice sounded calm over the intercom channel. "They are beginning an attack run."

"Wait," Khalid replied. "*Wait!* No one is to fire without my direct order!"

He was in the Ship's Security Office, watching the approaching helicopters on a monitor displaying the feed from a camera mounted on the ship's Deck Nine fantail, looking aft across the swimming pool there. Three of the four helicopters in the lead were angling off to the left, toward the starboard side of the *Atlantis Queen*. The remaining lead aircraft, plus the other four, larger and heavier aircraft, continued to approach from astern.

So predictable, he thought.

Khalid and the Operation Zarqawi planning staff had expected something of the sort, of course. The Americans and their British lapdogs weren't about to let the *Pacific Sandpiper*'s cargo go without at least a show of force.

He held a microphone in one hand. "Barakat! Are you ready?"

"We are ready, Amir! We have target lock."

"Hold steady. Track them, but do not fire!"

"Yes, Amir!"

"Shawi! Are your people set?"

"Yes, Amir! The gun ports are all open, as you commanded. We're tracking them with the stern gun!"

"Do not fire until I give the order."

"As you command, Amir!"

"Let me see Camera Ninety-five," he told Hamud Haqqani, seated at the monitor immediately in front of him. That camera was located on the terrace overlooking the pool and sundeck on Deck Eleven, between the bridge superstructure and the ship's smoke stack. The camera angle could be controlled by Haqqani from Security and was looking now out across blue water as three of the four lead helicopters flew past. The fourth was centered on the view from the fantail, steadily moving closer.

"Amir! This is Fakhet, in the radio room!" a voice called over the intercom. "They are transmitting. They say they want to check on the condition of the passengers and the crews of both ships! They say this is not an attack, and that they are willing to negotiate!"

"Ignore them," Khalid snapped.

The enemy would be using the transmission as a ploy, hoping to get as close as possible. Those four leaders were gunships; he could see the TOW missile launchers slung from outrigger pylons to either side of each helicopter.

The three lead attack helicopters were visible in full broadside now, passing the *Queen*'s starboard side where the *Sandpiper*'s guns couldn't reach them.

He keyed his microphone. "All stations . . . *fire*! Fire *now*!"

Grotto Pool, Deck Eleven, *Atlantis Queen*
47° 48' N, 40° 46' W
Tuesday, 1847 hours GMT

"Fire *now*!" Khalid's voice called over the radio in Ahmad Khaled Barakat's earphone.

He raised his hand, then snapped it down. *"Fire!"*

The five men with him on the Grotto deck stood along the starboard rail, each balancing a one-and-a-half-meter-long tube over his shoulder. Three of the men fired their weapons, the back-blasts spitting bursts of white smoke across the suddenly churning waters of the pool. Three missiles leaped from the launch tubes, kicked out by small ejection motors that carried them a safe distance from the shooters before the main, solid-fuel rockets fired. They dropped a few feet before the main engines engaged, giving them an odd, swooping look as they streaked out and up toward their targets, the motors white-hot on the leading tips of their gently curving contrails.

The weapons were American-made FIM-92 Stinger shoulder-launched antiaircraft missiles, a type well known to the mujahideen fighters of Afghanistan during their war against the invading Soviets. All six of the men standing behind the railing were veterans of that war. Barakat himself had stood on an icy, wind-blasted precipice north of Kabul and brought down a Russian Mi-8 helicopter with one, over twenty years earlier, and he'd trained all five of the others in their use at various camps across the border in Pakistan.

Ironically enough, it had been the American CIA that had provided these missiles, a means of striking at the Soviets through their mujahideen proxies in Afghanistan over twenty years earlier. The Americans had supplied as many as two thousand Stinger launchers to mujahideen camps in Pakistan and taught Barakat and others how to use them. Later, when the hated Soviets had at last been sent scurrying north beyond the Kotal-e Salang, the money-crazed Americans had actually tried to *buy back* the unused launchers.

As if Allah's holy fighters would ever surrender such magnificent weapons!

Three targets, three missiles. The other two men stood ready, launchers balanced on their shoulders, waiting to see if the first three would find their targets or if they would need to fire more. The missiles streaked low across the water, their infrared homing sensors drawing them relentlessly toward the hot engine exhaust ports on either side of each Super Lynx's engine.

The first Stinger struck the lead helicopter squarely in the engine just below the main rotor, the three kilograms of high explosives in the warhead detonating with a sharp flash and a spray of fragments. The aircraft staggered in mid-air, rolling to the right as its main rotor began to come apart, then plunging nose first into the sea with a vast white splash.

The other two helicopters had started to shear off toward the north, but a second Stinger missile found one of those and exploded against its fuselage as well. Smoke boiled from a hole in the aircraft's side. The third Super Lynx released a string of flares like dazzling stars as it turned away, struggling to gain altitude. The last Stinger started to follow it up, then veered off, tracking a flare instead.

"New weapons!" Barakat yelled, pointing. "Now! And you two! Go aft! Quickly! Quickly!"

Arif and Nejmuddin, the two men who'd not yet fired, hurried toward the right, running past the white loom of the cruise ship's smokestack. The other three dropped their empty launchers and snatched up three more. A pile of cases had been laid out in a neat row beside the swimming pool, opened and ready, all of them covered by a large tarpaulin to keep the weapons hidden from the prying eyes of American satellites.

They would reload the empty tubes later. Right now, it was faster to grab new launchers. Several BCUs, or Battery Coolant Units, rested on the deck nearby. Each man plugged a tube from the BCU into the hand guard of his new weapon, charging it with argon gas and preparing it to fire.

Over the years, many of the weapons had become useless. Those battery packs needed careful maintenance to keep them charged; the argon gas canisters sometimes leaked. But enough had been kept in working order, or been refurbished by parts brought from other sources. There were even *American* weapons dealers willing to break their own laws and sell fresh battery packs to Saudi buyers, for enough money.

What was it Lenin had said about selling Capitalists the rope with which they would be hanged?

Astern, there was a flash, and a missile came streaking in low above the ships' wakes. The fourth helicopter had just fired a missile, which was arrowing straight toward the stern of the *Pacific Sandpiper*. At almost the same instant, Nejmuddin fired his Stinger at the hovering aircraft. Arif fired his weapon an instant later.

The trick here was to make the helicopter pilot veer off before the wire-guided missile struck its target, a deadly game of chicken. The British pilot held his figurative ground, however, dropping a string of bright-burning flares and holding his position until the TOW missile slammed into the open gun port above the *Sandpiper*'s fantail and detonated with a savage blast. Only then did he swing his aircraft's nose to the right, beginning a hard turn away from the battle, but before he'd completed the turn the first Stinger streaked into the fuselage just behind the cockpit and exploded.

Barakat raised a pair of binoculars to his eyes, studying the retreating Super Lynx. The first round of the battle had certainly gone to the jihadist fighters, but only one aircraft had been shot down, and though two of the others were damaged, they were still in the air, and all three were still armed and deadly. There were also four more helicopters in the air, the troop transports, still a couple of miles out.

The battle wasn't over yet.

Art Room
NSA Headquarters
Fort Meade, Maryland
Tuesday, 1348 hours EST

"It's not over yet," Jeff Rockman said, his eyes on the big screen, along with those of every other man and woman in the Deep Black ops room. Amethyst Two had just gone down into the sea.

"Yes, it is," Rubens replied softly. "They've lost the element of surprise."

On the enormous monitor filling much of the wall in front of the Art Room consoles and workstations, the battle unfolded in eerie, green-lit silence. The images this time were coming not from a U.S. spy satellite but from an aircraft currently orbiting nearly two hundred thousand feet above the North Atlantic, on the very edge of space.

Once, that aircraft had been known by the code name Aurora, and some insiders continued to refer to it as such. The actual name had been changed in 1985, when a military censor had missed the mention of "Aurora" in a Pentagon budget request to Congress, and the very existence of such an aircraft remained one of the U.S. government's most closely guarded secrets. With pulser ramjet engines fueled by liquid methane, the hypersonic Aurora could accelerate to mach 6 and reach altitudes of sixty miles or more, qualifying the handful of Air Force pilots flying them for astronauts' wings. This aircraft had left Groom Lake—the fabled Area 51 in southern Nevada—in the wee hours of Sunday morning, arriving at its operational airfield in Machrihanish, Strathclyde, on the tip of the Kintyre Penninsula in Scotland, just over an hour later.

From there, it had deployed out over the ocean to the targeted operational area for the past three days, tracking the *Atlantis Queen* and the *Pacific Sandpiper* closely. From its perch almost forty miles up, the dead-black, triangular aircraft remained invisible and unheard; its array of sophisticated cameras, imaging radars, and other senses gave observers at the NRO, the Pentagon, the CIA, and the NSA unprecedented resolution, better even than the best views afforded by the Argus series or other spy satellites.

On the big wall display, the view had zoomed in on the flat, open deck between the *Atlantis Queen*'s bridge house and Deck Twelve Terrace, and the open passageways leading aft on either side of the smokestack. There was a light cloud cover between the spy plane and the ship, so the view was illuminated in greens and gray tones, a computer-synthesized blending of radar, IR, and UV imaging.

When the terrorists pulled back the tarpaulin, the Stinger missile launchers in their opened crates had been easily identifiable. So were the BCU units on the deck, bleeding cold argon gas under IR wavelengths in thin, black clouds. Three of the terrorists, seen from almost directly overhead, ran aft past the smokestack.

Voices called back and forth from the Art Room's overhead speakers.

"This is Amethyst Three! Target lock!"

"Amethyst Three, Talisman One! Take your shot!"

"Three, firing!"

"Pull back," Rubens said. "Let's see the helicopters."

The view zoomed out, the two hijacked ships dwindling to side-by-side mismatched green rectangles against a black sea. Two helicopters were turning away to the north, one trailing hot smoke, while a spreading patch of white-on-black marked the crash site of Amethyst Two. Amethyst Three was dead astern of the two ships. They watched in silence from the Art Room as a wire-guided missile streaked away from Amethyst Three toward the stern of the *Sandpiper*, as, an instant later, the contrails of two Stinger missiles drew white lines out from the *Atlantis Queen*'s superstructure toward the British helicopter gunship.

The TOW missile struck, the explosion of white fog from the back of the freighter's deckhouse silent and sudden. Before the Super Lynx gunship could turn away, one of the Stingers struck it, the second missing and falling into the sea.

"Amethyst Three, I'm hit! I'm hit!"

"Amethyst Three, Talisman One. Break off! Break off!"

"This is Amethyst Two! I'm losing power! Mayday! Mayday!"

A second helicopter plowed into the ocean, a gentler

impact than the first as the pilot tried for a controlled touchdown.

"Talisman Two, Talisman One! Get in there and see if you can help Amethyst Two! All units, break off the attack. Repeat, break off! Break off!"

"Damn!" Rockman said.

"They had no choice," Rubens said.

"But they got the number three gun on the *Sandpiper*," Sharon Tollerton said from the next console over. "They could still go in with the Merlins!"

"Not with the hijackers fully alert and waiting for them with automatic weapons," Rubens said. "The commandos would be cut to pieces before they could fast-rope to the deck. We'll need to try something else."

Unfortunately, Rubens thought, *the British debacle might have just slammed the door shut for Black Cat.*

Pyramid Club Casino, *Atlantis Queen*
47° 48' N, 40° 46' W
Tuesday, 1854 hours GMT

Carolyn Howorth slipped into the casino, glancing left and right for any signs of terrorist gunmen before moving into the crowd. There were fifty or sixty people in the room, she estimated, most of them staring out through the broad glass windows overlooking the ship's fantail. The room was dead quiet, the tension palpable.

Outside, she saw helicopters in the distance, black specks against the glare of the westering sun.

Howorth had been in her hideaway—a rather traditional place for stowaways, she thought, the interior of one of the *Atlantis Queen*'s lifeboats—when she'd heard the whoosh of rockets and peeked out in time to see a British helicopter shot down into the sea. She decided then that she needed to get inside and mingle with the passengers.

It had been just twenty-four hours since she'd escaped

from her stateroom over the balcony railing as armed terrorists had burst into the compartment, gunning down
Thomas Mitchell and Ghailiani. The man who'd opened
his stateroom's balcony door had let her into Cabin 5087,
which was directly beneath hers.

The man—he introduced himself as Adrian Bollinger
and the much younger woman with him as Tabitha
Sandberg—had bombarded her with questions, most of
them about how she'd managed to get to his private balcony outside, but she'd stopped him by the simple expedi-
ent of placing her palm across his mouth. He'd spluttered,
then gone silent when she told him terrorists had taken
the ship and that now they were hunting her.

"We wondered," the Sandberg woman had said. "All
those men with guns . . ."

"They're going to be coming down here in just a second," she told them. "You never saw me, okay? They'll
think I fell into the sea."

"But where are you going?" Bollinger had asked. "You
can't just—"

"I can and I will," she'd said, opening the cabin door
and checking both ways outside. "Remember! You haven't
seen *anyone*!"

Bollinger turned and locked the glass sliding door.
"We haven't seen a soul."

Howorth had made her way to a service stairway, then,
and gone down one more deck. Most of the staterooms on
Deck Four didn't have balconies like the one she'd scrambled onto on Deck Five, because that space was taken up
by long lines of lifeboats slung from davits.

A door opened onto the Deck Four starboard promenade, which gave her access to the lifeboats. She'd been
hiding in Number 5 ever since, eating emergency rations
and making herself comfortable on a jury-rigged mattress
of life jackets and blankets. She needed time to think, and
consider her next move.

Howorth had to assume that Mitchell and Ghailiani

both were dead . . . though she wasn't sure about the Moroccan crewman. She'd seen him drop to the deck when the gunmen broke in, but she hadn't seen bullets ripping him open like they had Mitchell, who'd caught a full burst through the splintering door. It might, she thought, be a good idea to assume Ghailiani was *not* dead but in terrorist hands. Did he know anything about her that might help the enemy? Other than the fact of the two of them, her and Mitchell, Ghailiani didn't know much at all.

Her ID card had been on the bedside table in her cabin. The terrorists would have it now. With luck, they'd checked out Bollinger's cabin and assumed she'd fallen into the ocean. The only way they could spot her now was if she wandered into a restricted area of the ship, one with sensors that would pick up her movement and body heat. If she stayed in those parts of the ship open to passengers, she thought, she ought to be okay.

Her computer was gone, hurled into the sea to keep the terrorists from getting it. She was out of touch with her headquarters. Briefly she'd considered going down to Connexions in the Deck One mall and using one of those computers to contact GCHQ, but she'd swiftly dropped that idea. She'd seen them capture one man there—Mitchell's partner—and if those computers were still online, the terrorists up in the computer center would be watching them for activity.

By transmitting the little she and Mitchell had been able to discover so far before the gunmen had burst in on them, she'd probably done all she could. The trouble was, Carolyn Howorth wanted to do *more*, and she couldn't do it while hiding in a damned lifeboat.

Then the helicopters had flown up the *Queen*'s starboard side, missiles had lashed out from one of the upper decks and slapped one of the aircraft into the sea, and she'd heard a thunderous boom from the other side of the ship. Quickly she'd scrambled out of the lifeboat and found service stairs going up. She reached Deck Nine and headed aft, entering the Pyramid Club Casino. Alone, she would invite suspicion, or simply harassment by any terrorists who might see her. In a group, she could blend in. Each time she'd been there, there'd been passengers in the Pyramid Club, sometimes lots of them.

Attendance in the casino was way down this afternoon, but there *were* people. None were playing at any of the tables, however. They seemed stunned by the sudden, brief battle with the helicopters. Outside, by the Atlas Pool, two armed terrorists watched the distant helicopters circle far out over the sea.

She spotted one man sitting alone at the bar, a nerdy-looking sort with heavy-rimmed glasses and a distracted expression. Then she took a second look. He had a laptop computer on the bar in front of him and was hard at work typing at the keyboard.

A computer was definitely promising. She walked over to the bar and sat down next to him.

"What," she asked, "are you doing?"

"Huh? Oh. Coding."

"Coding what?"

He nodded toward a kind of kiosk at the rear of the casino, not far from the sliding doors. She blinked. The kiosk encircled a vaguely humanoid figure, a *woman's* figure complete with a plunging neckline between large plastic breasts, robotic arms, and an eerie face on a TV monitor mounted where the head should have been.

"That," he said. "Rosie."

She'd read something about the machine in a brochure in the travel package they'd handed her at Southampton. "That's the card-playing robot?" she asked. "The one that plays blackjack?"

"The one and only."

"Um . . . I don't know how to say this, exactly," she said carefully, "but you *do* know we've been captured by hijackers, yes?"

"Of course. We all heard the announcement."

"So why are you doing *that*?"

He stopped typing and looked up, looked around, then looked at her. "We need guns," he said, his voice low, a conspiratorial whisper. "A way to fight back! Maybe Rosie can help us get one. She's *very* strong."

"How? She doesn't look very . . . mobile."

"She's not. She's bolted to the deck." He started typing again.

"By the way, I'm Janet Carroll," Howorth told him.

"Jerry Esterhausen."

"Listen . . . I know it's a lot to ask, but can you connect with the ship's Internet with that thing?"

"Of course. It has a built-in router."

"Jerry," Carolyn said, lowering her voice in a deliberately and sexually provocative manner, "you and I need to talk!"

Forward Deck, *Atlantis Queen*
47° 28' N, 42° 16' W
Tuesday, 2001 hours GMT

"The attack by unknown helicopters appears to have been beaten off," Sandra Ames said, speaking earnestly into the microphone as the freshening wind caught and tousled her blond hair. "We don't have any more details at the time, but at least one helicopter was shot down by missiles fired from the *Atlantis Queen*'s upper decks, and at least two more were damaged. The rest of the helicopters— witnesses said they saw between five and ten additional helicopters off the ship's stern at one point—appear to have left the area."

The three of them, Fred Doherty, James Petrovich, and Sandra Ames, were standing on the forward deck under the watchful and dispassionate gaze of one of the terrorist gunmen. They were losing light fast. Doherty wasn't sure what time zone they were in right now, so he didn't know the local time, but the sun was approaching the horizon in a blaze of sunset color and gilded clouds astern.

"Amir Yusef Khalid, the leader of the terrorist group, gave this news team permission—it was more of an order, really—to come outside onto the ship's forward deck and film this report. I don't know what—wait. Amir Khalid has just come out onto the deck. Perhaps he has something to say to us on-air. . . ."

Fred Doherty turned and looked aft, toward the ship's superstructure. A grim-faced Khalid had just emerged onto the forward promenade. Behind him were two of his thugs carrying AK-47 rifles, and an older man, his hands bound behind his back. At the sight of the civilian passenger, Doherty felt a sharp chill that was not due to the wind.

They marched the civilian up to the ship's railing and forced him to his knees, facing out to sea. With the camera rolling, without any preamble at all, Khalid pulled an automatic pistol from his belt and stepped up behind the prisoner. The passenger sensed the movement and started struggling, but the guards kept his arms pinned. Khalid brought the pistol up to the base of the man's skull and pulled the trigger.

Ames screamed as the sharp crack of the gunshot echoed back off the ship's superstructure. "Oh, my God, no!" Petrovich said. The passenger pitched forward into the railing and slumped to the deck, blood pooling beneath his head.

Khalid turned and stalked toward the camera, eyes burning with a ferocity Doherty had not seen before. Glaring into the camera, Khalid pointed back over his shoulder at the body as the two thugs lifted it between them, balanced it upright for a moment against the rail, then heaved it over the side. "That," Khalid said, "was one of the ship's passengers. His name was Arnold Bernstein, of Los Angeles, California. You—the governments in Washington and in London—may take comfort in the fact that we of the

Islamic Jihad International Brigade are merciful and did not kill every man, woman, and child on board this vessel tonight as a result of your idiotic posturing and chest-thumping! Attempt another such attack, however, and over thirty-three hundred more people will die!

"We know you have two warships closing with us. Those ships are to keep their distance. Come no closer than twenty miles with any ship or aircraft to the *Atlantis Queen* and the *Pacific Sandpiper*, or we shall begin killing more passengers!"

Khalid turned suddenly and walked away, back toward the ship's superstructure. "And cut," Doherty said quietly.

Beside him, Sandra Ames quietly muttered, "That fucking raghead son of a bitch."

He'd never heard her use that kind of language before.

22

"THERE WE GO," ESTERHAUSEN said. "You can send your e-mail now, and the terrorists up in IT won't have a clue."

"Excellent!" Howorth said. "You slowed down the packet rate, you said?"

"Yes." The man was almost preening, quite proud of his computer savvy. Howorth knew her way around computers and IT networks as well, but she'd reined herself in as she'd talked with Esterhausen, asking pertinent questions and making suggestions, but letting him think he was doing most of the work. It was, after all, his computer, and she needed access if she was going to pull this off. She had the impression that he didn't often have the opportunity to show off to people.

Especially to girls.

"My wireless card can connect with the ship's Intranet, of course," he continued, "but anyone monitoring the network up in the ship's IT department would know if we tried sending a message out. I've got pretty good encryption—they wouldn't know what you were saying— but they'd be alerted that someone on board was talking with the shore. But by slowing the transmission rate way, way down, they won't see it in IT. It'll look like routine background traffic."

"Perfect! That's wonderful, Jerry. Thank you!" She checked her watch. It was just past midnight-thirty back home. The two of them had been at this all evening, bent over Esterhausen's laptop. They'd moved from the bar to a booth some hours ago, to give themselves a bit more privacy.

The hour didn't matter. They would pick up her message both at GCHQ and at Fort Meade, middle of the night or not. She started typing.

"So what is this important e-mail you need to send, anyway? What are you trying to do? You said you worked for the government. . . ."

"I do. The less you know about it, the better."

"What, MI5?" His eyes lit up. "MI6?"

That reminded her of Mitchell, and it hurt. "No. Like I said, the less you know, the better. As to what I'm doing . . . have you ever heard of a drive-by download?"

His brow furrowed above the heavy black frame of his glasses. "Uh, no. I don't think I have."

"I'm hoping the tangos on the bridge haven't, either," she said. "And if they don't know we're transmitting down here in the first place, the surprise will be that much sweeter. . . ."

National Security Council
White House basement
Washington, D.C.
Wednesday, 1010 hours EST

"Leon Klinghoffer," Debra Collins said.

"Who is that?" Donna Bing asked.

"A passenger on the cruise ship *Achille Lauro*," Rubens told them. "An old man in a wheelchair, murdered by the terrorists when they took over the ship in 1985. They shot him in the head and in the chest, then forced a couple of the ship's crew to throw the body and the wheel-chair overboard."

"The news media is playing up that angle," Collins added. "Bernstein was Jewish, like Klinghoffer."

"Is that why they killed him?" Bing wanted to know. She sounded horrified. "Because he was *Jewish*?"

"Of course," Gene Carter, one of the regular NSC members, said. "Terrorists have sequestered Jewish hostages before, and threatened to kill them first. Entebbe is a case in point."

"It's possible, I suppose," Rubens said. "Mostly, though, I think Khalid just wanted to send a message to show he was serious. Bernstein might have just been a convenient, random target. It is true, though, that the terrorists appear to have access to Ship's Security records on the passengers. They might have identified Bernstein from those."

"The . . . public aspect of this crisis is getting out of hand," Wehrum pointed out. "FOX has trotted out the *Achille Lauro* affair, pointing out the similarities with the *Atlantis Queen*, and is doing these damned man-on-the-street interviews with people saying we have to go in and kick Khalid's ass." He glanced at Bing, who gave him a sharp look. "Sorry."

"It's true," Thomas Elton said. He was a small, prissy man, the NSC's liaison with the State Department. "The other networks are starting to take it up as well. With this . . . this cold-blooded murder airing on every news channel over and over, people are wondering why we're not doing something about the situation."

"They're starting to look at Reagan and his response to the *Achille Lauro* hijacking," Wehrum said. "They want the President to do something."

"Maybe he should," Rubens said.

"The *Achille Lauro* hijacking," Bing said carefully, "was resolved without bloodshed. Without more bloodshed, I should say. We didn't go in all guns blazing. The Egyptians negotiated with the terrorists, and they went ashore peacefully. Reagan's response was to force the suspects' plane down in Sicily, and precipitate an international incident."

"With respect," Rubens said, "the *Atlantis Queen* crisis really has very few similarities to the *Achille Lauro*. None at all, actually, except that both hijackings involved cruise ships.

"In fact, the PLF terrorists who took over the *Achille Lauro* weren't intending to hijack the ship at all. There were only four terrorists on board—some sources suggest there were two others who stayed in the background—and they apparently were using the ship as a staging platform for launching a raid on Israel from the sea. A ship's steward spotted their cache of weapons and explosives, though, they panicked, and they took over the ship. They threatened to blow the ship up unless fifty Palestinians being held in Israel were released, but everyone involved knew that wasn't going to happen. When Syria refused to let the ship dock at Tartus, they were stuck. A classic example of a full-blown clusterfuck."

"Mr. Rubens, please," Bing said.

He shrugged. "The Egyptians *did* negotiate, or they pretended to, and the terrorists went free at Port Said, supposedly before anyone ashore knew about Klinghoffer's murder. They, and the mastermind of the operation, Abu Abbas, got on a seven-thirty-seven headed for Libya. At Reagan's orders, the plane was intercepted by F-fourteens and forced to land in Sicily.

"This situation is different on almost every level. This time, the terrorists clearly targeted both the *Atlantis Queen* and the *Pacific Sandpiper* from the start. The operation was large—Carrousel estimates at least twenty hijackers on board the *Queen*, and a similar but unknown number on the *Sandpiper*. It was well armed, their weapons including a number of Stinger shoulder-launched antiaircraft missiles and, we're guessing, several tons at least of high explosives smuggled onto the ship at Southampton. It was well equipped, including a helicopter. And it was superbly planned. The op included the suborning of at least one of the security officers on board the *Queen*, the murder and replacement of two Japanese nationals on board the *Sandpiper*, and the replacement or the suborning of at least one of the crewmen on board the *Ishikari*."

"How do you know that last?" Wehrum asked.

"Because of the timing. The destruction of the *Ishikari* was deliberate, timed to allow a helicopter full of terrorists to touch down on the *Sandpiper* and take her over just before the *Queen* arrived in the area. The tangos have been carrying out this plan of theirs step by step by meticulous step . . . and they've been staying one step ahead of us the whole way."

"So what are you suggesting, Mr. Rubens?" Bing asked him.

"First, that we not allow the perceived similarities of this situation with the *Achille Lauro* hijacking to deter us," he said. "Second, that we pay attention to something important—the fact that, whatever Khalid claims, the tangos aren't simply holding the crew and passengers of the *Queen* for ransom. They didn't need to take over the *Pacific Sandpiper* for that. So we can assume they have something bigger in mind. Something flashier."

"New York City," General Barton said. "A huge dirty bomb in New York Harbor."

"That seems the likeliest possibility right now," Collins said. "The IJI Brigade is almost certainly aligned with al-Qaeda, and might be an operational branch of it. Al-Qaeda *always* goes for big, spectacular operations with high body counts. The 1993 World Trade Center bombing . . . which was supposed to bring down both towers *and* release a cloud of poison gas, though that part isn't generally well known. Operation Bojinka, which was discovered and stopped before it could be carried out—the simultaneous hijacking and destruction of ten or twelve commercial aircraft over the Pacific Ocean. The attack on the USS *Cole* off Yemen. The embassy bombings in East Africa. The nine-eleven attacks. Typical al-Qaeda operations don't have religious overtones, and they don't demand ransom money or the release of hostages. They're designed to punish the West for supporting Israel or for acting as 'oppressors.' And they're designed to grab world attention and hold it."

"Maybe this is a first time for ransom demands," Bing suggested. "Al-Qaeda might need money. We've been putting the squeeze on them by seizing their assets every time we can identify them."

"Or it might not be al-Qaeda after all," Wehrum added.

"*Or* the demand for two billion dollars and the release of Muslim prisoners might be nothing but a smokescreen," Rubens said, "a means of spinning things out, to let the hijacked ships get close enough to a U.S. city to do some serious damage."

Bing considered this. "The President is still . . . reluctant to authorize military action against the hijackers," she said. "But he also says that the *Atlantis Queen* and the *Pacific Sandpiper* must not be allowed to enter American waters. To prevent that, he *will* authorize deadly force against both ships."

"My God," Barton said. "Are you saying what I think you're—"

"A *Los Angeles*–class submarine is shadowing those two hijacked vessels," Bing said. "The *Newport News*, part of the *Eisenhower*'s strike group. If necessary, she will be given orders to destroy both ships."

"There *must* be another way," Admiral Prendergast said. "We can't kill over three thousand civilians!"

"If they've breached those MOX containers," Elton added, "it could also mean an unprecedented ecological disaster. All of that radioactive debris adrift in the Gulf

Stream? It could poison the North Atlantic . . . contaminate the entire Atlantic coast of Europe, at the very least."

"All of which the terrorists are probably counting on," Rubens pointed out. "My guess, ladies and gentlemen, is that that's exactly what Khalid and his people intend . . . to force us to destroy those ships ourselves in order to protect our cities. Remember the nine-eleven conspiracy nonsense?"

They did. In the aftermath of the September 11 attacks on the World Trade Center and the Pentagon, conspiracy theories had begun floating about on the Internet to the effect that Flight 93 had been shot down by U.S. military aircraft, that the WTC attacks had been staged by the U.S. government, even that what had crashed into the Pentagon hadn't been a hijacked airliner at all but a missile launched by an American combat plane. The possible motives for such a conspiracy were fuzzy, of course, but generally had to do with creating an excuse to invade the Middle East in order to secure and control the sources of Arab oil.

So far as Rubens was concerned, the people spreading those conspiracy theories on the Internet and even in video documentaries were little better than traitors, dishonoring the memories of the thousands of Americans who'd died in those attacks and the brave Americans who'd gone on to take the war to the enemy. By blaming the recent and unpopular Bush Administration with ignorance, distortions, and outright lies, they'd given aid and comfort to the real enemy, apparently for nothing better than political point-making.

It was still a free country, and free speech was still the law of the land, but that kind of domestic political propaganda was damnably close to shouting, "Fire!" in a crowded theater. Oliver Wendell Holmes would not have been amused.

"You're saying we're playing into Khalid's hands," Bing said.

"As I said, Dr. Bing, they've been keeping just ahead of us right along, ever since before the crisis started. I think they're using misdirection now in order to delay, that they have no intention of taking the money even if we give in. They want to offer us a choice of two and only two options—they sail into New York Harbor and set off a dirty bomb that will kill thousands of people and contaminate the entire city, or they force us to sink those ships ourselves, be seen by the world killing three thousand civilians, and possibly contaminating the European shoreline, everything from Ireland to Spain and Portugal."

"So what are you suggesting, Mr. Rubens?" Prendergast asked. "Your military insertion option?"

"I would suggest, first, that you negotiate. Tell them that we *will* give them the money and the prisoners. See if they'll halt those ships mid-ocean if we make that promise. If they do, then I'm wrong. We can continue to negotiate . . . or launch a military option, whatever you and the President think best."

"That seems reasonable," General Barton said.

"With an important caveat," Rubens said. "They could still blow those ships up out there even while we're in the middle of negotiating with them, and *claim* we did it. There would be plenty of people who would believe them. And radioactive contamination of western Europe and the poisoning of fish throughout the North Atlantic would still kill thousands, and result in tens of billions of dollars of damage. It would give al-Qaeda the propaganda victory it's looking for.

"So while we talk, I do still think we need to get a team on board those ships."

"To launch an assault?" Bing asked. "Or for reconnaissance?"

"For reconnaissance first," Rubens said. "We have to have decent intel. How many terrorists are there? Where are they? What is the situation of the hostages, and where are they? Are there explosives in place? We need to know."

"Your last report said that you were again in contact with one of your agents on board," Wehrum said.

"Carrousel, yes," Rubens said. "She sent a message through confirming that she's okay, and suggesting some electronic options we might be able to take."

"Then she can get us the intel we need," Barton said.

"No, unfortunately. She can't. We need to see places that passengers aren't allowed to go. The bridge. The cargo hold. She would be picked up by the ship's sensors, and an alarm would sound in Security.

"What we have in mind is to put two teams on board, one on each ship. They could check areas closed to passengers, and give us a picture of just where the bad guys are. They would then be in position when a full-scale assault is launched. Our working plan so far is to have them take down terrorist leaders before they can order the detonation of any explosives in the ships' holds. An alternate possibility is to send the recon teams to those holds and have them disarm any explosives before the actual assault begins."

"And you think this operation could be kept low-key?" Bing asked him. "The President still wants to downplay any American involvement."

Politics again. "Yes, Dr. Bing," Rubens replied. "In fact, what we would recommend is that the SAS get another crack at those ships. As you said the other day, it's their ship, their responsibility. And a success here would go a long way to repairing their public image. And it would keep our people out of the public eye."

"*I'm* not so sure this is a good idea," Wehrum said, looking at Bing. "If the assault force screws up, the ships could be destroyed anyway. And it *would* look like it was our fault."

"Doing nothing guarantees failure," Rubens pointed out.

"I'll take this up with the President," Bing said. "No promises . . . but have your Black Cat unit positioned and ready to go. How long will it take to get them in position?"

"They're ready now," Rubens said. When Bing raised her eyebrows at that, he grinned. "It seemed a worthwhile precaution to put our team in place for an op, just in case. They're on board the *Eisenhower* now. We also have a SEAL team on the USS *Ohio*, shadowing the hijacked ships."

"We'll still need Presidential approval," she said.

"Of course," Rubens said. "There's one thing more, though."

"What is it?"

"Met reports from that part of the ocean are not encouraging right now. The wind is up to ten knots with gusts at fifteen, the sea state is at three, and there's a storm front moving down on those ships from the north. Weather conditions are expected to deteriorate dramatically over the next ten to twelve hours."

"What does that mean?"

"That we are not going to be able to launch a parachute insertion onto those ships with winds over about ten to twelve knots. And SEALs on board an ASDS trying to come alongside will not be able to board them if the seas are higher than about sea state three to four. We need to go now, within the next few hours . . . or we'll need to wait until the storm passes."

"Tell your team to stand ready," Bing said, standing suddenly. "I'll get back to you with the President's decision."

"At last report, the *Atlantis Queen* was one hundred and eleven miles southeast of Mistaken Point, Newfoundland," Rubens said. "That's a bit over five hundred miles from New York. We don't have much time."

The meeting was over.

"I need to know I can still trust you," Khalid said.

"I told you . . . I didn't tell them anything! They . . . they grabbed me and Rawasdeh so quickly, and then Rawasdeh was knocked down the stairs. I didn't have a gun—"

"Yes, yes, we have been over all of that," Khalid said, placing a fatherly hand on the man's shoulder. "It wasn't your fault."

Ghailiani's right arm was in a sling, heavily bandaged, and he had another bandage wrapped around his torso beneath his open Ship's Security shirt. The ship's doctor had patched him up after Aziz and Nehim had shot him in the woman's stateroom.

It would, Khalid thought, *be safest to shoot Ghailiani right now.* The problem was that Khalid's personnel assets were stretched to the limit right now. He needed technical people—people who knew computers—in the IT department and in the ship's Security Office.

Things had been tight before with twenty-four Brigade fighters on board each of the two captured vessels, a total of forty-eight. Now Rawasdeh was dead. So was Wahidi, transferred to the *Sandpiper* on Saturday to work with Bekkali and Moritomi in the special technical unit.

Wahidi's death had been . . . horrible, a three-day agony of vomiting and diarrhea as the radiation poisoning he'd received had eaten away his guts. Bekkali was dead as well, the same way, and two other fighters soon would be. The KKD atomic expert, Moritomi, had shot himself when the first radiation poisoning symptoms had set in hours after the transfer of nuclear material to the *Atlantis Queen*. And two more men had died in the *Sandpiper*'s stern gun position, when the British helicopter had blasted it with a wire-guided missile.

Eight dead so far. Counting himself, then, there were twenty-nine Brigade fighters remaining on board the *Atlantis Queen*, eighteen on the *Pacific Sandpiper*. Khalid had expected to take losses, of course; the sacrifice of the special technical unit had been expected, a part of the operational plan.

But Khalid had just five men on board the *Atlantis Queen* with the training and experience to operate both the ship's computers and the security monitors—and that number included himself. They were working now in staggered eighteen-hour shifts, with one man catching a few hours' sleep at a time. He *needed* Ghailiani to help fill in, because he'd been trained in the *Atlantis Queen*'s security systems. With some minor changes to the programming of the computer running the ship's security section, Khalid would need fewer men as guards, would be able to control all of the thousands of people on board this ship watching through cameras and the ship's sensors, instead of with armed men standing at specific points like the fantail, the Promenade Deck, and up on Deck Eleven.

With the repulse of the helicopter strike, Khalid was sure that they would have at least a day or two before another attempt was made. According to the colored symbols on the electronic chart table, the enemy ships were keeping well back, none closer than about 250 kilometers.

His big concern now was controlling the ship's thirty-three hundred passengers and crew.

Ghailiani trembled under Khalid's hand.

"Have you seen your e-mail yet today?" Khalid asked, dropping his hand.

The man, his eyes screwed tightly shut, managed a jerky nod.

"Then you know your wife and daughter remain safe. Our original bargain still stands. You help us to the full extent to which you are capable. And your wife and daughter will not be harmed."

"I will do anything you command, Amir. *Anything*."

"I know you will. And soon this mission will be over, and you will rejoin your family as a very wealthy man. For now, though, I need your help in security. I know this ship has sensors to monitor when people have wandered into areas where they should not go, yes?"

Ghailiani nodded again.

"Good. And I would like you to . . . extend the list of such places, so that we can know immediately when one of the free passengers wanders into a stairwell, say, or the deck outside."

"I can do that, Amir."

"Good. Do it, then."

A sudden blast of wind struck the bridge windows as Ghailiani departed, followed by a rattle of rain. The weather was turning ugly, the sky turbulent and overcast.

Good. That meant even less likelihood of an enemy attack.

High up next to the ceiling of the ship's bridge, a TV monitor was displaying CNN, via a satellite feed. A woman was talking earnestly into the camera, telling of a rumored deal being struck between the U.S. government and the *Atlantis Queen* hijackers.

Khalid smiled.

The Americans had fallen all over themselves in transmitting a radio message accepting the IJI Brigade's terms. The promise of $2 billion and the release of several hundred Islamic prisoners . . . that in itself was a sweet victory, almost victory enough to leave Yusef Khalid believing in a beneficent and all-powerful Allah.

Almost. This victory had been won with daring, imagination, sacrifice, and a great deal of money from al-Qaeda's financial backers in Saudi Arabia, Pakistan, and elsewhere. It wasn't necessary to drag God into the equation.

Still, knowing that the Americans had capitulated filled Khalid with a surging sense of power, of purpose. A handful of fighters willing to sacrifice themselves in the name of Allah had brought the world's so-called sole superpower to its knees.

It was a shame, really, that he wouldn't be accepting the American offer. He'd given orders to maintain radio silence, to refuse to respond to any signal from the Americans or the British.

Later, when they were closer to New York City, he would begin to negotiate, but only to drag things out and give them the opportunity to take these vessels and their radioactive cargos all the way into the port and cram them up America's ass.

Khalid wasn't interested in money or in freed prisoners. He was interested solely in revenge.

Hangar Deck, USS *Eisenhower*
43° 54' N, 54° 18' W
Wednesday, 1625 hours GMT

"Another delay?" Charlie Dean asked.

"I'm afraid so," Rubens' voice replied in his head, speaking over his communications implants. "But this time it's the weather."

Around him stretched the gray recesses of the *Eisenhower*'s hangar deck, a high-ceilinged cavern filled with the crouching forms of aircraft, wings folded, quiescent. The two Black Cat assault teams crouched nearby in front of Lieutenant Richard Taylor, who was drawing with a black marker on a large whiteboard with side-by-side deck schematics of the two ships printed on it.

"Conditions are still decent here," Dean said. He'd just come down from the ship's Met Office.

"But your target is sailing through a squall line right now. They're telling us to expect high winds and unfavorable sea states along the *Queen*'s course for the next twelve hours at least."

And by the time the bad weather had passed, dawn would be approaching. The insertion *had* to take place at night to have any chance at all of success.

"So we're looking going in at sometime tomorrow night," Dean said.

"Use the time to study those deck plans and photos," Rubens told him. "And we'll be developing our contact with Carrousel."

"Tell her to keep her head down," Dean said.

"Rubens out."

Bridge, *Atlantis Queen*
44° 49' N, 54° 10' W
Wednesday, 2114 hours GMT + 4

"What the hell is that noise?" Khalid demanded.

Phillips, the ship's captain, stood before him between two armed men. "What noise would that be?"

"You can't have not heard it."

Khalid had ordered Phillips brought to the bridge. Much of the time, he and the other bridge officers were kept confined in a watch room down the passageway behind the bridge. One or another of them could be brought to the bridge any time there was a need for their advice. Khalid didn't like the look in Phillips' eyes, however, and since he and a few trusted Brigade soldiers could handle the ship's wheel, watch the compass, and keep an eye on the electronic chart table and radar, there was no need for the regular ship's officers on the bridge at all.

"I don't know what you're talking about," Phillips replied.

As if on cue, then, a long, low, grinding rumble sounded, transmitted through the steel deck of the bridge. The ship itself gave a lurching shudder.

"That noise," Khalid growled. "Will you tell me what it is, or shall I put several of your passengers overboard?"

The threat seemed to batter down Phillips' defenses. "The sea is getting rougher," he said. "The two ships, this one and the *Sandpiper*, are of different lengths, and different drafts, so they ride the waves differently from one another."

Khalid walked to the port bridge wing and looked aft. It was dark and raining, but in the haze of glowing mist illuminated by the *Pacific Sandpiper*'s deck lights, he could see the smaller ship grinding unevenly against the *Atlantis Queen*'s side.

"Are we in danger?"

"I don't know. It's hard to tell. If the sea gets any rougher, the *Sandpiper* could stove us in, I suppose."

"What can we do about it?"

Phillips gave a halfhearted shrug. "You could bring both ships about into the wind," he said. "Cut our speed until we're just barely making way, and ride out the storm."

"We do not need the delay," Khalid said. "We have a schedule to keep." He gestured toward the officer. "Take him back to his quarters."

As Phillips was led away, Khalid called the radio watch. "Sadeeq! Raise the *Pacific Sandpiper*."

"Yes, sir."

"Tell them we are going to separate the ships. Our time together is over."

The two would proceed to their respective targets separately from here on out.

23

Stateroom 4005, *Atlantis Queen*
North Atlantic Ocean
42° 58' N, 61° 54' W
Thursday, 1320 hours EST

"WHO *DO* YOU WORK FOR?" JERRY Esterhausen asked. "SAS? The American Delta Force? I know! The CIA!"

"Believe it or not, I'm a relatively low-level clerk," Carolyn Howorth told him. If he wanted to jump to the conclusion that she was CIA, that was fine with her. "I just happened to be at the wrong place at the wrong time."

"Or the right place, right time," he said with feeling.

They were seated at the desk in Esterhausen's stateroom. Late last night, he'd brought her down here, and she'd slept here. *Only* slept; Esterhausen had gallantly let her have the queen-sized bed while he took the double-wide love-seat sofa. It was, Howorth was forced to admit, infinitely better than blankets and life jackets in a lifeboat outside.

She'd been up early, however, sending more reports back to GCHQ and NSA Headquarters and also trying to raise Mohamed Ghailiani.

He was alive. She was fairly certain of that, now. According to GCHQ, which was closely monitoring every transmission in and out of the *Atlantis Queen*, another JPEG photo of Ghailiani's wife and daughter had been transmitted to his e-mail account on Tuesday, again on Wednesday, and then yet again that morning. The images weren't piling up in his in-box, either, but were being opened each morning. With Ghailiani's e-mail account password, she could check that. If he had been killed, there would have been no reason to keep Nouzha and Zahra Ghailiani alive, no need to keep e-mailing photographs of them with a fresh copy of the *Guardian* each morning. Both women would have been dead within hours of Mohamed Ghailiani's death.

The question was whether or not she could develop the guy as an agent-in-place. He'd been co-opted by the terrorists through threats to his family; perhaps he could be turned if those threats could be eliminated. However, he'd been so terrified the other day, so broken, that she wasn't sure he would be of any use even if she could elicit his cooperation.

Early that morning, she'd finished typing out an exploratory e-mail, addressed it to Ghailiani's account, and clicked send. The slow packet transmission rate meant that it would take a while to get there, and she had no idea when he would again be checking his shipboard account.

But right now she had nothing but time. Her fingers clattered over the keyboard and, suddenly, a mail icon popped up. She clicked on it.

Who are you?

She stared at the three words for a long moment. The e *should* be from Ghailiani himself, but there was always the possibility that someone else, one of the terrorists, was reading his e-mail for him. It was possible that they didn't trust him to access his e-mail without someone reading over his shoulder. So *Who are you?* might be from Ghailiani, or it might be from a tango.

A friend, she typed back. *You know me. I can help you.* She pressed send.

It would take a while for Jerry's computer to send the message at its deliberate electronic snail's pace.

She waited.

Waterhouse Lane, Millbrook
Southampton, England
Thursday, 1910 hours GMT

They'd been watching them all day.

MI5 had found the flat two days before, on Tuesday afternoon. A policeman had called in the black sedan with its license registration of Y9WE83K, parked on Waterhouse Lane in front of a line of two-story brownstone row houses in an aging section of town. The neighborhood was just three miles across town from the Ghailiani residence, an easy drive out the A3057.

MI5 agents had questioned neighbors, learning from them that two men, foreign-looking and secretive, had moved into the vacant flat only two weeks earlier. The two apparently kept to themselves—and that of itself was enough to attract attention and elicit comment in a clannish and close-knit community such as Millbrook.

MI5 had talked to the people living next door, a newly married Indian couple named Rajeesh. The two had been temporarily evicted on Tuesday, moved to a hotel in Southampton for the duration, and with the promise that the government would take care of any damages. MI5 had moved in, entering the flat from the rear two at a time in order to try to avoid alerting the residents at Number 1240 next door. Lia DeFrancesca and Ilya Akulinin had arrived on Wednesday, setting up a satellite radio link with both MI5 and GCHQ.

Early on Thursday morning, while it was still dark in the hours before dawn, the SAS had arrived as well. The takedown, code-named Imperial, was a go.

The upstairs of the Rajeesh apartment had been

transformed into a military command post, the furniture moved downstairs, the carpets rolled up, and folding chairs and tables brought in for the banks of computers and monitors being used by the HRT personnel. Two technicians had used silenced electrical saws to cut through the south wall, which, according to architectural plans from the local planning-board office, should back up against the north wall of the suspect's bedroom. Working with extreme and methodical care in absolute silence, they brought down a seven-foot-high, nine-foot-wide section of lath and plaster wall, exposing the back side of the suspect's wall and the nine-inch gap between the two.

A hand drill was used to very, very slowly bore into this final barrier, a sheet of aging lath and plaster half an inch thick. The resultant hole was scarcely wider than a finishing nail, but it accepted the stiff end of a boroscope probe, connected by a fiber-optic cable to a TV monitor on a folding table several feet away.

The boroscope's fish-eye lens revealed nearly all of the room next door, and it provided the final proof that MI5 had found the right place. Two women could be seen tied on the bed. Two and sometimes three men came and went. Sensitive microphones placed against the wall's interior side let the HRT team hear everything that happened, every word that was spoken. A couple of Arabic-speaking translators were brought in, who sat and listened to everything as the recorders rolled.

But Imperial couldn't go in immediately. Clearance needed to be won from higher levels of the bureaucracy, and unless the two victims were in immediate danger, an entry warrant needed to be approved by the local magistrate. The watchers at first couldn't see either of the women's faces, and there was at least a small chance that MI5 was peeking in on a kinky sex scene rather than an actual kidnapping.

So they watched, and they recorded. Both women were positively identified when their captors temporarily released them to let them use the toilet or to allow them to eat. The warrant didn't come through until late Thursday, however. The government was still stinging from allegations of abridged citizens' rights and illegal surveillance issues, and magistrates were being a lot more cautious now to safeguard citizens' rights to privacy.

And so MI5, the SAS HRT, and the two American liaisons had watched and listened as, early Thursday morning, one of the men photographed the women in the bed with a folded newspaper, then downloaded the image onto a laptop computer and sent it off. They watched in helpless and steadily building fury as the captors talked among themselves or described to the two helpless women in gruesome detail just what they were going to do with them when they were no longer needed.

Captain Burns, in charge of the HRT, was ready to go in without a warrant on the assumption that the women *were* in imminent danger. He was convinced to wait by Ronald Harriman, the senior MI5 officer on the scene. If the HRT went through that wall and things went badly, if the tangos on the other side of that wall were able to get word to the terrorists at sea, Mohamed Ghailiani might become a liability and die . . . and that might mean repercussions that would result in SAS casualties on the *Atlantis Queen* as well. In the wake of the abortive helicopter attack on Tuesday, *everyone* was being super-cautious and playing it strictly by the book.

And so they waited.

The warrant and final approval for the assault came through by mid-afternoon on Thursday. Burns and Harriman both agreed that they would wait a few hours more. The tangos seemed to have established a routine; each evening, one of their number would leave the flat and buy take-out food. On Wednesday night, they had watched the terrorists gather in a group, all three of them standing together around a table on the far side of the bedroom from the captives. If they followed the same pattern on

Thursday, that was when the hostage rescue team would go in.

At around six-thirty, one of the tangos left to get dinner. By this time, the SAS troopers had placed a large loop of yellow det cord against the interior of the lath and plaster wall, with extra lumps of C-4 placed as cutting charges against the exposed studs. Detonators were placed at several points along the det cord and in every C-4 charge, with all of them carefully woven together by wires to the firing box in the middle of the room. The HRT unit prepared for the assault, each man wearing black battle dress, combat harness, balaclava, and gas mask and carrying H&K MP5 submachine guns.

Lia DeFrancesca sat with the MI5 technical people, watching the screen. Harriman signaled that spotters outside were watching the man who'd left to get food and was returning, and four SAS troopers took their place at the jump-off, facing the old plaster wall and detcord-woven studs. Two more stood to either side of the detcord loop, well back from the blast zone but ready to move in support of the four-man unit. A military doctor and a pair of medical specialists waited in the rear, as seconds dragged by and the Imperial HRT waited for the final signal.

A moment later, clearly visible on the monitor, the man who'd gone for food entered the bedroom with a brown paper bag, which he took to the table. The other two tangos had been sitting beside the bed teasing their prisoners. Both of the men stood and walked to the table, still laughing. They had pistols tucked into their belts; three AK-47s had previously been spotted leaning against a wall beside the window overlooking the street, as though the tangos were ready for a police siege.

As they began removing cartons of Lebanese takeout from the bag, DeFrancesca gave Burns a thumbs-up and Burns pointed at the trooper manning the firing box. The man pressed a button, and the det cord exploded, a dazzling, lopsided circle of fierce white light accompanied by a startlingly loud blast as the wall disintegrated in plaster dust, smoke, and splinters.

On the monitor, all three men were swatted back from the blast; the four troopers on point rushed through the sudden opening while plaster and chunks of wood were still falling, their H&Ks tucked up against their shoulders, already firing as they moved.

Two of the terrorists, the two with pistols, were hit and killed instantly. The third, sprawled on the debris-covered floor, groped blindly for one of the AKs. One of the troopers brought his boot down on the man's arm and shoved the muzzle of his weapon against the man's skull. The other troopers moved to different corners of the room, then positioned themselves to cover the door leading to the hallway and stairs outside.

"Clear!" one of the HRT troopers yelled.

The entire assault had taken less than three seconds.

Stateroom 4005, *Atlantis Queen*
43° 20' N, 60° 53' W
Thursday, 1535 hours EST

Howorth read the last message from Ghailiani: *how cani truist you?*

The answer, of course, was that he couldn't . . . any more than she could trust him, no matter how badly spelled his e-mail reply was. She wondered if he'd composed that last while actually talking with one of the terrorists, pretending to work, perhaps, while typing quickly and blindly before hitting the send key.

But she'd moments before received confirmation from GCHQ that the Imperial assault had gone down without a hitch, and that the proof Ghailiani needed before committing himself was already being transmitted.

Take a look at the next mail from home, she typed. *Open it as an HTML document and click on the link.*

She hit send.

Security Office, *Atlantis Queen*
42° 42' N, 62° 36' W
Thursday, 1625 hours EST

Ghailiani sat at his workstation, staring at his in-box folder for his e-mail. Haqqani was with him, seated at another console. He couldn't see Ghailiani's screen.

This latest e-mail was from an unknown sender, someone ashore. The woman, Janet Carroll, had told him it would be coming, however, hinting that it would have the proof he needed.

He held his breath as he clicked on the mail icon.

A photograph opened in front of him, a somewhat grainy image of the sort taken by a cell-phone camera, but still in full color and with a level of detail that left his arms and knees weak, left him trembling, had his heart pounding in his chest.

It was yet another digital photograph of Nouzha and his beloved Zahra, but this time, instead of being another in a sickening series of photos depicting a slow, ongoing nightmare of a striptease, Zahra and Nouzha were free, *free.* . . .

The bedroom in which they'd been held was utterly trashed, with pieces of wood scattered everywhere and a layer of plaster dust over everything and everyone, including both of the two women. His wife and daughter were standing up, blankets over their shoulders and wrapped close around them as British military personnel helped them walk. Several of their rescuers were visible in the photo, anonymous in black military jumpsuits and bulletproof vests, knit balaclavas, and full-face gas masks.

Both women were crying, the tears streaking the film of plaster dust on their faces like makeup. Underneath the photo, someone had typed: *They're okay. On way to hospital for checkup. Both safe.* Following that line were two blue-highlighted words: *Click here.*

They were safe! . . .

"What's wrong?" Haqqani asked, his voice sharp.

Ghailiani realized that tears were running down his own face, that his hands were shaking. Somehow, he managed to reach out and hit the key that closed the image. "I . . . I'm thinking about my family," he said. "How I might not see them again. . . ."

"Do what we tell you and they'll be safe," Haqqani said with a shrug. "Allah will keep them safe."

He already has, Ghailiani thought. *Allah, and someone named Janet Carroll.*

Pyramid Club Casino, *Atlantis Queen*
41° 17' N, 67° 08' W
Thursday, 2215 hours EST

"So . . . am I ever going to get my computer back?" Jerry Esterhausen asked.

They'd come back up to Deck Nine and the casino earlier that evening, ordering dinner and sitting with the handful of passengers who seemed to have made the Pyramid Club their preferred gathering spot. So far, their terrorist captors had made no move to sequester them or to limit their freedom to move around, save to ban them from a handful of key shipboard areas. The armed intruders went about their work or stood guard in certain spots scattered about the ship and for the most part didn't interfere with the passengers when they went out to get meals or to sit in small groups in places like the casino and talk.

Questions about the safety of people who'd disappeared were ignored or, at best, shunted aside with a curt statement that they were safe so long as the rest of the crew and passengers made no trouble.

And none of the hijackers would reply to questions about how much longer this drama would play out or what was going to happen to the passengers of the ship when they arrived at their unknown destination.

"Just one more moment," she said. Howorth looked around the casino, checking to see if anyone was watching. One tango was standing inside the glass doors leading out to the pool deck, and two more were visible just outside in the spill of light from within the room. No one was paying attention to her or Esterhausen, seated in a booth in an out-of-the-way corner. She opened the latest e-mail from Ghailiani and read it.

Saw picture. Thank you. From bottom of heart thank you. Clicked HTML page. Nothing. Now what? And this one was signed: *Ghailiani.*

Just wait, she typed back, and then clicked send. The clock on Esterhausen's laptop, which was still set to GMT, read: "10:18 PM." If the mission GCHQ had mentioned in its last e-mail to her was on schedule, they should be seeing some action here within just a few more hours.

There was a sudden commotion at the forward door to the casino. Several passengers—a handful of elderly women and men—had been on the point of leaving, but they were being ordered back into the casino by one of the hijackers. "No! No!" the man shouted. "You stay here, now!"

"What's the meaning of this?" another man demanded.

The hijacker pushed him back with a jab from his rifle. "All of you, stay here now! No move anywhere!"

"What the hell?" Esterhausen asked.

"I think they're getting nervous about us moving around," Howorth told him. "Maybe they're watching our aircraft out there, following us."

"What does it mean?"

"That things are going to start happening damned fast, now."

Howorth set up one final e-mail, this one addressed to GCHQ and the NSA: *Ghailiani clicked HTML page. Carrousel in casino, Deck 9, 2218 EST. Two tangos outside by Atlas Pool, one inside casino. Ready to receive visitors.*

Again she hit send. The message was encrypted using a GCHQ cipher originally created at Fort Meade, so in the unlikely event that someone in Ship's Security was aware of her mail, they weren't reading it.

"Okay, Jerry," Carolyn said, closing the e-mail account and sliding the computer across the table to Esterhausen. "It's all yours."

"What did you do?"

She shrugged. "Nothing much. Called down the wrath of God on the unbelievers, maybe. Just a little."

"I don't understand."

"You will," Carolyn Howorth said. "Just be patient, and you will."

Osprey Cambridge One
40° 19' N, 69° 06' W
Friday, 0442 hours EST

The V-22 Osprey droned through the night, its enormous twin props in the forward flight configuration, driving the aircraft along at just over 270 knots. On the red-lit cargo deck, twenty-four men in combat dress that gave them the look of malevolent beings from another world quietly waited, their rucksacks parked between their booted feet.

"We're approaching the drop zone, Mr. Dean," the cargo master said over the intercom. "Ten more minutes to drop."

"Right."

Dean looked aft along the twin lines of black-garbed

and masked men seated in the blood-tinted glow of the
Osprey's cargo deck. Members of the ultra-secret Black
Cat Bravo assault force assigned to the NSA's Deep Black
program, they were the National Security Agency's pre-
mier military strike team—or would be after tonight.
This would be their first operational mission.

Over the past several years of Deep Black's operational history, Desk Three agents had been limited in
combat to the firepower they could carry on their
person—generally a semiautomatic pistol. The standard
wisdom of covert ops held that if you actually needed to
use a firearm, your mission had failed.

There were times, however, when something more was
needed than a sound-suppressed pistol, a means of delivering major firepower with surgical precision. Various
branches of the U.S. military had such units—the Army's
Delta Force, Rangers, and Special Forces, the U.S. Marines' Force Recon, the Navy's SEAL Teams—and Deep
Black's Desk Three had worked with all of them, generally through the auspices of USSOCOM, the U.S. Special
Operations Command.

But for the past two years Rubens and Charlie Dean
both had been pushing for a special-capabilities unit an-
swerable solely to Desk Three. The need had become
particularly evident last year, when Dean had undertaken
a Desk Three op in the Arctic far north and the takedown
of a Russian ship illegally holding American personnel
who'd been operating an ice cap weather station. A SEAL
assault unit had taken the ship, but difficulties in command control, in communications, and between individual personnel had caused difficulties that Black Cat was
designed to prevent.

The Black Cat units, Alpha on the West Coast, Bravo
on the East, were the result.

Technically, the team members were, like Dean,
civilians—"technically" because although the NSA was

subordinate to the U.S. Department of Defense, with either a lieutenant general or a vice admiral as director, the Agency operated in a kind of twilight world straddling both the civilian and the military defense communities.

Of course, the NSA officially didn't even have a field-active component or human intelligence capabilities. Its original charter called for the Agency to handle electronic and signals intelligence—SIGINT—only, which it did by monitoring radio broadcasts, phone and satellite communications, and Internet connections worldwide.

But Desk Three existed because sometimes a human being had to place a listening device in a telephone or an intercept unit inside a computer keyboard to eavesdrop on communications. And sometimes those humans needed a lot of firepower, fast.

Hence, Black Cat.

"Cougars!" Dean called over the team's radio channel. "Switch to tank oh-two!"

The Osprey's cargo deck had already been depressurized, and every man there was breathing pure oxygen through an attachment to O_2 lines along the cargo deck's internal fuselage walls. They'd been breathing pure oxygen for the past forty minutes in order to flush all of the nitrogen out of their bloodstreams. Each man now made the switch-over to his own, personal oxygen bottle, throwing a connector switch, then unthreading the aircraft supply line from their oxygen system. At these altitudes there simply wasn't enough oxygen in the air to keep a man aware and conscious for more than a few minutes.

One by one, the men along the starboard side each raised a black-gloved fist with the thumb extended up. The Osprey could carry twenty-four passengers in two rows of seats, more if they were floor-loaded. Dean and his eleven men were Cougar Team. The twelve men on the port side comprised Jaguar Team and would remain in reserve.

"Cougars! Prepare for jump!"

The eleven men along the starboard side of the aircraft stood as one.

The bad guys had thrown the team a curve just over twenty-four hours ago by separating the two ships that, until now, had been lashed together. The *Atlantis Queen* was still less than half a mile away from the *Pacific Sandpiper*, but the two vessels would have to be taken down separately now.

And so a second assault force was approaching the *Sandpiper* on board the USS *Ohio* with an ASDS riding piggyback on its after deck and Navy SEALs preparing to deploy. Jaguar Team, which originally had been intended to land on the *Sandpiper*, would now hang back in the orbiting Osprey and jump where they were needed.

The Cougars began going through their final checkout.

Dean pressed a key on the panel strapped to his left forearm, and the LED screen lit up with pertinent data—his altitude above sea level, now 22,745 feet; the temperature outside, minus twenty-three degrees; the wind speed downloaded from the Osprey's computer; the atmospheric pressure . . . it was all there, right down to the wind speed above the water at the target. He pressed another key, and the atmospheric data were replaced by a bio stats screen, including, again, the outside temperature, as well as heart rate, blood pressure, and the flow rate of O_2 through his face mask.

He pressed a third key, and those data were replaced by a navigational screen showing his precise longitude and latitude, plus his current velocity—271 knots—as clocked by NAVSTAR-GPS satellites in medium Earth orbit, eleven thousand miles overhead. Most important was the tiny, glowing red arrow on the extreme right, by his wrist, accompanied by the numerals 96845, the last three of which were flickering so quickly they were blurred as the number dwindled. It was the range, in yards, to the target, which now lay about fifty-five miles to the northeast. The arrow gave the direction to the *Atlantis Queen* and was now pointed at the front of the Osprey's troop bay.

The wrist pad gave him all the data he needed to conduct a HAHO paradrop and landing on what otherwise would have been an impossible target—a *moving* target, in pitch-blackness, that was just seventy feet long and about fifty wide.

Each of the other men in the assault had the same device, and each was cycling through the different screens now, making sure they were operational. Once certain that their electronic systems were good to go, they began the time-honored physical check, with each man checking the straps, weapons, gear, and buckles of the man beside him, then standing still as the two switched roles.

Each man in the assault team wore a black GORE-TEX jumpsuit over a Polartec liner, cold-weather gloves and overboots, and an HGU-55/P parachutist's helmet with a built-in communications system that would allow him to talk to the other team members and, via a relay through a nearby AWACs aircraft, with Desk Three. His lower face was covered by an MBU-12P pressure demand oxygen mask. His left eye was covered by an AN/PVS-14D night-vision monocular, which left his right eye dark-adapted in the dim red glow of the Osprey's cabin lights.

They carried a mix of weapons. Four, including Dean, carried the ubiquitous H&K SD5 with infrared laser targeting mounts and an integral sound suppressor. Four others carried a fairly new entry in the U.S. military arsenal, the AA-12 automatic combat shotgun, while the last four carried CAR-15 assault weapons. Each man also carried a SIG SAUER P226 with a sound suppressor screwed tight to the muzzle.

Dean finished checking the straps and harness fastenings on Tom Fredericks, the man immediately in front of him, making sure in particular that his combat shotgun was secure on his back and the hose from his O_2 cylinder was clear and not going to be torn by an opening parachute. Then Dean clapped Fredericks on the shoulder and allowed the other man to check him.

Final checkout complete, the twelve of them stood single file, facing the still-closed boarding ramp of the aircraft.

And then there was nothing to do but wait.

24

THE MINUTES PASSED, AS they always do just before a step into emptiness, slowly.

The Osprey had reached its service ceiling of about twenty-four thousand feet. HAHO parachute jumps usually took place at altitudes over twenty-five thousand feet, but that could always be tailored to fit mission requirements. Cougar would be steering to target across a distance of only five miles, rather than the more usual thirty to fifty. They droned along now in level flight, steadily closing on the waypoint designated Charlie One.

"What's the word, Mr. Rubens?" Dean asked, keeping his helmet comm gear switched off while he used his implant to talk to the Art Room. "We've got about two minutes to go/no-go."

"The President still hasn't gotten back to Bing," Rubens said. He sounded tired and not a little exasperated. "This may be a CYA hand-me-down."

"Shit."

Dean hadn't been paying a lot of attention to the bureaucratic games in Washington lately, but he'd heard enough from Rubens over the past several days to make a pretty fair guess as to what was happening. The current administration didn't want to be seen as militarily adventurous at a time when it was trying to disengage from Iraq. The United Kingdom had rejected an offer of help by the United States with Harrow Storm, and that had been fine with the President. He wanted to stay out of what publicly was a British crisis if he possibly could.

But the two hijacked ships were now just two hundred nautical miles from New York City. Rubens was convinced that the real goal of the IJI Brigade terrorists was to force the United States to step in and either attempt a bloody takedown of both ships, one that might well end in hundreds or thousands of casualties and risk radioactive contamination of the entire North Atlantic Gulf Stream, or, failing that, sink the two ships out of hand to keep them out of American waters or ports, an act that would show the U.S. military murdering thousands of hostages *and* contaminating the ocean, all live on the nightly cable news.

By doing nothing, the administration might be hoping that someone else took the responsibility of actually making a decision. If Rubens decided to launch Operation Neptune on his own, he would give the President options. If Neptune was a success, the President could accept the praise. If it was a disaster, he could always "disavow all knowledge of their actions," as the old TV spy show so succinctly put it.

As Rubens said, a CYA hand-me-down of responsibility—cover your ass, and let someone else take the responsibility.

"Neptune," Rubens said after a moment, "is a go. On *my* authority."

"Copy," Dean replied. "Neptune is go." At that moment, he was very, *very* glad he did not have Rubens' job. Success would mean someone else got the praise and he, most likely, would get a severe dressing-down for exceeding his authority. Failure meant political crucifixion and quite probably legal action as well. If Neptune turned sour, they would be looking for scapegoats in the morning.

"Good luck, Charlie."

"Thanks. And . . . don't worry. We'll do our best."

"I know you will."

The aircraft cargo master slapped Dean on the shoulder and switched his headset back on. "The tangos just called to wave us off," the cargo said over Dean's helmet radio. "Guess they're nervous about us flying so close."

"What'd you tell them?"

"That we were a fat, stupid UPS plane en route to Boston," the cargo master replied. "Just like we planned it."

"Any reply to that?"

"Negative. But you can bet they're watching us!"

"Yeah, but a cruise ship's radar isn't going to spot man-sized targets. They can watch all they want."

The cargo master held a hand up as he listened to an intercom transmission from the cockpit, then nodded and gave Dean the ready sign. They were coming up on Charlie One. The pitch of the Osprey's rotors changed as the aircraft slowed sharply.

With a shrill grinding sound, the rear ramp to the Osprey's cargo deck opened, dropping to create a descending ramp leading into darkness.

Dean opened his communications channel again. "We're good to go, people," he said. "Light your strobes." At the back of the helmet of each man in the line, an IR beacon began winking on and off, invisible to the unaided right eye, visible as a white, pulsing flash through the NVG monocular each man wore over his left.

The sudden wind from outside whipped at the legs of Dean's jumpsuit. The oxygen coming through his mask was cold and unbearably dry. More seconds crawled past, and then the cargo master said, "Okay, people! We're coming up on jump point Charlie One in five . . . four . . . three . . . two . . . one . . . *now!*"

"Go!" Dean yelled. *"Go! Go! Go!"*

The line of twelve black-clad men moved forward swiftly, passing the line of empty seats to their right, the line of watching comrades still seated on their left. They hit the lowered ramp one close behind the next, launching one after the other into the night.

Dean was the last man out . . . and then he was falling through the dark.

Starboard Boat Deck, *Atlantis Queen*
40° 47' N, 69° 59' W
Friday, 0448 hours GMT

"This way," Johnny Berger, the steward, whispered. "But be *quiet*!"

Andrew McKay nodded and passed the whisper back to Nina, and she passed it on to the others following. There were twelve of them strung out in a long line, emerging one by one from the door onto the Starboard Boat Deck. Eleven would be taking the lifeboat; the twelfth, Dr. Barnes, was bringing up the rear. He would help them keep a lookout and actually operate the davits that would lower them into the sea.

"Mommy, I'm sleepy," Melissa said.

"Shh, dear. Not now."

Their escape had been put off one time after another. Not long after their secretive meeting up in Kleito's Temple on Tuesday afternoon, the helicopter attack had thundered out of the east. Several of them, including McKay and his family, had seen the helicopter shot down off the starboard side. The escape, which had been planned for that evening, was put off. The hijackers would be on their guard, and it was too dangerous to go wandering around on deck.

There were rumors that a passenger had been shot afterward, but no one in the group had been able to confirm that. They'd agreed, though, that the terrorists might decide to lock all of the passengers up at any time—perhaps put them with Harper and Bernstein and the ship's captain and the Cruise Director and everyone else who seemed to have vanished during the past five days.

But then the wind had picked up and it had started raining. Berger had pointed out that they did *not* want to try to drop into the sea from a moving ship. The maneuver would be dangerous enough even if the water was calm.

And so they'd put the escape off for another night.

That afternoon, however, the rain had lifted and the wind had died down as the ship had emerged into sunshine from a long line of squalls. Barnes had checked some maps in the ship's library earlier. He'd pointed out that—given their speed and course since Sunday—they ought to be somewhere off the coast of Massachusetts by now, probably less than fifty miles from shore; they could start rowing northeast and hope to strike land within a day or two, even if the military didn't pick up their emergency signal and come get them.

Tonight, they'd all agreed, would be the night.

Turning right, they moved along the safety railing toward the loom of the first lifeboat, hanging just above the deck. Barnes used his security key to swipe through a reader. Everyone else had left their ID cards in their staterooms; if the hijackers were tracking people by the locations of their passkey cards, they likely wouldn't notice the ship's doctor on the boat deck, where they would definitely come investigate twelve passengers and crew out here late at night.

A ready light winked on, and Barnes pressed a button. With a grinding whine, the lifeboat swung across the deck and over the railing.

"Let's get the women and children on first," McKay said, nudging Nina and Melissa forward. He knew it sounded silly—a bit of melodramatic nonsense—even as he said it. But the stress was building inside him to the point where he could hardly stand still. He needed to get them off the ship *now*. . . .

"Wakkif!" a harsh voice barked from farther aft . . . and then three flashlights switched on, pinning the party of passengers against the railing. "Stop! Stop where you are!"

"Aw, shit!" Carmichael said. Turning, he started to run forward, but a hijacker with an AK-47 stepped out of the shadows and knocked Carmichael down with a rifle butt to the jaw.

Stunned, the civilians could only stand there, helpless as a half-dozen armed men came toward them both from forward and from aft. A few of the civilians raised their hands.

"Put hands down," one of the hijackers said in heavily accented English. "We know you no have weapons. Now move! That way! You will come with us!"

And the hijackers herded the twelve of them forward along the deck, back toward the door from which they'd just emerged.

Assault Team Cougar One
40° 47' N, 69° 56' W
Friday, 0458 hours EST

They fell to twenty thousand feet before releasing their chutes. With a shock, Dean's parachute opened above him, rapidly slowing his terminal velocity from free fall to a gentle drift through the night.

Grabbing his left and right steering toggles, Dean brought his parafoil into a gentle left turn. His parachute was an MC-4 ram-air military chute, two night-black rectangular canopy sections joined by seven air cells to create a double wing, one just above the other. Ram-air chutes had astonishing glide and control characteristics that allowed the parachutist to steer them with extraordinary precision. The red arrow on his forearm display was showing the direction toward the *Atlantis Queen* and the range . . . now about four and a half miles.

He could see the other jumpers ahead of him in a ragged and uneven curve, the bright wink of their IR strobes showing their positions in the sky as they slowly began adjusting their positions relative to one another. Vic Walters and David P. Yancey had point and would be going in together; the rest were spacing themselves out so that they would come in one at a time, about five to ten seconds apart.

Dean would come in last.

His rate of descent was steady at fifteen feet per second, his speed twenty-five knots. The wind was light—about five knots from the southwest. The sky had been clear earlier, when they'd left the *Eisenhower*, but was becoming overcast again swiftly.

With the *Queen* steaming away from him at twenty knots, it was going to take him some time to catch up with her.

Art Room
NSA Headquarters
Fort Meade, Maryland
Friday, 0502 hours EST

Rubens stood in the Art Room, looking up at the big screen. Deck plans provided by Royal Sky Line had been turned into computer-graphic schematics showing every deck on board the ship, Decks One through Twelve above, Decks A through D below. The sheer size and complexity of the target meant that Neptune was going to have to be carried out in sections. Cougar was only the first wave. Jaguar was in reserve, the *Ohio* was closing with the *Pacific Sandpiper*, and the SAS had just reported that they were ready to go with Operation Harrow Lightning.

But the critical part was getting those first few men down safely onto the *Atlantis Queen*'s deck.

He listened to the chatter from the string of parachutists. There wasn't much. The team had drilled endlessly and didn't need to say much as they lined themselves up for the approach to their target.

"Cougar Two," a voice said, identifying itself. "Slowing descent. Winds picking up a bit. Eight knots."

"Copy."

So far, everything was going perfectly by the book. Rubens was already composing his resignation letter in his head, however. By ordering Neptune to go in without authorization from the President or the Pentagon, he was committing a decidedly illegal act, dropping a dozen armed men onto the deck of a cruise ship belonging to another nation and running the risk that his actions would precipitate disaster. If Khalid decided to blow up either ship out there, radioactive fallout would easily stretch along the prevailing winds three hundred miles across southern Newfoundland, while seaborne contamination might wash across beaches from Newfoundland to Ireland and possibly the rest of western Europe as well. It would be an unprecedented ecological and radiological calamity. That he'd given the order while the U.S. government was supposedly carrying out negotiations with the hijackers, or trying to, would only cast his decision into a sharper, harsher light.

But the alternative was to let the *Queen* keep coming, with the New England coast now less than six hundred miles away.

It was an alternative that simply didn't bear consideration.

"How about it, Kathy?" he asked the woman seated at a computer console nearby. Kathy Caravaggio was one of his best handlers. "Ready to raise the stakes?"

"We have full admin control," she told him. "They

don't know it yet, but *we* have control of their security systems now."

"Do it," Rubens said.

Security Office, *Atlantis Queen*
40° 45' N, 70° 07' W
Friday, 0510 hours EST

"What is wrong with it?" Khalid demanded.

"Amir . . . I don't know. The security system appears to be running normally, but all of the security cameras have just switched off!"

"That's impossible, unless you shut it down here!"

"I did not, Amir! I swear!"

"Let me see the deck displays."

Hamud Haqqani touched a switch, frowned, then hit it again. "Sir . . . we don't have those screens, either."

Khalid felt a cold twist in his gut. The deck display screens should have been able to show him points of light for every person on board the ship—red for passengers with ID, blue for people sensed in various areas of the ship without ID, green for the hijackers and the members of the crew. If he couldn't see where the hostages were, he was losing control.

"There was a large group of hostages in the casino, yes?"

"Yes, Amir," Haqqani said. "Last time I looked, there were around fifty passengers and a few crew members there. Tahir and Faruk are on the deck outside there, and El Hakim is inside the casino."

"Are there other large gatherings of passengers?"

"No, sir. A few in the Kleito Bar . . . four or five, perhaps. Most passengers are in their staterooms, except for the ones in the theater."

"We may be facing an attack," Khalid said. "Get those screens working!"

Assault Team Cougar
40° 45' N, 70° 06' W
Friday, 0510 hours EST

They were picking up speed. The maximum forward velocity of a standard ram-air chute is about 25 miles per hour. The team's MC-4s had been modified, however, to improve their speed in horizontal flight. They could manage about 34 miles per hour, now, which meant they were closing on the *Atlantis Queen* at about 14 miles per hour . . . or roughly twelve knots. Four and a half regular miles was a little under four nautical miles. Four nautical miles at twelve knots—twenty minutes.

Which meant they were getting damned close by now.

Guided by the GPS-controlled readouts on their wrists, the strike force steadily closed on their target, now less than half a mile ahead. The *Queen* was running with her lights on and so made a splendid visual target.

"Okay, Cougars One and Two," Dean said over the squad channel. The men were identified by their order in the stick. "You've got the call."

"Cougar One. I see the Atlas Deck. I see two, repeat, two tangos close in by the windows, as expected. AK-47s and cigarettes."

"Cougar Two, roger that. Two tangos in sight."

"Doesn't look like they're expecting us," Cougar One, Vic Walters, added.

One point of HAHO drops was that the parachutes opened so far from the target that the crack of unfolding fabric grabbing air couldn't be heard at the target. Another was the ability to literally fly to the target, within certain fairly broad parameters.

"Cougar One, Two, this is Twelve," Dean said. "Take them down at your discretion."

There was no going back now.

Neptune Theater, *Atlantis Queen*
44° 27' N, 59° 13' W
Friday, 0511 hours EST

"Inside!" Rashid Abdul Aziz said, nudging one of the Westerners with the muzzle of his AK-47. "Sit down and no make trouble!"

The twelve captives meekly filed through the door and into the theater, escorted by Nejmuddin and Sadeeq, one of them, the black one, still clutching his forehead where Baqr's rifle butt had clipped him.

Stopping in the hallway outside the theater entrance, Aziz pulled out his radio and called the bridge.

"What is it?" Fakhet's voice replied.

"This is Aziz. We've caught them all," Aziz told him. "We're putting them inside the theater now."

"Any trouble?"

"None at all."

"Good. The Amir wants you to—" The voice broke off.

"Bridge? Are you there?"

There was a moment's silence, and then Fakhet's voice sounded from the radio again. "There is a . . . problem," he said. "Listen. Take all of your men to Deck Nine, then aft to the casino. The Amir wants all of the people gathered there to be rounded up and moved to the theater as well!"

"Why?" Aziz asked. "There must be fifty or sixty—"

"Just *do* it, Aziz! All of our security cameras have just switched off! The Amir says there may be an attack coming at any moment!"

Cougar One
44° 27' N, 59° 13' W
Friday, 0513 hours EST

Victor Jeffery Walters was an old hand. Forty-eight years old, now, he'd joined the Army Special Forces as soon as he'd made sergeant and eight years later had been selected for Delta Force. He'd seen action in both Afghanistan and Iraq, been promoted to staff sergeant, and finally retired after twenty-two years.

His retirement had been illusory, however . . . or, at best, in name only. An NSA recruiter had approached him last year, and he'd volunteered for paramilitary service with the Deep Black program and Desk Three. Since then, he'd been training with the Cougars, keeping up his weapons skills, keeping up his jump certification.

And now it all was paying off.

Not that this jump was an easy one. He'd done it time after time in training, and his heart still felt like it was trying to climb up out of his throat. He'd once heard a Navy aviator friend talk about the difficulties of landing at night on an aircraft carrier . . . a huge vessel that during the approach appeared to be about the same size as a postage stamp, *and* it was moving.

His friend, he thought, had nothing on him. This was a *lot* worse.

Through the NVG monocular he could clearly see the Atlas Pool and the large deck around it, positioned at the rounded back end of the *Atlantis Queen*. Light spilling from the casino inside made the deck area as bright as day; he could see the two hijackers clearly. They appeared to be relaxed, weapons slung, the red star of a burning cigarette in the mouth of each.

Thirty feet from the *Queen*'s taffrail, he hauled back on the brake toggles of his parachute, spilling air and speed. As he drifted forward at the uncertain edge of a stall, he pulled his H&K, which he'd released during the jump to hang by its straps from the right side of his body, up to his shoulder.

The touch of a gloved thumb switched on the infrared laser targeting system; through his monocular, he saw the ruby-bright point of light, invisible to the naked eye, dancing across the torso of the terrorist on the right.

"Cougar One," he whispered. "Target right."

"Two. Target left."

"Take 'em!"

It was tricky taking a shot while trying to control a parachute just thirty feet from touchdown, especially with some turbulence kicking up as he flew through the cruise ship's slipstream. He had to release the parachute control toggles while in a sustained near-stall, raise his weapon, aim, and fire, all before he stalled completely and lost control. The IR laser made aiming simpler; as the red dot slipped swiftly up the tango's body, from left hip to right shoulder, Walters began squeezing off shots, the H&K's integral sound suppressor muffling each shot to a loud, hissing snap.

The terrorist jerked backward, chin going up, hands clawing at his chest as he slammed into the glass at his back. Walters managed five shots before he dropped his weapon and grabbed the control toggles again, allowing himself to pick up airspeed once more and glide toward the open deck. To his left, Dave Yancey seemed to hover motionless in mid-air for a second or two as he continued pumping near-silent rounds into his target, then dropped his weapon as well and continued his glide in for a landing.

The deck came up to meet Walters' booted feet. He misjudged his speed, though, which was a little high. He touched down running, dragging down the toggles and collapsing the ram-air chute behind him, then slammed full body into the glass doors leading into the brightly lit casino.

Pyramid Club Casino, *Atlantis Queen*
40° 45' N, 70° 07' W
Friday, 0513 hours EST

Jerry Esterhausen jumped at the slam of something heavy hitting the door leading out to the Atlas Pool. Howorth stood and turned, trying to see, but it was dark outside and the lighting, though low, had wrecked her night vision. She thought she saw movement out there, however, a shadow in the blackness.

And she saw the two outside guards as well, crumpled on the deck.

The hijacker guard who'd remained inside the casino had been sitting at a chair up against the aft-starboard bulkhead. He'd started at the thump as well, and was moving toward the door to investigate.

He was five feet from Rosie, Esterhausen's card-playing robot.

"Jerry!" Howorth hissed. "We need a distraction! Fast!"

"Huh?"

"Your robot! . . ."

Jerry typed a command into his computer, then dragged his fingertip across the touchpad. Rosie, who'd been sitting lifelessly in her kiosk, awoke suddenly, her metal arms snapping up and out, her torso spinning to face the hijacker.

Cougar One
Atlas Pool deck, *Atlantis Queen*
Friday, 0518 hours EST

Behind Walters, David Yancey stepped onto the deck alongside the swimming pool at a gentle walk, his forward velocity perfectly matched to the speed of the ship.

"Army klutz," Yancey said. David Yancey was a former U.S. Navy SEAL.

"Fuck you, squid!"

Walters struggled to unhook the harnesses holding the parachute to his body. As he looked up, however, he saw movement . . . and the flash of a weapon. Their last briefing had mentioned a tango inside the casino.

And suddenly a man screamed, and Walters heard the sharp clatter of a weapon firing full auto.

25

Pyramid Club Casino, *Atlantis Queen*
Thirty-three miles south of Nantucket
40° 45' N, 70° 07' W
Friday, 0518 hours EST

THE TERRORIST HAD TURNED at the noise, looking up to
see Jerry Esterhausen's robot leaning toward him, arms
outstretched.

The man panicked. He screamed and the AK in his
hand went off; he was holding the weapon one-handed,
and the muzzle climbed sharply with the recoil, out of
control. People in the club screamed, some diving for the
floor as stray rounds slammed into bulkheads and the ceiling. Bullets cracked and whined, some shattering the plastic
woman-shaped torso shell of the robot, some ricocheting
from tooled steel. The monitor at the top of the unit exploded in flying glass.

But as Jerry Esterhausen had pointed out on another
occasion, the robot's computer brain was located in the
machine's base. From across the room the engineer
pressed a key and swiped his finger across the touchpad
once again, and the machine's arms snapped closed like a
trap, moving with mind-numbing speed, gathering in the
terrified hijacker and his weapon and smashing him close
against its torso in a metal embrace.

An instant later, the glass door behind him slid open and a nightmare shape entered—all in black, the form turned monstrous by heavy clothing, combat vest, helmet, and mask. The man advanced with a submachine gun tucked up tight against his shoulder, moving as though weapon and man were one and the same.

The terrorist gave a strangled scream, struggling against the relentless, backbreaking steel hug. The black-clad apparition pivoted slightly at the sound and fired, putting two rounds into the terrorist's head, the shots no louder than a sharp click. Spent brass tinkled and danced along the casino floor in the deathly silence that had followed the parachutist's entrance.

"*Please*, sir! You're making me blush!"

With that, a number of civilians started to rise. Someone cheered, the cheer joined by another, and then another.

"*Quiet!*" Carolyn Howorth startled herself with the strength of her bellow. Her voice cut through the rising crowd noise and brought the mob to a halt. "*Everyone quiet!*"

"Everyone stay down!" the black apparition by the door shouted. He kept the submachine gun up against his shoulder, pivoting this way and that, giving the appearance of being a machine himself, one seeking its next target. "Everyone stay down, stay calm, and we'll get you out of this!"

A second man in helmet, mask, and combat gear entered the open door and the two separated, putting their backs against the bulkheads to either side of the rear wall.

"Don't shoot," Howorth called. "You got them all in here!"

"Atlas Pool deck clear!" one of the figures said. "Casino clear! Three tangos down!"

And another black figure touched down on the deck outside, moving too fast. He took three running steps as he tried to come to a halt and fell into one of the two hot tubs set to either side of the swimming pool.

Security Office, *Atlantis Queen*
40° 45' N, 70° 07' W
Friday, 0520 hours EST

"In Allah's name, what is happening?" Khalid demanded. He held the radio against his ear. "Tahir! Report!" He shook the radio in frustration, then put it to his ear again. "El Hakim! Come in! This is Khalid. Talk to me!"

There was nothing, no response but static.

He changed channels. "Aziz! Are you there?"

"Yes, Amir!"

Khalid felt, first, relief at hearing the voice, followed almost at once by a deadly and cold sense of purpose. A radio failure by itself he would accept as accident—a dead battery, perhaps—but to have all three of the men guarding the stern deck area of the ship go silent at the same time that the security cameras *and* the shipboard monitor system switched off could not be coincidence.

"We have lost touch with the guards at the back of the ship," he said. "We may have unwanted visitors aboard. Where are you?"

"Grand Staircase, going up," Aziz replied. He sounded out of breath. "Deck Five!"

"Get to the casino as quickly as you can. Watch out for an ambush!"

"Yes, Amir!"

"Keep me informed! Out!"

Khalid thought for a moment more, studying the four men seated at the Security Office consoles. Beyond, the door into the IT center was open, and he could see two more men there . . . Hamud Haqqani and Ghailiani. Slipping the radio into its belt holster, Khalid strode into the IT center.

"What has happened to the security systems?" he demanded.

"Amir, we don't know," Haqqani said. "The main computer may have gone offline for a moment."

"Would that turn off the security cameras?"

"Amir, *I don't know*!"

"Ghailiani? You know these systems! What's happened?"

Ghailiani turned in his seat, his eyes locking with Khalid's. "I don't know, either," he said. "All systems appear to be functioning normally, except for the cameras and the security scanners. We could try to reboot. That will take about twenty minutes."

Khalid considered Ghailiani for a second. The man was . . . calm, *icy* calm, when everyone else in the Security-IT suite was stressed to the point of near hysteria.

What had the man done?

Probably nothing. Ghailiani was weak and indecisive, paralyzed by the threat to his family. He wouldn't have done anything on his own. His current calm was probably simple fatalism . . . a numb acceptance that things were out of his control.

But Khalid would definitely ask some more probing questions later, perhaps after having the men at the Millbrook safehouse work on Ghailiani's daughter for a time and send him some more photographs of the process.

"Twenty minutes is too long," Khalid said. "You have five minutes to tell me what is happening to the security systems on this ship."

He turned and left, walking swiftly through the Security Office and out into the Deck Eleven passageway. Through the security doors—he was relieved to see that they, at least, were still working as he swiped his key card—and up the service stairwell beyond. He emerged, seconds later, in the passageway leading to the radio room and the bridge.

"The Americans are continuing their transmissions,

Amir," Fakhet told him as he passed the open door to the radio room. "They say they will give us whatever we want, but that we—"

"Ignore them," Khalid snapped. He used his card to go onto the bridge. Three of his men looked at him curiously, Obeidat, Mohawal, and Abdallah. Abdul Mohawal was at the ship's wheel.

"Come hard right!" Khalid ordered. "Steer north!"

"Yes, Amir!"

"Fakhet!"

"Yes, Amir!" the radio operator called from the next compartment.

"Call the *Pacific Sandpiper*. We need them!"

"At once, Amir!"

It wasn't yet too late.

Cougar Twelve
40° 45' N, 70° 07' W
Friday, 0522 hours EST

"This is Eleven. Target is changing course," sounded in Dean's helmet receiver.

"Stay with him."

Dean saw the ship turning, but the movement was slow and ponderous. The hijackers were probably hoping to throw off the landings of any more parachutists, but a cruise ship of that size simply couldn't maneuver like a speedboat. Dean watched the silhouette of Gene Podalski, Cougar Eleven, touch down on the brightly lit pool deck now just a few hundred feet ahead. He tugged slightly at the ram-air chute's controls, bleeding off some of his forward speed, and held his breath as the deck swooped up to meet him.

He touched down on the hard wooden planking, taking a few steps to keep his balance, then collapsed the chute behind him. The other Cougar team members crouched on the deck, either forming a defensive perimeter, moving inside, or gathering up their chutes and jump gear.

They'd all made it! Some of the op planners, he'd known, had insisted that it would be impossible to get all of the chutists down safely onto that tiny aft deck of a moving ship. In fact, part of each man's gear included a tightly packaged, inflatable one-man raft, just in case he missed the target and ended up in the sea. It looked like Brisard had managed to fall into one of the aft deck pools, but he was the only one who'd gotten wet.

Dean unsnapped his harness, let his billowing chute, reserve chute, and harness go over the side. As he stepped inside the casino, he saw Carolyn J. Howorth and felt a further surge of relief.

"Hey, CJ," he said, pulling off his oxygen mask, then raising his monocular. "Enjoying your cruise?"

"Charlie!" Her eyes were wide. "What the hell are you doing here?"

"Rescuing you," he said. "Unless you insist on doing it yourself."

Art Room
NSA Headquarters
Fort Meade, Maryland
Friday, 0524 hours EST

"Looks like trouble headed their way, sir," Caravaggio said.

Rubens looked at the big screen with its side-by-side schematics of the *Atlantis Queen*'s decks. A tight group of green dots was clustered in the Grand Staircase on Decks Seven and Eight. They appeared to be going up, toward Deck Nine.

"Dean?" he said.

"Yeah. Copy."

"You've got eight hostiles one deck down, coming up the main staircase. They're moving slow, but you don't have more than a couple of minutes."

"Right."

A *drive-by upload*, the GCHQ woman had called it. Send an e-mail in HTML format to a target computer. Get someone with access to that e-mail to open it and click on a hypertext line. The result was an influx of code into the target computer—a carefully crafted virus, in fact—that took over that computer and gave the sender administrative control.

In short, the *Atlantis Queen*'s security and IT computer network was now being run by the Art Room, almost a thousand miles away. So far as the hijackers were concerned, everything was running normally . . . or it had been until Rubens had ordered the cameras switched off and the security overwatch display rerouted to the Art Room and switched off on the ship.

It gave Dean and his men a technological edge where they most needed one.

Cougar Twelve
Pyramid Club Casino, *Atlantis Queen*
Friday, 0524 hours EST

"Keep us posted," Dean said. Swiftly he started peeling off his clothing.

"What the hell are you doing?" Howorth asked.

"Plan A," Dean replied, standing on one foot as he peeled off the jumpsuit. "Walters! You're with me!"

"Got it."

Dean had to sit down to peel off the Polartec long johns. "The rest of you . . . police the area and get yourselves and all of your gear behind that bar. And . . . someone get that guy down off the robot."

Operation Neptune had come in with two possible

mission plans, depending on the situation they discovered when they got on board. While they were prepared to launch a general assault—Plan B—with some of them heading down to the cargo hold and the rest heading for the bridge, they were also prepared to carry out the original plan, which had been to infiltrate the ship by posing as passengers. Each of the Black Cat parachutists had a change of civilian clothing—jeans, pullover sweaters, socks, tennis shoes—rolled up inside the rucksack he'd carried secured to his harnesses during their jump.

"They're all on Deck Nine," Rubens' voice said in Dean's head. "Looks like they're sorting things out among themselves."

Dean fastened his jeans and tugged his shoes on—to hell with the socks. As he dressed, he glanced around the casino, looking at the crowd surrounding them, trying to take their measure. A number of them were elderly. Others were younger but scared. There was always the possibility that one or more terrorists had infiltrated themselves among the hostages. In fact, in a normal hostage crisis takedown, the rescue team would be using zip strips to immobilize *everybody* they found inside the objective, just in case.

That simply wasn't practical here—or desirable, given that they might need to move these people out quickly. But Dean was alert to the possibility that not all of these civilians were innocents.

He pulled his sweater down over his head, unholstered his pistol, a SIG Sauer P226, screwed the sound suppressor onto the muzzle, and tucked it into the waistband of his jeans at the small of his back, tugging the sweater's hem low to hide it. Nearby, Walters did the same.

"Listen up, people!" Dean called. "When they come in here, as far as you know, a bunch of guys in black shot those three, then headed up the steps outside. We'll be watching, in case they try anything, okay?"

The crowd responded with a murmured assent.

"When are you getting us off the ship?" an older man called.

"As soon as we can. Be patient."

"What if they're coming to kill us?" Howorth asked.

"We don't plan on letting them," Dean replied. "Your e-mails said they were probably taking people who got in the way to the theater, right?"

"That's right. Deck One, toward the bow."

"If that bunch of tangos coming aft don't find us, either they're going to herd you all forward to be with the rest, or . . ."

"Or what?"

"Or we'll take them down here," Dean said. He wouldn't admit to her that those tangos could be an execution squad. That was unlikely, though. The terrorists wouldn't start killing their hostages until they *knew* things were going bad.

Ten of the Black Cat team members vanished with weapons and gear into the bar area to one side of the casino, ducking low to stay out of sight. It wouldn't hide them if the tangos searched carefully, but Dean doubted that they would be in a patient mood.

The young man with glasses who'd been hovering near Howorth did something with his laptop, and the robot near the outside door opened its arms. Walters dragged the body to a spot near the door onto the deck and left it there with the AK beside it.

"Remember!" Dean told the quietly watching people. "Guys in black came in, you're not sure how many. Maybe five or six. They shot these three, then went up the outside stairs." According to the ship's deck plans he'd been studying, there were two sets of curving steps, port and starboard, leading from Deck Nine up to Deck Ten and an outside promenade running forward to the Kleito Bar. It would be a quick and immediate way to reach the bridge and the Security Office, an obvious attack route.

"They're coming your way," Rubens said in Dean's ear. "They're at the door. . . ."

Dean and Walters mixed in with the civilians, urging them to scatter more around the casino rather than provide a bunched-up target. The door at the back of the casino banged open, and six men in khaki with AK-47s burst inside.

They came in with their guns raised, ready to start shooting. "Everybody stay where you are!" one shouted, his voice shrill. "Everybody don't move!"

"Don't shoot!" Dean yelled. "They're not here!" This was the critical moment. If this was an execution squad, they could start shooting in an instant. Dean wanted to get them talking instead.

"*Who* is not here?" one of the gunmen yelled back. The others advanced cautiously, weapons up.

"A bunch of guys all in black parachuted down on the pool deck!" Howorth called out. "They . . . they shot your men! . . ."

"They're not here," the guy with the laptop added. "They all went back outside and up the stairs to Deck Ten!"

"How many?" the hijacker demanded. "How many were there?"

"I'm not sure," an elderly woman on the other side of the room said. "Maybe five or six?"

The tangos advanced, then, some moving among the passengers, roughly shoving them aside, others making for the door leading outside. One checked the dead terrorist inside; another checked the two on the deck. One of them had a small, handheld radio and was talking into it in rapid-fire Arabic.

Dean watched as the terrorists gave the room a cursory check, though they never even approached the bar. The one with the radio began gesturing and shouting. "All of you! We move you to safe location."

"Wait!" Howorth said. "Where are you taking us?"

"We take you someplace safe. Now move! *Move!*"

Dean allowed himself to be herded along, one of the passengers. The skinny guy started to pick up his laptop, but one of the gunmen jabbed the muzzle of his AK against the guy's side. "No! You leave it!"

"But that's my computer!"

"*Leave* it, Jerry!" Howorth said. "Damn it, you can get it later! . . ."

The crowd of civilians began moving out into the passageway, hurried along by their captors.

A group of eighteen or twenty of the civilians in the casino were older people, in their sixties or seventies or even older. One was a man in a wheelchair. Several of the women had walkers, and more were leaning on canes. As the gunmen hurried the mob forward toward the door, the group swiftly fell behind, unable to keep up. One of the gunmen shoved an elderly woman and knocked her down. The gunman snarled something and raised his rifle as if he was going to strike her with it.

Dean whirled and caught the terrorist's arm, stopping him. The man gaped at him, eyes wide.

"Don't," Dean said in a firm voice. "*Don't*. They're old; they can't hurt you."

The gunman wrenched his arm free, then swung the butt of his rifle at Dean's face. Dean sidestepped, but the stick grazed the side of his head, knocking him back a step. The gunman hovered there, as though trying to decide who to kill, Dean or the old woman.

" 'Do no harm to the elderly, and do not strike the infirm, for it is hateful in the eyes of Allah,' " Dean said, touching the wound on his scalp with his fingertips. They came away slick with blood. "Isn't that what your Qur'an says?"

"You . . . you know the holy book, the words of the Prophet?"

"A little. I know it teaches you that if you kill the innocent, you burn in Hell!"

The man's eyes widened a bit more. "Leave them, Rashid!" another gunman said.

Turning suddenly, he waved the elderly group away. "Go back!" he said. "All of you! Go back! Stay here!"

Dean helped the woman up off the deck. "Thank you, young man," she said. "Just like Bruce Willis!"

A passenger, an older man, took her hand. "Come along, Ms. Jordan. Let's stay out of their way."

One of the gunmen was left behind to collect the three dropped AK assault rifles. The others urged the younger captives forward. One nudged Dean in the ribs with his rifle. "Now move! Quick! Yallah!"

Dean let himself be nudged along.

"That was very brave," Howorth said quietly, moving close beside him as they moved into the passageway. "Do you really know the Qur'an?"

Dean glanced around to make sure none of the terrorists was within earshot. "No," he whispered, "and neither do they. Most of them, anyway."

"What do you mean?"

"In my experience, most Christians don't know the Bible very well. My guess is that most Muslims are the same with the Qur'an. The fundamentalists like to pick and choose which verses they'll use, and argue about interpretations . . . but only the scholars know the book well. Just like with most Christians."

"And my guess is that you're damned lucky!"

The group hurried forward through the ship.

Bridge, *Atlantis Queen*
40° 45' N, 70° 07' W
Friday, 0528 hours EST

"Very well," Khalid said, speaking into the radio handset. "Hurry!"

He handed the microphone back to Fakhet, then

stepped back out onto the bridge. The *Pacific Sandpiper* was a mile away, and it would take her time to complete her turn.

Khalid considered keeping the *Atlantis Queen* on the same heading, due north. The coast of Massachusetts was out there, the islands of Nantucket and Martha's Vineyard. If he ran the *Queen* aground there, it would create an appropriately spectacular disaster.

But not, perhaps, spectacular enough. Al-Qaeda's message would be so much sharper, so much more to the point, if it was delivered to Manhattan. "Bring us back to the left," he told the man at the helm. "And reduce speed to ten knots." Khalid wanted the *Pacific Sandpiper* to catch up with them.

Aziz had reported in moments before. Passengers in the casino said they'd seen black-clad men parachute onto the pool deck—probably SAS. They'd apparently killed three guards back there and now were on Deck Ten, moving forward.

Khalid retrieved his AKM assault rifle from the electronic chart table and checked the action. Let them come. He was ready for them.

As for the passengers, he'd ordered them moved to the Neptune Theater. If there was going to be a firefight, he wanted them in a controlled place, where he could have his men begin shooting them if the attackers got too close.

And as a last resort, he would detonate the radioactive canisters in the hold.

Neptune Theater, *Atlantis Queen*
Friday, 0529 hours EST

Yaqub Nehim grinned down at the struggling woman. "Perhaps you would like it if we tied your hands again?" He let his hand move along her leg, caressing.

"Get your hands off of me, you asshole!" the woman

screamed. She tried to slap him, and he blocked the clumsy swing easily.

"You son of a bitch! Leave her alone!" The ship's chief security officer lunged at him, but Nehim whipped the muzzle of his pistol around and caught the man on the side of his face.

"Yaqub!" Ra'id Hijazi called from farther up the theater aisle. "Leave the woman alone! This is not the time!"

"Mind your own business, Ra'id! I've been looking forward to this since we came on board!" Yaqub gave a harsh, bitter laugh. "It's not like any of us will survive this voyage, right?"

"Women are a trap of Satan!" Hijazi said, quoting an ancient *hadith*, a traditional quote from the sayings of Mohammed.

"'Forbidden are married women,'" Nehim replied, "'except those you own as slaves!' Surah Four-twenty! We can do as we like with these whores!"

It wasn't rape and it wasn't illegal when the woman refused to be properly dressed. These Western bitches paraded around half-naked all the time, putting themselves on display. Often they did not even go out accompanied by a husband or another male relative. They deserved whatever they got. In fact, most fundamentalist Islamic regimes condoned forcing condemned female prisoners to have sex, since the holy Qur'an forbade putting a virgin to death.

He doubted that these women were virgins, but they all were certainly under a sentence of death. It wouldn't hurt to make sure, just with one of them. . . .

Yaqub Nehim cared little for the Sharia or the tenets of his religion, and his knowledge of the Qur'an extended just far enough to provide a rationalization for what he would have done anyway. He'd gotten into trouble with the authorities in his native Saudi Arabia over his attempt to have sex with a foreign woman, an Italian, in Medina five years ago. The *ulema* hearing Yaqub's case, the religious judge, had offered him a choice—prison or joining a jihadist group dedicated to destroying the enemies of Islam.

He'd accepted recruitment. He *knew* what Saudi prisons were like.

As for accepting martyrdom . . . well, there *was* still time. Perhaps one of the lifeboats . . .

The door at the back of the theater banged open, and passengers spilled inside. Nehim let go of the struggling woman and stood, raising his AK-47 in case this was the vanguard of a prisoner revolt. Then he saw Aziz and Baqr and others of his mujahideen comrades, funneling the prisoners in through the door.

"What have you brought us, Rashid?" he asked Aziz. There were attractive women in this group as well. One in particular . . .

"They were in the casino," Aziz replied. He glanced at the woman in the seat next to Nehim, who was trying to straighten her clothing. "None of that, Nehim," he snapped. "We have work to do. *Holy* work!"

"What work?"

"The enemy has boarded the ship! Three of our brothers are dead! Guard the prisoners well, and keep your pants buckled. There will be time for games later!"

Nehim helped herd the new batch of prisoners down the aisle as Aziz and the others turned and headed back out into the Deck One mall area. Hijazi was giving Nehim a smug, I-told-you-so look, but he wiped his mouth with the back of one hand and ignored him.

That was the problem. There would be no time later, not if the enemy was already coming on board the ship. Nehim had been hungering for one of the half-naked bitches for a week, and in all likelihood the hijacked liner was going to be blown to bits within the next few minutes. Damn Khalid, and damn the sanctimonious Saudi *ulema* who'd put him here!

He was going to have one of these bitches before he

died, no matter what Hijazi or Aziz or the Amir himself might say.

The question was, which one?

Art Room
NSA Headquarters
Fort Meade, Maryland
Friday, 0531 hours EST

"Face the front of the theater," Rubens said, looking closely at the schematic showing the Neptune Theater. Pinpoints of red light representing forty more passengers had just entered the room and were moving down toward the front.

"Okay," Dean's voice came back from an overhead speaker. The dots representing him and Walters were green. Both were carrying ID passkey cards provided by Royal Sky Line before the mission. There were well over a hundred colored pinpoints already within the theater, a mingling of red and blue.

Not counting the blips representing Dean and Walters, there were eighty-eight green, people carrying crew-member IDs. Many of those would be terrorists, but most would be prisoners, crew members brought to the theater. Separating the two was going to be tough.

"We've identified five tangos surrounding your group," Rubens said, "the ones who brought you in. They're at twelve o'clock, two o'clock, five o'clock, six o'clock, and nine o'clock."

"Rog. Got 'em spotted."

"You have four shooters in the Deck Two balcony. Two o'clock, four o'clock, eight o'clock, and ten o'clock."

Again there was a pause. "Okay. I have them. And I saw two outside the Deck One doors. Any more?"

"There may be others mixed in with the prisoners. We can't differentiate here."

"I see one, yeah. One o'clock, thirty feet away. He's hassling a couple of women. Damn it . . . one of them is CJ! Our GCHQ contact!"

Rubens checked the indicated area. Two green blips overlapped, close beside several blues. "We see them."

"Ten targets. That'll take some shooting."

"Charlie, I recommend that you wait. The tangos who brought you down here will probably be leaving soon. And Brisard and three men are on their way on Deck Two. They'll be there in a few minutes."

"Rog. We'll wait." Almost a minute later, Dean spoke again. "Listen . . . that son of a bitch mixed in with the hostages. He's just grabbed a woman . . . no, *two* women! CJ and someone else! He's leading them up the other aisle!"

Ruben saw the dots, one blue, two green, moving closely together toward the door. "I see them."

"We need to take him now."

"You need to sit tight, Dean. Brisard's's almost there."

"*Damn* it, Bill!"

"By the book, Dean. *By the book*."

The three points of light moved through the door and into the passageway.

"They're gone," Dean said.

"You'll have your chance in a moment."

Brisard and the other three operators were nearly at the theater's Deck Two entrance. . . .

26

DEAN AND WALTERS WALKED all the way down the aisle, to a point where they could see all four of the terrorist shooters in the second-floor balcony. The five who'd brought them here were all leaving, at the top of the aisle and filing through the doors.

"Brisard's at the door on the second deck," Rubens' voice warned.

"Right. Walters? Get ready!"

Together the two men reached behind their backs and drew their pistols, sitting down in theater seats on opposite sides of the aisle as they did so, keeping the weapons carefully hidden.

The theater was a gaudy, glitzy explosion of Baroque architecture, heavy on the gold paint and curlicues, filled with Nereids and dolphins, seashells and seahorses, nets and tridents. An enormous figure of Neptune—the Roman Poseidon, the god who'd supposedly founded Atlantis—emerged from the bulkhead directly above the stage.

Their guards were leaning on the balcony railings, looking down into the auditorium, but they seemed to just be watching, not preparing to massacre the hostages. If any of them took aim, Dean was ready to pull out his weapon and begin firing, Brisard or no Brisard.

Dean was angry about the one tango he'd seen leaving the theater with two captives. For Dean, the horror of extremist Muslim fundamentalists wasn't their religion; so far as he was concerned, people could believe what they wanted. He knew that moderate Islamic clerics taught justice and equality, including equality for women, a fairly advanced concept for a Prophet born in the sixth century. The problem was that too many fundamentalists of *all* religions relied not on their scriptures but on local custom and belief . . . and then went through their holy books looking for isolated verses that would justify those beliefs. If your culture already believed that women were second-class citizens or worse, it wasn't hard to make the Qur'an support your prejudice.

As a result, there were Muslim societies where women were forbidden to go to school, where their genitals were mutilated, where rape victims were imprisoned and even killed, where a woman who didn't wear the veil was automatically responsible for whatever a Muslim male decided to do to her.

All in the name of Allah, the merciful, the all-knowing.

"Keep tracking those three," he murmured to Rubens.

"We are. Stand by. Brisard is coming in."

"Walters!" Dean snapped. "Ready . . ."

Cougar Six
A Deck, *Atlantis Queen*
Friday, 0532 hours EST

"We're at the infirmary," Yancey said. Behind him were five of the jumpers in a strung-out line. They'd ditched their oxygen bottles and masks but were still in their combat blacks. Their NVG monoculars were in place, their gain tuned down to allow for the ship's ambient lighting but still revealing the aim points for the IR laser sights.

"Copy that," Caravaggio replied. "We have you on the board. The passageway is clear ahead of you, all the way through the galley. You have one green light standing next to the far door inside the galley, probably a tango guard, and ten more in small groups left and right—probably galley staff."

"Roger that." They would have to sort tangos from crew members when they went in.

Hiding there behind the bar up in the casino had been one of the toughest things David P. Yancey had ever done—and he'd been through SEAL training and Hell Week, through a deployment in Afghanistan and two tours in Iraq, none of it exactly easy duty. Crouching there in silence, looking up with weapons ready to open fire if they were discovered or if the tangos started slaughtering hostages, they'd waited out the confrontation in the casino, emerging only after one of the elderly women—a Ms. Caruthers—had called out "Ally ally outs in free!"

There were ten of them, now, with Walters and Dean on their way forward with the terrorists. After briefly consulting with the Art Room, Tom Brisard had taken three of the men and headed forward, intent on following Dean and Walters to wherever the hostages were being led. Yancey took the remaining five and, guided by Caravaggio back in the Art Room, found a service stairwell that would take them all the way down to A Deck.

They emerged in a passageway outside the ship's infirmary. Several civilians, including two of the ship's doctors, clustered around them. "Are you here to rescue us?" one, an older woman, asked.

"We're going to try, ma'am," Yancey had replied. "All of you stay here and stay down!"

"Dr. Barnes! Have you seen him? The terrorists took him. . . ."

"We'll take care of it, ma'am." Brushing aside other questions, they'd moved aft down the central passageway leading from the infirmary to the massive watertight door leading to the galley.

Coulter and Yancey took the lead, since both of them had suppressed H&Ks, while Boone and Michelson carried combat shotguns, and Daniels and O'Brien had assault rifles. He took a stance, weapon braced against his shoulder, and said, "Go!" Daniels swiped an ID card through the reader, and Michelson pushed the door open.

Beyond was the gleaming expanse of the galley for the Atlantia Restaurant, one deck above. At the far end of the room, a lone man in a khaki uniform and holding an AK slouched in a chair, looking bored. Both Coulter and Yancey opened up with sharp, precise three-round bursts, their fire guided by the infrared dots visible through their monoculars. The man sprawled backward, arms flying to either side and weapon clattering to the deck as he slammed against the door at his back, then spilled from the overturning chair and sprawled in front of it in an untidy heap.

"One tango down," Yancey said as the six Black Cats rolled through the open door in swift succession, keeping their weapons up. Cooks, stewards, and galley assistants stood to either side, some screaming, some taking cover behind tables and food prep stations.

"Stay down!" Coulter barked. "Everybody down! Hands on your heads!"

There was no time to check for terrorists mixed in with crew members; Yancey saw no obvious tangos anywhere else in the galley, but that didn't mean they weren't there. So long as he saw no weapons, however, he kept moving forward, H&K at his shoulder, making for the far door.

"There . . . there are terrorists in there!" one young woman called out.

"We have four tangos inside the after hold," Caravaggio said over his radio headset. "All together, all toward your right as you go in, at roughly two o'clock."

"Stay down! Nobody move!" O'Brien called out, moving backward across the galley as he brought up the rear. Yancey and Coulter both dropped their half-empty magazines and popped in fresh ones, took stances in front of the door, and waited for Boone, Michelson, and Daniels to get into position between and behind them. "Go!"

The door to the aft hold opened, and Yancey stepped through, immediately pivoting to keep his weapon and its dancing IR spot aimed toward the four tangos inside. From the door, however, all he could see was an enormous stack of massive crates and cardboard boxes, bank upon bank of refrigerators, steel shelves, and piles of canned goods and boxed food.

"They heard you," Caravaggio warned. "Two targets, moving toward you and toward your right."

The trouble was, Yancey knew, that back in the Art Room they were looking at nice, clean deck schematics and they couldn't see the mountains of supplies that were providing cover at the moment for four jihadist tangos. It was comforting knowing how many tangos they faced and what their general direction was, but that didn't make getting at them very much easier.

"Boone! With me!" Yancey started forward, following the main open pathway leading aft from the door.

"Rest of you with me!" Coulter added. He broke to the right and started climbing a pile of wooden crates fifteen feet high.

"Watch out for hot tubs," Yancey said, grinning. Coulter's jumpsuit was still sopping wet from his accidental immersion in a spa on the Atlas Pool deck.

"Yancey!" Caravaggio said, her voice urgent. "Two tangos *right in front of you*! *Range ten feet!*"

What was right in front of him was a line of refrigerators forming the right-hand wall of the passageway he and Boone were following. It looked like there was a cross-passage just ahead, however. Gun still tight against his shoulder, Yancey broke into a run.

Swinging around the corner of the last refrigerator, he came face-to-face with two bearded men, khaki-clad, both holding AKs at port arms. Reflexively his finger tapped the trigger before his brain had fully processed what he was seeing; a three-round burst of 9mm bullets slashed into the face and throat of the closest man, spinning him roughly aside.

An instant behind Yancey's burst, Boone opened up with his AA-12, the combat shotgun set on full auto. With a fire rate of three hundred rounds per minute, the weapon loosed a thundering barrage of four blasts in less than a second, the 12-gauge shot ripping into both terrorists and cutting them apart. Blood splashed across the refrigerator, stacks of crates, and the deck.

"Two more down!" Yancey called, stepping across one of the bodies. Ahead he could now see the inside of the main outer doors to the cargo hold. Fifty feet to the right of those were three trucks, with enclosed cargo decks and open tailgates.

But he couldn't see the other two tangos.

Neptune Theater, *Atlantis Queen* Friday, 0532 hours EST

A door opened on the second-level balcony in the back of the theater. There were two tangos back there, one to the left, one to the right, and they both turned at the sound.

Dean lifted his SIG Sauer, dropping into a kneeling crouch and bracing the weapon in a two-handed stance, aiming at the gunman on the right-side balcony forward. The man had also heard the door and was turning to face it, raising his AK.

The range was a good fifty feet from the front-row seats to the front balcony one level up, a long shot for a pistol. Long hours on the practice range, however, had let Dean qualify as an expert, both with his beloved accurized M1911A1 and with the SIG Sauer P226. Releasing his pent-up breath halfway, he squeezed with his whole hand.

The shot came as a surprise, as it should in careful marksmanship. The terrorist lurched to one side, twisting, as the AK in his hands went off, the muzzle flash long and stuttering in the theater's dim light.

People in the theater screamed, some bolting in panic, others trying to duck down among the rows of seats. Dean reacquired and fired again, and the terrorist dropped out of sight behind the balcony railing.

At Dean's back, Walters fired again and again as his target jackknifed over the railing, then dropped twenty feet to the deck. Brisard and his people were moving down the balcony aisles at the same moment, firing at the two terrorist gunmen there. Dean pivoted, ready to add his fire to theirs, but both tangos were already dropping.

The back doors to Deck One swung open, however, and two more terrorists rushed in—the guards who'd been standing outside, obviously brought in by the burst of AK fire. Dean dropped his aim and fired twice at one, then pivoted to aim at the other . . . but held his fire. Panicking civilians were everywhere, scattering as one of the newly arrived terrorists opened fire with his AK.

"Get down! Everybody down!" Dean yelled.

One young man stood up, shirtless, waving his arms.

Aft Cargo Hold
A Deck, *Atlantis Queen*
Friday, 0533 hours EST

Omar Mohammed Ra'd heard the echoing *thud-thud-thud-thud* of a heavy weapon close by and leaped toward the trucks.

Aram and Fahaj had left moments before to investigate the opening of the door to the galley. No one was supposed to come through that door unless word came from the Amir himself that it was okay. In retrospect, it might have been better for the men guarding the trucks in the hold to have stayed in place, concealed and ready to open fire on any intruders . . . but the four of them had not been chosen for their combat experience or their tactical expertise.

Ra'd was the oldest of them, and he was just nineteen. He was Egyptian, the son of a poverty-crippled family in a suburb of Cairo. He'd joined the revived Gama'a al-Islamiyya, a militant Egyptian group that had united with al-Qaeda in 2006. From a training camp in Egypt he'd been sent to the Bekaa Valley in Lebanon, where he'd first met Amir Rahid Sayed as-Saadi and transferred to the Islamic Jihad International Brigade.

Ra'd and the three with him had been chosen, as-Saadi told them, because of their faith.

And Ra'd was dedicated to the way of submission, to Allah and Islam and the word of the Prophet. Ra'd had welcomed the opportunity offered by the Amir to guard the trucks and their tons of high explosives and to detonate those explosives if at any time the enemies of Islam tried to take them. The four of them had been warned not to wander too close to the trucks, that there was a deadly poison inside the trucks on top of the explosives, but if enemy forces tried to break into the ship's hold, they were to detonate the explosives immediately.

The detonator lay on a small folding table set up next to one of the trucks, at the end of a long, black coil of rubber-sheathed cable. A car battery rested in the deck beneath, connected with a tangle of electrical cables leading into each vehicle. All he needed to do was turn the arming key on the detonator and press the red button.

Behind him, Said Shalabi snatched up his rifle. "Go, Omar! Go, and I will cover you!" To his left, Aram and

Fajah tumbled across the deck in an explosion of wet scarlet, as two ominous figures in black rounded a line of refrigerators holding foodstuffs for the galley.

One of the figures shouted something . . . but Ra'd spoke no language but Arabic—specifically the Egyptian dialect. He'd had trouble understanding his brothers from Syria and Morocco.

The thunder sounded again, and something shrieked off the bulkhead behind him. Heart pounding, he snatched up the detonator and turned the key. . . .

Neptune Theater, *Atlantis Queen*
Friday, 0533 hours EST

"Everybody get down!" the shirtless man screamed, and then a burst of AK-47 fire tore through his body, knocking him over the back of a theater seat. As he fell, Dean had a clear shot at the shooter and took it, firing three rounds into the gunman in rapid succession as Walters opened fire as well. The gunman collapsed, and Dean swung, aiming his weapon across the crowd. It was still possible that there were other terrorists here on the main floor, sheltering among the hostages.

And there he was, bolting for the door at the top of the aisle, one remaining gunman.

Screaming people continued to clog the aisle, blocking Dean's shot, and the man was underneath the back balcony now, out of the sight of Brisard and the others. The terrorist knocked several people over; a young woman panicked and ran, and the gunman spun, raising his AK. An older man leaped and knocked the woman flat but was hit himself by a burst of full-auto fire as the gunman emptied his AK into the shrieking mob. Then he spun and vanished out the door just as Walters fired twice, the bullets slamming into the closing door behind the fleeing hijacker, spraying splinters.

Cougar Six
Aft Cargo Hold, *Atlantis Queen*
Friday, 0533 hours EST

David Yancey heard the yammer of an AK. Bullets screamed off the refrigerator, and he felt a hammer's blow against his right side, slamming him to the left. Boone opened up with his AA-12, the first rounds going high. Staggering with the slam to his side, Yancey kept tracking the figure by the truck, loosing a three-round burst from his H&K, then another, then a third.

The gunman with an AK off to the right was continuing to fire and Yancey was hit again, but the man by the trucks collapsed as Yancey and Boone both kept firing.

Yancey dropped to his knees; he wasn't in pain, exactly, but he was having trouble breathing. Boone shifted his aim and brought down the other gunman as Coulter and the others climbing up onto the crates reached an overlook and joined in as well. Caught by 12-gauge shotgun blasts, 9mm, and 5.56 rounds from several directions, the gunman crumpled in a heap on the deck.

Neptune Theater, *Atlantis Queen*
Friday, 0534 hours EST

"We've got one runner," Dean called as the fleeing gunman banged out the theater door just ahead of Walters' shots. "First Deck, heading aft!"

"Let him go," Rubens said.

"Clear here!" Brisard called from the balcony. His men were checking the bodies, making sure the three tangos up there all were dead.

"And clear here!" Walters called. He'd moved over to the left side of the theater and was checking the body of the man who'd fallen.

"Five tangos down, theater," Dean added. "We have at least two civilian casualties. No . . . make that three . . . correction . . . four." Several people had been hit by the indiscriminate spray of AK fire from the top of the aisle.

"One of you stay with the civilians," Rubens said. "Help the wounded and keep the rest quiet. The rest need to head for the bridge."

Dean moved up the aisle to the wounded man, easing him down off the seats and onto his back on the floor. He was wearing swim trunks. He had a savage gunshot wound in his stomach, hidden by fast-welling blood, and a second wound higher up, in the right side of his chest, bubbling as he tried to breathe. Dean, the ex-Marine, had seen enough combat wounds in the field to recognize a sucking chest wound.

"I've got him," an older man said, kneeling at Dean's side. "I'm the ship's doctor." The man had his shirt off and was pressing it against the bloody abdominal wound. "Cigarettes!" he yelled. "Anyone here have cellophane cigarette wrappers?"

Several men and women offered the wrappers from their cigarettes. The doctor accepted two and slapped them over the bubbling holes, entry wound and exit wound, in the man's chest and back.

"Listen . . . ," the wounded man said. His voice was weak, and it sounded like he was gargling. "Those two women . . . He took them. . . ."

"We saw," Dean told him. "We'll get them!"

"Sharon Reilly. Janet Carroll. Please, *please* . . . help them. . . ."

"We'll do our best."

Cougar Six
Aft Cargo Hold, *Atlantis Queen*
Friday, 0534 hours EST

Coulter jumped down off the wall of boxes and jogged toward the truck. The terrorist with the firing switch lay in a fetal curl in a spreading pool of blood; emotionlessly Coulter put another 9mm slug into the man's skull, just to make sure. "This one's dead!"

"Four tangos down!" Boone called. "Team member down!"

"I'm okay," David Yancey said, rising unsteadily. He reached up under his harness, probing the heavy weave of his Kevlar combat vest, then pulled a slightly flattened 7.62 slug from the weave. "Gonna have a bruise or two, though. . . ."

"Stay put. We'll check the trucks."

He lurched to his feet, still clutching his side. "Fuck that. I'm with you."

Daniels was scrambling down off the crates. He was waving a handheld Geiger counter in front of him. "It's hot!"

"We're copying the radiation readings here," Rubens' voice said. "Our advisor with the AEC says one man at a time, no more than fifteen minutes' *total* exposure for any of you. Understand?"

"Roger that," Yancey said. "Coulter! Get away from there! All of you guys, clear out. Set up a defensive position on the other side of the galley door."

Unsteadily he approached the trucks, looking for signs that the explosives were booby-trapped.

While the Islamic militants in Afghanistan and Iraq had acquired a reputation as bad boys with improvised explosive devices—IEDs—their best was rarely very sophisticated. They were proficient at planting mines that could be set off remotely, from a distance, or with trip wires, and they'd been known to pull cute tricks like pull-

ing the pin on a hand grenade and leaving it beneath a
dead or injured man, the firing lever compressed and held
in place by the weight of the body. Elaborate booby traps
involving choices between multiple colored wires and
which order to cut them in were generally the provenance
of Hollywood . . . and usually *bad* Hollywood at that.

Yancey had gone through quite a bit of training with
the SEALs, in both the creation and the disarming of improvised explosives. He'd also trained for a time with the
Navy's Explosive Ordnance Disposal people, the EOD. He
approached the trucks carefully, tracing the electrical wiring by eye. There was the battery, beneath the table, a pair
of wires leading up and into the back of the truck. Yank-
ing those wires ought to be all that was needed to safe the
bomb.

Ought to be. You didn't make it in the SEALs or the
EOD without acquiring a bit of paranoia. He knew radiation was burning him—he couldn't feel it, but it was
burning him nonetheless. Every instinct he possessed told
him to yank those battery cables and get the hell out of
there.

But he followed the two battery wires up onto the back
of the nearest truck. The flatbed was piled high with non-
descript cardboard boxes, each one holding block upon
block upon plastic-wrapped block of C-4 explosives. One
of the battery leads was connected to a larger cable, and
that ran back through loop after loop to the firing box in
the dead tango's hand. A second lead emerged from the
firing-box cable and was connected to a solid-pack electrical detonator embedded in a block of C-4. Another
wire connected the battery directly with the detonator. So
far, so good. Arm the firing box by turning a key, press
the red button, the circuit completed, the blasting cap
went off, and with it went several tons of plastic explosives.

But a part of the wire directly connecting the battery
with the blasting cap was hidden under a large box of

C-4. He was reaching for the wire to pull it out when he stopped. In this line of work, paranoia was good.

Shaking his head, he backed off. Returning to the battery on the deck outside, he unscrewed the caps and removed the wires. The blasting cap ought to be harmless, now, its connection to the battery gone.

But he still didn't trust it.

He switched on his radio. "Art Room! This is Cougar Six!"

"Go ahead, David," Rubens' voice replied. "What've you got?"

"It's definitely rigged as an IND," he said. The acronym stood for "Improvised Nuclear Device" and referred to radiological material designed to be spread by a conventional explosion. Quickly Yancey described what he could see of the circuitry and told them what he'd done. "But I don't trust it," he said. "Part of the battery lead is hidden, and I can't get at it. Not without lifting a stack of cardboard boxes as tall as I am."

"Go ahead and get out of there, David," Rubens told him. "The SAS assault lifted off from the *Ark Royal* twenty minutes ago, and we have more helos inbound from the *Eisenhower*. They should be there in another ten. We have a NEST on the way with the American helicopters."

"NEST" stood for "Nuclear Emergency Support Team," the unit under the jurisdiction of the U.S. Department of Energy tasked with responding to all types of accidents and emergencies involving nuclear material, including bomb threats.

"Roger that," Yancey said. He felt exhausted. He wondered if he was already feeling the effects of the radiation.

Before he left, though, he took another look at the back of the truck. Odd. The boxes of explosives weren't stacked neatly and squarely. Maybe that was what had been tugging at his subconscious . . . the fact that several boxes were jammed in every which way, carelessly, and several were tipped up on one edge, leaving space beneath. Reaching into the back of the truck, he grabbed one of the tipped boxes and lifted it, dragging it aside.

A hand grenade had been placed underneath the box, its pin already pulled. Yancey saw the metal arming lever pop off, saw the grenade skitter across the flatbed, its three-second fuse already burning. . . .

27

Bridge, *Atlantis Queen*
Thirty miles south of Nantucket
Friday, 0535 hours EST

KHALID GLOWERED AT THE night, which was just beginning to show the faintest flush of light in the east. He'd just lost touch with his men in the theater and in the A Deck hold aft. The attackers were moving too fast, too precisely, for his men to manage a coordinated defense. On the chart table he could see the blips of approaching aircraft—helicopters, most likely, from the British and American task forces that had been dogging them.

It was time to give up on the dream of setting off the explosives inside New York Harbor, of spreading death and revenge across Manhattan and much of New England. If Ra'd and the others in the hold were not answering, they must be dead . . . and Ra'd had failed to press the button on the detonator.

The booby traps set within the trucks might yet set off the entire load of explosives, *would* set them off if any of the attackers were foolish enough to try to dismantle the battery wires.

But Khalid still needed to make sure, and there was one way to do that.

Striding to the door leading to the radio room, he snatched up the radio and pressed the transmit key. "Ramid! Ramid, are you there?"

There was a crackle of static. Then, "I hear you, Amir."

"Execute *Ya*."

Everything said over the radio was in code or in very carefully phrased speech; the enemy, Khalid knew well, was listening to everything. *Ya* was the final letter of the standard Arabic alphabet, and as the end of the series it carried the same sense of finality as the Greek *omega*, the English *z*. *The ending*.

"Execute Plan *Ya*," Abdel Ramid echoed from the *Pacific Sandpiper*. "Allah be praised!"

Khalid did not reply. Allah, if He existed at all, had thwarted Operation Zarqawi, as He had thwarted so much else.

Allah, if He existed, would have no part of this ending.

Cougar Six
Aft Cargo Hold, *Atlantis Queen*
Friday, 0535 hours EST

David Yancey saw the armed grenade bounce across the flatbed of the truck. If it exploded there, next to tons of explosives and at least one primed and ready blasting cap, sympathetic detonation would cause all of the C-4 in all three trucks to explode. He dived on the grenade instantly, scooping it up and rolling toward the open tailgate, whipping it around in his right hand as he rolled and flinging it as hard and as far as he could, even as he fell off the back of the truck.

He was aiming high, for the far side of that line of refrigerators if he could make it. The grenade exploded in mid-air before it reached them.

The explosion was piercingly loud in the cavernous

metal-walled vault of the A Deck hold. Shrapnel rattled off the truck and the bulkheads and something struck his leg and his side as he fell and slammed full-length into the deck.

He lay there for a long moment, panting, rejoicing in the pain because it meant he was still alive.

Cougar Twelve
Deck Eleven, *Atlantis Queen*
Friday, 0537 hours EST

Up past Kleito's Temple on Deck Ten, Dean led three men spiraling up the service stairwell. It had been all he could do to pull the others from the theater and lead them up here. CJ and the other woman might be killed as soon as their value as hostages was outweighed by the trouble they caused . . . and knowing CJ, she was capable of plenty of trouble. But Rubens had ordered Dean to play it by the book, and the book said to gain control of the ship's bridge, where the terrorist commander would almost certainly be trying to put together a last-ditch defense of the hijacked vessel.

Dean decided he would have to trust that CJ would take care of herself.

But, damn it, she was a desk jockey, a computer geek, not a trained field agent.

At Deck Eleven, someone with an AK-47 opened fire from above, loosing an entire magazine on full auto down the stairs.

Brisard had brought along Dean's H&K, combat harness, vest, and helmet, and he'd pulled those on over his civilian clothing, giving him an oddly mismatched look with his jeans and tennis shoes. Snapping a fresh mag into his H&K, he loosed a burst up the stairwell. The tango responded with another burst of AK fire, bullets screeching wildly as they ricocheted off steel railings, steps, and bulkheads. Tim Morgan cursed as a fragment off a railing scratched his face, leaving a thin trail of blood.

"Where are they?" Dean asked Rubens, sheltering under the steps. "And how many?" The bad guys could hold them pinned here all day.

"You have four people in the Security-IT suite, Deck Eleven," Rubens told him. "There are six on Deck Twelve. That's three on the bridge, two in the radio room, and one in the stairwell above you. Five more are outside, on Deck Eleven, further aft."

"Waiting to ambush us between the casino and here," Dean said. "What about the two guys who left the theater?"

"We're tracking them. One is taking the two women down a passageway on Deck Four. He might be looking for a stateroom. The other is going up the Grand Staircase, passing Deck Five now. We're tracking them both." There was a hesitation. "One tango left Security a few minutes ago. You just missed him by a few seconds. He went down the stairwell you're in now. Deck Ten."

Dean tried to hold the described positions in his mind, a three-dimensional map of the enemy's positions. On the one hand, having the Art Room peering into the ship and identifying the locations of each person on board did a lot to lift the age-old fog of war.

On the other hand, it was damned tough to keep track of it all. "What about our people in the hold?"

"The situation there is under control." Rubens sounded stressed as he said it, though, and Dean wondered what he was hiding. "Helicopters are inbound, about ten minutes out. A NEST is on board."

"Okay, then," Rubens said. "Throw the switch."

"Done. . . ."

By injecting the HTML code into the *Atlantis Queen*'s computer system, the Art Room had turned all of the computers in the ship's IT section into zombies—that was what the techies called them—and admin control now rested with the Art Room. Not only did they have control of the security cameras and computer displays, but they also had control over every one of the automated door locks on the ship, all of which normally were programmed from the IT department but which now were being controlled by Rubens' team at Fort Meade.

They'd just locked every key-card door on the ship.

Another burst of gunfire thundered down the stairwell. Dean slapped Henderson on the shoulder. "Hit him with the frag-12s."

Sam Henderson, a former Army Special Forces staff sergeant, nodded and pressed the release catch for the ammo drum on his AA-12 combat shotgun. Dropping the 32-round drum with its normal load-out of 12-gauge shot, he pulled out a smaller, 20-round drum loaded with frag-12 rounds.

The frag-12 had been developed especially for combat shotguns, a 19mm grenade with four tiny, curved stabilizing fins that unfolded as it left the weapon's muzzle. The armor-piercing versions could blast through a half inch of steel plate, and a barrage of the deadly little slugs fired at three hundred rounds per minute created a firestorm of death and devastation.

Henderson chambered the first round. Dean leaned out from under the cover provided by the steps overhead and opened fire with his H&K, spraying wildly to make the gunman overhead duck back. Henderson stepped past Dean, raised his AA-12, and fired a long burst of frag-12s into the upper level. Explosions cracked and banged overhead, and someone screamed as an AK-47 bounced and clattered down the steel steps. Henderson fired another high-explosive burst, and then Dean and the others pounded up the stairs.

The tango lay on the deck in front of a partially wrecked door, covered with blood and trying to pull a pistol from his belt. Dean shot him twice in the head and kept moving.

In the passageway beyond the broken door, a second

security door blocked the way. Beyond were the radio room and the bridge, and five cornered tangos. . . .

Ohio **ASDS**
Approaching *Pacific Sandpiper*
Friday, 0538 hours EST

The Advanced SEAL Delivery System, a dry-deck submarine sixty-five feet long and displacing sixty tons, was a relatively new addition to the combat inventory of the U.S. Navy SEAL teams. On board, besides the two submarine officers serving as pilot and navigator, were sixteen Navy SEALs equipped for VBSS operations, the acronym standing for "Visit, Board, Search, and Seizure."

Over an hour before, they'd left the warmth and security of the USS *Ohio*, a former ballistic missile submarine converted to Navy Special Warfare service, now a transport carrying up to sixty-four SEALs and the ASDS on her afterdeck. The SEALs had climbed a ladder up into the midget sub's spherical air lock and taken their places in the closely fitted seats aft. The *Ohio* had taken them to a rendezvous point just ahead of the oncoming *Pacific Sandpiper* and released them.

For an hour, now, the ASDS had played tag with the *Sandpiper*, attempting to close for boarding. The *Sandpiper* had changed course several times, however, and currently was heading almost due north, toward the *Atlantis Queen*, almost half a mile away.

When the *Sandpiper* had swung north, however, the ASDS pilot, anticipating the vessel's attempt to close with the cruise ship, had been able to aim for a point well ahead of the *Sandpiper*, then turn north, with the transport pounding down on the midget sub's wake.

Guided by satellite tracking systems, the sixty-foot submarine had allowed herself to be overtaken by the 322-foot freighter bearing down on her at twenty-two knots.

The miniature submarine's maximum speed, while classified, was in excess of eight knots—about half of the plutonium transport's best speed. There was no way for the minisub to catch the freighter in a stern chase, but a bit of luck and some skillful seamanship on the part of the pilot and navigator had put the ASDS in the perfect position for an intercept at speed.

As the freighter passed the submarine's starboard side, pushing the tiny vessel along on its bow wave, Gunner's Mate Chief Randolph Kellerman had popped the ASDS's upper hatch, leaned out into the cold, slashing spray, and fired a grappling line high into the night. He was aiming for the top of the high, dark, wet steel wall passing a few yards away. The grappling hook missed its hold on the first shot; he dropped the gun over the side, took a second from RM1 Garrison, who was clinging to the ladder inside the air lock just below him in the hatch, and took aim for a second shot.

This time, the grapple snagged hard on the *Sandpiper*'s port railing. The near end of the line was secured to a deck cleat and drawn taut. Inexorably the ASDS was drawn close alongside the larger vessel. Kellerman deployed several fenders to keep the hulls from grinding together, secured a second line aft, then unshipped a boarding hook. The device was a twenty-four-foot telescoping pole that extended and locked with a hook on the end, and a snap-down two-footed brace at the foot to hold it out from the hull.

Swinging the hook over the railing directly overhead, Kellerman gave it an experimental tug, then started to climb.

Bridge, *Atlantis Queen*
Friday, 0538 hours EST

Khalid hated the night.

It hadn't always been that way. But six years earlier, he as Rahid Sayed as-Saadi, and his two older brothers,

Hammed and Abdul, had been part of an insurgent team in Iraq, working with the Tanzim Qaidat al-Jihad fi Bilad al-Rafidayn, known to the West as al-Qaeda in Iraq. The three brothers had been on a mission with three others in a suburb of Baghdad one night, well past midnight.

They'd been told in the training camps that the night was their friend, that the American and Coalition forces feared the night and would fear the soldiers of Allah who made the night their own. The six of them had been crouched beside a pickup truck and a ruined mud-brick wall, preparing an old Russian artillery shell as an IED. The plan was to bury the shell beside the road, then detonate it by radio when an American patrol passed in the morning. With the bomb prepared, the six of them had knelt in a circle to pray.

But first, the young as-Saadi had excused himself and walked a few meters away to urinate on the other side of the wall. The bomb—he'd been told later it must have been one of the damnable American "smart bombs" guided to their target by laser—had glided out of the night and landed squarely in the middle of the other five fedayeen as they prayed for success, exploding with savage ferocity and precision.

He'd found himself almost ten meters away, unharmed but stunned, his ears ringing and blood streaming from his nose. The wall had been leveled, the truck shredded. By the firelight of the burning fuel tank he'd found Abdul's head, lying on the road, the eyes wide and staring.

They'd never even had a chance to strike a single blow in the holy name of Allah.

And that had been the beginning of the end of as-Saadi's faith. His brother fedayeen claimed to see the hand of God everywhere, with each victory won against the invading Coalition forces, with each American killed, with each enemy vehicle destroyed . . . and yet, step by step, battle by battle, the war in Iraq had been lost. *Lost.* It was unthinkable.

And al-Qaeda hadn't exactly fought the war with

intelligence and cunning. Savage, wasteful attacks against rival militias, against the Shia heretics, even against the growing Iraqi police and military forces, the American puppets, seemed to have a negative effect. The ordinary people of the villages and towns and city suburbs, the people al-Qaeda *needed* in order to hide, to move, to fight . . . as the years passed, those people had begun turning against the insurgents.

Eventually Rahid as-Saadi had moved up in the al-Qaeda hierarchy, attracting the attention of several of the Leader's senior lieutenants. As-Saadi had submitted a plan to seize a British plutonium transport ship . . . then amended it to include the cruise ship. By sailing both ships together into New York Harbor, he would ensure one of two outcomes would ensue. Either the radioactive cargo, or part of it, could be scattered across all of Manhattan as a deadly, poisonous dust on the wind, the poison blowing as far up the coast as Maine . . . or the Americans would be forced to sink both ships and kill over three thousand innocent people to prevent that far greater disaster. America would be humiliated before the world.

And Yusef Khalid would die on the *Atlantis Queen*'s bridge, claiming vengeance for Abdul and for Hammed, but, more important, focusing the cause of Jihad back where it belonged . . . not on religious extremism, not on the differences between Sunni and Shia, but on the need to strike the hated West again and again and yet again at the points where they were most vulnerable.

Iraq and Afghanistan had bled al-Qaeda nearly dry. A successful attack, one killing thousands, perhaps tens of thousands, from New Jersey to Maine and crippling the American economy by poisoning ships and docks and ports and cargoes all along the northeastern seaboard . . . *that* would bring fresh and eager recruits flocking to the Cause. They would come, they would train, they would strike, and they would continue striking until America was humbled, until America was destroyed.

And Hammed and Abdul and Rahid himself would again have peace.

In the meantime, he dreaded the night, and the Americans who'd made it their own. . . .

SEAL VBSS Force Cold Steel
Pacific Sandpiper
Friday, 0538 hours EST

Kellerman had practiced this climb hundreds of times, but he'd not expected to be making it while the ship he was boarding was surging ahead at twenty knots or more. Twice he'd nearly fallen, but at last he grabbed the lowest line of the safety railing along the ship's bulwark and rolled himself over onto the deck.

They'd deliberately positioned the ASDS alongside the *Sandpiper* directly beside the aft end of the deckhouse. The midget sub was invisible to radar and all but invisible optically to any lookouts. Unless their luck was *very* bad, the SEALs should be able to get aboard without being seen.

But Murphy is an uninvited guest at every military evolution. Forward, just five yards away along the covered passageway between deckhouse and railing, a watertight door swung open and two men stepped out. Both had AK-47s slung over their shoulders.

Kellerman was wearing standard VBSS gear, including combat harness and black wet suit, his face blacked, a AN/PVS-14D night-vision monocular over his right eye and a watch cap over his head. He was carrying an H&K SD5 strapped to his back along with a rolled-up caving ladder, but getting his primary weapon unhooked and into play would be too noisy, with too much movement, with the enemy just a few steps away. If they turned to face aft . . .

Kellerman was already unholstering his pistol, the Navy version of the P226, a sound suppressor already screwed over the muzzle. One of the men leaned against the railing, looking out over the sea as he struck a match and lit a cigarette. The other turned and looked straight at Kellerman.

"*Min haida?*" the man said. The words sounded calm, perhaps curious. It was so dark he probably wasn't seeing anything more threatening than a shadow crouched on the deck. Two-handed, Kellerman fired and kept firing, snapping round after round into first one man and then the other, shifting his aim back and forth as the two tumbled back from the railing. One tried to reach for his rifle, then slumped with two holes side by side just above his left eye.

Swiftly Kellerman reloaded his pistol, then holstered it. He unhooked the caving ladder from the back of his harness, attached the free end to the railing, and let the roll deploy itself down the side of the ship. Garrison was already climbing the boarding hook, coming up hand over hand as Kellerman had done. Lieutenant Rogers was already in the ASDS hatch, securing the base of the caving ladder and preparing to come aboard.

The two bodies were dragged aft and sent tumbling over the fantail. Kellerman then unshipped his H&K and took up a security position forward of the ladder, waiting as the rest of his team came on board.

Cougar Twelve
Deck Eleven, *Atlantis Queen*
Friday, 0540 hours EST

Dean stood beside the massive security door, exchanging glances with the other three, Brisard, Morgan, and Henderson, close behind him. "Ready?" he asked, and all three nodded.

Dean and Brisard carried H&Ks, Morgan a CAR-15, and Henderson his full-auto shotgun, still loaded with 19mm frag-12s. The door was locked, of course, and the ID key cards they all carried no longer worked.

But they had another means of entry. Dean reached into his retrieved combat harness and pulled out a small, waterproof pouch. Inside was a laminated card a bit larger than a postage stamp. Taking the card, he positioned it over the thumbprint reader and pressed the activation button.

Their secret door-opening device was actually nothing more than a laser photocopy of the thumbprint of David Llewellyn, the ship's chief security officer. His prints, of course, were on file back in Southampton, and Sir Charles Mayhew had arranged to fax them out to the *Eisenhower*. Since Llewellyn's thumbprint was the default print for all print readers on the ship, it gave them access to all doors with print readers.

What Dean had never known before was that a print reader could be spoofed by a photocopy; so much for Hollywood and its use of bad men's fingertips to access the things.

The machine hummed, a band of light moved along the touch screen, and the door clicked open. Dean stood aside as Henderson and Morgan rolled through. Forward was a short passageway leading past the radio room on the left, with the bridge itself just beyond. The radio room door was open, and Morgan opened up with his CAR-15, firing short, precise bursts that cut down two terrorists seated at the console side by side. A second door was open, leading onto the bridge; Morgan pulled a flash-bang from his combat vest, pulled the pin, and tossed it through. Brisard, meanwhile, went up to the first bridge door, still closed, and braced against the bulkhead.

The flash-bang went off with a shrill explosion of sound and a literally blinding chain of dazzling flashes, the charge designed to stun, blind, deafen, and disorient anyone within range. Henderson rushed through the radio room door, followed closely by Morgan, as Brisard and Dean went through the other. Explosive shotgun blasts shredded one terrorist near the chart table, who was fumbling with his AK; Morgan cut down the tango at the helm.

Dean caught a flash of movement at the door leading out onto the port wing of the bridge. "I've got him!" he yelled.

"Radio room, two tangos down!" Morgan snapped over the combat frequency. "Bridge, two tangos down. One runner. Bridge secure!"

Dean rushed out into the night, looking around. A ladder led down.

Khalid was below, descending.

SEAL VBSS Force Cold Steel
Pacific Sandpiper
Friday, 0542 hours EST

Kellerman led the way to the *Sandpiper*'s bridge. Five SEALs followed him as Lieutenant Rogers led the rest down into the bowels of the ship, splitting into three fire teams to hit the engine room, the crew's quarters, and the common room—the largest compartment on the ship save for the holds forward, and the likeliest place for the *Sandpiper*'s crew to be held.

Kellerman pounded up a ship's ladder, reaching the top just as two men burst from a cabin farther down the passageway. One threw a hand grenade, which flew past Kellerman's head and clanged off the deck below. "Cover!" QMI John Podesta yelled as the other four SEALs crouched and turned away to minimize the effects of the blast. Kellerman opened up full auto on the two tangos in front of him, the sound-suppressed rounds snapping as they slammed through both men and took them down.

Both, Kellerman noted as he passed, were Asians, Japanese, he thought. Odd. His briefing had said they'd be facing Islamic fundamentalists, not Japanese. Where the hell had *they* come from?

He would photograph them later, after the ship was secure. If there *was* a later.

Cold Steel had been sent in with the assumption that the tangos would not have explosives set around the remaining radioactive material forward. Those one-hundred-ton canisters bolted to the hold's deck were simply too huge, too thick-walled, too well cushioned, to breach with anything less than a few hundred tons of explosives. The VBSS team was concentrating, then, on securing the bridge, engineering, and the crew.

But there were never any guarantees in this line of work, and the tangos were perfectly capable of pulling off an unexpected and last-second kick to the nuts.

There was nobody else in the room from which the two Japanese had emerged. Kevin Smith was injured, his ears bleeding from the grenade blast. He sat on the lower step of the ladder while the rest of the SEALs continued their climb.

The bridge was just ahead, and two decks up.

Cougar Twelve
Deck Eleven, *Atlantis Queen*
Friday, 0543 hours EST

Khalid was ten feet below the port side bridge wing, swiftly descending the vertical ladder past Deck Eleven. Dean leaned over the railing and fired, but the ladder had safety hoops encircling it every few feet, and the bullets ricocheted into the night. An instant later, more bullets snapped in, these coming from somewhere aft. Dean looked up and saw the muzzle flashes—gunmen hidden on Deck Eleven, just in front of the ship's smokestack, which was just barely visible in the darkness.

Dean was fully illuminated by light spilling from the bridge behind him, a perfect target.

Khalid reached an open platform on Deck Ten; according to the plans he'd studied, there was a door there leading into Kleito's Temple.

A bullet struck Dean's vest, slamming him painfully back a step. In a second or two, Khalid would be back inside the ship, and if he discarded his passkey, it would be easy to lose him.

A bullet grazed Dean's left arm, a fierce burn; Dean vaulted the railing and fell. . . .

Cougar Six
Aft Cargo Hold, *Atlantis Queen*
Friday, 0543 hours EST

David Yancey lay on his back, fighting back the pain. The bruise where the tango had hit Yancey's vest was throbbing, and he thought there might be a broken rib there. Kevlar vests were lifesavers, but they weren't *perfect*.

More serious were the wounds in his side and leg, where shrapnel from the grenade had missed the vest and punctured him. His fingertips came away wet with blood when he touched those spots.

Oh . . . and there remained the little matter of radiation from the opened MOX canisters in the trucks. He'd been here . . . how long? Ten minutes, maybe.

"How are you doing, David?" Rubens' voice said over his helmet radio.

"Okay, sir. Listen . . . I think I have it doped out."

"David, you need to crawl away from those trucks. The farther you are from the MOX canisters, the better."

He tried to move, and gasped as the pain hit him. He shook his head, trying to clear it. "Listen . . . don't want to pass out. They have those crates of C-4 just tumbled inside the trucks every which way, y'know?"

"The EOD and NEST people will be there soon. They'll take care of it."

"That grenade popped out from under a box. I think they have a *lot* of grenades inside all three trucks, sir. It would be a simple way to booby-trap them . . . put eight or ten grenades under those boxes and between boxes and tucked in everywhere, all of them with the pins pulled. . . ."

"The EOD people will take care of it, son. You just try to get away from those trucks."

"The thing I can't figure is . . . I can feel the ship rolling a little right now, the deck moving under my back. If the weather got rough, like it was the other night, some of those boxes could shift. All it would take would be one armed hand grenade to set off *all* the grenades, all the blasting caps . . . and the whole mountain of C-4 would go up. . . ."

28

Cougar Twelve, Dean
Deck Eleven, *Atlantis Queen*
Thirty miles south of Nantucket
Friday, 0543 hours EST

DEAN PLUMMETED THROUGH the night, feetfirst, his H&K
in his right hand, his left outstretched for balance and to
grab at Khalid if he missed.

He *almost* missed, coming down immediately behind
the Saudi terrorist, grabbing as he fell, crashing against
the man and slamming both of them sideways against a
railing. White pain shot up Dean's leg with the impact.
The H&K went spinning into the night. Khalid snarled
and twisted and tried to turn, bringing his AK up; Dean
slammed the heel of his palm against Khalid's nose,
slammed it as hard as he could, and felt cartilage snap
with the blow.

Khalid yelped and tried to pull away. Dean held tight
with one arm and slammed Khalid's face and jaw again
and again until the terrorist finally managed to hit Dean
hard in the chest with the muzzle of his AK and break
free.

Dean felt the pain screaming up from his left ankle; he
must have broken it in the fall. Khalid took an unsteady
couple of steps backward, his face a mask of blood, his

teeth showing bright through the blood as he raised his AK-47.

The gunshot was startling and unexpected. . . .

SEAL VBSS Force Cold Steel
Pacific Sandpiper
Friday, 0544 hours EST

Kellerman signaled to Podesta and Vance, counting down the seconds, three . . . two . . . one . . . *go*! Jakowski tossed a flash-bang in through the open door, and Podesta and Vance rolled through into the darkened room filled with smoke and screaming. Kellerman and Jakowski were next, with Herrera bringing up the rear.

Sound-suppressed gunfire snapped and hissed. A tango at the helm crumpled and collapsed; another lying on the deck, covering his ears, jumped and twisted and lay still; a third fired blindly with his AK, spraying high until two 9mm rounds punctured his skull. Two more tried to run out onto the port side wing of the bridge and were cut down at the door.

"Cold Steel!" Kellerman called over the combat channel. "Bridge clear! Bridge secure!"

Herrera was at the ship's wheel, his eyes startlingly wide against thc blacking on his face. "Madre de Dios!"

Kellerman followed the other SEAL's stare ahead, across the ship's forward deck to the black water beyond. The *Atlantis Queen* was there, looming huge out of the predawn darkness, lights aglow at her bridge.

And the *Pacific Sandpiper* was headed straight toward her at twenty knots.

Cougar Twelve, Dean
Deck Ten, *Atlantis Queen*
Friday, 0544 hours EST

Dean flinched as the first shot rang out. The smile on Khalid's bloodied face froze, then melted as the terrorist leader took a step to the side, half-turning. The man standing in the doorway to Kleito's Temple fired his handgun once again, and Khalid collapsed to the deck.

The man emerging from the bar was wearing a Royal Sky Line security uniform. Tucking the pistol into his waistband, he stooped to help Dean.

"Thanks," Dean murmured. Reaction was setting in, adrenaline thundering through his body, and he was starting to shake.

"No," Mohamed Ghailiani told him. "Thank *you*."

Deck Five, *Atlantis Queen*
Friday, 0545 hours EST

Yaqub Nehim had been looking for one of the empty staterooms, a place to hide with his two personal hostages until the enemy came for him or the ship was blown to bits. He'd bound both women's wrists at their backs with plastic zip strips and herded them along the passageways with his Russian-made Makarov pistol. There were a number of empty staterooms here, and if the explosives in the hold didn't explode, it would be hours before anyone found the three of them. *Plenty* of time . . .

On Deck Four, he'd discovered that his key card no longer worked. None of the doors he'd tried would open.

Something, he knew, was going seriously wrong. For several minutes the radio on his belt had sounded with several sharp calls in Arabic, and once he'd heard the chatter of an automatic weapon. On Deck Five he'd met Ra'id Hijazi, panting and wild-eyed, who'd confirmed that enemy commandos had killed all of the fed-ayeen brothers in the theater moments after Nehim had left with his captives, that only he had managed to escape.

Nehim's thoughts of venting his lust on the two women melted instantly. "What should we do?" he cried. A new thought struck him. "We should kill these two!"

"No!" Hijazi said. "There are hostages in the gambling place, old people, many of them. We will take these two, gather up the other hostages, and wait. We can use them to bargain for time."

Hijazi's sanctimonious quoting of the Qur'an had always irritated Nehim. "What happened to dying the martyr's death?"

"The plan is wrecked. We will never reach New York. But the ship may yet explode at any moment. We need *time*."

"The children in the hold must be dead by now."

Hijazi gave him a measuring look. "Yesterday, at the Amir's orders, Aziz, Al-Shafi, Haqqani, and I went down to the hold. We . . . arranged things so that the explosives will detonate easily. *Very* easily."

"How?"

"Never mind. But if the enemy commandos attempt to tamper with the crates on the trucks, if this ship runs aground, if we hit anything or anything hits us, believe me. The trucks will blow!"

"Perhaps one of the lifeboats . . ." Nehim was thinking furiously. He could take one of the women as hostage, lower a boat—

"Fool!" Hijazi snarled. "In minutes these waters will be filled with enemy ships, the sky filled with their helicopters! No, if we hold many hostages at gunpoint, they will try to negotiate. We can kill a few at a time, to prove we mean business, to keep them from attacking. And while they negotiate, their people will attempt to dismantle the explosives in the truck."

"And we shall die."

"Martyrs' deaths, Yaqub." He gestured at the two disheveled women glaring at them from a few feet away. "We will find better than *them* in Paradise!"

Nehim had serious doubts about the Prophet's description of what awaited true believers in Paradise, but Hijazi's plan offered at least the possibility of escape. They were in the middle of an empty ocean. There was no chance that the cruise ship would run aground out here, or that anything would hit them.

He might survive yet.

SEAL VBSS Force Cold Steel
Pacific Sandpiper
Friday, 0545 hours EST

"Podesta!" Kellerman barked. "We need to turn *now*!"

QM1 John Podesta took the ship's wheel, spinning it hard to the right. "We won't stop in time," he said. "But the *Queen* is moving forward. Maybe we can miss her by passing astern!"

Kellerman hesitated, his hands above the two throttle levers, one for each of the *Sandpiper*'s screws. His instinct was to throw the ship into reverse, to try to stop the leviathan before it collided with the ship now just five hundred yards ahead.

But with the rudder hard right, with the bow now slowly swinging to the right, toward the other ship's stern, throwing the screws in reverse would actually act against the turn. He remembered reading about some confusion on the bridge when the *Titanic* had spotted the iceberg, about how an attempt to turn away from the ice had actually swung the bow of the doomed ship toward it.

"That one," Podesta said, pointing at one of the side-by-side levers. "All back! The other one, full ahead!"

In the old days, these levers would have been engine

telegraphs, telling the crew in the engine room what to do. Nowadays the throttles were handled directly from the bridge—a good thing, since Kellerman hadn't yet heard the word from the lieutenant that the engine room was secure.

"Why aren't we turning?" Kellerman asked after a moment. The *Atlantis Queen* still loomed enormous just ahead.

"You don't turn these things on a dime, Chief," Podesta replied. "Or stop 'em on one, either. What the hell?"

Podesta was standing on tiptoes, looking down at the forward deck immediately ahead of the deckhouse. In the darkness, a half-dozen men were running forward, some clambering into the helicopter parked midway down the deck, others unfastening the lines securing the aircraft to the deck.

"This is Cold Steel Two," Kellerman called. Grabbing his H&K, he jogged for the port side bridge wing. "We have tangos on the forward deck! Looks like they're making for the helo!"

"It'll take 'em an hour to get that thing ready to fly," Vance told him.

As Kellerman left the enclosure of the bridge, he heard the shrill, rising whine of the helicopter's engine, saw the main rotor begin to turn. Two more tangos were running from the deckhouse as others climbed aboard. He shouldered his weapon and began firing. One of the hijackers fell. Another was hauled through the open doorway by a friend already on board.

The bastards had had the aircraft warmed up and ready.

The question was where they would go. The SEAL unit's pre-mission briefing had mentioned the helicopter, pointing out that by now it was probably so low on fuel it would be useless. Land lay forty miles to the north. They *might* make it . . . but would find themselves immediately surrounded by the authorities.

What the hell were they trying to do?

"Cold Steel, Cold Steel," Rubens' voice said over Kellerman's radio. "Take that helo down! *Now!*"

"Yes, sir!" He switched his H&K selector switch to full auto, raised the weapon, and began firing. With the integral suppressor, the H&K made little sound against the rising thunder of the helicopter's main rotor.

Jakowski was joining in from the opposite bridge wing, but the 9mm rounds had little punch to them. With an unsteady lurch, the helicopter lifted from the forward deck, its rotor arc barely clearing the traveling bridge gantry forward.

Kellerman kept firing until his magazine ran dry. He dropped the empty, slapped home a fresh magazine, chambered a round, and began firing again. By now, though, the helicopter was turning away, and Kellerman felt a cold chill of realization.

That helicopter wasn't headed for the mainland.

It was dropping low, low over the black water, nose down and accelerating as it headed straight for the cruise ship ahead.

Pyramid Club Casino, *Atlantis Queen*
Friday, 0545 hours EST

Yaqub Nehim shoved one of the women hard ahead, sending her sprawling onto the floor as they entered the casino. "Nobody move!" he screamed, holding the other woman close against his chest, the Makarov pressed up against the side of her head.

"Move to the back of the room!" Hijazi added, gesturing with his AK. "Quickly! Quickly!"

The old people did as they were told. "I hope you assholes know you're both going to die," one old woman said.

"And you will die with us, crone," Hijazi said. He strode closer to the crowd. "But if you all do exactly what we tell you, you might live a little longer!"

Nehim was feeling more confident now, more in control. They had twenty hostages here, all of them old people or women. The enemy commandos wouldn't dare attack them now.

And he might yet get out of this.

"Please!" the young woman in his grasp begged, twisting, whimpering. "Please let me go!"

He let her turn around until she was facing him, then squeezed her close with his left arm. To Nehim's eyes, to his culture, the whore was half-naked, her legs bare, the swell of her breasts clearly defined beneath the Western T-shirt she wore.

"No, whore," he told her. He brought his left hand up to grab the long hair at the back of her head, dragging her face closer to his. His right hand, holding the pistol, waved at the darkness beyond the casino's windows. "You and I have the rest of the night to enjoy!"

He tried to kiss her.

Her knee came up hard, a sharp, savage shock squarely into his groin.

Gunfire cracked, two shots. At first, the sagging Nehim thought that Hijazi had opened fire . . . but as he dropped to his knees he saw that a man had been hiding an AK-47 behind the back of another elderly man just in front of him, that it had been he who'd brought the weapon up and fired two rounds into Hijazi, who was collapsing onto the deck.

Nehim started to raise his pistol, but one of the elderly women nearby whipped her cane up and around and cracked it hard across his wrist, sending the gun flying. An instant later, the cold, black muzzle of a second AK slammed hard against the side of his head. Out of the corner of his eye, he saw a woman who might have been his grandmother beaming at him.

"Yippee-ki-yay, motherfucker," she told him sweetly. "Arnie Schwarzenegger said that, in *True Lies*—"

"It was Bruce Willis in *Die Hard*," another grandmother,

the one with the cane, said. "Get your movie quotes straight, Anne."

She picked up the dropped Makarov and smiled at him.

Cougar Twelve, Dean
Deck Ten, *Atlantis Queen*
Friday, 0546 hours EST

Dean sat with his back against the railing. "You're Ghailiani?"

"Yes, sir," the Ship's Security officer said. He quirked a smile. "Nice trick with the computer virus, and locking all the doors."

"How'd you get out of Security?"

"The others were distracted, trying to figure out what you did. I slipped out, took a gun, and came down to Kleito's Temple before your people locked the doors."

"Why Kleito's Temple?"

He nodded at Khalid's body. "Because I knew *that* bastard would run if the bridge was threatened. If I went up there myself, I'd never have gotten close to him. But if he ran, if he came down here . . ." Another shrug. "I just had to wait and see which ladder he came down, port or starboard."

"Your family's okay, by the way," Dean said. "SAS released them yesterday. They weren't hurt."

Ghailiani smiled again. "I saw. It's been . . . a nightmare."

Motion and a flutter of sound pulled at Dean's eye, and he looked out over the water, toward the south. The sky was growing lighter in the east—the approaching dawn—and the other ship, the *Pacific Sandpiper* was there in the south surging directly toward them, her bow wake a white mustache against the darkness.

Worse, a helicopter was flying toward them—an Agusta

Westland Super Puma. It had just lifted off the *Sandpiper*'s deck and was accelerating straight toward the *Queen*.

There were still tangos on the *Queen*'s upper areas, outside on Deck Eleven, the ones who'd been shooting at him a moment ago. Possibly the helicopter was flying to pick them up . . . or to bring reinforcements for the terrorists from the other ship, but Dean had a feeling that the bad guys had something else, something deadlier, in mind.

"Rubens!" he called over his comm implant. "They're trying to ram! The *Sandpiper* . . . and there's a helicopter that looks like it's lining up to crash us!"

"We're on it," Rubens replied.

"Tell them to turn the *Queen* to port!" By turning into the attack, the *Queen* might be able to swing her stern out of the way. Her Azipod thrusters gave her a lot more maneuverability than a ship her size with conventional screws.

"We're on it," Rubens repeated.

The helicopter was closer, *much* closer, looming huge . . . close enough that Dean could see the pilot at the right-seat controls. . . .

The missile streaked in out of nowhere, coming from the west on a slender white contrail. It struck the Super Puma squarely in its starboard fuselage, exploding in orange flame . . . and then a far larger explosion followed, a vast and thundering boom across the water as the aircraft was completely engulfed in flame and black smoke. Burning chunks of wreckage scattered through the air, and something struck the *Queen*'s hull with a metallic clang a few yards away.

The fireball plunged suddenly down, striking the water twenty yards clear of the ship. Dean released the breath he'd been holding; the size of that explosion meant the terrorists had had explosives inside the helicopter, a last-ditch effort to detonate the explosives in the *Queen*'s hold and scatter radioactive death across New England.

It had been *that* close. . . .

With a roar, a British Sea Harrier flew in low above the water, banking as it passed the surging circle of white water where the Super Puma had gone down. Dean heard shouts from farther aft, and the rattle of automatic weapons.

Shit. There were still tangos back there, and they might still have Stinger missiles.

"Help me up!" He'd lost his H&K, but he had Khalid's AK-47 and Ghailiani's pistol. The terrorists were on the Deck Ten pool area, behind Kleito's Temple and the ship's health club. Once on his feet, Dean found he could manage a halt-footed limp. It wasn't broken then, just sprained . . . but getting around was going to be damned tough.

With Ghailiani helping him, he plunged back inside the ship.

Cougar Three, Brisard
Deck Eleven, *Atlantis Queen*
Friday, 0548 hours EST

Guided by Rubens and the Art Room, Tom Brisard had left one man at the ship's helm and led the rest aft, down one level to Deck Eleven, then out onto a raised promenade overlooking the Deck Ten Atlantean Grotto Pool area. Through their night-vision monoculars they could see five tangos there—three of them standing guard, the other two opening one of the long dark olive crates lying on the deck.

Brisard had been Army Delta Force before signing on with Black Cat . . . and before that he'd been an Army Special Forces staff sergeant, with experience both in Afghanistan and in Iraq, none of which had required him to parachute into swimming pools or hot tubs, thank God. He knew the others weren't going to let him live that one down, and he was briefly tempted to take out his embarrassment on the tangos in his sights.

"Take prisoners if you can," Rubens' voice reminded Brisard over his headset.

"Roger that," he replied in a whisper. The Black Cat personnel's emergence from the ship was silent, and the tangos never heard their approach. At the moment, all of them were staring off to port, where an approaching helicopter had just fallen into the sea and a British Sea Harrier was drifting slowly closer toward the ship's side. The terrorists appeared mesmerized by that shrieking, hovering apparition.

"Wakkif!" he shouted, targeting one of the thunderstruck men below. "Halt! Do not move!"

For a heart-pounding instant, commandos and terrorists faced one another across fifty feet or so of emptiness. A second Sea Harrier appeared, followed by the thunderous beat of more helicopters.

Then, faced by the Sea Harriers' cannons, incoming helicopter transports, *and* the aimed weapons of the commandos on the railed balcony above them, the terrorists began dropping their weapons and raising their hands.

Health Club
Deck Ten, *Atlantis Queen*
Friday, 0548 hours EST

Fred Doherty put a hand on James Petrovich's shoulder.

"Don't worry, man," Petrovich said before Doherty could say a word. "I've got it and it's fucking great!"

Leaving Ames in the room, they'd emerged cautiously from the wardroom cabin where the terrorists had been keeping them along with Phillips and other bridge officers, slipping out after hearing what sounded like muffled shots or explosions and finding the guard posted outside of their room was gone.

There'd been no guards in front of the storage room

where their cameras were being kept, either. They couldn't access the security door leading to the bridge and decided they didn't want to tangle with whoever was in there— Khalid or whoever had just stormed the ship. A body lying in the forward stairwell showed that a takedown was under way.

Instead, they'd made their way aft down Deck Ten, through the Kleito bar-restaurant area, and then past the cruise ship's large and rather formidably equipped health center.

Through the large glass windows at the aft wall of the exercise room, Doherty could see several terrorists standing pinned in a glare of light from the sky. There were helicopters as well; his time in the Navy years before had taught him to recognize both British Merlins and U.S. Navy Seahawks, and the pair of British jump jets hovering off the side of the ship were a nice, if noisy, extra touch.

Using his camera's night settings, Petrovich had started filming as the first black-clad commandos had begun fast-roping onto the deck. . . .

Cougar Twelve, Dean
Deck Eleven, *Atlantis Queen*
Friday, 0552 hours EST

It took him almost five minutes, with Ghailiani's protesting help, to hobble through the bar and into the health club farther aft. Two men were standing by the large glass windows, one with a camera balanced on his shoulder.

"Halt!" Dean had snapped, raising the AK. "Who the hell are you two?"

One of the two turned, raising his hands slowly. "Uh . . . press!" he said. "News reporters!" He seemed to be trying to decide whether Dean and Ghailiani were terrorists or rescuers.

The other man continued filming through the window.

"Get the hell down!" Dean said, deciding that the two were what they claimed to be. They would sort things out later.

Moving past, Dean and Ghailiani emerged cautiously on the open deck again. By that time, helicopters were arriving, filling the sky in every direction, British Merlin transports and Super Lynx gunships, this time, along with gray U.S. Navy Seahawks off the *Eisenhower*. British SAS troopers were fast-roping down from the cargo deck of a Merlin hovering above the *Queen*'s smokestack onto the Deck Twelve Terrace. Other soldiers stood on the Atlantean Grotto Pool deck, their weapons aimed at a half-dozen ragged-looking tangos on their knees, their fingers interlaced behind their heads. A pair of Sea Harriers, hovering practically wingtip to wingtip, stood overwatch off to port. Evidently, the last group of tangos had surrendered rather than face those chain guns.

A pair of SAS troopers, anonymous in gas masks and balaclavas, confronted Dean with raised weapons as soon as he limped through the door. Dutifully he surrendered the AK and raised his hands.

"It's okay!" Walters called. He was standing next to a stack of tarp-covered Stinger missiles, along with Brisard and several other Black Cat team members. "He's American! He's one of ours!"

With his rather unmilitary blend of civilian clothing and combat vest, Dean decided he was lucky the Brits hadn't shot first and checked for ID later. SAS troopers were already shoving past him through the door, returning a moment later with the two newspeople in tow.

To port, the *Pacific Sandpiper* slowly passed the *Queen*, moving bow to stern, one of the SEALs standing on the bridge wing, waving. Between the *Queen*'s turn to port and the *Sandpiper*'s slowing and turn to starboard, the oncoming plutonium transport missed the cruise ship by a good eighty yards. Hell, it hadn't been close at all. The *Queen*'s Azipod thrusters were *good*.

Cabin 27, *Pacific Sandpiper*
Friday, 0559 hours EST

Fuchida was waiting for them in the cabin where poor Moritomi had died.

He'd been able to hear as the commandos stormed through the ship, hunting down the remaining hijackers, alone or in small groups, and killing or capturing them. He suspected that both Inui and Yano were dead by now; they'd both been determined to take as many of the enemy with them as they could, and to die fighting.

Kozo Fuchida, however, had been thinking since Moritomi had taken his own life, had been thinking a lot.

The Kokusaiteki Kakumei Domei had been born from the ashes of the Japanese Red Army, which had sought only to humble the West and to support the Palestinians in their cause against Israel. The reborn KKD, however, had begun with a more focused cause—the end of Japan's atomic energy program.

There were millions of Japanese who supported that aspect of the KKD's program. Japan and the Japanese people had always been sensitive to that issue, thanks to Hiroshima and Nagasaki. Fuchida had gotten his start demonstrating against nuclear-armed and nuclear-powered warships of the U.S. Navy being based at Sasebo, right across the bay from Tokyo itself. He and Moritomi had sworn an oath to help al-Qaeda carry out its plan for nuclear terror, exploding a dirty bomb in New York Harbor that would poison tens of thousands, perhaps millions, of Americans.

But Fuchida's *omi*, his burden of obligation, still rested with the leaders of the KKD. By now it was clear that the Americans had stopped Operation Zarqawi—named for a pathetic terrorist captured and killed by the Americans in Iraq. The world would not now see the object lesson of a radioactive dirty bomb exploding in a metropolitan area, would not learn the dangers inherent in the PNTL shipments.

His choice now was to die with the others . . . or to surrender.

Non-Japanese still thought of the Japanese people in light of World War II, of kamikaze and banzai attacks, of ritual seppuku and a disregard for life. What Westerners never seemed to understand was that the Japanese had a very high regard for life; they simply had a higher regard for the requirements of *omi*.

The cabin door burst open, and a black-clad arm appeared, holding a flash-bang grenade.

"Don't shoot!" Fuchida yelled. "I surrender!"

There would be a way, *somehow*, to continue the fight another day.

Cougar Twelve, Dean
Seahawk medevac
Friday, 0615 hours EST

Almost twenty minutes later, with the sun just rising above the horizon, the OED team and NEST had reported that the explosives in the hold were secure. By that time, Dean was on board a Seahawk medevac chopper, along with an unconscious Llewellyn, a half-conscious Yancey, and several other wounded personnel and Black Cat operators, and on his way back to the *Eisenhower*.

America was safe. But the debrief, Dean thought, was going to be a bitch.

The hijackers should never have been allowed to get that close to American waters.

He suspected that there would be some policy changes in the very near future.

29

"LADIES AND GENTLEMEN, this is your captain speaking. Welcome to New York City."

Captain Phillips hesitated, uncertain as to what to say. He exchanged glances with Charlie Vandergrift, who shrugged and looked away. Behind him, the man in the business suit, a "Mr. Johnson" of the State Department according to the ID card he'd flashed, stood listening as well.

Outside, the armada of boats and small craft that had descended on the *Queen* as she made her way north into the mouth of the Hudson River continued to circle and hover; horns, bells, whistles, and a cacophony of noise continued to sound from the fleet. The entire city, it seemed, had shut down in order to welcome the *Atlantis Queen* to her unexpected berthing at the city's passenger ship docks—Luxury Liner Row, as they were known to the crews of the ships that used them. Nearly all major transatlantic liners had docked here over the years, including the RMS *Queen Mary 2* and the MS *Freedom of the Seas*.

"The nightmare is over," Phillips said at last. "As you can tell from all of the commotion outside, we're being given a truly magnificent welcome to the United States. For those of you who wish to debark, our agents ashore will see to it that you make the appropriate travel connections. Those who wish to remain aboard are welcome to do so. We expect to remain in New York City for approximately one week for maintenance and service, before returning to Southampton.

"Arrangements have been made with several major hotels in New York City for those of you who wish to stay. Transportation will be provided at the head of the pier, and your luggage will be sent along to your rooms later.

"I'm sure all of us join together in giving thanks to the brave British commandos who carried off an unprecedented, truly incredible rescue of this ship, and of all of us aboard . . . while we were hundreds of miles out at sea." He glanced again at Mr. Johnson, who nodded. "As I'm sure you all can imagine, the press will be eager to interview anyone who was aboard the *Atlantis Queen* during the hijacking. Remember that you have the right not to speak with the press. You've all been through an extraordinarily trying week. You don't need to face that particular gauntlet unless you so wish.

"Royal Sky Line deeply regrets the circumstances of this past week. Our representatives will be in contact with you in regard to any and all monetary or legal claims that may have arisen as a result of this . . . incident.

"Thank you. *All* of you."

He hung up the intercom handset. "Satisfied?" he asked Johnson.

"You did fine, Captain Phillips. Our government thanks you."

"I do not like lying."

The man shrugged. "It's necessary, sometimes. As are oaths of secrecy."

Phillips hadn't liked that part, either. He and his bridge

crew had been required to sign documents promising not to divulge certain pieces of information, under penalty of twenty years in prison and a one-hundred-thousand-dollar fine. He still wasn't sure of the legality of that. Phillips was, after all, a British subject, not a citizen of the United States, and he wasn't sure the U.S. State Department *could* require him to sign such an oath. A phone call to the British consulate in New York City that morning for clarification had ended with instructions to sign . . . and that the legal work would all be sorted out later.

Frowning, he walked over to the bridge window and looked down on the surging mass of cheering, waving people gathered at the head of the pier. It looked like Twelfth Avenue had been blocked off to accommodate the crowds.

He suspected that some sort of fix was already in the works. Two hours after his conversation with the British consulate, he'd received a phone call from another cruise ship line, one of Royal Sky's competitors . . . and the offer of a new command.

And *what* a command! Late last year, the first of a new class of cruise ship had been launched—the magnificent *Oasis of the Seas*. She was bigger and more luxurious than anything yet afloat: 360 meters long, with a displacement of over one hundred thousand tonnes, sixteen passenger decks, and a capacity of 5,400 passengers, with a crew of 1,500. She had a five-deck-high area in the center of the ship called Central Park, open to the sky and filled with lush tropical vegetation, shops, and upscale restaurants, and featuring the Rising Tide Bar, which would actually travel up and down through three decks. Arched glass domes in Central Park called the Crystal Canopies would channel sunlight into the ship's public areas below. The *Oasis of the Seas* and her sister vessel were astounding triumphs of marine architecture and art.

And Eric Phillips was being offered her captaincy.

Apparently, both the Ministry of Trade and Sir Charles Mayhew expected Royal Sky Line to file for bankruptcy. The company had been running close to the wire to begin with, and the company's solicitors were expecting a storm of lawsuits engendered by the hijacking, not to mention the loss of tens of millions of pounds in returned fares. The company, after all, had not made good on its promise of a luxury cruise through the eastern Mediterranean.

And that despite all of the new state-of-the-art security systems.

It would be quite an honor to command the *Oasis of the Seas* . . . but Phillips wasn't sure he would accept. During the hijacking, he'd been forced to choose between the safety of his passengers and the safety of those thousands of people down there on Twelfth Avenue. His attempt to ground the *Queen* and the *Sandpiper* off Newfoundland had failed, and he'd spent the rest of the voyage locked up in the wardroom area until those commandos—*American* commandos—had freed him that morning.

Eric Phillips felt . . . broken.

He wasn't sure he could ever face the responsibility for almost seven thousand souls. Right now, he wanted nothing more than to retire and never go to sea again.

But he also knew that once the sea was in your blood, it never let go. Now was too soon to make anything like a final decision. He needed time.

But he *did* know that he would not accept his next command as a bribe for his silence.

Pier 88
Passenger ship docks
New York City
Friday, 1730 hours EST

Andrew, Nina, and Melissa McKay walked down the starboard gangway together, stepping onto the passenger ship pier off of West 48th Street in west Manhattan. It was a brilliant, clear, crisp September afternoon. Seagulls wheeled and shrilled overhead, and the air smelled of mingled salt and big city. In the distance, a roar like heavy surf echoed back from a wall of skyscrapers.

As Nina stepped onto the concrete of the pier, her knees almost gave way. God, it was *so* good to be home.

"Look, Mommy!" Melissa cried, pointing excitedly to a massive, looming gray shape alongside the pier directly ahead, just beyond a quay converted into a park. The park was filled with cheering, waving people, as was the deck of the ship behind it. "An aircraft carrier! Maybe it's the one that rescued us!"

"No, I don't think so, sweetheart," Andrew replied. "That's the USS *Intrepid*, and she's a part of a naval museum now. The ships that helped us are still out at sea."

He started pointing out to her two other exhibits at the Intrepid Museum—a submarine tied up at the near side of the *Intrepid* pier and the bizarrely out-of-place droop-snooted bird shape of a Concord SST, rising on its raft next to the dock.

Nina smiled. By all rights, Melissa should have been somewhere between exhausted and unconscious, but she was showing no signs of running down. Andrew had taken her to the ship's library that morning to look at a book about aircraft carriers when she learned that their black-clad rescuers had flown in off of a British carrier called the *Ark Royal*.

After the dramatic rescue of the passengers and crew of the *Atlantis Queen* early that morning, there'd been neither time nor inclination for sleep. The three of them had been interviewed by some men in conservative dark suits while the ship was still cruising west past Long Island. Apparently, everyone on board was going through a thorough debriefing before they could go ashore; the McKays and the other passengers who'd been held in the ship's theater had gone through the screening first, so they were among the first to be allowed to leave . . . thank God.

A polite but very serious gentleman from the U.S. State Department had asked the questions, but the men standing behind him, Nina thought, were from a different government agency. FBI? CIA? There'd also been several armed soldiers present. She wasn't positive, but she was pretty sure that the purpose of the interview was to make sure none of the surviving al-Qaeda terrorists walked off the ship pretending to be legitimate passengers.

Nina watched Andrew take Melissa's hand as they walked across the pier for a closer look at the *Intrepid*, and wondered—yet again—what the future held for them.

Andrew, Nina thought, had been uncharacteristically subdued since they'd been caught by the terrorists at the lifeboat early that morning. The memory sent a small shudder through her; the small group of passengers had been herded forward at gunpoint, and their captors had argued loudly with one another in Arabic. She'd thought they were trying to decide whether or not to kill the would-be escapees then and there.

Instead, they'd been roughly shoved into the theater with dozens of other captives and told they'd be "dealt with" later.

Nina had watched Andrew struggle with the situation. The man had always been so damnably competent, so frustratingly *right* about everything . . . a white knight convinced he could handle any situation, and who always knew the right way to do it. During the hijacking, though, he'd been helpless—they'd *all* been helpless—and she'd seen that knowledge torture him. He'd wanted to gallop in on his charger and save her and Melissa from the bad guys, and his best attempt to do so had only made things much, much worse, had almost gotten them all killed. It hadn't been his fault, certainly; apparently the terrorists had set the Ship's Security system in such a way to alert them to just such an attempt by the hostages, and there was no way any of them could have known that.

But since their capture Andrew had been taking his helplessness badly.

Trying and failing might even have been good for him.

Nina walked up beside him and took his free hand. "Will you have dinner with us tonight?"

Andrew looked down at her, surprised. "Sure," he said, the word a mumble. "If you want."

"No promises," she said. "But I really do want to talk."

"No promises," he agreed. "But . . . hell. We've just been given a new chance at life, right? At living?"

"We'll see where it takes us," she told him. And she squeezed his hand.

★   ★   ★   ★

Andrew McKay felt the squeeze of Nina's hand and squeezed back. He was still sorting through what needed to be done. They'd told them on the ship that hotel rooms were being reserved for all of the liberated passengers off the *Queen—and how many tax dollars had* that *cost?* he wondered. Still, it would give him and Nina a chance to talk.

They hadn't done much of that on the *Queen*. Things had been moving too quickly, too desperately, for that.

Just like the past six months.

A soldier in full combat gear and holding a rifle was standing a few yards down the pier, waving them along, so Andrew tugged gently at Melissa's hand. "We've got to move along, honey," he told her. "Mommy and I are talking about having dinner tonight together. Do you think you'd like that? Or do you want us to go to the hotel and let you sleep?"

"How can I be sleepy, Daddy?" Melissa said. "We're *home*! Well . . . almost. But we're in *New York*! And we didn't get to see New York when we flew out to England!"

That seemed to explain everything.

He wondered if he and Nina could make things work. He honestly wasn't sure he *wanted* to go back. So much had been said, so much had *not* been said . . . and so much trust had been lost.

He'd always thought of himself as able to make things work. Everything but his marriage, apparently. And his life. But they *had* been given a second chance.

And it was certainly worth exploring.

Mall Concourse
Deck One, *Atlantis Queen*
New York City
Friday, 1737 hours EST

"No, I don't think you understand," Fred Doherty said, angry now. "Do you people have *any* idea who I am?"

"We know who you are, sir," the man in the dark suit said. "But your equipment has been impounded."

"That's, like, a hundred, a hundred-twenty thou worth of gear, man!" Petrovich cried. "Counting the computers and the transmitter! And it'll come out of my salary if I don't turn it back in!"

"We've already given you a receipt for your equipment, Mr. Petrovich. And your people can pick it up after we've had a chance to go through your recordings."

"To do what?" Doherty demanded.

"To determine whether or not there is material there that could be prejudicial to national security," the man said.

"Everything we shot has already been broadcast," Doherty said, trying to keep his voice patient and reasonable. "Including the terrorists' demands. The people already know al-Qaeda was trying to blackmail us. What else could we release that they haven't already seen?"

"I am not going to comment on that, Mr. Doherty. But I will ask you for your cooperation. So far as the government of the United States is concerned, this story is *over*."

Doherty looked around the mall concourse. It was becoming crowded as more and more passengers and crew members were released by the government officials who'd been questioning them. "Come on, Jim," he said. "We won't get anywhere here."

"But . . ."

"Come *on*."

Sandra Ames was waiting for them at a café table in front of the shipboard Starbucks. She still looked pale and withdrawn, and had said little since they'd witnessed the brutal execution of Arnold Bernstein. "No luck?" she asked, looking up from her espresso.

"It's a cover-up," Doherty said. "I can smell it."

"A cover-up of what?" Petrovich wanted to know. "And *how*? They can't silence all of these people on board. And everyone *knows* the ship was hijacked."

"Yeah," Doherty added. "And there was Khalid's ultimatum. We broadcast it!"

"Fuckin'-A!" Petrovich was becoming more wound up by the moment. Without a camera on his shoulder, he could become quite animated at times. "Everyone knows about the plutonium!"

"I think they don't want Americans to know just how close we came to losing New York City," Doherty said. "It took us, what? Another nine or ten hours to reach port after the commandos took down the ship this morning? I don't know what that translates to in miles, but we *had* to be pretty damned close to Massachusetts and Connecticut to be able to make it the rest of the way here that quick. *That's* the story, I think."

"I wish we'd been able to uplink the footage we got this morning," Petrovich said. "You know they're not going to release those shots of the hostage-rescue people coming in. Shit, you'd think they'd *want* people to see that stuff!"

"Let them have their damned secrets," Sandra Ames said, sagging back in her chair. "I just want to go home."

Doherty looked at her in surprise. "You don't want to follow up the story?"

"I don't want to follow up *any* story. I'm going *home*. To Elk Grove, Illinois. And I don't ever want to set foot on a boat again in my life."

"It's a ship, Sandra," Doherty said. He started to say something more, something to make her change her mind . . . and then changed his own. Her experience on the *Atlantis Queen*'s forward deck seemed to have sucked the life out of her. Hell, they taught you in journalism school that you were supposed to be objective as a reporter. Unfortunately, there were things, *experiences*, about which it was impossible to remain objective.

"I took a job with CNE to interview stars and celebrities," Ames added. "To gossip about which airhead was dating which fool in Hollywood, whose movies were getting rave reviews, and whose career or marriage was on the rocks! Not to . . . not to . . ." She couldn't continue.

"I hear you, Sandy," Doherty said.

No matter. There were plenty of talking heads in the biz who could tell the story on-camera.

And he thought he knew where to go to start digging. If the authorities were clamping down on the story on this side of the pond, there was always the British. When he'd checked the Internet news services that morning, they'd been full of the story of how the British SAS had taken down the pirated cruise ship and the plutonium transport. An interview with someone at Royal Sky Line might be productive . . . especially if he could talk to members of the crew.

Khalid's ultimatum had threatened to blow up the two ships, no more. But what if that madman had planned on blowing them up right *here*, on the Hudson River next to Manhattan's West Side? Or a few miles south, alongside the Statue of Liberty, for instance? How much plutonium had been involved? How far would the radioactive cloud have traveled up the New England coast? How badly, and for how long, would the fallout from a dirty bomb of that size have crippled American trade and business at a time when her economy was already teetering on the brink?

Just how close had the *Queen* and the *Sandpiper* come to that particular Ground Zero? And why was the presence of American commandos in the rescue being covered up? Doherty had heard one of the men on Deck Ten shout, "He's American." And Doherty knew he'd seen American helicopters in the sky that morning.

God, there was a story here, a *huge* story! If he couldn't sell the story to someone at one of the major news networks, then he would write a book.

The hell with entertainment. And the hell with government suits.

The people had the right to *know*. . . .

Pier 88
Passenger ship docks
New York City
Friday, 1740 hours EST

Tabitha Sandberg walked down the gangway, unseeing, unfeeling. New York City was her home—she'd met Adrian here at that party at her sister's place just a few blocks uptown, on 67th Street—but right now Tabitha didn't feel like she would ever be home again.

God, Ade, I miss you!

It had happened so damnably fast. She and Adrian had been in the ship's theater, where the terrorists had led them at gunpoint last night. There'd been that burst of noise from up in the rear balcony . . . and then gunfire, people screaming, people running. She'd been sitting with Adrian in one of the theater seats, had jumped up when the shooting had exploded and started to run.

Adrian had jumped up, launched himself at her, and knocked her down.

And when she'd rolled him off of her, he'd been dead.

Damn it, it was so *senseless*!

They'd been talking about a new life together, a new chance, a new start. She had relatives, her sister included, who hadn't cared for the May-December relationship thing, and there were relatives on his side who'd thought Tabitha was just after his money.

Fuck them. Fuck them all. They didn't know. *Couldn't* know. Adrian had loved her and she'd loved him, and he'd died trying to protect her.

Just like he'd stood up to those terrorists who'd broken into their stateroom Monday night, looking for the young woman who'd come in over the outside balcony. He'd tried to protect Tabitha then and gotten clubbed in the face.

She shuddered at the memory, wrapping her arms tight across her chest.

Alone, she started walking up the pier. The massed skyscrapers rose like a cliff face beyond the massed throng of New Yorkers packed onto Twelfth Avenue behind the police barricades.

They'd offered her professional counseling. Therapy. The doctor on the ship had been especially sympathetic, had suggested that she seek help for post-traumatic stress disorder.

But that would mean having to talk about it, and Tabitha didn't know if she would ever be able to face that.

She knew a lot of the passengers were taking Dr. Barnes up on that offer, though. There was the young woman she'd met while they'd been prisoners in the theater . . . Tricia

Johnson. The twit had actually fallen for one of the terrorists . . . and she'd been in hysterics when she learned the kid had been killed.

Stockholm syndrome. Tabitha had heard about it. People held prisoner in hostage situations for more than a few days often developed deep feelings for their captors. After all, the terrorists literally held the power of life and death over their prisoners, and when you were consumed by feelings of helplessness your mind could get pretty messed up. The guy standing over you with a gun became a strong figure of stability and of protection . . . not a sick bastard who might rape or kill you in the next few seconds.

Tabitha was, she knew, in absolutely no danger of falling in love with those . . . those monsters.

Even her hatred and her bitterness, though, seemed . . . distant. More than anything else, she was numb.

God, Ade, what am I going to do?

They'd offered to ship her luggage to one of the hotels where they were putting up the passengers off the *Atlantis Queen*, but she'd opted to go to her sister's place instead. She'd be able to get a cab right over there at West 48th and Twelfth.

She'd survived this city for twenty-five years before she'd met Adrian.

She would survive this.

Somehow.

Concourse deck, *Atlantis Queen*
Pier 88, New York City
Friday, 1752 hours EST

"What do you think, Reggie?" Jake Levy asked.

"Dunno, man. She's . . . different, that's for sure."

"Arnie Bernstein's death really hit her bad, I guess."

"I know she had a thing for him. Bossed him around

like nobody's business, but she kind of loved him, I think."

"Ah, you *know* he was just about the only guy in the group who wasn't banging her, right?"

Carmichael shrugged. "No big deal either way, right? That's just banging. Not love."

Levy suppressed a wry smile. Carmichael had been Harper's current boyfriend for all of . . . what? Two months? But he'd never seemed jealous of the woman's dalliances with other men in her entourage. An open relationship, she'd called it.

It took all kinds.

They were watching Gillian Harper leaning against the railing, watching the crowds. They'd expected her to want to leave the ship immediately; she'd always been drawn to crowds and seemed to have a special fascination for press conferences. Anything that would give her exposure and media attention.

But not, it appeared, this time.

"I think it did hit her, Arnie's death, I mean," Levy said. "And I think she was damned scared. Maybe for the first time in her life. She told me this morning she didn't want to go through with 'Livin' Large.'"

"Shit no, man! She's under *contract*!"

"Maybe she's just thinking about someone other than herself for a change." Levy hesitated. It sounded like Carmichael was more worried about the money than about Harper's affections. "We'll see how it works out. Maybe we can interest her in a new project."

"Just so long as it doesn't have to do with boats, man," Carmichael said. "I ain't never gonna get on one of these things again!"

New York Presbyterian Hospital
New York City
Friday, 1810 hours EST

"How's the wrist, Ms. Caruthers?" Donald Myers asked.

Elsie Caruthers was sitting up in the hospital bed, her right arm encased in a lightweight plastic cast extending almost to her elbow. Anne Jordan hovered nearby. They'd flown all of the injured off of the *Atlantis Queen* early that morning, flying them by helicopter to New York Pres on Manhattan's West Side.

"I keep telling them I'm *fine*," Caruthers said, petulant. "That young doctor on the ship fixed me up just fine."

"Well, they wanted to make sure everything was okay," Myers said.

"Why wouldn't it be?"

"You managed to break your wrist!"

"Just a crack. Hairline fracture, the radiologist called it." Caruthers' mouth worked in what might have been a smile. "I'd have whacked that young son of a bitch harder if I could've!"

"Now, Elsie, you don't mean that!" Jordan said.

"I do mean it. This wasn't a damned movie, Anne. It was real, and those men would have killed us if they could've. Or killed those girls . . . or worse." She shook her head. "I'd do it again!"

"Well, you won't have to, will you?" Myers said. "No more cruises for you!"

"Who says?" She looked up at him sharply. "I signed on for a tour of the Mediterranean, and I intend to have it! God knows I may not have that many more years, and I'm going to go there before I die! Greece. Turkey. Egypt. I'm going to *see* them!"

"Well, I'm sure that can be arranged," Myers said, startled. "Another Walters tour group, maybe."

"Exactly! And you'll take us, Mr. Myers, won't you? As our guide?"

"Ah . . . er . . ."

"Because, you know, I've always *loved* your lectures, even when you got the facts a little confused, sometimes."

"Of course, Ms. Caruthers," Myers said. He felt an odd mix of resignation and enthusiasm. "I'd be happy to."

Pier 88
Passenger ship docks
New York City
Friday, 1812 hours EST

Jerry Esterhausen walked down the gangplank with Janet Carroll. "So . . . will I be able to see you again, Janet?"

Carolyn Howorth gave him a sidelong look. "Jerry, you don't even know my real name!"

"Because you won't tell me!" he said. "*Or* who you really work for!"

She laughed. "My friends call me CJ," she told him. "That's all you need to know."

"Okay, am I your friend?"

"Of course!"

"Then . . . CJ, will you have dinner with me tonight?"

She didn't answer immediately, and he must have taken her hesitation as a negative. "I mean, *just* dinner! I've just never known a girl who knows her way around a computer like you! And . . . and what you did to crack the ship's computer system was just brilliant! I'd just like to—"

"It's okay, Jerry," she said. "Yes."

"—be able to talk. And it calls for a celebration, y'know? Rosie's gonna be famous, y'know, and I had a call this morning from the company about how someone wants to put her on a new cruise ship that's operating out of Florida, a real giant named the *Oasis of the Seas*, and . . . huh?"

"I said 'Yes.' I'd love to have dinner with you."

"Uh . . . oh!" He swallowed and adjusted his glasses. "Gee, great!"

She laughed. He was *such* a stereotypical geek. "No promises," she told him. "I have to be in Washington tomorrow."

"Uh, sure! No promises! I just . . . uh . . . well . . . I don't know what to say!" He frowned. "I guess I'm better at talking to robots than I am to girls."

"You do just fine, Jerry," she told him. She took his hand as they turned to walk down the pier toward the waiting crowd. "You do just fine."

EPILOGUE

DEAN WAS SEATED AT A TABLE in one of the building's cafeterias with Lia DeFrancesca and Carolyn Howorth when William Rubens walked in. "Don't get up," he said as Dean started to rise. "Stay off of that ankle."

Dean grinned ruefully and patted his cane. "That's something they never covered in boot camp," he said. "Do *not* jump off a twenty-foot ladder."

"Remember that next time," Rubens said. "How is it?"

"Bad sprain, nothing more."

"The idiot could have killed himself," Lia said. But she was grinning.

"Good. Thought you'd like to hear, Charlie," Rubens said. "David Yancey has a good chance. They're putting him through a series of bone marrow transplants . . . but they say that the truck beds themselves gave him a measure of shielding. He's young; he's strong; he should make a full recovery."

"I'm glad to hear it," Dean said. "He deserves the Medal of Honor."

"That might be a problem," Rubens said. "Technically

he's a civilian. I plan to nominate him for the Congres
sional Gold Medal, though."

Dean chuckled. "That's one way to get the 'Congres
sional' bit in there legally." The Medal of Honor was often
but incorrectly, referred to as the *Congressional* Medal o
Honor, since it was awarded by the President on behalf o
Congress. The Congressional Gold Medal, however, wa
one of the two highest medals to be awarded to a civilian
"for an outstanding deed or act of service to the security
prosperity, and national interest of the United States."

"How about a medal for every man on the Neptune
strike force, and every SEAL off that submarine?" Caro
lyn Howorth said. She'd arrived from New York tha
morning on a business commuter flight.

"They *all* did a hell of a job," Charlie Dean said
"Medals aren't the same, though, as knowing the job go
done."

"And done with so little collateral damage," Lia added

"We got lucky," Dean said. "*Very* lucky, in fact; only
one passenger and one crew member killed in the assault
And . . . what? A dozen wounded out of thirty-three hun
dred?" That didn't count the one passenger and severa
members of the ship's crew killed before Neptune ha
gone in, of course. Still, total casualties—*collateral dam
age*, as Lia put it—had been incredibly light.

Poor David Llewellyn. He'd died before they'd reache
the *Ike*.

"I'm glad you're just interested in the job," Ruben
said, "since this op will be so highly classified, you boy
won't be allowed to show your medals off."

"It's being buried?" Dean asked. "Why?"

"Interests of national security. Translated as . . . 'th
politicians don't want anyone to know how close we cam
to losing New England.' "

"I'd think the people would be dancing in the streets
Judging from the news footage I've been seeing, they *ar
dancing in the streets!*"

"The official story is that the *Atlantis Queen* and the *Sandpiper* were still 'several hundred miles off the coast.' Not thirty miles from Martha's Vineyard."

"I don't understand that," Howorth said, shaking her head.

"Some folks think it's better that we stay fat and happy. And that we not know about our politicians playing cover-your-ass."

"In light of that," Dean said, "you might want to reconsider your resignation letter." Rubens had confided in Dean shortly after he'd gotten back aboard the *Eisenhower.*

Rubens snorted. "I don't know yet. I'm not sure I *want* the job anymore, not when I spend more time fighting with the people who are supposed to be on our side. Since you pulled off Neptune, the NSC probably won't want my head on a platter. Not this time, anyway."

"I'm glad to hear it."

"It helps that we caught so many of the hijackers alive. A half-dozen or so prisoners from the *Atlantis Queen*, and another twelve from the *Sandpiper.* We're already learning a lot of new stuff about the Islamic Jihad International Brigade and how it fits in with al-Qaeda. And his new Japanese group, the KKD . . . that's going to bear watching. Fuchida has been talking. Looks like al-Qaeda's trying to branch out, forge new alliances." He grinned. "The Japanese have already disavowed the group. They want nothing to do with them."

"Moderate Muslims have been disavowing al-Qaeda for years," Dean pointed out.

"Oh, Lia," Rubens said. "You might be interested to know that your op in Lebanon has drawn some official attention."

"Oh? Are they after *my* head?"

"Not at all. Remember your friend Colonel Suleiman?"

"Scorpio. Sure."

"Guess who Yusef Khalid's contact in Lebanon for the two-billion-dollar ransom was supposed to be?"

"Suleiman?" She looked puzzled.

"None other. We found out about it through that back door you planted in the Syrian network for Collins."

"What does Syrian Air Force intelligence have to do with al-Qaeda?" she asked.

"Normally nothing. There's a perception in the Islamic community at large, though, that al-Qaeda has gotten *too* violent, that it's out of control. Some other Islamic militant groups may be trying to rein them in. Seems that their biggest, flashiest ops tend to *alienate* moderate Muslims, not inspire them. Suleiman was acting as the IJI Brigade's money man in hopes of getting control of the group. Apparently he didn't know that Khalid had no intention of accepting the ransom, that he was going to try to blow those ships no matter what we did."

"Makes sense," Carolyn Howorth said. "A few out-of-control crazies make it harder for everybody." She slapped Dean's shoulder. "Attracts tough old birds like *this* one to come in and kick arse."

"I still think it would be better to publicize what happened," said Charlie Dean. "Show the bastards that we can fight back. That we'll stop them, no matter what they try."

"Oh, I imagine the word will get out," Rubens said. "The passengers are being processed in New York City now. Among them are three CNE news team people—the ones who first broke the story."

"I ran into them at the end," Charlie Dean said. "Filming the final takedown."

"The news services already know there's more to it than the government is saying," Rubens said. "I imagine the powers-that-be will have trouble covering it up. We'll have to see how it plays out over the next few days."

"Meanwhile," Reubens said, ". . . I don't speak for you, Ms. Howorth. You don't work for me. But *these* two have some leave coming."

"Sounds good," Lia said, grinning. "You know, I've been thinking for some time, Charlie, that I'd really like to go on a vacation cruise."

Somehow, Dean managed to keep a straight face. "Sure. The Persian Gulf, perhaps?"

Playfully she punched him.